Chasing the Wind

California Rising
Book 3

PAULA SCOTT

CHASING THE WIND by Paula Scott
www.psbicknell.com

This is a work of fiction. Names, characters, places, and incidents are products of the author's imagination or are used fictitiously. Any similarity to actual people, organizations, and/or events is purely coincidental.

Cover Designer: Jenny Quinlan
Editor: Jenny Quinlan, Historical Editor, historicaleditorial.com
Cover Image Credit: © TJ Drysdale / Trevillion Images
Typesetter: Jeff Gerke, www.jeffgerke.com

International Standard Book Number (13): 978-0692069424

Printed in the United States of America

Part One

"I will betroth you to Me forever; yes, I will betroth you to Me,
in righteousness and justice, in loving kindness and mercy;
I will betroth you to Me in faithfulness,
and you shall know the Lord."

Hosea 2:19-20

Chapter One

Marysville, California, 1850

Peter looked at his cards one last time. There it was. The king of hearts. Unbelievable. He glanced at the girl. She stared at the golden crucifix the Californio tossed onto the table. The Californio had lost his gold claim in the round before this one. The girl tore her gaze off the rosary and whispered in Spanish to the Californio, "That is Maria's." She didn't know Peter understood every word they said.

"I will win," the drunken Californio assured her. "I will not lose the rosary, *niña*. Or you. Dios is with us tonight."

But God had decided the Californio would lose. With that king of hearts, Peter had just won the rosary and the girl. His survival instincts kicked in. Mick wasn't going to like it. They'd saved each other's lives on countless occasions, but they had tried to kill each other a time or two as well. Reaching down to his holster, Peter coughed to cover the sound of clicking the hammer back on his Colt pistol. He would need every second when Mick saw that king of hearts in his hand.

He'd ridden with Mick a dozen years. Fought the Mexican War with him. Had seen Mick shoot men for lesser offenses than taking his card. That king of hearts would have been Mick's if he had bowed out of the game as any sane man would have when the girl was offered up, but Peter couldn't fold. It was as if God himself tapped him on the shoulder and said, "Hold 'em, Peter."

The Good Lord probably didn't speak to gamblers, but that's what he heard in his gut, and he had no explanation for it aside from the Almighty. Mick had a lightning draw and a temper just as fast. He might die today over a golden crucifix and the prettiest Indian girl he'd ever seen. Killed by his best friend. Maybe it was time he stopped riding with Mick. In a gunfight, there was no man he'd rather rifle with than Mick, unless it was Kit Carson himself, but drinking and carding with Mick was a whole different matter. When Mick was in his cups, he would rather kill you than lose.

"Let's see them, boys." The dealer flipped over his cards. Only three men remained in the game: the old Californio, out of his mind on brandy, Mick, whose confident grin had disappeared when that last round of cards was dealt, and he with his miracle hand.

Sweat ran down Peter's back and beaded on his forehead. He could smell the booze. Everyone was well into their cups. The tent reeked of unwashed bodies and alcohol, but in spite of it all, the sweet scent of the girl with the slanted blue eyes filled his senses. Where did she get those strange blue eyes? Her hair was black as midnight. Her skin smooth and golden brown, without blemish. She spoke perfect Spanish and carried herself like a white woman, but he could see the Indian in her. That's why the Californio could gamble her away. Plenty of mountain men took squaws for wives and sired half-breed children who were treated poorly by the white population. Perhaps the girl was the Californio's daughter, but he doubted it. Californios weren't keen on mixing their fine Spanish blood with the Indians.

Six years ago, he'd ridden with John C. Fremont and Kit Carson against the Californios during the Bear Flag Revolt. From what he'd gathered, the Californios were a proud breed that didn't take to squaws. The Spanish had turned the California Indians into slaves, though they called them servants. Without their Indian laborers, the Californios wouldn't have been able to run their vast ranchos, but with the American takeover—and now the gold rush—the Spanish culture was dying.

The Indians were dying too, entire tribes wiped out, largely due to the white men's diseases and guns. He hoped the blue-eyed Indian girl lived a long life. He'd never seen eyes like that on an Indian before. He couldn't stop looking at her. All the men stared at her. She kept her gaze mostly on the wood-planked floor, remaining quiet, except when she protested the rosary thrown into the pot.

Why the rosary and not herself?

These days, you could buy a beautiful Indian girl for five hundred dollars in Marysville. Nobody was going to interfere when the girl was offered up, except maybe the man standing behind Mick. The one they called the preacher. He had a long gray beard, but his hair wasn't gray. A fine head of brown hair lay under his hat, from what Peter could see. Peter had no idea how old he was, forty or sixty, who knew. The man looked strong and fit and ready to hold Mick and Peter to their word. When the drunken Californio tossed the girl in the pot, he'd made sure each man promised to marry her if they won her. Mick had laughed like the devil, slapped his knee, and said of course he'd marry the girl. Sure, he'd marry her. The way Mick looked at the girl made Peter's skin crawl. Mick wasn't nice to Indian girls.

Peter had silently nodded his acceptance of the marriage proposal when the preacher pinned him with avenging eyes. The girl with long black hair in two neat braids didn't deserve this. No woman did. In a town of mostly tents along the convergence of the Yuba and Feather Rivers, every man here was hungry for gold. And that hunger for gold was only outweighed by a hunger for women. The truth was, gold was far easier to come by than a beautiful half-breed.

Drunken laughter filled the tent. Peter glanced at the girl before flipping his cards face up on the table. She looked scared. As soon as he threw his cards down, he sprang up from his chair, kicking it out of the way so he could shoot any man who came at him. He expected Mick to fight and wasn't surprised when his friend flung his chair back too and braced himself for a gun battle. By then, Peter's gun was leveled on Mick's forehead.

"You took my card," Mick snarled, staring down the barrel of Peter's Colt with his hand gripping his own pistol.

"It's my card," Peter said in his soft, certain way. He'd always been a soft-spoken man. You didn't need to make a lot of noise to make yourself known in this world.

"You were gonna fold until that golden crucifix caught your eye." Knowing Peter had gotten the draw on him, Mick holstered his gun and spit on the preacher's boot. He didn't mean to spit on the man's boot, but the preacher stepped between them as other men scrambled out of the way in a hurry.

The Californio was telling the girl in his drunken Spanish that he'd lost everything. She must marry the winner because he had nothing left for her. They would starve to death.

"You promised to take me to San Francisco," the girl said in Spanish, tears filling her eyes.

Peter could hardly hear the girl's soft whisper over the murmur of men. Her tears moved him. He hated seeing her cry. Mick began laughing and couldn't stop. His manic laughter raised all the hairs on the back of Peter's neck.

Peter hadn't touched spirits in over a year, not since leaving Taos with Jedediah and all those blasted sheep they'd brought over the Sierras when the snow melted in the passes. Why he'd given into the devil's brew tonight, he didn't know. His sudden thirst for firewater came over him this way. He'd resist drinking for a long time, and then the need for whiskey would spring upon him like a grizzly roaring from the willows.

Mick had that look in his eyes. Like he was full of the devil tonight. "You got yourself a squaw," Mick crowed. "Pete just won himself a squaw." Mick howled with laughter. He'd won the old Californio's gold claim in the previous hand. Now that his rage had vanished, Mick was in a fine mood. A celebrating mood. He patted backs and shook hands and was ready for a wedding like he was the best man.

The preacher put a hand on Mick's shoulder, pushing him aside. He stepped forward, his piercing gaze on Peter. "You going to make things right here, son?"

At twenty-seven years old, Peter didn't feel like anyone's son, but to the gray-bearded preacher he must have seemed young. The preacher reminded him of Jedediah. All sober righteousness. The preacher didn't belong here. And Peter didn't like being told what to do.

The tent erupted in another wave of raucous laughter. Peter didn't know what was so funny. He glanced at the girl. She looked pale, her golden complexion drained of color, her eyes wide and shining with fear. The Californio stood beside her, looking like a beaten dog as all the Mexicans were in California with the American takeover.

Fremont had ridden right through this valley, killing the Indians to keep them from siding with the Californios during the Mexican War. Peter had scouted and hunted for Fremont under his boss, Kit Carson. He didn't like to remember how they'd set upon the Indians in their peaceful villages along the Sacramento, slaughtering men, women, and children in their tule huts beside the river. When it came to killing, nobody did it better than Carson. He didn't kill for pleasure. He killed for his country. Carson was set on taming the West. Winning California for the United States was his aim, and Indians weren't gonna stand in his way. Peter wondered what tribe the girl came from. She was tall for an Indian woman, and slender; perhaps she was from the north.

She wouldn't look at him now that he'd won her. An hour ago, she'd snuck glances at him when she thought he wasn't paying attention. When she'd watched him that way, his stomach had grown tight with longing. If she was the kind of woman who could fulfill his need tonight, he'd know just by looking into her eyes. But as soon as he'd caught her gaze, her cheeks had blazed with color, and she'd looked away like a girl you'd meet in church. There would be no fulfillment with her. He'd have to head on down to Clara's place after the game like he'd planned.

That was an hour ago. Now the girl stood in front of him, handed over by the Californio. "She is yours, señor. Marry her," said the drunken fool.

Peter reached across the table to scoop up the golden rosary, but the preacher grabbed his wrist. "You can't have that until you marry up."

He shook off the preacher's hand. He had nothing against the man, but he didn't like anyone touching him—unless it was a woman in a bed of his choosing. He didn't trust men, or women either for that matter. "I'll marry up when I'm ready," he said, gripping the golden rosary as he stared down the preacher.

Men hooted and hollered the way drunken men do when entertained. Peter didn't like being their entertainment. He supposed the girl didn't like it much either.

The preacher pulled a small leather Bible from under his belt. Most men carried a gun or knife tucked into their belts, but this preacher carried only the Good Book. "I'm all about making things right here," said the preacher. "How about you, Peter?"

Peter, do you love me? Take care of my lambs. The whisper whirled through his mind when the preacher said his name. Jedediah had said that to him as they looked after the sheep on a high mountain pass. The wolves had howled that night as his father read straight out of the Bible. *Peter, do you love me? Take care of my lambs.* He'd told his father that night he didn't want to listen to the Bible. "Keep that book to yourself," he'd said to Jedediah. He preferred to call his father by his given name. The tension between them had been there all of Peter's life. He'd never had a mother. She'd died giving birth to him. Why he thought about this now, he didn't know.

The men in the tent no longer laughed. They wanted a wedding. "Come on, Brondi," a man called as the tent quieted down. "If you won't marry the girl, I will!"

"I'll marry her!" cried another.

"We'll all marry her!" a man shouted.

Everyone laughed. The men were so drunk. Peter felt far too inebriated to think straight. Sweat dribbled down his chest under his buckskin shirt. He longed for some fresh air. The tent was stifling. And stank to high heaven.

"You should hear the Bluebird sing. I'd make her sing every night before I bedded her and every morning while she fixed my chow," said a bearded miner standing near the preacher.

"You gents quiet down," the preacher commanded. He held the Bible above his head and smiled, revealing several missing teeth. "We're gonna have ourselves a wedding tonight." He turned to the girl.

Her calico dress was threadbare and strained against her feminine curves. The dress was too short, revealing the dainty turn of her ankles and the pair of worn-out boots that covered her small feet. The girl was lissome and graceful, reminding him of a shy doe, with enough flesh in all the right places to please him. Heat pooled in his belly and made the journey to his loins. He knew fate had given him that king of hearts. God must want him to have this beautiful girl. Desire washed over him, and he took a deep breath, trying to gain his bearings.

She wouldn't look at him. Instead, she kept her gaze on the floor. In the lantern light, he noticed red strands in her hair and found that unusual. He'd seen Spanish women in California with red hair. Certainly, her blue eyes came from some

European mixed in her. How old was the girl? Had she ever lain with a man? He figured she hadn't been treated too kindly up in the gold camps, but she certainly didn't look abused. She looked young and innocent and so pretty he couldn't think straight.

Before he knew it, the preacher was reciting Christian vows. None of this seemed real. What kind of man would gamble a girl away? Perhaps this had happened to her before. Maybe the Californio had won her in a card game as well. Maybe she'd been passed from man to man up in the gold camps. The urge to protect her rose up in him. He reached out and put his fingers under her chin, tilting her face up so he could look into her eyes. Her features were finely wrought, her mouth lush and inviting. Long black lashes feathered her cheeks when she closed her eyes. "Open your eyes," he softly commanded.

She obeyed. Their gazes met, and that settled it. In her frightened blue eyes, he saw his future. He'd take this lamb for his own. He wasn't about to let her go to a wolf like Mick. He could tell Mick wanted her badly. Every man in the tent lusted after the girl. It made him all the more determined to keep her for himself. He cupped her cheek in his hand and marveled at the softness of her silken skin against his calloused fingers. Her eyes widened when he ran his thumb lightly across her lips. Her mouth opened in surprise, and heat flooded him. More sweat trickled down his body under his buckskins, and his knees grew unreliable.

The preacher kept on about God's good plan for their lives. Peter longed to tell him to hurry it up. He wrapped his arm around the girl and drew her closer to him. She leaned back, gazing up at him with a mixture of trust and terror in her eyes. He gave her a bit of a smile, hoping to ease her fears. She tried to smile in return but gave up and closed her eyes, her lips moved in what he recognized as a Hail Mary spoken in Spanish. She must be Catholic, like Carson's young wife. Realizing he still clasped her rosary, he squeezed it in his hand. The golden cross cut into his palm as he pulled her against his tall frame, fearing she might bolt or faint. The feel of her excited him. She fit him perfectly, her nubile curves pressing all the right places. He'd give her back her rosary as soon as this was over. Staring at her face, he had a premonition of sorts, like he already knew her. It came to him that she was meant to be his. "You going to let me kiss my bride?" he interrupted the preacher.

"I declare you man and wife." The preacher grinned like he'd just won a foot race. "Go ahead. Kiss your bride."

Chapter Two

Instead of putting a ring on her finger when the preacher declared them man and wife, her new husband handed her back Maria's rosary. Isabella groped for her skirt pocket, trying to tuck the rosary there. Peter—she must get used to his name—pulled her against his hard frame. He was tall, broad-shouldered, and strong as a bear. His beard felt soft on her face before his lips engulfed hers. He tasted like brandy and wasn't shy about kissing her. When she tried to lean away, feeling shamed with all those drunken men cheering, he cupped her cheek in a big, rough hand so she couldn't escape his mouth. He kissed her so thoroughly her knees buckled, and a wave of heat overcame her.

The tent rang with brawny cheers. Miners in blue shirts and broad pants tucked into tall leather boots pounded her new husband on the back, spewing congratulations and words so unseemly Isabella wished she didn't have ears.

The preacher followed them out of the tent and untied his horse, hitched to the rail alongside her husband's painted horse. She knew it was her husband's horse because she'd seen him ride into town that afternoon. She'd thought him a sight for sore eyes on that painted Indian pony. Not the California Indians, but the fierce Indians of the plains she'd read about in a dime novel one of the miners had given her. The preacher's horse was once a dappled gray but was whitening now with age. She could see this all under the full moon. Her husband's painted horse's white markings stood out in the darkness. It nickered when her husband came near with her anchored to his side, his arm a vise around her waist, drawing her away from the boisterous men. She frantically searched for Don Pedro. She'd taken to calling him by his name since he didn't act like her padre anymore. He wasn't really her father anyway, which pained Isabella to think about, even though she was leaving him.

Don Pedro spilled out of the tent with another drunken man, stumbling like he was about to sprawl on his face in the dirt. The other man did just that, landing in the dusty street with a dull thud. The moon was so bright it was like a midnight sun illuminating adobe buildings constructed by a man named Cordua, who'd built a trading post here. A number of buildings in the town were brand new, constructed of wood and bricks, looming several stories high above the tents. They called this new city Marysville after one of the founders' wives, a girl who'd survived the ill-fated Donner Party. It was rumored starving folks had eaten their dead to survive the winter when their wagons got stranded in the snowy Sierras.

Isabella didn't want to think about the ill-fated Donner Party. It was too terrible to fathom. After living in the mining camps this past year, doing Don Pedro's washing, and other miners' laundry too, she understood how hard life could be. She missed the rancho with its sleepy siestas, cheerful fiestas, and her once happy family. That was all gone now. She hadn't lived at peace since the American takeover.

The Yankees were everywhere. Marysville was becoming a booming trade center due to its location on the convergence of the two rivers. Boats unloaded passengers and wares headed for the goldfields. They came from San Francisco and Sacramento City daily. She looked down the street at the sprawling tent city lit by lanterns. Music from the saloons jangled her nerves. Don Pedro stumbled around as if blind. Her husband's big hand on her back urged her over to his painted horse.

"Get on up in the saddle." His voice was raspy, soft, and firm. "These drunken louts have had enough fun with us. We need to move on."

The preacher tucked his Bible back into his belt before he climbed up into his saddle. "You be good to your bride," he admonished. "She's a gift from God. A fine wife is from the Lord, you hear?"

Her husband lifted her up into the saddle as if she weighed no more than a sack of feathers. "I hear," he told the preacher as he untied his horse from the post.

"Please, I need my things from our mule." Isabella tried not to sound terrified, but she was. Fear tightened her throat. She found it hard to speak.

Her husband walked over to the mule tethered nearby. He stared at the broken-down animal for a moment and then walked to Don Pedro. He handed Don Pedro a small sack he pulled from his pocket. "For my wife's mule," he said.

Without waiting for a reply, Peter led the mule over to his painted horse and tied the mule's rope to his saddle. Then he led Isabella, along with the mule, down the street, away from the hooting, hollering men.

Isabella couldn't stop looking back over her shoulder. She was leaving everything she knew with a stranger she didn't know at all. A man who kissed her so thoroughly she'd nearly fainted. She'd never been kissed before and couldn't believe she was really married.

Don Pedro did nothing to stop their leaving. He looked relieved to be rid of her. She was so thankful the other frontiersman hadn't drawn that king of hearts. Had the man, Mick, won her, she would have jumped in the river to escape him. She could tell just by looking at Mick that he was a bad man. She'd thought her new husband and him were friends or even brothers because they dressed the same and knew each other well, but as the card game spun out, she realized Peter didn't trust Mick. The two were about the same age, dressed in deerskins and draped in weapons, men who put the fear of God into other men.

She was surprised her husband walked while she rode his horse and the mule plugged along behind them. A Californio would never walk if a horse was available. She knew Peter had drank too much. She'd watched him all night consuming alcohol, yet he moved so graceful and quiet, like an Indian. His moccasins hit the ground without a sound. What did he look like without that beard covering the lower half of his face?

She imagined her real father, a Russian fur trapper, had looked much this way—tall, burly, and strong as the mountains he came from. Would her husband abandon her as well once he tired of her? Both her fathers had bartered her away.

Her Russian father when she was a babe at Fort Ross, and now her Californio padre, the only father she'd ever known.

Tears flooded her eyes. No man wanted her because of her Indian blood. She reached into her skirt pocket and took hold of the rosary, praying her new husband would be a good man. When their eyes had met in the tent during the taking of their vows, she'd seen kindness. His eyes reminded her of a stormy sky before the rain. He was so serious, but he'd given her a small smile as they wed. She had been too scared to return his smile and had instead closed her eyes and prayed.

Outside of town, he led the horse and mule over to a shadowy oak grove along the river. "We'll camp here for the night." She liked the sound of his gravelly voice. He talked softly, but there was nothing soft about him other than his deep, sure voice, and perhaps his beard. She'd never felt a man's beard on her face before. Or been in any man's embrace. She still trembled from his passionate kiss.

A nighthawk screeched from the trees. The air was pleasantly cool after the stifling heat of the gambling tent. Oak branches created a canopy over their heads. Through the branches, she could see hundreds of shining stars in the dark heavens. The smell of the river came to her on a gentle breeze. It was a fetching summer night. Her husband stepped over and helped her down from his mount. His hands were possessive on her waist, like he already owned her, as he placed her on the ground.

"You don't weigh much." She wasn't sure if that was a smile under his beard or a grimace. He reached out and captured one of her braids, stroking it between his fingers, staring into her eyes the way he had during their vows. Something hot and heady and hopeful spread through her. She shivered, her insides

15

whirling with nerves and fear and perhaps excitement. This was her wedding night after all.

"I'll make us a fire." He dropped her braid and turned to lead his horse over to one of the trees, where he deposited his saddle and tied the animal to a low-hanging branch. He secured Old Amigo, her mule, beside his horse.

Isabella wasn't sure what to do next. The way he'd looked at her while stroking her braid sent fire to her cheeks and other parts of her body as well. There was a sure, confident way about him she admired. He didn't seem drunk, though she suspected he was. From the moment he'd ridden into town that afternoon, she hadn't been able to take her eyes off him. It felt like her fate to be here with Peter Brondi. Her destiny to become his wife. *Isabella Brondi.* Turning her back to him, she tried the new name on her tongue.

True to his word, he had a fire crackling in no time. He pulled some jerked beef out of his saddlebag and handed it to her. He gave her a bota, letting her drink her fill of water before he drank, all the while watching her. She grew more nervous with each passing second. When he walked over to his saddle and returned with his bedroll, unfolding it alongside the fire, her insides twisted into a tangle.

"You sleepy?" He looked her over from head to toe, his gaze consuming her.

She shook her head. She wasn't sleepy. She was scared. His desire was tangible, but he made no sudden moves. Reaching into his saddlebags, he pulled out a hair brush, settling himself on his bedroll. "Come sit with me." It wasn't a request, but a gentle command.

Isabella had always done as she was told. On trembling legs, she walked to him, easing down beside him on the woolen blanket. Without a word, he pulled the leather straps off the ends of her braids, using his fingers to loosen her hair before sliding his hands through the tresses like he'd done it before. Never had a man's hands been in her hair. She could hardly breathe when he leaned in close and whispered, "You've got real pretty hair. Soft as a beaver pelt."

She shivered with his warm breath against her ear.

He began to brush her hair. Slowly. Tenderly. She didn't know what to make of it. "Did you ever trap beaver?" she finally gathered the courage to ask.

"I trapped my fair share when I was younger."

She took a deep breath, trying to calm herself. "My father was a trapper."

"So the Californio is not your father?"

"He adopted me when I was a babe."

He stopped for a moment. "The Californio wasn't a good father. You're better off rid of that foolish man." Then he continued to brush her hair.

She didn't argue. Don Pedro had protected her virtue in the gold camps, but that was about all the fathering he did. A woman's virginity to the Californios was worth dying for. Don Pedro told any man who looked at her twice that his pistol was loaded and he would use it.

"You old enough to be married?" His question interrupted her thoughts.

"I'm older than my mother was when she married my father." Isabella clasped her hands together in her lap to stop them from shaking. She couldn't see his face, but the fire cast a golden glow over the two of them, and their shadows merged on the ground in front of her. She could feel his breath on her hair. The heat of his body warmed her more than the fire.

"I won't hurt you," he promised.

She closed her eyes in relief. She believed people until they proved themselves false. She'd spent the past two years believing Don Pedro's promises that they were going to become rich in the goldfields. They would buy back Rancho de los Robles and live like kings among the Americanos who'd taken their land. They would get everything back, all the horses, cattle, and sheep. They would return to Monterey and have their fiestas. That was such a lie. Now all she had were precious memories of that bygone way of life and a wedding in a gambling tent.

Peter stopped brushing her hair. He took her gently by the shoulders, easing her down onto the bedroll. Stretching out beside her, he rolled onto his back, folded his hands across his chest, and stared at the stars shining through the oak branches overhead. "So your name is Belle, and you can sing real pretty."

She let out the breath she'd held when he lay her down. "I suppose so." She could hardly remember who Isabella was, the cherished daughter of Califorinos, though she wasn't sure if she even had a drop of Spanish blood in her. She was half-Russian. Her mother was a Creole. That's what they called the mixed-blooded people of Fort Ross. Under the sun, her skin turned the color of sunbaked clay. As she grew older, her cheekbones became prominent. Her hair, like her cheekbones, was definitely Indian. Men found her beautiful, but they didn't respect her the way they did white women. Don Pedro had tried passing her off as his Spanish-blooded daughter when they'd first arrived at the camps, but he soon gave up and embraced the miners' measure of her. A blue-eyed Indian who could sing like a bluebird. That's what they called her in the camps. The Bluebird. Nobody called her Isabella anymore.

Don Pedro didn't find much gold, but he discovered her singing could keep them from starving after washing men's laundry in the cold mountain streams about killed her last autumn. As the days wore on, Don Pedro nearly died in the freezing mountain streams too, a pan in his hand as he searched for gold. All their vaqueros left, melting away last spring like the snow in the Sierras, until it was just the two of them. Every last bit of gold Don Pedro found he traded for brandy. It was a miracle she still had her virtue, surrounded by men who stared at her like hungry wolves. She'd always known it would come to this, a man would have her whether she agreed to it or not. She was just grateful this man made her his wife before making her his woman. And he wasn't repulsive. She found him quite handsome, even though he made his home in the mountains and appeared as wild as the wilderness he'd stepped out of.

"Will you sing for me, Belle?" He rolled onto his side and looked at her in the firelight.

"Right now?"

Singing had become a way of keeping men at bay, but something was growing inside of her that didn't want to keep him at bay. He wasn't forcing himself on her. He was showing her nothing but tenderness. She hadn't had her hair brushed by anyone since they'd left Rancho de los Robles. Servants had always brushed her hair. When he was brushing her hair, it opened up a deep longing in her to be loved by another human being.

"Perhaps in the morning. Do you remember my name?" he asked.

"Peter," she breathed, her eyes gazing into his, her fate sealed in that moment.

"Say my name again. I like how it sounds on your lips." He propped himself on his elbow. In the firelight, just as in the sunlight of this afternoon, she found him so appealing, but fear returned. She'd never lain with a man before.

"You are Peter," she whispered.

He rolled close, and his lips covered hers. He kissed her so thoroughly she felt unmoored. Like she dreamed the kiss. His body trembled, and she trembled with him. His mouth tasted of brandy, something she never dared drink. The way he kissed her told her there was no turning back. He meant to make her his wife in earnest, and a strange mixture of excitement and grief filled her. She'd always dreamed of a grand wedding fiesta, like the parties she'd grown up with, but the Americans conquering California had done away with all the Californios' joyful celebrations. Guitars and violins would not serenade them tonight. There would be no dancing. No feasting and laughter.

His hands loosened her ragged dress. The ground was hard under her back. In the distance, music carried down the river from Marysville. No longer would she have to sing to keep men at bay. Her new, strong husband would keep them at bay. There wasn't an ounce of softness about this man. His chest felt like a rock wall above her. She considered pushing him away, but she knew he had every right to do what he was doing, and a part of her savored this closeness with his big, warm body. Oh, how she longed to be loved.

She could no longer think with his mouth on hers, his hands gently roaming her body, removing her dress. Her awful dress. It hardly fit anymore. She was no longer a girl. Anything of value that had once been hers, Don Pedro had gambled away. Only this morning, he'd found Maria's rosary that she'd kept hidden in her shoes at night. When Peter gave it back to her after they wed, she was so surprised. Only a good man would return a treasure. Only a good man would brush her hair. Only a good man would be this tender with her.

It felt like he was consuming her slowly. With patient passion. True to his word, nothing he did hurt her. Pleasure began to weave through her like wool turning into a blanket under his skillful hands. The more she responded to his caresses, the more he took his time. He kissed her and stroked her until she could hardly stand it. Until all she wanted was him.

Her wedding night was so much more than she'd ever dreamed it could be. She was desired. She was loved. Unable to stop herself, she whispered in Spanish that she loved him. Because in that moment, she did. Something was weaving their souls together. It wasn't just their bodies joining, their spirits united as well. She'd never felt so close to another human being in her life. Tears of surprise and joy filled her eyes.

He paused when she whispered that she loved him, like what she said startled him, but she wasn't worried he understood her breathless words. He didn't speak Spanish, and she wasn't about to repeat herself in English. That night Peter Brondi not only claimed her body, he claimed Isabella's young, tender heart as well.

Chapter Three

Peter awoke with the girl pressed against his chest. Birds sang with the sunrise, yammering on as happy as folks headed to church on a Sunday morning. For a moment, he thought he'd dreamed last night. Then he was afraid to open his eyes because he knew, with everything inside him unfurling, it wasn't a dream. The girl was real, and she wasn't Maggie or Clara.

The urge to rise up and run nearly overcame him. He had a wife now. He'd married the blue-eyed Indian girl he'd won in the card game last night. And they'd become one flesh in the moonlight. The memory of their union sent a bolt of heat through him. Had their lovemaking really been that astounding?

Steeling himself, he opened his eyes. Dark, silky hair spilled across his naked chest. He'd brushed that hair in the firelight last night, remembering the fear in her eyes, her face an appealing mix of Indian and European. Not wanting to wake her, he remained perfectly still, his body pressed against hers. Her warm skin excited him all over again. He tried to ignore his body's response to her. Last night's dream had turned into a nightmare this morning.

Were they legally married?

He didn't believe so. The first thing he'd do was head back to find the preacher. If he really was a preacher at all. He remembered how the men had howled with laughter during the ceremony, as if everyone was in on the joke but him. Was the girl a part of it as well? They'd called her the Bluebird. When a woman had a nickname in the camps, that only meant one thing, she earned a living on her back, like Clara's girls.

He gazed down at all that silky black hair. Her bare shoulders were paler than her arms and face, exposed to the sun, her smooth olive skin as pleasing to him as her velvet hair. At least she was a beauty. It could have been worse. She could have had teeth like a horse's and a mule's disposition. He remembered now he'd bought her mule. A poorly animal he'd probably have to shoot sooner than later. At least the girl's disposition wasn't mulish. She'd submitted so sweetly. Never had a woman been so eager to please him. Her voice was soft and submissive, even when the Californio had tossed her into the card game, trying to win back his gold claim last night. Her eyes had gone wide with horror, but she hadn't said a word against that foolish man.

Peter couldn't figure out if she was a prostitute or the man's daughter or even his woman. Though right away he rejected that last notion. The thought of her with anyone else didn't sit well with him. He'd rather think of her as a whore than another man's concubine. He hoped she was the Californio's daughter, but he just couldn't imagine a man gambling away his own child. What kind of man did something so despicable?

He'd seen desperation on the Californio's face last night when he'd tried to win back his gold claim. Peter wanted to find the drunken Californio and beat some sense into him. And then he'd give him back the girl. That fool didn't deserve her back, but what else could he do? She wasn't his wife. She couldn't be. No legitimate marriage took place in a gambling tent.

He closed his eyes and listened to the girl breathing softly in sleep. With each breath she took, her body caressed his. The delightful feel of her was almost more than he could handle. This wasn't the first fix he'd gotten himself into while into his cups. He once drank firewater with a band of Indians, and when he'd returned to their village to trade with them, the chief insisted he marry his daughter because Peter had offered the chief two swift horses for welcoming him so finely. He'd been twenty-one years old at the time, still a greenhorn in the Rocky Mountains.

By the skin of his teeth, he'd escaped that marriage after embarrassing the chief by offering such a powerful gift as two horses, not realizing the chief would have to give him an even greater gift in return. He'd told the chief he'd marry his daughter after he bathed for the ceremony in a creek a mile away. When he'd hit that creek, he kept riding as fast as he could. The last thing he wanted was a squaw for a wife.

He'd hightailed it back to St. Louis in '45, where he met Maggie. The thought of Maggie filled him with sorrow. She was a minister's daughter with shiny brown hair and a dimpled grin. It hadn't taken him long to propose marriage. But Fremont was on his third exploratory expedition with fifty-five volunteers when his old boss, Kit Carson, convinced him to join up since he'd been on Fremont's second mission as a hunter and never failed to return to camp with meat for the men. Peter thought they were headed back into the Rockies to survey the mountains as they'd done before and promised Maggie he'd return to marry her before she knew it. But at the Arkansas River that summer, Fremont abandoned his survey project in the mountains and pressed hard for California.

Peter was shocked. What was Fremont doing? He wrote to Maggie, asking her to wait for him. In the Great Salt Lake Desert, they all nearly perished. He didn't know if he'd survive this second expedition with Fremont. Carson rescued the small army by riding sixty miles ahead in search of grass and water. Peter rode along with him, and they'd cut a mule's ears and drank its blood to bolster their strength before attempting the long trek across the desert.

At a distant mountain, they discovered water and plenty of grass for the livestock. They built a signal bonfire to encourage Fremont to cross that stretch of no-man's-land. By the winter of 1846, they conquered the Sierra Nevada Mountains and dropped down into the Sacramento Valley, assuring the American settlers around Sutter's Fort that should war break out with Mexico, Fremont's army troops would protect the settlers.

The expedition's real mission filled Peter with pride. Defending American settlers gave him a sense of honor he'd never had before. He wrote Maggie again, telling her how proud he was to be riding with Fremont and Carson. They would stretch their great nation from sea to shining sea, but nobody, including Carson, who was deeply devoted to his country, was openly talking about Fremont's real mission, which appeared to be an act of war with Mexico.

At Gavilan Peak, a mountain near the Coastal Range northeast of Monterey, they erected a rough fort in a matter of days and hoisted the American flag, daring the Mexicans to kick them off the mountain. General Castro obliged, gathering hundreds of Californio soldiers in the valley below to do just that.

Somewhere along the way, urged on by Carson, Fremont decided their fort building and flag hoisting was war enough for now, and they slipped off the hillside under the cover of darkness and left California in early March, riding all the way to Oregon, where they ended up camped on the southern shores of Klamath Lake that April. With a heavy heart, Peter wrote Maggie they'd lost three brave men beside those strange turquoise waters of the Klamath. The Indian attack came so unexpectedly. It was a wonder they all didn't die in their beds that night beside the lake.

Peter had been rolled in his saddle blanket, much like he was now with the girl, on a cold spring night. He awoke to the sound of a dull thud where Basil lay sleeping. Carson rose up, calling out to the Frenchman, "What's the matter over there, Basil?"

When Basil didn't answer, Carson jumped up, pistol in hand and ran to their sleeping friend. But Basil wasn't sleeping; his head had been cleaved in two by a hatchet. Everyone was on their feet by then, looking around for Basil's killer.

"Indians!" Carson cried.

They fired their pistols into the darkness as arrows rained down. Two of their Delaware Indian scouts, Denny and Crane, died with arrows buried deep in their chests beside the campfire. Peter thought they would all perish, but after the war party's leader, the bravest Indian Peter ever saw, rushed in and fought valiantly, the chief went down in a hail of gunfire, the battle-ax that killed Basil still strapped to his wrist. The chief's skin was elaborately painted, and a feathered war bonnet was on his head. With their chief dead, the war party finally disappeared as silently as they had come out of the dense Oregon forest. Only then did Peter check himself for injuries.

An arrow had ripped through his deerskin pants but hadn't drawn blood. Another arrow had skinned his left ear. He still had a scar there. He couldn't believe these Indians had attacked since just days before they'd given gifts of tobacco, meat, and knives to these very same Indians, who'd appeared happy to receive their hospitality.

"A treacherous race," Carson proclaimed, wondering out loud if the British had instigated the Klamaths to ambush them after Carson examined the British-made battle-ax the dead chief had used on Basil. As their guide, Carson took Denny, Crane, and Basil's deaths particularly hard, especially Basil's, who he'd ridden with on numerous expeditions with Fremont.

Peter had become especially fond of Basil and was glad they'd killed the Indian that killed him. Even before this Klamath raid, and the bloody Indian battles that followed in California along the Sacramento River, where Fremont's men killed every Indian they came across in retaliation for the deaths of their men in Oregon, Peter had distrusted Indians. Fremont claimed all the killing was a warning for the California Indians not to side with the Mexicans against the Americans in the Sacramento Valley. Several Bear Flaggers died at the hands of the Californios, and Fremont's men killed a couple of Californios near San Francisco, which hadn't sat well with Peter, but in the end, the only serious fighting they'd done was in the south at the battle of San Pasqual. Peter had killed men there too. Could he ever return to Maggie with all that blood on his hands?

He tried to convey all this to her in his letters and ended each appeal with a promise to marry her just as soon as he got home. But after killing so many men, Peter realized he might never return to Maggie. At least the man he'd been would never return. After that night on the Klamath, he hated Indians even more. He couldn't remember a time when he didn't hate Indians.

And then there was Paul and his treacherous Indian mother.

The woman had joined them one last time in New Mexico, bringing a boy, insisting he was Jedediah's son, though Peter knew his father doubted her. But Jedediah accepted the boy, changing his Indian name to Paul, cutting Paul's long, dark hair, and dressing him as an American child. Paul turned out to have American in him indeed, though he didn't have the Brondi cleft in his chin like Peter and Jedediah. Paul's eyes were dark, like his mother's, instead of the Brondi blue, which was really steel gray. When Paul grew older, he told Jedediah and Peter his real father was an outlaw his mother took up with after leaving Jedediah. Paul said his mother had lied to Jedediah, wanting someone to take him off her hands. This rang true when Paul's mother took up with another bad man in New Mexico, disappearing for good. Paul cried for days over her desertion. Peter did his best to comfort the little Indian boy. They never saw Paul's mother again.

Peter felt sorry for Paul when they were young. At least Peter knew Jedediah was really his father; he looked just like Jedediah, with golden-brown hair and that dimple in his chin and those Brondi blue eyes. The Brondis also had slashing eyebrows that made them look hawkish, though women still found them appealing. Paul's dark eyes were always dancing. He had that charismatic way his mother had, something powerful that drew folks to them. Paul had drawn Maggie like a moth to flame.

Thoughts of Maggie and Paul left him sick, as it always did. She was the only girl he'd ever loved, and Paul had killed her.

The girl began to stir in his arms. He quickly untangled himself from her, pulling the blanket up over her shoulders to cover her nakedness before grabbing his buckskins and heading for a nearby thicket. His head pounded from the whiskey and brandy he'd consumed the night before. He cursed the brandy. Whiskey he could handle. He should have stuck to whiskey when he reached Marysville, but Mick had insisted they drink brandy too. Mick had ridden with Fremont and Carson as well, grinning as they gunned down the California Indians on the Sacramento, slaughtering women and children along with the men.

Mick had bragged, "It was the prettiest battle I ever saw," after the last Indian was dispatched by a blow from the butt of Mick's rifle. Peter didn't see it as a battle at all. What happened along the Sacramento was a massacre, plain and simple. It haunted him still.

He shook his head, trying to clear his mind of butchered Indians and Maggie dying while giving birth to Paul's baby on a wagon train bound for California. Most nights Peter had nightmares about Maggie dying or him killing or being killed by Indians. The girl he'd left rolled in his blanket looked nothing like Maggie. The only thing they shared was an uncommon beauty. But somehow the half-Indian girl had touched something deep inside him he never wanted touched again after Maggie. The desire to love and be loved.

He tried not to think about the girl saying she loved him in Spanish last night as they coupled. He told himself he dreamed that part of it, along with the intensity of their lovemaking. He'd never experienced that kind of union with a woman before. He knew he'd joined more than his body to her last night. A part of his soul was sealed to her now. It disturbed him a great deal.

The summer morning was warming fast. The Yuba River ran clear and cold and blue. He knew that river was chilly because he'd bathed in it often enough. He left his buckskins at the water's edge and dove in, swimming across the river underwater like he'd learned from the Indians along the Missouri River. Reaching the other side, he turned and swam back underwater, where the current wasn't so strong, grateful he knew how to swim this way. Most white men didn't.

Rising out of the water, he wondered what he would do when he stood face-to-face with his brother. Paul had a thirst for whiskey and gambling that far outweighed his own sudden urges for the vices. He'd come to visit Clara too. She was good at satisfying his desire for a woman with no strings attached.

The cold water of the Yuba cleared his head. He'd fetch the girl and return her to the Californio or the preacher. How dare those two old men saddle him with her when he was too drunk to know better. Back in his buckskins, with his knife and his pistols strapped around his waist, another knife tucked into his moccasin boot, Peter felt almost like himself again.

He strolled back to camp, set on working free from the girl just as fast as he could. He found her braiding her long black hair by the smoldering remains of their campfire. He could smell the smoke—campfire smoke always pleased him—and she was such a pretty sight. Her gaze locked on him as soon as he stepped from the trees. She smiled as he approached, her teeth straight and white, a rare thing in a woman.

When he didn't return her hopeful smile, the welcome slid off of her face. He wondered if the Almighty had done this on purpose. A way of reckoning him to the last thing he wanted to be reckoned with—the hate he carried for his half-breed brother and all Indians like this girl.

"We need to saddle up; we're burning daylight," he said without a trace of the anger roiling through him. No reason to be hard on her. She appeared too young and innocent to be a part of this nasty joke they'd played on him, but he knew she had to be privy to it. Last night she'd pretended not to know what to do with a man, though she'd been willing enough to learn.

He never took what a woman didn't freely offer and despised men who did. Truth be told, he had enjoyed her company a great deal. Did the Californio rent her out the way Clara sold her girls? Clara had just built herself a three-story brick hotel in Marysville. She called it a lodging post, but most men couldn't afford to spend the night there. Just a half hour in one of Clara's fancy new rooms was about all most men could afford. Of course, they weren't alone in those rooms, and they sure as the sun shined weren't sleeping, but Clara never charged Peter a dime for her company.

He knew Clara loved him. They'd met in Missouri before Clara migrated west, perhaps searching for him. Back then, she'd worked alone, her fine red hair and buxom figure drawing men to her like beaver to a scented trap. Clara was older than him by about ten years, her youthful beauty waning as her shrewd mind figured a better way to do business—getting other girls to work for her instead of doing the work herself.

While securing his saddle and then bridling Mel, he watched the girl when she wasn't watching him. She reminded him of a doe in the forest, shy and graceful and far too vulnerable with hunters around. He told himself he hadn't hunted her down. He never shot does when he'd been employed to feed Fremont's men. He didn't want the responsibility for a fawn starving to death without its mother. Had he been sober last night, he never would have agreed to take the girl with him. Nor would he have stood for that make-believe wedding to entertain a bunch of drunken louts.

Worst of all, he remembered the way he'd coaxed her into love-making like he had to coax Mel across every river using a gentle hand and plenty of sweet talk to get her there. Afterward, the girl had cried in his arms. He hadn't been sure what to make of it, so he'd just held her until she cried herself to sleep. He'd been sobering up by then and almost told her she didn't have to pretend to be anything but a girl like Clara's girls, though she sure didn't act like a soiled dove. Her tears struck him as sincere. It had taken him a long time to fall asleep with her in his arms. Long enough to regret bedding her, that was for sure.

He motioned the girl over, and she came with that look of trust on her face he already hated because it made him feel like a rogue. When he put his hands on her slender waist to lift her into his saddle, one of her long silky braids brushed his forearm and sent a bolt of heat clear through him. He'd been with his share of women, but this girl had completely captured his fancy. Thoughts of their night together was like a fever in his veins.

Instead of walking and leading her on his mount as he'd done last night when he was drunk, he put his boot in the stirrup and swung up behind her. "Where were you born?" he asked, hoping talk would provide the answers about who she really was as they rode the river road back to Marysville.

"Fort Ross," she said and didn't elaborate.

"You still have family at Fort Ross?"

"I don't know."

Peter frowned. He knew the Russians had abandoned the fort, selling it to John Sutter, the indomitable Swiss who ruled the Sacramento Valley. But now Sutter was having trouble holding on to his empire with all the gold rush squatters overrunning his land.

California was firmly in the hands of the United States now, the Russians and British had bowed out, and Mexico was completely conquered in Alta California. Spanish was the girl's native tongue, though she spoke English fair enough. He decided to never let her know he understood her Spanish. He didn't want to hash out why she'd said she loved him last night. Perhaps a man had never satisfied her and she enjoyed the pleasure he'd given her.

It was better they parted more as strangers than anything else, though he couldn't escape the bond he felt with her now. Like their souls had joined along with their bodies. It was a mystery he didn't understand and certainly didn't want to dwell on.

She didn't say any more about her life at Fort Ross, and his frustration grew. She wasn't a talker, which in other circumstances he would have appreciated. He preferred quiet women these days, though Maggie was anything but quiet, and neither was Clara. But he needed this girl to talk. What he really wanted to know was if she was in on the joke on him last night.

It was a pleasing day, the sky clear and cobalt blue, wild-life teeming and birdsong along the riverbanks. He didn't take pleasure in the beautiful day as he normally would have. If the girl wasn't going to fess up about who she really was, he'd just give it to her straight. "Did you make any money on me last night?"

She stiffened. He knew he'd offended her, but she didn't provide an answer.

He leaned forward, whispering in her ear, "I don't take kindly to jokes." He gritted his teeth, not wanting to say more he'd regret later.

"I don't know about a joke." Her voice unfurled soft and sweet but guarded.

He backed off. "I was drunk out of my mind last night. I hardly remember what happened." He was lying. He remembered last night well enough, and his guilt was growing.

"You didn't seem drunk. Not like the others."

"I was dead drunk," he assured her.

She stiffened even more, drawing her body as far away from him as she could in the saddle. She knew exactly what he meant. Saying he didn't remember what they'd done in the moonlight, in the firelight, was a boldface lie. He couldn't shake the feeling he'd done her wrong. He remembered her soft, surprised moan—not in pleasure, but in pain when he finally made her his. He didn't want to believe she was a maiden. Perhaps she was a good actress. Soiled doves were like that, pretending to be whatever a man wanted them to be. If she wasn't in on the joke, he was more than a lout. How could a beautiful half-breed keep her virtue in the gold camps?

"Do you remember marrying me?" she ventured. He could hear the heartache in her voice, and it pierced his conscience.

So this was how it would be between them. Even though he was sober now, she'd pretend to be a virtuous young woman he'd ruined last night. It was going to be a long ride back to Marysville.

He'd hoped she'd confess to being a prostitute, and they could part ways laughing this off. He could even visit her when he came to Marysville, though he'd have to keep that from Clara. "I don't believe we're truly married," he finally told her, having a hard time thinking straight with her in front of him in the saddle. He didn't want to talk anymore. He just wanted to find the make-believe preacher or the drunken Californio and plow his fist into their faces.

Chapter Four

Isabella tried not to touch him in the saddle after he made it clear he didn't think they were married. Memories of last night flooded her, filling her cheeks with searing heat and her heart with stinging hurt. Hot tears filled her eyes. She did her best to blink them away. She stared straight ahead, unwilling to let her feelings show. She'd learned a long time ago to hide her emotions. Peter believed he'd been tricked, not just by the minister and those men, but by her as well. She felt betrayed too. She had surrendered everything to him. She'd awoken thinking not only were they husband and wife, but that they were in love. Only two people in love could do what they'd done last night.

She'd watched him rise from their bedroll when the sky was still rosy, the heat of his body no longer keeping her warm, but she wasn't worried about him leaving. Not after what they'd shared. He was probably going hunting for their breakfast, since it was obvious he made his living off the land. But when he returned with that look on his face, she knew something was terribly wrong. All her life, she could read people's faces. What she read on her new husband's face tore her hopes asunder.

She was doing everything she could now to avoid touching him. She'd grown up on horses and knew how to move with her mount, but she wasn't used to a large, brooding man behind her. He reminded her of her brother, Roman, before he married Rachel. A man at war with the world. Her fretting was interrupted when a fox bolted from the undergrowth beneath the horse's feet. The paint mare skittered sideways. Peter wrapped his arm around her waist, drawing her up against his hard frame as he reined in his mount. Even after the horse settled down and the fox was gone, Peter didn't release her, but kept her pressed tightly against him.

All she wanted was to escape. The beating of his heart pounded against her back, matching the pounding of her own wild heart. There was nothing soft or cold about this man. He felt like a warm wall of muscle and bone behind her, his arm like a band of steel around her middle. They were headed back to Marysville, of that much she was certain. Would Don Pedro be there still? Or the minister who had married them?

What was Peter planning to do in Marysville?

It never occurred to her until he said as much that their marriage was a farce. In the camps, she'd seen these kind of sudden unions between strangers. Not in gambling tents, mind you, but men and women leapt into matrimony without knowing each other all the time in the goldfields. A host of strange men had sought her hand in marriage, but she'd turned them all away. She'd never met a man she wanted to build a life with until Peter Brondi rode into town on his painted horse yesterday. A mare. He rode a mare. Californios rode stallions. What kind of man tamed a mare? A mount he fondly called Mel? She blinked hard, and two scalding tears rolled down her cheeks when she recalled how tender he'd been with her last night, and yet how his passion had consumed her. She wiped the tears away as his arm loosened, but he didn't let her go.

"No need to cry," he softly said against her hair. "I'll return you to where you belong, and we'll put this all behind us."

Anger and frustration finally overcame her. "Our gold claim is gone. We have nothing left. Don Pedro doesn't even want me anymore. Where will I go?"

"Home," he said and added no more.

"I don't have a home." How could she explain her home was gone? Rancho de los Robles had been overrun by the Americans. She could certainly return to Roman and Rachel and their brood at Rancho El Rio Lobo—if she could make it there alone—but she had hoped to build a life of her own with a husband of her choosing. She feared Roman wouldn't allow her to choose her own mate. Surely, her brother would follow the way of the Californios and marry her off to a man he chose for her. Don Pedro had promised to let her choose a husband for herself, but that was months ago when he wasn't drunk every day. When he was still finding bits of gold in their claim and still had hopes of striking it rich and buying back Rancho de los Robles.

Peter suddenly spoke to her in a language she'd never heard before. She didn't respond because she had no idea what he was saying.

"You don't speak Indian?" He leaned in close, leaving her shivering with his warm breath against her ear. "I thought you were Indian."

"I only speak English and Spanish, and some Russian," she admitted.

"Say something in Russian."

"Are you my father?" she asked in Russian. She didn't speak fluent Russian anymore, but Lupe spoke more Russian than Spanish, and when Isabella was small, the Indian servant from Fort Ross who ran the Vasquez household had been more a mother to her than anyone else. Lupe had always spoken Russian when they were alone together.

"Sorry, I don't speak Russian. What did you say?"

Her throat constricted so tight she could hardly speak anymore. She'd always dreamed of being reunited with her Russian father. "It doesn't matter," she murmured, doing her best to stop crying. She knew Peter would leave her. Like every man left her. She closed her eyes, aching inside. The thought of being on her own in Marysville terrified her. If Don Pedro wasn't there with his pistol, and Peter left her by herself in the town, she would probably fall prey to the next man who came along. What if that man was Mick? The thought horrified her.

"It matters to me. Tell me what you said in Russian." His voice was softer now, his arm around her gentle. She knew he had bathed because he'd returned to camp with wet hair, slicked back as if he'd just come out of the water. He smelled clean and wild and looked so handsome this morning. Isabella loved to swim and imagined how wonderful it would be to find a bathing hole and spend the whole afternoon, just the two of them, splashing around like carefree children. Peter was still her husband, even if he didn't like the idea. There was no way he couldn't be her husband after last night. They would always be married in her mind. And perhaps now she would bear him a babe. The thought bolstered her spirits. She longed for a child.

"I said, 'Are you my father?' Someday I will return to Fort Ross to find my real father."

"The Russians sold the fort several years ago. Most of the Russians have departed California," he told her.

"That can't be true."

She tried to keep the distress from her voice, but it must have come out because he said, "I'm sorry. But it's true. The Russians are gone." He drew her back against his body once more as if he would comfort her. She let him embrace her, unable to resist his strength anchoring her close.

"You shouldn't hold me this way if you don't believe I'm your wife." The realization that her real father could be gone from Fort Ross stunned her. What did she have left? She could go to San Francisco to Maria, but Maria had her own life with Dominic and the children.

"I'm sorry about last night," he said, and the regret in his voice made her ache.

As confused as she was about what had happened between them, she didn't harbor regret the way he did. How could she regret last night? He was a part of her now and always would be. Peter was her husband. She would not give up on him. "I'm not sorry," she whispered.

Why did he talk this way and insist on keeping her pressed against him? She wedged her elbow back, trying to get him to loosen his hold on her.

"Mel is a little shy, like you. I don't want you falling off if we come across another fox in the brush and Mel bolts. So I'm going to hold you."

"I've never fallen from a horse in my life." She shoved her elbow hard into his midsection, which felt like stone.

He laughed.

It surprised her.

"You do have some spunk after all."

She could tell her blow hadn't hurt him a bit. "I don't understand you."

"You aren't the first woman to say that." He wasn't laughing now and still wouldn't let her go.

"I can cook. I will wash your clothes. If you own a book, I'll read it to you."

"You can read?" He sounded surprised.

"I wasn't raised in a gold camp. I grew up with tutors in a grand hacienda. The Californios adopted me when I was very young. I was raised with wealth and privilege and servants."

"Well, aren't you something."

"I'll make you a good wife." It took all her courage to tell him that.

He loosened his hold on her. She could feel him pulling away with Marysville looming in the distance. New brick buildings, wooden stores, and the shorter canvas tents filled her vision. The morning sun reflected off the two rivers where they joined at the edge of town. It really was a pretty spot for a city there, where the waterways converged. Schooners came up the river every day from Sacramento City and San Francisco, delivering goods and miners and anyone looking to make their fortune in the nearby hills.

They rode into town in awkward silence, passing the tent where he'd won her, and moving on down the street with her mule in tow. She'd nearly forgotten about Old Amigo. In Peter's presence, she could hardly think of anything else but him.

At a new brick hotel with a freshly painted sign that read, "Clara's Place," Peter climbed off his horse and helped her down. He stared into her eyes for a moment, and the look on his face sent foreboding through her. The hotel door swung open, and a red-haired woman swept out onto the porch. She wore a fine silk dressing gown the color of green grass and looked like a grand lady. Clearly, she hadn't been out of bed very long. She wasn't even dressed yet but didn't seem to mind.

"Peter Brondi," she scolded, "I haven't seen you in a month of Sundays." She stepped right up and kissed Peter's lips with Isabella standing there slack-jawed beside him. "Who is this little girl you got with you? You never told me you had a baby Indian sister. She looks like Paul with all that ebony hair and them Indian cheekbones." The red-haired woman reached out and pinched Isabella's cheek none too gently. Like one would pinch a child's cheek but harder.

Isabella stepped closer to Peter. She read the scorn in the woman's flashing green eyes. And a challenge too. This woman considered Peter hers. That was apparent.

"You know I would have told you if I had a sister, Clara." Peter put his arm around Isabella's shoulders.

She leaned into him, hoping he'd protect her. The woman had a pleasant smile on her face, but Isabella sensed she'd just made an enemy.

"So is she Paul's baby sister?"

Isabella couldn't stop staring at the woman's dressing gown. The robe of green silk made her eyes blaze green. She had a surprisingly small waist, curving hips, and very buxom breasts. The top half of her breasts were exposed for all to see. Once upon a time, she must have been the most beautiful woman on earth, but age was stealing her beauty.

"Don't play games with me," said Peter. "I know you heard about last night. Nothing happens in this town you don't know about, Clara." He kept Isabella close to his side, which eased her fears a little.

Clara laughed. "Mick said you stole his king of hearts."

"Is Mick here?" Peter left Isabella's side and tied his horse and the mule to the rail in front of the hotel.

"He headed into the hills to stake his new claim about an hour ago. Thinks he's gonna fill his pockets with gold."

"Do you know where the Californio went? This is Belle. She belongs with that old fool."

Clara fell silent. The look on her face changed. She turned sympathetic eyes on Isabella.

"You got some bad news?" Peter asked Clara before flashing Isabella a look of concern. "Did he already leave town?"

"He's dead." Clara's eyes lingered on Isabella.

Was that pity or hate she saw in that green gaze?

"The greaser shot himself last night. Lickidy scooped him off the street and is looking for someone to pay the bill for his undertaking."

Isabella gasped.

Peter wrapped both his arms around her before she fell down. He scooped her up and carried her past Clara into the hotel. "Give us a room," he growled, heading up the stairs with Clara on his heels.

The swoosh of Clara's skirts and Peter's feet on the stairs filled Isabella's ears. The sound of his moccasins surprised her. She'd grown accustomed to him making no sound in those deerskin boots. But he was in a hurry and didn't seem to care that his feet hit the stairs with thud after thud. He took her to the third-story room where Clara directed and laid her down on the bed.

She curled onto her side and stared at the wall in shock. The room reminded her of an attic but had a big glass window with sunlight pouring through and was done up real pretty. Lace curtains and all.

How could Don Pedro be dead?

She could hear Peter whispering and Clara whispering back, but she couldn't make out what they were saying. The two left the room together and returned with a bottle and several glasses.

"To ease your pain," Peter said, but Isabella refused the glass of amber liquid he handed her.

Clara insisted she drink it, so Isabella gulped down the fiery stuff. Perhaps it was medicine, but then Clara poured Peter and herself a glass too, and both she and Peter sat on the edge of bed and sipped their drinks.

"Do you want to talk about your pa?" Clara asked.

"He wasn't her pa," Peter answered for her. "Belle's father was a Russian from Fort Ross."

"That's where she gets them looks," Clara said, like Isabella wasn't even there. "I heard about the likes of her from a German from Fort Ross who stocks my shelves from time to time. He said the Russians have mixed with the Indian women for years. It's created a real pretty race of black-haired, blue-eyed Creoles. They're intelligent too, but haven't learned to keep themselves clean. They don't live very long on account of the germs."

Isabella began to weep as Clara talked that way about her.

"I think you should give me some time alone her with her," said Clara. "Unless you plan on keeping her. Everyone knows Old Will ain't a real preacher. The whole town's had a good laugh on you, Pete, I'm sorry to say."

Peter stood up and downed the rest of his drink. Clara did the same and poured Peter and herself another round. She filled Isabella's glass back up too, even though Isabella shook her head that she didn't want anymore.

Peter stared at her for a moment before asking, "Where's Old Will?" His face had gone hard, and his voice was emotionless.

"He's gone. Never stays long when he's here. Don't know what to make of Old Will. I think he's a crazy coot."

"Does he visit your girls?"

Clara chuckled. "I don't tell who comes and goes here. You know that, Pete."

"Can you tell me where he was headed?"

"You plan on searching for him?"

"Maybe."

"Well, you're burning daylight. You best get going if you want to catch Old Will. He's headed to Sacramento City. I'll take care of your Creole. I've been wanting a black-haired, blue-eyed Fort Rossy here. It will be good for business."

"She's not a working girl." The certainty in Peter's voice reassured Isabella.

"Everyone earns their keep around here," Clara insisted. "This fine building ain't going to pay for itself."

"She cooks and washes and knows how to read. Put her to work doing that until I return," Peter said firmly.

Clara smiled. "Never had a girl here who could read. Maybe I'll have her recite Shakespeare for the gents. Wouldn't that be something? Shakespeare at Clara's Place. I might have to hang another sign."

Peter downed his drink and handed his glass back to Clara. "If I hadn't been drunk last night, I wouldn't have gotten tied up in this mess. Don't give me any more whiskey. I need my wits about me today."

Clara stepped up to Peter and put her hands on his face, stroking his beard, looking into his eyes. "I told you to stay away from other girls. Only a woman like me can make you happy. I'll fix this for you. Go get Old Will. I know you need to find out if he's a real preacher or not."

Peter stepped away from Clara and walked to the door. "You told me he's not a real preacher already." His voice sounded accusing. He looked at Isabella on the bed. She didn't want him to leave, but she didn't say anything to stop him. The shock wouldn't leave her.

"You don't quite believe me, do you?" Clara's question turned Peter's attention back to her.

He glared at Clara. "I don't know what I believe anymore," he said and then walked out the door.

Chapter Five

Three days later, after not finding the preacher at Sutter's Fort or down in Sacramento City, he returned to Marysville. What else could he do? Old Will had turned into a ghost, and he was in a foul mood, convincing himself that perhaps even Clara was in on the joke. The Californio was dead. He couldn't account for that, but Clara had admitted she wanted a Creole girl, and Belle hadn't done anything but cry at Clara's Place, which left Peter at a loss on figuring this whole thing out. He just wanted to pass through Marysville and keep on riding back to Jedediah and make sure his father was still alive. There was no sign of Paul in Marysville or Sacramento City, though his brother was known in both places. Peter worried Jedediah wouldn't get to make amends with Paul before he died.

His father had never given up on Paul. It was something Peter hated and admired in equal measure, Jedediah's unquenchable love for his lost son. Paul often referred to himself as the dirty Indian boy of the Brondi family. "We all know

I'm not really your son. I'm an outlaw's bastard, and you're done with me!" Paul had yelled at Jedediah when Peter and Paul had come to blows over Maggie. The two brothers nearly beat each other to death that day, with Jedediah shooting them both to end the brawl.

Jedediah was a deadeye with a firearm. He'd only winged his boys. Paul rode away wounded. They hadn't seen him since. Jedediah doctored Peter up. It was only a flesh wound and healed fast. But Peter's heart hadn't healed. The fight left him with a wound that festered deep inside. Jedediah expected Peter to forgive Paul. "Maggie was as much to blame as Paul," Jedediah said. "And you're carrying your own blame as well. You chose Fremont and Carson over Maggie. She knew it. Paul knew it. I'm just surprised you didn't know it."

"I was serving my country," Peter had retorted. "We won the West thanks to Fremont and Carson and the fine men I rode with in '46."

"We all make our choices." Jedediah stared into his soul. "Then we live with those choices. Maggie chose your brother after you left. It wasn't Paul's fault she died. That broke your brother's heart. And Paul didn't just lose a wife, he buried a son too. You need to forgive him and get on with being his brother. Paul loves you dearly and you know it."

After Peter mulled over the mess with Paul and Maggie, he replayed the tent wedding in his mind as he rode back to Marysville, trying to figure out if there was a chance the marriage was legitimate. Again, he concluded there was no way he'd really wed Belle officially, yet he couldn't get her out of his mind. She was his last thought before he fell asleep at night and his first contemplation come morning. When he awoke was the worst because he wasn't prepared for her memory. Recalling her long black hair sliding through his fingers sent an ache right through him. He wanted to kiss her again. Make love to her again. And then hold her if she cried. He could still see her almond-shaped blue eyes shining with tears. It wasn't just her beauty that ensnared him. She really did need him. He wasn't used to being needed by anyone.

And maybe he needed her too.

Reaching town, he stopped by Lickidy's to collect her mule. The animal looked in better shape, and he thanked Lickidy for feeding him so well. Lickidy said he'd used the old mule to transport the Californio to the graveyard on the outskirts of town. "The mule seemed to know he carried his master and walked with his ears pricked and his step proud. It was a fine send-off for such a foolish man," Lickidy said. "I sure hope you ain't gonna leave that pretty little gal at Clara's Place."

"She isn't my gal." Peter hurt just thinking about Belle. "Everyone knows they pulled a fast one on me." He took the mule's lead rope and tied it to his saddle. He thought he saw Lickidy tuck away a smile, but when he stared hard at him, Lickidy's face grew solemn.

"You got a lot to learn, boy," he said.

"Everyone wants to teach me something. I don't like it," Peter answered.

"I'd say the Good Lord is teaching you something, so you'd best listen up." Lickidy smacked the old mule on his hindquarters, and the animal brayed. The mule's protest surprised them both.

"Why'd you smack that poor old mule?"

"Because I'd like to smack you, but that poor old mule's a lot smarter than you. He won't smack me back and start a fight. But you might."

"You already started a fight." Peter unballed his fists, knowing he could never hit an old man like Lickidy. Especially since he was the town's only undertaker. It wasn't really Lickidy he was mad at. He couldn't find a man to vent his anger on. The Californio was dead and the fake preacher long gone.

"I'm not fighting you. I'm trying to talk some sense into you. A man would be lucky to end up with that little blue-eyed, half-breed gal. She's about the prettiest thing I ever seen," Lickidy said.

Peter climbed into the saddle. "I'm not lucky."

"It was standing room only at Clara's last night. All the men wanted to see your girl."

Peter tipped his hat to Lickidy. "Stop calling her my girl. She isn't."

He wasn't about to tell Lickidy that he would have ridden over to Clara's to fetch Belle right now if not for his pride. He'd never taken kindly to being laughed at. He just wanted to forget this whole thing. At least with Clara he could ride away the next morning without any regrets. They didn't owe each other a thing. He felt like he owed Belle something. At least an apology for the Californio's death, and he should return her mule too. But she wouldn't need the mule if she settled in at Clara's Place. He'd feel better knowing she had some gold. He could pay her for the mule, though he'd already bought the mule from the Californio. It bothered him far more than he cared to admit that he didn't know Belle's real history. The thought of other men tasting what he had tasted with her didn't sit well with him at all. He hadn't been possessive of a woman since Maggie. Each time he thought of Belle, he got confused and mad. She seemed so innocent, but that just couldn't be true. Innocent women weren't won in card games.

He looked at the mule trailing behind Mel and realized the animal might come in handy. Jedediah had been wanting a mule to guard the sheep. This wasn't the kind of mule Jedediah had in mind. A young jack to bond with the sheep was what his father wanted, but Peter liked the way the old mule was willing and patient and didn't give him any grief. A lot of patience was needed for sheep, and he could see the old mule had patience in spades.

He stopped by the barber shop before going to Clara's. For some reason, he wanted to spruce up before seeing Belle again. Truth was, he was nervous to face her. Inwardly, he chastised himself. She was just a girl and hopefully wouldn't have the same effect on him when he was sober. Maybe when he saw her, he'd realize she wasn't special. She was just a good actress, like Clara's girls, and the nightmare he'd fallen into would end. Any man would think him crazy for buying the mule a second time, but he needed to put some gold in Belle's pocket before he left. The mule seemed the best way to do it.

"Go ahead and shave off my beard," he told the barber before he changed his mind. "I want to make sure I still have the Brondi cleft. I haven't seen my chin in years."

"A dimple don't go away," said the barber, sending him over to the bathhouse to wash up before the shave and haircut. When Peter returned, the barber used a straight razor to remove all his facial hair and cut his hair too.

"You're younger than I thought," the barber said when he finished and happily weighed the gold Peter paid him on his own scales. Peter hadn't used coins in a long time. Everyone dealt in dust and nuggets in California.

Feeling fancy, he purchased a new set of clothes as well. He'd promised Jedediah he'd give homesteading a try and planned on settling down with his father and the sheep until Jedediah passed on. If only Belle wasn't half-Indian and perhaps a prostitute.

He pushed the thought aside as he shrugged into the fine cotton shirt and light gentlemen's trousers. It amazed him that Marysville had this kind of mercantile, where a man could dress finely if he wanted to. Brick buildings were going up faster than tents, and there were several nice restaurants now. Eating alone wasn't something Peter enjoyed, so he put away his noon meal as fast as possible without being rude. He wasn't much of a talker, but he asked everyone he saw if they knew Old Will. A few said they did, but none could say for certain if the man was really a preacher.

"Old Will's a funny one," said one man. Another man told him, "I saw a Bible in his belt. He's a religious man."

Jedediah was a religious man, but he wasn't a preacher ordained to marry folks. That's what Peter really wanted to know. Could Old Will actually marry them in the eyes of God and man?

He knew Clara's Place didn't stir until late in the day, so he found a nice shady spot on the edge of town with grass for Mel and the mule. He staked the animals out to eat and then pulled one of his favorite novels from his saddlebags. He'd spent the past several days in turmoil. For the most part, his anger had cooled. It was hard to stay mad at a man he'd paid to have buried and a preacher he couldn't find. And he couldn't be angry at Belle. Was she really what she claimed to be? Did she really know how to read? He didn't know many folks who could read in California. Jedediah had taught him and Paul to read and then put the Bible in their hands when they were boys. "There's nothing better than the Good Book," Jedediah had said. "You'd best read this while you're young. If a man can read, he can change his world."

His father meant a man could find a better place in the world, but Peter took what Jedediah said at face value. He liked reading about other worlds, forgetting the hardships of his wilderness life and savoring the gentile surroundings he found in novels. Of course, those gentile surroundings weren't real, but they seemed so with his nose buried in a book.

He made himself comfortable in his spot by the river, leaning back against a large cottonwood tree, where he spent several hours reading. Finally, he closed his eyes for a spell.

When he awoke with the sun sinking low in the sky, he decided it was time to go see Belle. His nerves were a jangle, and he hated feeling this way. The truth was, he wanted to be alone with her again. He imagined their camp in the oak grove, the two of them wrapped in his bedroll, and groaned. "You're a lovesick fool," he chastised himself as he rode back to Clara's Place.

When he got to Clara's, her place was surrounded by men. It was standing room only on the front porch, and he had to wait in line to get inside. By the time he made it through the door, he was back in a foul mood. Stale smoke, strong perfume, and the stench of beer filled his nostrils. When he saw Belle sitting on the stairs in a fancy dress, all dolled up like one of Clara's girls, her shoulders bare, reading a book to a passel of men, his heart stopped and then pounded hard.

Of course she was all dolled up and thick with the men. How foolish could he have been the past few days? She probably made every man feel the way he felt about her. Her shiny black hair was no longer in braids. It was pinned up like a fancy lady's hair. He didn't like it.

"She's quite the draw," Clara whispered in his ear, pressing her soft curves against his back.

"Reckon she is," he replied. He turned and accepted the kiss Clara planted on his lips.

"Why don't we go upstairs for a while. It's been too long since I've seen this dimple." Clara pressed her finger into his chin and then kissed him again, a kiss meant to stir a man's passions. He felt nothing. He tried to smile for Clara, though he was sick inside. Glancing over his shoulder, he saw Belle was no longer reading. Her gaze was locked on him. The men around her stared at him too. The look on her face was one of shock and grief. He almost went to her right then to carry her out of here.

Clara grabbed his chin and turned his face back to hers. "Don't tell me that girl's any match for me." The look in Clara's eyes was something he'd never seen before. Not once had he noticed Clara jealous of another woman, but tonight she was, and something in her green eyes gave him pause. He decided he needed to convince Clara that Belle wasn't a threat. Clara was good to her girls if she liked them.

He forced out a laugh. "Of course, she's no match for you, darlin'. I didn't even try her out. I just feel bad for the way men have treated her." He was speaking of himself treating Belle badly, but he would never admit that to Clara.

"Let's go to my room. I'll make you forget all about that Creole."

He squeezed the crystal glass of whiskey Clara handed him. "I've got the Californio's blood on my hands. Even though he wasn't really her father, I feel terrible that he's dead."

"That old fool took his own life because Mick got his gold claim. It wasn't about the girl. Don't carry that burden."

"If I hadn't taken her from him, he wouldn't have killed himself."

"Why did you take her?"

He needed to shake Clara off her notion that he desired Belle. "She reminded me of Paul's mother, the only mother I ever knew." Peter downed his drink. He wasn't used to lying.

Clara looped her arm through his and walked him over to the bar. The smell of stale beer was stronger there. "Billy, give Pete a bottle of whiskey. He's gonna need it tonight."

Clara's bartender, a big, good-natured New Yorker, slid Peter a brand new bottle of Clara's finest whiskey.

Take the girl and go.

The thought came out of nowhere and hit him like a warm gust of wind. The voice reminded Peter of the intuition that had saved his life on countless occasions. A voice he couldn't hear, but heard all the same.

"Did you find Old Will?" Billy asked.

Peter found it hard to concentrate on what the bartender was saying. The voice deeply disturbed him. He usually only heard it in the midst of battle. And he always did what it said. He attributed still being on this earth to obeying that voice.

Clara had been sidetracked by a smooth-talking gambler who wanted a girl. "She must speak French," the gambler was saying.

Clara had her back to Peter, so he took the opportunity to see what Belle was doing. Over on the stairs, she was reading to the men again, but she looked up as if she knew he stared at her. Did she recognize him without his beard and buckskins? From across the room, their gazes collided, and he heard the voice again.

Take the wife I have given you and leave this place. He swore he felt a warm wind on his face for a moment. His cheeks flushed with heat and conviction. He shook his head, trying to clear it.

"Clara tells me you had yourself a wedding after stealing Mick's king of hearts." Billy laughed and then grew serious. "I'd marry Belle," he said softly. It was obvious he didn't want Clara to hear.

"You ever seen Belle before in Marysville? Is she a soiled dove?" Peter gulped down his whiskey, trying to act like he didn't care about Belle and hadn't heard the voice. He was unnerved, but he didn't want anyone to know it.

Billy shrugged and poured drinks for two men who stepped up to the bar. "She ain't taken a gent to her room yet. I've been watching since she got here. Belle's new to Marysville, I can tell you that."

"Is she having a good time? Does she act like the other girls here?"

Billy grinned. "No. She drinks milk and won't touch champagne or any spirits at all. And she talks real sweet when you can coax her into a conversation."

Clara had walked away from the bar with the gambler, trying to appease him since both her French girls weren't in the parlor, which meant they were already upstairs doing business.

Peter refilled his drink and held on to the bottle Billy passed him. "Do you know how old she is?"

"Hard to tell," said Billy. "Old enough, I suppose."

Peter was doing his best to forget about that voice. Especially since a young miner was kissing Belle's naked shoulder now. She hadn't stopped reading to the men and would no longer look his way. He took a seat at the bar and proceeded to drink hard and fast, his gaze on Belle. He wanted to kill the young miner for touching Belle. He fantasized about beating the man senseless and carrying Belle away.

"I got more comfort for you than what's in that bottle, Pete." Clara leaned over, and the scent of her French perfume didn't stir him like it used to. He accepted her kiss again, but all he could think about was Belle.

Take my lamb and go. I have given her to you. She is your wife.

Peter jumped out of his seat. "No," he said vehemently.

Clara was taken aback. "It won't cost you a dime, you know that, Pete. You ain't my customer. You're my lover."

He placed his empty glass down harder than he intended on the well-polished wooden bar. "I didn't mean you, Clara." He pointed at the young miner caressing Belle's bare shoulder. "She's here to read or cook or clean. She's just a girl—I told you that. She was in braids when I brought her here. Now you got her wearing silk. Entertaining your gents. I don't like it. It's not right to put an Indian girl in that kind of dress. Find her some calico."

Clara was even more stunned by his outburst. "I've never seen you this way. She's gotten under your skin. What is going on with you and that Creole girl?"

"I brought seven thousand sheep across the mountains. Paul could be dead for all I know. And my father's dying. I won her in a card game, and now she's orphaned because of me."

"We're all orphans." Clara tried to calm him down. "You don't have a ma. You can barely stand your pa. I never knew my own folks. Billy, you got any family back East?"

Billy shook his head.

"See, all of us are alone in this world. I know what you need. You've been on the trail for too long without a woman. Let me be sweet to you. After a night with me, you won't be thinking about anyone else. And don't you worry about Paul. He was here less than a month ago. Fine as a fiddle and randy as a Billy goat. He'll be back around soon enough and when he comes, I'll send him on home to Jedediah."

Peter could feel the whiskey getting a hold of him. Another drink and he'd be the one kissing Belle's shoulder like a smitten fool. Or taking her back to the oak grove. She needed him, and he needed her, and they'd found something particular together. But he didn't want to lose Belle like he'd lost Maggie. He just wanted to forget all about Belle and get on with his life.

What he really needed was a night with Clara to clear his head. Clara was right. He'd been on the trail for too long without a woman. That's why his night with Belle had plagued him so badly. "Billy, put that whiskey away before I drink the rest of it." He slid the bottle back to the bartender, who caught it with one hand. "Come on, Clara. Let's go upstairs."

Clara smiled in triumph. "Now you're talking, Billy, give us a bottle of champagne for the room. Me and Pete's celebrating tonight."

Chapter Six

"All the world's a stage, and all the men and women merely players; they have their exits and their entrances, and one man in his time plays many parts, his acts being seven ages. At first, the infant, mewling and puking in the nurse's arms. Then the whining schoolboy, with his satchel and shining morning face, creeping like a snail unwillingly to school. And then the lover—"

Isabella stopped reading when Peter and Clara walked up the stairs. Peter's beard was gone. His hair cut short. He looked like a fine gentleman. So handsome he stole her breath away. The men gathered around her moved out of the way so he and Clara could pass by. Clara put her hand on Isabella's head when she reached her. "Go to bed, honey. You're done reading for the night."

The men protested, but Clara stood firm. "Belle's my schoolgirl. It's past her bedtime. I'll have her pick up reading for you gents where she left off tomorrow night."

"Good evening, Belle." The way Peter looked at her made Isabella remember his lips on hers, the way he'd brushed her hair beside the fire before making her his woman.

She closed her eyes, willing the scalding tears away. Why was he with Clara tonight?

"You gonna say hello to Pete?" Clara drawled. "I told you my rules. Everyone's nice to the gents."

Isabella swallowed hard and whispered, "Hello," though she didn't look at Peter. She kept her burning eyes on the stairs. A hand returned to her head, and she knew it wasn't Clara's. Peter gently stroked her hair.

"Leave her be," he said, tenderly caressing her for a moment.

Hot tears splashed down her cheeks. Peter stepped past her and headed up the stairs.

"Get to your room," Clara commanded. Her voice was soft, but Isabella could tell Clara wasn't happy.

She rose to her feet, cradling the book of Shakespeare against her chest. The men began telling her good night. "We love you, Belle," a man said, and she tried to smile as she wiped away her tears.

Peter's broad back filled her gaze. He looked so spruced up. Obviously for Clara. This was so confusing. She couldn't stop thinking of him as her husband and wanted more than anything to leave with him. To build a life with him. Have his children. Take care of his home. Fall asleep in his arms every night. Her heart was breaking.

"You gents go get a whiskey on the house," Clara told the men lingering on the stairs. She took the book of Shakespeare from Isabella's trembling hands. "Why are you upset?"

"I'm not upset." But her heart was shattering into a million little pieces. Would Peter brush Clara's hair too? Would he be tender with her? Cover her with kisses and give her pleasure beyond measure?

"Well, stop crying if you're not upset. Get yourself to bed." Clara pushed her up the stairs none too gently.

Isabella stumbled in her haste to escape Clara's wrath.

Peter caught her as she dashed up the stairs, nearly falling at his feet in her haste to do Clara's bidding. "Slow down. You're going to hurt yourself." Peter picked her up as if she weighed no more than a mite and set her feet on the landing, where the hallway stretched in both directions with rooms. After steadying her, he reached out and plucked several pins from her hair.

Clara came up the stairs with an unreadable look on her face. She stretched out her hand, and Peter placed the pins there. "I don't want her hair up like that again. Put her back in braids. It's how she belongs," he said in his quiet, raspy way.

The meager light of the upstairs landing's oil lamps illuminated the turmoil on Peter's face. Isabella bowed her head, unable to look at him anymore. Everything in her wanted to plead with Peter to be his wife. She didn't care if their wedding wasn't real. She didn't care if they weren't really married. She just wanted to ride away with him and never see this place again.

"I'm trying to figure all this out," Clara said. "You either think Belle's your long-lost sister, or you got it bad for her. If you got it bad for Belle, you may as well tell me now."

Isabella wanted to hear Peter's answer as desperately as Clara did.

"I suppose you're right," he said. "Belle's not my sister, but I feel responsible for her, and I can't stomach men fawning all over her. I don't like her in that fancy dress with her shoulders showing. She doesn't belong in doves' clothing."

After speaking to Clara, he turned to Isabella, and in that moment she didn't believe that he merely felt responsible for her because Don Pedro was dead. She knew Peter cared for her. She could read it on his face.

Why was he fighting those feelings? Why not just try to make a life together? In the goldfields, they could do anything they wanted. Nobody would talk. That's just the way things were with everyone gold crazy. It was live and let live in the gold camps. A tear streaked her cheek. She desperately wanted Peter to change his mind and accept her as his wife. She wiped the tear away before another took its place.

"Now don't go crying. Clara will be real good to you on account of me. Won't you, Clara?" Peter gave Clara a smile.

Clara smiled in return, relief on her face. "Should we change her name to a sisterly name? All of my girls take on new names when they come here. She could do that too."

Peter said something in an Indian tongue. Neither Clara or Isabella understood what he said.

"Is that a name?" Clara asked. "We don't speak Indian."

"It means Girl Who Flies on the Wind," said Peter. "It's the perfect name for Belle, but she won't need a new name. She not going to do anything anyone's ashamed of here, so she can keep her real name. I'd be obliged, Clara, if you treated her like my baby sister."

Isabella was tempted to tell them her real name wasn't Belle, but she held her silence and stared at Peter, begging him with her eyes to keep her as his wife.

While looking into her eyes, Peter said in perfect Spanish, "You remind everyone here you're my sister. Especially Clara. If another man touches you, I'll kill him. You tell every man I said that. I'll be back around to check on you."

"Why are you speaking Spanish? What did you just say?" Clara put her hands on her hips. A frown returned to her lips.

"I told Belle when an Indian loses a child, they sometimes replace that child with another child they kidnap and adopt into their family. These kidnapped children become the tribe's beloved children. This is why white children survive when taken by the Indians. They become sisters and brothers to the Indians. Belle's my sister now. I expect everyone to honor her and not treat her poorly. She's a guest here, and I'll pay her board as long as she stays. She doesn't have to earn a dime."

"Well, that's real sweet. You think Belle speaks Spanish?"

Isabella hated how Clara talked about her like she wasn't even there. Clara had been doing that for days, but that's not what left her stunned now. Peter had just spoken to her in perfect Spanish. Heat filled her cheeks. Her stomach churned. He'd understood when she said she loved him. And now he'd just straight out lied to Clara. Peter was giving her a message he didn't want Clara to hear.

He took a small pouch from his pocket. He handed it to Isabella, then reached down to his belt and pulled out a long, sharp knife. "That gold is for your mule. You got no purpose for the animal now, and I need a mule to mind my sheep. You hide that gold away. I don't want anyone taking it from you," he told her in Spanish.

In English, he said, "Some Indians cut their hair when they're mourning the loss of a loved one." He gathered Isabella's hair into his hands and spoke Spanish again, "I won't take much. I know you're mourning the loss of the man who wagered you away, but I want you to mourn the loss of me. Because I'll be mourning the loss of you."

After tucking the pouch of gold into her dress pocket, she reached up and grabbed Peter's hand that held the knife. "Take me with you," she whispered in Spanish. "I'll be a good wife. I'll do anything you ask me to do."

With her hand on his, Peter began to cut her hair. "I'm sorry about the other night. You deserve better. You deserve a real husband. Use that gold to go wherever you want. Find a good man to build a life with. A husband who loves you."

"I want to build a life with you," she whispered, holding on to his hand.

He took his hunk of hair and pulled his hand away from hers. "I'm not a good man."

"You are a good man. I see it in your eyes. Please take me with you, Peter."

"I'm with Clara." He tucked his knife away and shoved the hair into his pocket.

"That's enough," said Clara. "We kicked the greasers out of California. We all speak English here now." She turned to Isabella. "Get yourself to bed, little sister. Your brother and I got catching up to do." She stepped over and looped her arm possessively through Peter's.

Peter gave Isabella a half smile that didn't look happy at all. She realized he was drunk again. How could he be drunk when he didn't act drunk? She'd lived with Don Pedro long enough to know drunkenness, but Peter didn't act like other men when he drank. Giving in to the tears, she said, *"Vaya con Dios,"* on a sobbing breath.

"What did she say?" Clara's patience had worn thin.

"She told me to go with God." Peter's half smile disappeared. He stared at Isabella as if she'd slapped him.

Clara suddenly laughed. "Pete will think he's died and gone to heaven with me tonight. Too bad you don't know anything about that, little sister." She pulled Peter down the hallway. "Lock yourself in your room," she called to Isabella. "I don't want any gents bothering you up there."

Isabella turned and ran up the narrow set of stairs that led to her attic bedroom. She locked the door and threw herself onto the bed, sobbing in earnest now. She'd given everything to Peter, and he'd chosen Clara. Reaching under her pillow, she pulled out her golden rosary. She clasped it to her chest and began to recite the prayers she knew so well, squeezing the crucifix until it cut her hand. She cried until she couldn't cry anymore.

For the past several years, all she'd dreamed about was marrying. She'd thought Peter was the man of her dreams, but tonight it felt like a nightmare. He had rejected her. Just as her fathers had rejected her. First her Russian father, and then Don Pedro. She thought about ending her life. She could drown herself in the river, but she realized she wanted to live. Staring at the blood on her hand from the cut the cross had made in her palm, she remembered all the blood when she'd fallen down the stairs searching for Señora Poppycock. She'd loved that little red hen more than anything in the world. Someone had taken Señora Poppycock, probably one of those terrible men who'd come to the rancho and then rode away with Don Pedro and Roman to fight the Americans.

Sarita had died with her baby coming too soon the next day. They'd lost the war, and she'd never gotten over losing Señora Poppycock. The Americans' arrival in California had changed everything. Now Americans were everywhere. Building cities. Taking all the gold from the hills. Killing the Indians.

Putting down her rosary, she got up from the bed. All Clara's rooms had mirrors in them. She went to the looking glass and inspected her shorn hair. "I'll be mourning the loss of you," Peter had said. He hadn't taken much. She'd only lost a few inches of hair. One thing was certain, she would never wear her hair in braids again. Fingering the shorn ends of her hair, tears filled her eyes anew. Peter was loving Clara right now.

In the past few days, she'd learned so much about what happened in a brothel. She wasn't a starry-eyed girl anymore. She couldn't believe all the men who visited these women. Dutch Sadie told her nobody was really loving. It was more like pigs mating. Isabella hoped Peter and Clara were acting like pigs together. Imagining them in a bed of mud made her feel a little better.

Being here wasn't so bad. She liked the beautiful dresses and delicious meals and being admired by the men. It was so much better than the discomfort of the gold camps. She wasn't about to take men into her bed like Dutch Sadie and the other girls, but she didn't mind reading Shakespeare. And she could sing. Clara said everyone needed to earn a living here. She could earn a living with her voice. She didn't want Peter paying for her room and board. He could keep his gold and keep on being a pig with Clara for all she cared. She'd show him. She'd show them all.

Chapter Seven

Peter rode out of Marysville early the next morning. His head pounded from the whiskey and champagne he'd drunk. Though he'd spent the night with Clara, all he could think about was Belle. Her hair was in his pocket, not the new trousers he'd purchased to look like a civilized man for her yesterday, but his buckskins. He'd abandoned the fancy clothes in Clara's room. Clara had been sound asleep when he gathered his gear and left. He had been so tempted to go to Belle's room and tell her to get her things and come with him. He hated leaving her. He'd even walked to the foot of the stairs leading up to the attic, but standing there, he'd talked himself out of it. If he took Belle with him, he'd certainly bed her again, and he didn't want to do that. He couldn't bring himself to turn her into anything but a wife, and she wasn't his wife. She was just a girl he'd won in a card game. A part Indian girl. What would he do with her?

The old mule plugged along behind Mel. After a week of feed and rest, the animal looked a far sight better. Jedediah would be happy, especially if the mule took to the sheep and kept the coyotes and wolves at bay. He'd given Belle far more gold than the mule was worth, but it wasn't really about buying the mule. He wanted to help her start over. If only he knew a respectable woman in Marysville where he could place her, but he only knew whores.

Meeting Belle had revealed just how uncivilized a life he really led. He had no hearth of his own, no womenfolk to call kin. He'd killed more men than he'd helped. Jedediah had homesteaded in a pretty little valley outside of Nevada City and wanted him to live there too.

"Why not find yourself a wife and raise some young'uns," Jedediah had said before he'd left for Marysville.

"Why are you building this farm if you're about to die?" Peter wanted to know.

"I'll die when the Good Lord is ready for me to die," said Jedediah. "And I'd like to knock some sense into you. I don't know where I went wrong raising you and Paul. All you do is waste your strength on soiled doves. In the eyes of God, that's a disgrace."

"When did you get so high and mighty? The pa I knew took up with a half-breed whore and tried to make a mother out of her. That didn't work out so well for any of us, did it?"

"We got Paul, didn't we?" Jedediah scooped the Bible off his lap and held it out to Peter. "Start reading this book. Ask for forgiveness, and never take another drink. I wish I hadn't been a drunk when you were a boy. I'm sorry. Drink ruins a man."

"I know it ruins a man," Peter admitted.

"Well, if you know, then why are you still drinking every time you go to town?"

"Why do all those sheep lie down and let the wolves have their throats?" Peter hated how he couldn't control the urge to drink when he was around a saloon. Then he would gamble and seek out doves and the next day hated himself for giving into the devil's desires.

"Because they're stupid sheep," said Jedediah. "Sheep don't know how to fight, but they know how to die. That's why they need a shepherd."

"I'm a Brondi. I know how to drink. That's how I'll live until I die."

"That's a lie from old Lucifer. You ain't really living that way." Jedediah dropped the Bible back onto his lap because Peter wouldn't take it from him. "You need to settle down and raise a family and surrender your life to God."

Peter smiled ruefully. "I'm not the settling down kind."

Jedediah stroked his beard. "I've been praying for you. Change is coming. You're gonna get over what happened with Maggie and marry soon. The Lord told me so."

Peter could feel himself getting riled the way he always did when Jedediah got after him. "You think you're a prophet?"

"I do a lot of praying out there with the sheep. The Good Lord speaks to me. I know he's got good plans for you."

"Well, you can talk to the Good Lord all day long, but I'm not changing my ways. I'm a rambling man." Peter set his jaw. He wasn't bending, even for his dying father.

"All that rambling is just chasing the wind. You ain't gained nothing under the sun living that way," said Jedediah.

This memory of their conversation ate at him as he rode home. How could Jedediah know he would marry in

Marysville, even if it wasn't a real wedding? Did the Lord really speak to him? Or was age and sickness making his father crazy?

It scared him that Jedediah was dying. Once his father was gone, he'd have no one left. He regretted meeting up with Mick in Marysville. They'd ended up in that card game, drunk as two fools fresh off the ship. Now here he was headed back to tell Jedediah he hadn't found Paul and could hardly sleep over what had happened with Belle. He never felt so low, except when he found out Maggie had died giving birth to Paul's child. He'd searched for her grave along the lonely wagon trail through the mountains but hadn't found it.

A warm breeze kicked up and stirred dust into his eyes. He blinked hard, his eyes burning. His chest ached, and his throat was so tight it was hard to swallow. He should turn around and ride back to Clara's right now to fetch Belle. She'd replaced Maggie in his thoughts. His night with Clara hadn't cured him of Belle. He woke up sick with regret that he'd bedded Clara. All he wanted was to go get Belle and ride away, but what would he do after that?

He didn't even know Belle. Maybe she fooled men with feigned innocence in other towns the way she had him under the stars in the oak grove. Maybe there was magic in her touch. Maybe Belle seduced every man she came across.

As much as he tried, he just couldn't imagine her seducing anyone. If he were honest, he'd admit he'd seduced her. He'd taken a girl in braids and made her into a woman. He recalled their first kiss after speaking their vows. When he tasted her, a part of him had shifted, like snow thawing with the first signs of spring. Something was reborn inside of him with Belle he'd thought forever dead with Maggie.

Why had he ridden away from Maggie four years ago? He made his living scouting and hunting for Carson and Fremont—it was all he knew how to do—but he'd lost Maggie because of it. Carson and Fremont kept wives, and both men genuinely seemed to love their women, but they spent most of their time blazing trails, fighting Indians, and taming the West. That didn't seem fair to the womenfolk. Something had kept him from marrying Maggie. Perhaps riding with Carson and Fremont had meant more to him than Maggie back then.

In September of '46, Fremont had chosen Carson and his men, Peter among them, to bring the news of the conquest of California to President Polk in Washington City. Carson had promised to make the journey in sixty days, routing himself through New Mexico to see his wife Josefa. Men said Carson's wife's beauty was that of the heart-breaking kind. And it was.

They'd crossed the continent on mules, Carson being super- stitious that way. On long treks, he always rode a mule, insisting mules could detect water miles away and foresee Indian attacks and hail storms and the likes of any danger. Mules could also go farther on less feed than horses, withstanding extreme tem- peratures better than horses. Mules were more surefooted and could carry heavier loads, but Peter preferred horses, though he'd ridden a mule like Carson for that trip.

Fifteen men, including six Delaware Indians, made that journey east on mules to see Washington City, their saddle- bags stuffed with correspondence for the president. Delivering important correspondence was something Carson thrived on. He loved America and was set on winning the West for the United States. Peter was patriotic as well, believing what they did was for the good of the nation. He wrote to Maggie that he was helping America win the war with Mexico and was proud of it.

Just eleven days shy of Santa Fe, following the Rio Grande, they'd run into General Kearny leading his Army of the West to California. To Carson's dismay, the general ordered them to turn around and return to California with his troops. Kearny badly needed Carson's help to cross the unmapped desert. Carson knew the best route to forge the desolate land, as well as the Colorado River, which was Kearny's greatest obstacle to California.

Carson, Peter, and the rest of their small band was half starved by then, with Carson pushing hard to see Josefa and Peter eager to see Maggie in St. Louis, perhaps marry her, before blazing on to Washington City. After Kearny ordered Carson and his men to turn around, the letters for the president were entrusted to Tom Fitzpatrick, a courier both Kearny and Carson trusted. After seeing Maggie, Peter had hoped to see Washington City and meet the president, but he remained with Carson, guiding Kearny's troops back to California that fateful October.

They hadn't realized it then, but California was not conquered as they'd thought when they'd left there in September. An insurrection had taken hold, and the Americans had been kicked out of all the coastal towns up and down the territory. Mexico was back in power, and the only place the Americans still held in California was San Diego, where Commodore Stockton was dug in and had several warships anchored in the bay.

Peter wrote more letters to Maggie that he never mailed. By now he had a saddlebag full of messages for her. Pouring out his heart, sharing his hopes and dreams and his determination to acquire California for the Union. They forded the Colorado River, passing the southern tip of the Sierra Nevada Mountains, now dusted with snow. The mules kept on dying, and wolves now trailed the army, feeding on the dead livestock. It made for a dark journey.

The first week of December, they came within twenty-five miles of San Diego, where they met up with a small force of United States Marines under the command of Captain Archibald Gillespie, who'd slipped through the Mexican siege lines surrounding San Diego to welcome Kearny's army. The marines brought food and a small brass howitzer, which lifted everyone's spirits. Gillespie also brought troublesome news: a few hundred Californios led by Captain Andrés Pico were camped at the little Indian village of San Pasqual. The nearby village stood directly on the road between them and San Diego. It was decided they would surprise the Californios with a predawn strike, considering they were outmanned and outmounted, the Californios on well-bred horses, while most of the Americans rode dying mules or marched on foot now. Kearny's aim was to get the Californios' horses, which they badly needed.

Sometime after midnight, their surprise attack was discovered, and the Californios raced to their horses, yelling, *"Biba California! Abajo Los Americanos!"*

Under the cover of darkness, the Californios had no idea of the size of Kearny's small, exhausted army. Even united with Gillespie and his marines, the Americans were outnumbered and their ammunition damp and useless in the misty darkness. Mostly, they'd be relying on their swords in the close contact fighting they expected with the Californios. Peter didn't like any of it. With a rifle in hand, he was second to none. On a used-up mule with only a sword, he wasn't sure he'd survive.

It was during that long night that he vowed never to ride a mule again. He'd acquired Mel soon after the Battle of San Pasqual. They lost twenty-one Americans there, and many more were wounded. It was the bloodiest clash of the Mexican War on US soil. The Californios rode circles around them, sticking the men with long lances that seemed like something out of the dark ages. The Californios also used their riatas with brutal efficiency, lassoing the Americans and dragging them from their mounts to lance them on the ground.

Carson and Peter survived unscathed due to a twist of fate. Their mounts went down at the beginning of the fray. The two men crawled into the brush and were able to dry their rifles for use. They captured fleeing horses and caught up with the fight, abandoning their saddles for the cover of boulders, where they picked off the Californios from a safe distance away with their rifles.

The Americans beat back the Californios that foggy morning, but the lancers didn't retreat far. The next day the Californios fired on them from a nearby hill. Kearny ordered a charge, and Lieutenant Emory, along with Peter and Carson, succeeded in killing or wounding five Californios, putting the rest of their forces in full retreat. But San Diego was still thirty miles away. The wounded could travel no farther, and the Californios outnumbered their dragoons and hadn't gone far. Kearny decided they would dig in and defend themselves until help could be summoned. Everyone hoped the US Navy in San Diego would save them. Peter took a few moments to write Maggie a hasty letter, perhaps his last, stating his deep regret for not marrying her before leaving. Then he helped build fortifications of crude breastwork out of boulders and rocks and anything they could find in the desert, while other soldiers slaughtered the mules for food.

Their camp became known as Mule Hill. Peter thought they would be overrun by the Californios there. Of course, it was Carson who volunteered a rescue mission. He and a Lieutenant Edward Beale, along with a young Diegueno Indian guide known as Chemuctah, crept through enemy lines and made it to Commodore Stockton's camp in San Diego undetected. Just days later, two hundred reinforcements sent by Stockton arrived at Mule Hill. In the face of the fortified American forces, the Californios vanished into the hills. The siege was over. California had been reconquered. Peter couldn't wait to get back to Maggie and put the suffering and excitement of war behind him. Peter could hardly believe it. Filled with grief and fury, he'd attacked Paul.

He returned to New Mexico, meeting up with Jedediah and Paul in Carson's hometown of Taos. They'd just returned from the failed wagon train, leaving Maggie buried in the mountains.

Just a month after Peter's fight with Paul, Jedediah decided all those miners in California would need mutton and wool for blankets and clothing. He got the crazy notion to bring ten thousand sheep to California. Peter suspected his father wanted to get to California because he figured Paul was headed there. They ended up gathering seven thousand Churros and driving them across the barren desert and over the Sierra Nevada Mountains with the help of six lead goats, a handful of Mexican sheepdogs, and sixteen men Jedediah hired to help. Astonishingly, they'd only lost about a hundred sheep in the drive. "They'd never have to work again," said Jedediah after selling most of the sheep for seven thousand dollars.

They built a barn for the small herd of sheep his father kept before winter set in. Jedediah and Peter hunkered down in the barn with the animals until spring, when they'd constructed Jedediah's cabin. "I don't know why you're going to all this trouble," Peter told Jedediah. "You're dying, and I don't want to live here when you're gone."

"You just trust me," said Jedediah. "I've been talking to the Good Lord, and he's telling me to care for his sheep. And you too."

Peter walked away from the conversation because it was hard to stomach Jedediah's sickness and his growing religion. That spring, Jedediah had pestered Peter to go find Paul. "You and I both need to reconcile with your brother," he said. "You bring Paul here, and the Good Lord will take care of the rest."

"I'm tired of hearing what the Good Lord's going to do," said Peter. "Why not ask the Good Lord to take away your sickness?"

"My old tent may be failing, but my spirit's growing stronger every day," said Jedediah. "I want you to find your brother and apologize to him for what happened in Taos. Make amends with Paul before it's too late."

"Finding Paul won't bring Maggie back. I can't forgive him for that."

"I'm praying you make up with your brother before I die." Jedediah gave him a sad smile and went to bed.

Filled with frustration, Peter sat in front of a cold hearth contemplating finding his brother. He didn't believe Maggie just happened to fall in love with Paul. He believed his brother had seduced her. Paul knowingly took his fiancée and made her his own. Paul had done both him and Maggie a terrible wrong. He didn't deserve forgiveness. Why couldn't Jedediah see that?

Now here he was riding back to Jedediah. He still needed to find his brother so Jedediah could reconcile with him. Peter wasn't about to reconcile with Paul himself, but he wanted his father to die in peace. He thought about Jedediah's cabin in the pretty meadow. They hadn't just thrown up a temporary shelter. Jedediah declared he would die in California and wanted to be comfortable until he met his Maker. His cabin was rough-hemmed timber, spacious and fine, with a roaring stone hearth and real windows of glass instead of canvas. After freezing on the last leg of their journey across the Sierras in late fall with the sheep, Peter and Jedediah built that large stone fireplace and made sure the cabin was well constructed to keep out the cold. It was not furnished yet except for two beds they'd built out of timber. Jedediah was working on a table when Peter left a few weeks ago.

Peter especially liked the nearby creek that roiled through the meadow and provided fresh water for the homestead. Everything a man needed was there except a woman. His thoughts that had always veered toward Maggie went straight to Belle. He reminded himself it wasn't a real wedding they had in the gambling tent. The cabin in the meadow wasn't his home. And Belle wasn't his wife. She was a half-breed like Paul, and he couldn't trust an Indian, of that he was certain.

Chapter Eight

Paul sipped the whiskey Clara poured him and listened to the Bluebird sing. So here she was. The girl Peter had married. Paul laughed softly under his breath. It wasn't like Peter to be hoodwinked. Nobody got the best of his brother, but apparently the Bluebird had. Paul could see why. Her voice alone could lead a man to the altar.

"She's something, ain't she?" said Clara.

Paul set his whiskey down. He started laughing and couldn't stop.

"What's so funny?"

"Peter," Paul said. "You got her all dressed up, but that's a little Indian girl. Peter hates Indians." Wiping his eyes, Paul settled back in his chair, and picked up his glass, his gaze on the Bluebird. "She's a pretty thing, all right, but she's still an Indian. I thought a fine red-haired gal like you would be the one to tame my brother."

"Nobody's taming Pete. He's like the wind in the pines, making a woman sigh her life away."

"Are you sighing your life away over my brother, Clara?"

Clara laughed. "Not a chance." But Paul could see in her eyes she was lying.

"If it helps, I've never seen Peter stay till morning with any other woman but you."

"Thanks, it helps." Clara turned to watch the Bluebird. "I don't know what to make of her," she said over the music. "Belle has the looks and talent to become famous but doesn't seem to know a dang thing."

A Mexican vaquero strummed a guitar while the Bluebird sang her Spanish love songs in English. The men in Clara's Place were captivated, gathering around the stage like they'd never seen a woman before. Clara had her all dolled up in blue silk that made the girl's strange blue eyes shine in the lantern light and accentuated her lithe curves. Her silky black hair was piled on her head. Even covered in powder to lighten her skin, Paul could see she was a half-breed like him.

"Where did she come from?" he asked.

Clara picked up the whiskey bottle she'd brought to his table and poured herself a drink. "I don't know. Belle says she was raised in a grand hacienda down near Monterey, but I'm not sure if that's true. I know she came to Marysville with a Californio who's buried now in the town's cemetery. Peter said she was born at Fort Ross."

"What happened to the Californio?"

"Lost his gold claim to Mick, and your brother took Belle from him after he gambled her away trying to get his claim back. The Californio killed himself that night. Just this month, more men have committed suicide on account of losing their gold than I've ever seen in my whole life."

"Maybe he killed himself on account of the girl."

"I don't think so." Clara appeared disgusted. "That girl even reads. I can't get over it. Don't know where she learned to read."

Paul sat up straighter in his chair. "She can read?"

"You should hear her toot Shakespeare. The gents like it almost as much as her singing."

Few folks could read in California. Paul was grateful Jedediah had taught him to read. He wasn't like Peter and didn't carry a book everywhere he went. But knowing how to read, being able to sign his name instead of just leaving a mark like most men, always made Paul proud. He'd never met a woman who could read. And a half-breed at that. The white blood was obvious in her, but so was the Indian. He'd never seen anyone with her kind of beauty.

Clara seemed to read his mind. "She's a Creole from Fort Ross. Her father was Russian." Clara pointed to one of her customers sitting near the stage, a big blond man intent on the Bluebird. The man didn't have a drink in his hand like the other men. And he didn't appear to be one of Clara's normal customers. He looked like a farmer in his dusty boots. "That's Gunther. He's a German from Fort Ross. He says there's a race of half-breeds up there that look just like her. The Russians didn't bring women when they came to California. They mixed with the squaws, and now they got the likes of her there."

"I'll have to make a trip to Fort Ross." Paul grinned.

"Gunther wants to marry her. He's not the only one. She ain't got much meat on her bones to keep a man warm at night and knows nothing about pleasing a gent unless she's reading or singing. Gunther don't drink and won't take any of the girls upstairs. He says he's waiting for Belle to accept his marriage proposal, then he'll be on his way."

"Is she soiled?"

"Not yet, but her time's coming."

Paul could tell Clara was jealous. Must be on account of Peter. "You think my brother soiled her?"

Clara leveled her gaze on him. "Would that change your mind? I know what you're thinking."

Paul grinned. "What am I thinking, Clara?"

"You want to be the lucky gent to take Belle upstairs."

"I take all the girls upstairs."

Clara laughed. "Trust me. She wouldn't know what to do with you upstairs."

"Well, I can fix that."

"I don't think your brother would take kindly to you soiling her."

"So Peter really did marry her. I thought it was a tall tale. Of course, everybody knows Old Will ain't really a preacher. So the marriage wasn't real."

"Pete feels responsible for her on account of the Californio killing himself. I told Pete I'd take care of her, and he rode off looking for you."

"Peter's searching for me?" Paul didn't want to feel hopeful, but he did. He sorely missed his brother and father. What had really happened between the Bluebird and his brother? Everybody knew Peter rode away with her and then brought her back the following morning. Peter never took advantage of a woman. Guilt hit him as it always did when he thought about Maggie. He'd taken advantage of Maggie.

"Pete was looking for you but got caught up in that card game down at the Golden Eagle, where he won Belle. I've never seen him this way. I'm not sure what to make of it," said Clara.

"Well, it's not very often a man wins himself a wife."

"She ain't his wife." Clara's face hardened.

Paul laughed. "I know that, sugar. I just can't help rubbing it in. Of all men, I can't believe my brother got himself in such a fix. Peter's always been real cautious when it comes to women."

"Well, he's cautious because of you. I heard about Maggie."

Paul fell silent. He downed his whiskey. He didn't blame his brother for hating him. Or Jedediah for siding with Peter that day. It was the darkest moment of his life. Even darker than the day Maggie died. All his life he'd done everything he could to please Peter and Jedediah, and he always came up short. They were better men than him, and Paul was even more convinced now that they weren't really his kinfolk. The thought grieved him, as is always did. He was an outlaw's spawn. There was no way he could face Peter and Jedediah again knowing he didn't deserve to be a Brondi.

Clara waved the Bluebird over when her song ended.

Paul downed another glass of whiskey before she reached their table.

"I want to introduce you to someone," said Clara.

The Bluebird's eyes widened on Paul. She looked even younger up close. And scared. Paul grew nervous. He hadn't been nervous around a woman since Maggie.

"This is Peter's brother, Paul. You be sweet to Belle, you hear?" Clara said as she ordered Belle to sit down with him. "I'll have Billy pour you some milk. I know that's your favorite." Clara patted the Bluebird on the head like a child. "You did real good singing tonight. Look at all the gents—they're dying to be in Paul's boots. You're the lucky gent, Paul; don't disappoint me."

Paul found his smile. "I've always been lucky." He leaned across the table and took Belle's hand. He opened her fingers, lightly pressing his lips to her trembling palm. "It's mighty nice to meet you, Belle."

A blush scorched her cheeks. Paul could see that under the powder on her face. She was shaking like a leaf but smiled anyway. He was charmed. His stomach tightened, and heat washed his insides. It was apparent this girl had no idea of her power over men. "How old are you?"

"Old enough," she said and didn't elaborate. Her voice was hoarse from singing. Or maybe it was just sweet and low that way. He loved the sound of her voice and wasn't about to let go of her hand.

"Are you afraid of me, Belle?"

She shook her head, but he could feel the trembles running through her, and her gaze was wide and uncertain on him. He scooted his chair close to hers without letting go of her hand. "I've been wanting to meet you."

Sitting so near, the sweet scent of her filled his senses. It was hard to smell innocence in Clara's Place, but that's what he smelled. Over the perfumes of other women, he inhaled Belle's naivety.

"Why did you want to meet me?" she asked shyly.

"Because my brother married you."

Her cheeks grew even redder, if that were possible. She dropped her gaze to the tabletop, appearing relieved when Clara approached with her milk. "Drink up, little girl," said Clara. "We're trying to put some flesh on you."

"Her flesh is just fine." Paul squeezed Belle's small, cold hand.

"I see you got it bad. Mind your manners. She's not one of my doves."

Paul regretfully released her hand. "I just want to talk to her. I'll be a right fine gentleman."

"Make sure and walk her to the stairs when she finishes all her milk. I usually have Billy take Belle to her room, but he's real busy tonight." Clara pointed a finger at Paul and said, "Don't touch her."

Paul laughed, though it wasn't laughter he felt. His heart was pounding. He was smitten.

"So you're Peter's brother," she quietly said after Clara walked away.

"I am."

"You don't look like him."

"It's a shame," Paul agreed. "Peter's a handsome feller. Just like our pa." He tried not to think about Jedediah not being his real father. He wished more than anything Brondi blood ran in his veins, but he couldn't believe that anymore because it wasn't true.

Belle finally smiled again. "Peter doesn't smile like you do. Your eyes are merry."

He laughed, this time with real humor. "My eyes are merry?"

She nodded and drank her milk.

"Well, I'll be. I got myself some merry eyes."

"Peter's eyes weren't merry."

He could hear the hurt in her voice. So she was pining over Peter. "Did my brother kiss you? Peter don't kiss many girls."

Belle was speechless.

"I'm sorry. I'll stop teasing you." He pulled out a handkerchief and began to wipe the powder from her face. "You don't need all that paint. You got real pretty skin without it."

She allowed him to clean her up and then sat there, still as a fence post, as he pulled the pins from her hair.

"Good Lord," he said when he was finished and her hair tumbled all around her. "You got such pretty hair. Drink all your milk. Let's get you out of here."

Every man in the room watched them now. Clara marched over and took Belle by the elbow, yanking her from her chair. "I told you to mind your manners," she scolded Paul.

"I'm sorry, I don't know what came over me."

"I know what came over you. Go find my new French girl. She'll take care of what's come over you. It's Belle's bedtime."

Belle's eyes were on Paul, wide and luminous, shining with surprise. He reached out and touched her hair. "Remember, you're real pretty just the way you are. You don't need all that powder on your face. I got Indian blood in me too. There's no shame in it."

"You got hot blood in you; that's what you got," said Clara.

Paul gave her a crooked grin. "Doesn't every man in this room have hot blood? Isn't that why you're getting rich here?"

"I'm rich because I'm smart." She pulled Belle away from him.

"Good night," Belle said breathlessly.

"Good night, Bluebird." He couldn't stop smiling at her.

"Good night," she said again, smiling shyly in return.

Paul laughed and quickly stepped over, planting a kiss on Belle's cheek before Clara could stop him. "I'll be here tomorrow night. Will you sit with me again?"

Clara was shaking her head, a frown on her face.

"If Clara lets me sit with you, I will," said Belle.

"Who am I to stand in the way of true love?" Clara rolled her eyes and marched Belle out of the saloon like a schoolmarm.

Paul followed them to the staircase. He waved to Belle as Clara marched her up the steps.

"Good night, my Juliet," he called. If she read Shakespeare, she certainly would know what he was talking about.

She returned his wave and then followed Clara without looking back at him.

So now he knew. Peter hadn't lost his mind. The Bluebird really was worth marrying.

Chapter Nine

A month passed. Belle sang most nights instead of reading Shakespeare at Clara's Place. After her time on stage, she'd taken to sitting with Paul in the saloon. She'd come to count on her evenings with him. Paul was nothing like Peter. He was always laughing and teasing. She liked his sparkling brown eyes the best. It didn't take him long to convince her the marriage to his brother was a farce. "It doesn't speak any less of you," Paul assured her. "I'm just amazed Peter went along with it that night. Nobody marries in a gambling tent. And everybody but Peter knows Old Will ain't really a preacher."

"I don't know why Peter brought me here," Isabella confessed, her heart still aching over Peter's abandonment. "He could have taken me somewhere else. Somewhere respectable."

"My brother ain't the respectable kind. You probably scared the tarnation out of him. But that's no excuse for what he did to you. I wouldn't leave you Belle. You don't belong here."

"Where do I belong?" she asked, savoring her milk as Paul sipped his whiskey. That's one thing she loved about Clara's Place, fresh milk, eggs, and cheese every day of the week and delicious meals all the time. Clara had two full-time cooks and a kitchen full of Indian servants. Isabella had gained weight. She was finally filling out the fancy dresses Clara loaned her.

"You belong on a homestead with a handsome husband like me." Paul was grinning.

Isabella grinned back. Paul wasn't Peter, but as the nights wore on and Peter didn't return, she found herself growing attached to Paul.

Most of Clara's girls were jealous that Paul always sat with her. He was a favorite at Clara's, and the girls didn't appreciate her consuming all his attention. They didn't understand why Paul was content to just talk to her and then leave without going upstairs with anyone. That wasn't like Paul at all, the girls said, and they'd taken to whispering behind Isabella's back.

It really didn't matter. She didn't plan on staying here forever. She wanted her own home, with her own husband—and children. Isabella loved little ones. She would teach her young'uns to read and sing and would find a tutor for them like she had when she was young. Or perhaps her children would go to school. She'd heard schools were opening in California. She would make sure her children were educated, and never would she abandon them.

"How about you and I go on a picnic tomorrow?" Paul said. "I'll find some horses and we can hunt down a pretty spot on the river to enjoy a little sunshine together." Paul leaned against her shoulder, lightly stroking her arm.

She shivered at his touch. "Clara doesn't want me out in the sun. She says my skin's already too dark."

"You got real pretty skin. Everyone needs sunshine. Don't pay Clara no mind. She's just jealous because you're so pretty."

"Why would Clara be jealous? She's beautiful." *And she has Peter*, but Isabella didn't say that. She'd set her mind on forgetting all about Peter, but it was hard.

"Clara's beauty is fading, and nobody sings or looks like you. You're the prettiest girl I've ever seen. That's why I'm taking you on a picnic tomorrow."

"I'll have to find myself a hat. And I don't have any clothes to ride in. I'll need a riding outfit."

"Don't you worry about a riding outfit. I'll take care of everything. You do know how to ride, don't you?"

Isabella laughed. "I can ride a little," she teased.

"Well then, we'll have to have a race. I ride like the wind." Paul was grinning again. His teeth were straight and white like Peter's, his smile endearing. He really was a fetching man. Looking at him, you'd never know he and Peter were brothers. They didn't look alike at all. Peter stole her breath away, but Paul made her laugh. It felt so good to laugh again.

"I was raised in the saddle," Isabella confessed. "I could ride before I could walk. I will beat you in any race."

Paul threw back his head and laughed loud enough to capture the attention of everyone around them. "We'll see about that. May I walk you up to your room tonight?"

Isabella's smile eased away. "The girls will think I'm doing business. I don't do business. You know that." Each night Paul pushed a little further. He was stroking her bare arm again, sliding his fingers to her elbow and back down inside her arm. His touch made her shiver.

"We're not doing business. We're just being friends. I want to make sure none of the other gents bother you."

Men were indeed waiting for a chance to bother Isabella. The quiet German was back from the goldfields, proposing marriage once more, and Mick was here again tonight, looming nearby, watching her with that look on his face that frightened her. She always steered clear of Mick as best she could. "I guess they'd pay us no mind if you came right back downstairs once we get to my room." She looked around to see who watched them.

Paul's fingers moved down her arm and wrapped around her wrist. "I know what Peter did after that card game," he whispered, and Isabella lost her breath. "I know you've lain with my brother."

"Peter married me," she whispered back, her heart skipping a beat, wondering how he could possibly know that.

"I won't leave you like Peter did." Paul promised. His merry eyes were twinkling with something else tonight. A promise of getting her out of here.

At that moment, Mick walked over, the look on his face unreadable. He carried two glasses of whiskey and a small glass of milk, cradling the three drinks in his large, rough hands. "Mind if I join your party?" he asked Paul, not looking at Isabella.

"I mind." The twinkle in Paul's eyes vanished.

Mick set the drinks on their table and then gritted out a smile. "I spoke with Clara. She said you've been taking up too much of Belle's time. She wants other gents to get to know Belle too." Mick finally looked at her, and fear overwhelmed Isabella.

"You ain't no gent," said Paul.

Belle had never heard that kind of edge in Paul's voice before. It reminded her of Peter's voice.

"What's that supposed to mean? I thought we were friends on account of your brother. Peter saved my life, and I've saved his a hundred times. That should count for something." Mick hooked his thumbs in his gun belt.

Clara didn't allow men to wear weapons in her establishment, so Mick's guns were at the bar with Billy. He still looked incredibly dangerous even with his holsters empty.

"You ain't no gentleman. That's all I'm saying, and Belle's with me tonight."

"Does Peter know you're after his woman?"

Mick's gazed raked over her before he stared down Paul. Isabella just wanted to get away from him. She tried to flee, but Paul wasn't letting go of her wrist. Paul's grip on her tightened. Isabella could feel the tension in him.

"Belle don't belong to Peter. She belongs to me."

"I watched your brother marry her."

Paul laughed, but not with his usual humor. "Everybody knows Old Will ain't really a preacher. He rides through the camps shouting about damnation, but nobody listens to him. That marriage didn't mean a thing."

"It meant something to Belle." Mick's gaze slid back to her, stripping off her dress and her defenses. Whenever Mick looked at her, Isabella grew terrified. Mick was strong, smart, and mean. Clara's girls didn't like him much. Whenever he picked a girl to go upstairs, the other girls felt sorry for her. Only Dutch Sadie handled Mick well. Dutch Sadie was tough as nails, and drank like a man, so she was always half drunk.

Paul turned to Isabella. "You knew that wedding wasn't real, didn't you, Belle?"

Isabella swallowed hard. "Of course."

Mick stepped closer, looming over her. "Peter's the better man," he said softly, as if only she could hear him.

Paul stepped between them, bumping Mick with his chest. "You need to back up. Belle ain't your business. You leave her alone." Paul reached down and whipped a long, sharp knife out of his boot.

Mick smiled a deadly smile. "That's the Paul I know. Always breaking the rules. You ain't like Peter. He follows Clara's rules of no weapons."

"Peter ain't here, and I don't want you bothering Belle."

The saloon had quieted. All eyes were on Mick and Paul. Billy came to Paul's side. He had his big wooden club in hand. Isabella had seen Billy use that club to knock a man senseless because he'd gotten drunk and disrespected one of the girls.

"What's going on here?" Billy drawled, swinging his club.

"Nothing." Paul tucked his knife back into his boot.

"You know the rules," said Billy. "I'm gonna need your knife, Paul. I'll put it with your gun. You can have it back when you leave here."

"I ain't parting with my knife," said Paul.

"Well then, it's time for you to leave." Billy held up his stick.

Clara swished over in her satin skirts. "What's going on?" She stared at Paul, then Mick, then Billy, and back at Paul. Everyone knew Clara liked Paul, but she would always side with Billy.

"Your bartender wants my knife."

Clara turned to Billy. "Paul can keep his knife if he leaves the saloon."

"Me and Belle are going upstairs," said Paul.

Clara's eyes widened in surprise, and then a smile slowly spread across her face. "Guess our little Bluebird has found a mate. You two have fun upstairs."

Isabella's legs trembled when Paul took her by the hand. Mick's gaze raked over her a final time. He reminded her of a hungry wolf. Paul pulled her close to him. She felt safer with Paul.

"When I see your brother, I'll make sure he knows you've plowed with his heifer," said Mick.

Clara laughed, but there was no humor in her flashing green eyes. "Belle ain't Peter's heifer."

Mick pinned Paul with his hawkish gaze. "You sure about that, Paul? Don't make the same mistake twice. I'm trying to be your friend. Think about your brother."

"I'm taking Belle upstairs." Paul grabbed his glass of whiskey and downed it without letting go of Isabella.

She wasn't ready to go upstairs with Paul, but she didn't know where else to flee. Clara waved her hand, and a fiddler standing near the vaquero with the guitar kicked up a jaunty tune. Several of the girls grabbed partners and began to dance. Clara cocked a finger at Dutch Sadie. "Mick needs some company." She turned to Mick. "Sadie's on the house. Be good to her. She's gonna take that fire out of you."

"Is Belle gonna take the fire out of him?" Mick glared at Paul.

Clara laughed again. "I guess it's time."

"Where is Peter?" Mick asked.

"I heard he's herding sheep up in the hills." Paul kept his arm anchored around Isabella.

"Those sheep made your brother rich," said Mick. "Jedediah was smart to bring all those sheep to California, but I hear you're done with the likes of your pa. You found any gold in that washed-out claim of yours?"

"More gold than you've found," Paul said, and Isabella could tell he was angry.

"The Californio's gold claim is paying," said Mick. "And she should have been mine too."

Isabella took a step back when Mick's gaze returned to her. Dutch Sadie looped her arm through Mick's. "You men gonna yap all night? Or are we going upstairs for a good time?"

The last thing Isabella wanted was to end up like Dutch Sadie, who had arrived by ship in San Francisco just six months ago. Clara had brought Dutch Sadie to Marysville along with a dozen other girls to start her business. Dutch Sadie was a buxom blond, a hard worker, and friendly, though she drank whiskey and even used tobacco like the men. Still, Isabella liked her. She could tell Dutch Sadie was trying to help her.

"You first," Mick said to Paul, his eyes lingering on Isabella.

Paul pushed Isabella toward the stairs. She wanted to resist. Her life here felt so precarious. Mick came every night now. If she let Paul take her upstairs, would Paul keep Mick away?

The fiddler sawed on his instrument. The saloon was picking up. Men crowded not just the saloon, but the parlor now as well. They eyed Isabella in that hungry way. In California, men outnumbered women at an astonishing rate. It made Isabella feel unsafe. Every time she turned around, a man was breathing down her neck. She wasn't a cherished daughter anymore and had no father to protect her. Her once happy life with the Californios was over. She would go upstairs with Paul. What else could she do? Peter didn't want her. Why should she wait for him? She closed her eyes, agonizing over the decision.

Paul guided her to the landing and then on up the stairs. Mick and Dutch Sadie followed. Dutch Sadie laughed at something Mick whispered to her. The sound of Dutch Sadie's mirth set Isabella's neck hairs on end.

Oh, Peter, why did you leave me? Isabella had gotten her monthly flow a few weeks ago. She wasn't pregnant, as much as she had longed for that with Peter. She felt so cold tonight. And so alone and afraid.

At the top of the landing, Paul reached down and cupped her face in his hands. "I'll take care of you," he promised. "You'll see. We'll be happy together." He guided her up the final set of narrow stairs to her attic room.

She allowed his lips to cover hers as they stood in front of her door. Paul's kiss wasn't unpleasant. He rubbed his hands up and down her bare arms while kissing her, warming her up a bit.

Isabella closed her eyes against the tears and tried not to think about Peter's kisses. How fierce and yet how tender Peter's lips had been on hers. Paul's kisses weren't Peter's, but she'd get used to that. At least she wouldn't have to endure men like Mick if she belonged to Paul.

Paul opened the door and guided her into the room. The moon shone through the window so brightly there was no need to light the oil lamp beside her bed. Isabella felt sick over what might have been but did her best not to show it. Memories with Peter in the moonlight poured through her mind. She closed her eyes and imagined Paul was Peter for a moment.

"We got plenty of time to get to know each other," Paul said, his voice startling her back to reality. "You don't have to undress if you don't want to."

That strange feeling of cold hit her again, and she shivered, though it was August and far from chilly. A balmy river breeze poured through her open window, blowing the lace curtains about. Every window in Clara's Place had lace curtains. Clara liked lace. On the breeze, she could smell the river. It reminded her of camping along the Yuba with Peter. An ache of longing filled her she thought would never go away.

Her bed had been freshly made by one of Clara's Indian servants—the same Indians that had once served the Californios. They'd traded one master for another and were treated like the slaves of the South, even though California had declared itself a free territory. Indian children were kidnapped and sold to the Americans coming to California. Everyone of any means in California had an Indian slave. Well-off folks kept a number of Indian slaves, though they called them servants. Isabella felt sorry for the Indians. And sorry for herself. She couldn't see a way out this night. If only Peter hadn't abandoned her here.

Paul sat down on the edge of the bed and took off his boots. He laid his long, sharp knife on the nightstand beside the bed. "I've never trusted Mick," he said. "I don't know why he's Peter's friend. Must be on account of Kit Carson. Peter would do anything for Kit."

The name Carson froze Isabella. The Californios hated Kit Carson. They called him *el Lobo*, the Wolf. Carson had practically won the Mexican War all by himself in California.

Peter had ridden with Kit Carson?

She walked over to the window to look out at the moonlight splashing the town. She didn't want to know Peter had ridden with Kit Carson, an enemy of her people. The Americans were overrunning California. Each day more buildings went up in Marysville. Tonight, music drifted down the streets, spilling out of the saloons and gambling tents—even coming from the finer hotels. Downstairs, Clara's fiddler sawed hard, his frantic music filling Isabella with more regret. She could hear men dancing and laughing and abandoning themselves to all sorts of vice.

Paul's warm hands settled on her shoulders there at the window. He slowly turned her around. "You don't belong here in this brothel."

"Will you take me away?" Isabella's heart pounded so hard. Men had always left her. She hoped Paul wouldn't leave her too.

A smile spread over his face. "I'll take you anywhere you want to go." His mouth settled on hers again. He scooped her up, carrying her to the bed. The hotel shook with the pounding of the dancers' feet on the floor, just as Isabella shook with the knowledge of what she was about to do. She would surrender to Peter's brother. Peter had lain with Clara. Perhaps this was a way to get even with him. It was also a way to survive.

Chapter Ten

Autumn was nearly here, and California had just become a state. Parades livened every town. Americans sang patrotic songs in the streets. Peter helped make it happen, and he was proud his nation now stretched from sea to shining sea. To celebrate, Jedediah rode to Nevada City and brought home two collie pups and some cider. He named the female pup Goldie, in honor of the Golden State, and told Peter to name the other pup as they drank their cider together.

Peter had never seen dogs like these. They were nothing more than fluff balls, but knowing Jedediah, they'd come from good herding stock. They'd lost two of their Mexican sheepdogs on the drive to California because the dogs fought with a mad wolf and had to be put down. They had two old Mexican sheepdogs left that stayed with the herd and wouldn't let a man near them. Peter had given up trying to befriend the large, dangerous dogs.

"You get the male. Name him whatever you want," said Jedediah.

Peter didn't want his own dog. He tried to ignore Jedediah and the pups and walk away with his cider. The male pup whimpered and tried following him, tumbling over itself in the tall grass. He resisted the urge to give the pup a gentle kick so it wouldn't trail him.

"What's eating you?" Jedediah asked.

The last thing Peter wanted was to tell Jedediah about Belle. He'd remained on the farm the rest of the summer, avoiding Marysville because Belle was there. During the day, he helped with the sheep. In the evenings, when the sheep were gathered in the barn, he crafted furniture. Every piece of furniture Peter constructed with a woman in mind. Right now he was designing a rocking chair. He didn't want to contemplate why a rocking chair, but all he thought about was Belle as he worked on it. Was it possible she carried his child? The thought filled him with angst and something else. Was it hope? He should return to Clara's Place and check on her.

"There's talk your brother's back in Marysville." Jedediah set his pup on the ground, and she tumbled over to the other pup and sat down beside him, whimpering. The smell of pine was in the air today, and some of the oaks were shedding their leaves. It was such a clear, pretty day. Peter felt like he could see all the way to Marysville. At least he supposed that's what he saw down in the valley stretched below the foothills. Standing with Jedediah on a high ridge above the Yuba River, he could see that clump of middle mountains the Indians inhabited in the valley just past Marysville. Folks now called those middle mountains the Marysville Buttes. Farther on stretched the faint blue coast range and then the Pacific Ocean.

"So Paul's not dead." Peter tried to hide his frustration. At least Paul could come up here and show his face to Jedediah before the old man died.

Jedediah smiled. "Your brother has nine lives. Must be the Indian in him."

When Jedediah smiled, he looked healthier. He still had all his teeth, and he remained a tall man, though he was too thin now.

"Paul don't have many lives left." Voicing his fear of losing Paul before they could make amends helped. Since meeting Belle, the loss of Maggie didn't hurt so much, and his anger at Paul had cooled. He was ready to forgive his brother. That should make Jedediah happy.

"They say your brother has taken up with a girl at Clara's Place. They call her the Bluebird." Jedediah got down on one knee to pet the pups because they were yowling.

Peter nearly lost his breath. "Belle's with Paul?" he rasped. He bent down and picked up the male pup, tucking him close to his chest. He put his hand over the pup's mouth to quiet him. "You best teach your pup some manners," he told Jedediah. "All that noise will bring in the wolves." Holding the pup close eased some of the pain in Peter's heart. "Are you sure the girl's the Bluebird?" It felt like he'd been hit by an arrow straight out of the woods. How could this happen again?

"You know the Bluebird?" Jedediah scooped up his pup and shushed her too.

"I do," Peter admitted.

"You know her like the Bible says a man knows a woman?"

Peter wouldn't look at Jedediah. He stared down at the valley, his throat so tight he could hardly swallow. He imagined Belle in Paul's arms, and it hurt real bad. Everything he'd felt after losing Maggie rose up in him. But this time it was far worse. He'd never spent the night with Maggie the way he'd done with Belle. He couldn't escape that union with her. Somehow Belle had gained a part of him that night.

"The man who sold me these pups said the Bluebird's a beauty. Hair as black as night and eyes as blue as the Pacific Ocean."

"What do you know about the ocean? You've never seen the Pacific, as I recollect."

"Well, I can imagine it's blue," said Jedediah. "And I imagine that girl's eyes are blue enough to drown a man. Too bad you let Paul have your wife."

Peter swung around, ready to punch Jedediah. But when his gaze met his father's, all the rage rushed out of him. Grief flooded him. Feeling defeated, he said, "She's not my wife. That was a cruel joke. How do you know about this?"

"I got my ways."

"I should never have touched her. She wasn't mine. I did her wrong."

"Now your brother's with her." Jedediah's gaze filled with sorrow. "I didn't raise my sons this way. One of you is going to marry that girl right and proper. I'll see to it myself."

Peter shoved the male pup into Jedediah's hands, tossing one pup onto the other. "I'll see to it," said Peter. What if Belle died because of Paul, like Maggie had?

He wanted to kill Paul. He spun around and strode down the hill toward the barn. He had to get away from Jedediah. He needed to be alone to work out his feelings.

He saddled Mel in no time, then went to the cabin and packed what he'd need for the trail. By the time he returned to the barn, a gunnysack was tied to his saddle. The gunnysack whimpered and whined, thrashing about.

"No, thank you, Jedediah," he said to the gunnysack. He didn't want a pup. Frustration nearly made him hurl the sack into the pile of nearby straw. Instead, he untied Mel and led her from the barn, leaving the sack hanging from his saddle. He longed to get rid of the pup Jedediah had tied there, but the little critter settled down, accepting his fate in the sack. Peter mounted up and rode off, leaving Jedediah standing on the porch, holding his own collie pup, watching him go.

He was ready to find Paul for a reckoning. Certainly, Paul knew he'd wedded Belle after winning her. Even if the wedding wasn't legitimate, he was ready to beat Paul within an inch of his life. If not for Belle, for what he'd done to Maggie. Peter had wanted a family with Maggie and felt so betrayed that she'd died giving birth to his brother's son.

Now he was reliving that nightmare all over again. He never should have left Belle at Clara's. That was his mistake. He knew deep down the morning after bedding her that he should have taken her home. He'd gone against what the voice had told him. The few times he'd gone against that voice, he'd nearly died.

A feeling of despondency came over him. He hadn't prayed since he'd found out Paul had taken Maggie from him, but the urge to cry out to God overcame him now. *I know I've done wrong. I should never have left Belle. Please help me get her back. I'll marry her right and proper. I swear I will,* he told the Lord as he rode to Marysville.

The collie pup woke up a few hours into the journey and began to whimper in the bag. Peter untied the sack and pulled the pup out by the scruff of his neck. He sat the furry little thing on his lap and scratched its ears. "You'll make a fine wedding gift," he told the pup. And then he finally smiled a little, hoping Belle liked fur balls.

Isabella looked for Paul in the men crowding the saloon. She hadn't seen him in three days and was beginning to panic. Surely, he wouldn't leave her alone with Mick still hanging around. Mick was currently glowering at her from his seat at the bar as he downed whiskey like a thirsty man. He'd waved off Dutch Sadie when she'd tried to sit down beside him a while ago.

If only Paul would return. He'd been run out of Marysville after a card game gone wrong a few days back. At least that's what she'd been told. A group of gamblers wanted to kill Paul for cheating, Clara said, and Paul ran off into the night. Nobody had seen him since.

Paul had promised to marry her, but would that ever happen? She given up on Peter coming back. Paul had promised her children and their own little farm.

"We can get sheep from my father," he'd said, "and start our own homestead." But Paul was now gambling every night and drinking more heavily than when she'd first met him. It scared her. Paul's drinking reminded her of Don Pedro's. After getting drunk at Clara's, Paul would head down the street to one gambling tent or the next, where he spent most nights deep in cards. Then he'd stumble in near dawn, climbing into bed with her, wanting her affections, and afterward, sleeping most of the day in her attic room.

Even Clara had had it with him. She told Paul he was turning into a good-for-nothing gambler and she didn't appreciate him taking advantage of her hospitality. "When Peter comes back, he's not going to take kindly to you loafing about here, stringing Belle along with promises you don't intend to keep."

Paul had lost his temper when Clara said that. "I keep my promises," he'd railed back at her. "You're just an old whore in love with my brother. I feel sorry for you."

The exchange had shocked Clara and Belle. Paul had stormed out of Clara's parlor, and they hadn't seen him since because he'd gotten those gamblers riled and now was a wanted man. One way or another, Paul had abandoned her. Like everyone else abandoned her.

Isabella's songs were filled with heartache tonight, her heart exposed to anyone listening. She still grieved the loss of Peter, allowing herself to think about him first thing in the morning when she awoke, lying beside Paul when he was there. How sweetly he'd brushed her hair beside the fire and then made passionate love to her. She just didn't feel the same with Paul.

Tears filled her eyes and spilled down her cheeks as she sang. The saloon quieted. Clara walked over to the stage she'd built just for the Bluebird, but the Bluebird wasn't really Isabella. Isabella didn't even know who she was anymore. She felt like she'd sold her soul to the devil. Giving her body to Paul. Singing every night for Clara's gents. Living like a whore with the other whores here.

She never saw the sun anymore. She and Paul had gone on that one picnic to the river, but after that she hardly went outside. Clara said she must avoid the sun so the Indian in her wouldn't show on her skin.

"You're done for the night," Clara told Isabella when she reached the stage. "You're making the gents sad. Go to bed. Forget about Paul. I'm gonna make you into something special.

I may even take you to San Francisco to perform on a real stage."

Isabella stepped down from the wooden platform in the corner of the saloon and followed Clara out of the bar and over to the staircase in the parlor. "I'm gonna find you a singing instructor. You've got real talent, and we're gonna make you famous. So stop your crying."

Isabella stood there and cried some more.

"You got to learn to be strong, little girl. I got my heart broke too when I was young like you back in St. Louie. That's when I decided no man was gonna rule me. I'd make my own life out West. And I have. You don't see me slaving away on some man's farm, having baby after baby, getting all used up and dying young. No, I'm a queen now. And you can be a queen too someday."

"I don't want to be a queen," Isabella told Clara. "I just want someone to love me and never leave me."

"You don't know what's good for you. I'll make you into something. You don't need a man."

Out of the corner of her eye, Isabella saw Mick watching them with that look that terrified her on his bearded face. She turned away and hurried up the stairs.

An hour later, she was nearly asleep when her door cracked opened. She'd locked it, but Paul must still have his key. She'd left the oil lamp burning because she was afraid. When she sat up in bed to greet Paul, she was horrified to see Mick standing there.

"Hello, darlin'," he said, and her blood ran cold.

"You get out of here," she managed to tell him. She scrambled out of the bed.

"You look mighty pretty with all that hair down your back." Mick stepped over to the bed. "I don't know why you pin it up and paint your face the way you do. You look like a whore now."

Isabella's heart pounded like thunder in her ears. "Please go," she said in a stronger voice. "I'm Paul's woman."

Mick laughed, an ugly sound. "I don't mind seconds. I'm gonna show you what a real man is like. Those Brondis are no match for me." Mick unbuckled his belt.

Isabella screamed so loud she surprised herself.

When she started screaming, Mick dove across the bed and grabbed her by the hair. He yanked her down on the mattress and began to tear at her nightdress.

Isabella screamed until Mick slapped her. The blow cut her bottom lip. Blood ran down her chin.

He straddled her and told her to shut up. "You're just a squaw," he snarled. "I don't even know why I've got to have you. But you're gonna forget all about them Brondis. That king of hearts was my card. You should have been mine."

Isabella spit blood at him. Her terror was abating, and anger took over. She needed to get strong, like Clara said. She needed to get over thinking a man would be her salvation. Perhaps Dios would save her. She began to pray in Spanish, pleading with Dios to rescue her from Mick.

Mick just laughed. "Well, ain't you a little spitting Spanish cat. We're gonna have ourselves a fine time tonight, *gata pequeña.*"

Mick didn't notice Billy striding into the room. His club hit Mick square in the head, making a loud crack. Mick crashed down on top of her. Isabella thought he was dead. She used all her strength to scoot out from under his dead weight.

"I been waiting for this," Billy said. He laid down his club and dragged Mick from the bed.

Several girls stood at the doorway with worried faces. Clara appeared and swished past them into Isabella's room.

"I hope you didn't kill him," she said to Billy.

"I hope I did. Look what he did to Belle."

Isabella could feel the blood running down her chin. She scrambled to pull her torn nightdress together. She didn't want Billy seeing her breasts.

"You sure do bring out the worst in men," Clara told her. "We need to get that spirit that drives men mad off of you."

"I don't have a spirit on me." Isabella wiped the blood from her face. Talk of spirits frightened her. She believed in spirits and remembered how Sarita had said she was a gatherer. That men would be drawn to her and she would capture their souls for the devil.

Isabella shivered violently. Was Mick dead? His soul would go straight to hell. No doubt about that.

Clara ran her hand over the lump on Mick's head. "Thank our lucky stars he's still alive. I don't want no man dying in my house. It would ruin my business and get us both hanged in this town."

"No one's gonna hang us because of this mangy mountain man." Billy hefted Mick onto his back and lugged the unconscious man from the room. Mick's boots dragged the floor, making a clanking sound that rang in Isabella's ears. The girls moved out of the way to let Billy pass.

Clara grabbed Isabella by the chin and inspected her split lip. "Go wash your face. You'll be fine in a couple of days. We may as well start charging for your company. I can't have the gents wanting you and not being able to have you. All that breeds is angry customers. Since you've been giving yourself to the likes of Paul, you may as well earn your keep like the other girls."

"I sing for my keep." Isabella tasted blood in her mouth.

"You'll do more than sing if you're living here. You ain't so high and mighty. Nothing wrong with making a living on your back like the rest of us."

Isabella pulled her chin away from Clara's grip. Fear and anger drove her. "You promised Peter I wouldn't have to do that."

"I didn't know you were going to take up with Paul. Or drive Mick mad. Don't become more trouble than you're worth. And remember you got Indian blood in you. That's a dangerous thing for a woman in California." Clara straightened her shoulders and smoothed down her skirts. "We've all been beat a time or two. Comes with the territory. Ain't that right, ladies?"

The girls standing in the doorway nodded. They no longer looked as sympathetic. Isabella lowered her head, letting her hair fall over her face like a curtain. She didn't want to look at the girls or Clara. She just wanted to disappear.

Her lip throbbed and bled. She felt so forlorn she decided right then she was leaving. She still had the gold Peter had given her for the mule. She'd use that gold to get away. Mick had attacked her, but in a way, that was a blessing. She didn't need to fear men like Mick. Or find a man to take care of her. God had taken care of her tonight. Dios heard her prayers and saved her.

After Clara and the girls left, Isabella pulled out her golden rosary. She wrapped it around her hands and said her prayers. Her adoptive mother had made her and Maria say their rosaries every night. When they were little girls, saying the rosary had calmed Isabella's fears. And kept nightmares from plaguing her. Lately, she'd been having nightmares again. Waking up sweaty and shaking and chilled to the bone. It was the devil, of course. And the devil lived at Clara's Place.

Holding tightly to her rosary, she earnestly prayed that Dios would forgive her for what she'd done with Paul. Peter was different. She'd thought they were married. All she'd really wanted was to live on a farm beside a pretty creek with chickens and children, a milk cow and some horses and sheep, perhaps. She didn't need a grand hacienda with fiestas and feasts and all those fancy things from her past. She came to the conclusion she just needed Dios. She prayed he would show her where to go from here.

Chapter Eleven

When the pup started licking his hands, Peter realized he was thirsty. He stopped beside a stream and set the pup down beside the rushing water. He took to whimpering and Peter frowned. "Making all that noise will get you killed in the wilderness." He bent down and cupped some water into his palms. When he offered his palms to the pup, the pup licked every bit of it up. Peter smiled ruefully. Much as he hated to admit it, he liked the little collie's company. Petting the pup calmed him. He no longer wanted to kill Paul, just beat him good for taking up with Belle.

After watering the pup and Mel and drinking some water himself, he shared some jerked beef with the pup and set out again for Marysville. Last night the wolves had howled. He hoped they weren't bothering the sheep and was happy to have Belle's old mule with the herd now. Nothing was better than a mule for letting a man know something dangerous lurked in the darkness. A mule took to snorting when something disturbed it long before a man sensed the danger.

Peter liked where Jedediah had chosen to homestead. Wolves usually weren't in the area on account of men and their guns. Nevada City was an easy ride from the farm, but Peter stayed away from the town. He hadn't taken a drink since leaving Marysville, and he liked his clarity of mind. Winning Belle in that card game, wedding her, bedding her, and then leaving her at Clara's Place had all happened on account of his drinking. He'd come to realize the joke must be on her too. The more he thought about it, the more he concluded Belle had been an innocent and he'd been a complete rogue. Jedediah had spoken the truth. He was just chasing the wind, like so many men in California. Maybe he needed a good dose of religion, like Jedediah had gotten years before.

Recently, he'd mentioned this to Jedediah, and his father had said, "You don't need religion, you need Jesus."

"I'll think on that," Peter had replied, confused about the difference between religion and Jesus. He didn't understand, but he knew the road he was on had him headed for hell. His conscience plagued him over the kind of life he'd lived thus far. A selfish life, really. Aside from helping California become a state, he really hadn't done any good. Thinking about it bothered him a great deal. And his hatred toward his brother felt like poison running through him. Both Belle and Paul were part Indian. It was so much easier to hate a whole race of people than to reconcile his complicated feelings about Indians. And he didn't even want to think about Paul right now. He just hoped he didn't kill his brother when he found him.

Instead of riding straight to Clara's, he left Mel and the pup with Lickidy. The walk from the undertaker's wasn't far to

Clara's Place, and he stopped on the way and paid for a bath and a shave at the bathhouse. Then he went to the mercantile in search of a wedding dress for Belle and new clothes for himself. He was dead set on doing right by her and didn't care what Paul had to say about it. He wasn't about to relive what had happened with Maggie.

His new clothes fit all right, but he hadn't found a dress for Belle. "San Francisco's the place for wedding dresses," the shopkeeper said. "I could order one for you."

"Never mind." He didn't have time to wait on a dress. He wasn't about to let Paul have another night with Belle.

He steeled himself against Clara trying to talk him out of what he was about to do. She sure wasn't going to like it, but he'd decided this was how it would be and planned on marrying Belle right and proper before the day was done.

It was late afternoon when he walked into Clara's Place. It wasn't open for business yet, which he appreciated. Facing Paul, Belle, and Clara was enough. He didn't want a crowd of men around when he confronted his brother and Belle.

Nobody was in the parlor or the saloon. Though he wasn't in his buckskins, he hadn't left his gun or knife behind. His pistol was tucked in his belt and his knife in his boot. He said a prayer that he wouldn't kill Paul. He'd never be able to face Jedediah again if it came to that. He headed upstairs quietly, glad he still wore his moccasin boots with the fancy trousers he'd purchased at the mercantile. Nobody met him on the upstairs landing. He went right up the second set of stairs to Belle's room without interruption. He knocked softly on the door, but nobody answered.

Taking a deep breath, he opened the door, afraid he'd find Paul with her, but the bed was made up and the room was all set in order. Disappointment filled him. Was he too late? Had Paul taken Belle away? Was he headed out of California with her on a wagon train bound for Oregon or on horseback to New Mexico? Winter was coming. If Paul killed Belle the way he'd killed Maggie, getting her pregnant and then taking her on a dangerous journey, there would be no stopping him. Peter was ready for a reckoning. He hoped it would be today.

After closing the door to the attic room, he went down the steep stairs to the landing and then on down the grand staircase back into the parlor. Clara was at the bottom of the stairs in one of her dressing gowns. She was rumpled from sleep and appeared older standing in the afternoon light pouring through the parlor windows.

"You looking for me?" she asked with a smile.

"No," said Peter. "I'm searching for Belle and my brother."

The smile melted off Clara's face. "Come to the bar. I need a drink."

"I'm not drinking." He felt sweat break out on his brow. *God, help me. If you don't stop me, I'll be drunk before nightfall.*

Wiping the perspiration from his brow, he followed Clara into the saloon. Nobody else was there. Clara stepped behind the bar and pulled out a bottle of whiskey. She sat two crystal glasses on the counter.

"Who told you about Paul and Belle?" She poured amber whiskey into both glasses and pushed one toward him.

Sweat trickled down his temple. *Please help me, Lord. I don't want to drink anymore.* He ignored the glass Clara nudged in his direction and pulled out a barstool to sit down. "Jedediah heard the news in Nevada City."

"Nevada City?" Clark took a sip of whiskey. "I've never been there. Is that where you've been hiding?"

"I haven't been hiding." Peter wiped his brow again.

"Come on, honey. Have a drink with me. It's the least you can do since I can tell you're here to say good-bye."

Peter looked into Clara's wounded eyes and reached for the glass. Before his fingers could wrap around the crystal, it felt like a force out of nowhere hit him, and he tipped over the glass instead of picking it up.

"You getting clumsy?" Clara grabbed one of Billy's rags from behind the bar and wiped up the spilled whiskey.

With a shaking hand, Peter righted the empty glass. *Thank you, Lord. I know you did that.* He trembled with the realization that the force he felt was real. And unexplainable. He hadn't tipped over that glass by himself.

Clara refilled his glass. "If you're looking for Paul, he got chased out of town by some gamblers who were gonna kill him."

Peter took a deep breath, badly wanting the whiskey, but certain now the Lord would keep him from it. A battle was raging inside him, not just over drinking, but over believing in a God he couldn't see. He'd only felt the presence of God on a few occasions, usually when he was about to die. When his and Carson's mounts went down at the Battle of San Pasquel, he knew God had done that. God had saved his life a number of times. Perhaps God was saving him now from a life of drinking himself to death. He prayed God would help him find Belle. "Where's Belle?" he asked. "Is she with Paul?"

"They parted ways."

"Was Paul bedding her?"

The smile returned to Clara's face. "I couldn't stand in the way of true love, now could I?"

119

Peter's heart constricted. Now he knew. He reached for the glass. The crystal felt cold in his hand. He was about to down the whiskey when something rose up in him he wasn't used to feeling.

Was it peace?

A warm peace washed over him like a wind out of nowhere. Stunned, he set the glass back on the counter. "Can you tell me about Paul and Belle?" he asked.

Was that his voice that sounded so calm? He felt like a stranger in his own body.

"Belle fell in love with your brother. What else is there to say?" Clara drank more whiskey. Peter could see the lines etching deeper into her once beautiful face. Were they lines of regret of a wasted life?

"Does Paul love her?" He pushed the crystal glass around in front of him but didn't pick it up again. The desire to drink was gone. Just gone. He couldn't believe it.

"I think he does. But Paul's his own worst enemy. He'll get himself killed one of these days."

"So where's Belle now?" Peter looked around the saloon. For the first time in his life, he didn't like what he saw. Saloons had always felt like home to him, but this one didn't. His surroundings suddenly appeared dark and sad. He couldn't wait to find Belle and get out of this depressing place.

"She's gone." Clara was staring at him with wounded eyes.

"Gone where?"

"She left with Gunther."

"Gunther?"

"The German from Fort Ross."

"Where did they go?"

"Back to Fort Ross, I reckon." Clara wiped the bar with Billy's rag. She looked old and tired. Peter felt sorry for her.

"I never thanked you for comforting me after Maggie died." It wasn't like him to talk about his feelings, but he owed Clara something and didn't want to part ways with her on a bad note.

She kept wiping the bar. The counter was clean, but she seemed blind to that. Did she feel any of the strange peace he felt? He supposed not. She didn't look peaceful. She looked haunted.

"You're welcome. By the time you find Belle, she'll probably be married to Gunther. All that girl wanted was a husband. And that German is set on marrying her."

"Nothing wrong with wanting a husband."

"I've never been that way. I never wanted a husband. No man's ever gonna rule over me."

"I don't want to rule over Belle. I just want to do right by her."

"What did you do wrong?" Clara finally dropped the rag. She refilled her glass and sipped at her whiskey, staring at Peter with confusion in her eyes.

"I bedded her."

"Well, there's nothing wrong with that. You're the best I've ever had in my bed." Clara tried to laugh, but she sounded pitiful.

"I'm sorry for bedding you too," he said. "I've been selfish all my life."

"I'm not sorry. I'll take you to bed right now. We'll forget all about what we've just said. You got a fever, Pete? You ain't drinking. You ain't sounding right. What's wrong with you?"

"I don't quite know what's wrong with me," Peter admitted. The warmth and peace were leaving him. He was starting to sweat again and thirst for whiskey. "I got to get out of here. Did Belle leave by way of the river or by horse or wagon with the German?"

"They took a schooner."

"Headed for San Francisco?"

"I suppose so."

"If you see Paul, tell him to head up to Nevada City. He can ask around and get directions to Jedediah's farm. Tell Paul that Jedediah's dying. He needs to see our father before it's too late."

"What about you and me?" Clara's green eyes shone with tears. Peter had never seen her cry before.

"I'm sorry. I won't be back." Peter picked up the whiskey and handed it to Clara. "I'm done drinking."

"That's all right," said Clara. "You can still come see me. We don't need to drink. We'll just make love."

"I'm done with that too. I'm set on marrying Belle, if she'll have me."

A tear streaked Clara's cheek. "She's a fool if she won't."

"I should probably let her marry the German. He's the better man."

"There's no better man than you, Pete." Clara set her glass down on the counter. She leaned over the bar and took Peter's face in her hands. "I'll always love you, Peter Brondi." Then she kissed him.

Peter returned her kiss for only a moment, then rose from the bar to walk out of the saloon. He crossed the parlor, passing two sleepy-looking doves, and headed for the front door. When he stepped out onto the porch, he'd never been so happy in his life to feel the sun on his face. Sunset wasn't far off, but it felt like sunrise. *Thank you, Lord. I didn't take a drink. Maybe there's hope for a better life after all.*

Part Two

"There I will give her back her vineyards and will make the Valley of Achor a door of hope. There she will sing."

Hosea 2:15

Chapter Twelve

Isabella was terribly seasick. The journey on the schooner from Marysville to San Francisco hadn't bothered her, but here on the ship sailing for Bodega Bay, the ocean waves rolled, the wind howled, and rain fell in torrents.

Gunther had paid for her own private cabin while he bunked in steerage with other men. She hadn't planned to go any farther than San Francisco, but Maria and Dominic were not in residence, having gone to Boston with their children. It was a disappointing blow, but Gunther assured her she belonged at Fort Ross. Perhaps she could find her real father there.

"I'll ask for your hand in marriage when we find your father," Gunther had said, his blue eyes earnest and adoring upon her. The German was tall, powerfully built, hardworking, and quiet. Nearly twenty years older than her, but what did it matter? She had resigned herself to marry him if they found her father and Gunther gained his approval. She'd missed her monthly flow and hadn't kept down any food since boarding the ship. She hoped it was just seasickness making her so ill, but what if Paul's seed had taken hold? The thought left her despondent. Peter's child she would have gladly welcomed. She still harbored the impossible notion that he was her husband. Bearing Paul's child would ruin any possibility of ever reuniting with Peter. The realization crushed her.

Gunther knocked on her door and entered the cabin, bearing a plate of salt pork and bread. She could see the worry on his face, and it comforted her a little. The German appeared to genuinely care for her, and he wasn't ugly. He seemed a patient man with steady hands. She'd never seen him take a drink, which relieved her. She was tired of drunken men.

"You need to eat this," Gunther said as he set the plate on the table.

Isabella rested in the bunk, weak and pale, wishing her adventure to the goldfields hadn't turned out so poorly. "I will try." She smiled for him, but when she sat up, a wave of dizziness hit and she fell back on the pillows, her world spinning.

Gunther felt her forehead. "You do not have a fever. That is good. When we reach Bodega and return to land, you will feel better." He stepped back after tentatively touching her head, his cheeks red, a blush Isabella was coming to recognize as his way of responding to her. He wasn't shy about making his feelings known, but unlike Paul and Peter, Gunther was careful not to touch her. He was a respectable farmer, and Isabella knew he would not be in this cabin alone with her if she wasn't so ill.

"I will be better with my feet on solid ground," she assured him. Then she closed her eyes, praying her world would stopped spinning. She'd never felt so awful in her life. How long could a person go on without food?

"Please try to eat something." Gunther brought her plate to her bed. "Shall I feed you?"

She opened her eyes and tried once more to smile. "I will eat in a little while. Please just leave the plate here with me. When this dizziness passes, I will try my best to get something down."

"The day after tomorrow we will be on horseback riding to my farm. The storm is passing. The sunshine will be good for you. This time of year is mostly fine weather."

Isabella nodded and closed her eyes. She dozed off. When she awoke, Gunther was gone. A fresh chamber pot sat beside the bed, anchored to the wall along with everything else in the cabin. Choking down several mouthfuls of salt pork, she chewed slowly and then nibbled on the hard bread. It did calm her stomach, and she was able to sleep more soundly after that.

True to Gunther's word, they landed in Bodega the following day, spent one uncomfortable night in a barn that housed agricultural supplies, and the following morning found them on horseback. They weren't alone. Five other men rode along, two of the men vaqueros guiding them to the fort. Isabella used all her strength just to stay in the saddle and keep up with the men. The sunshine did make her feel better, but her dizziness didn't completely disappear. Eating still proved difficult.

Gunther watched her with worried eyes. It was a nine-hour ride to Fort Ross. Along the way, when the horses tired, new mounts were selected by the vaqueros, who herded along fresh horses. At the Slavyanka River, they stopped for lunch. Isabella was surprised two men were there who had prepared a picnic for them. They sat on logs and ate the first delicious meal Isabella had had since leaving Clara's Place. The food tasted so good, but before she could get back on her horse, she ran to some nearby bushes and heaved up her meal.

She tried not to worry about the reason for her sickness as she returned to her mount. The men were waiting for her, already astride their horses. Gunther was the only one not in the saddle. He came right over and helped her mount up, though she didn't need his help. He'd secured a sidesaddle for her, which Isabella rode as nimbly as the men rode astride, but her dizziness was back, and it took all her concentration to remain in the saddle as they left the beautiful river, with it's wooded, grassy banks and towering redwood trees, and returned to the windswept bluffs along the cliffs, where the sound of crashing waves filled Isabella's ears.

Puffy white clouds were swept across the sky by a breeze that had risen off the ocean. The land in the north was lusher than Bodega, the hills covered with tall woods and fields of grass, where cattle grazed on coastal hillsides. Every now and then vaqueros in the distance herded livestock. The vaqueros reminded her of her home near Monterey. As a babe, she must have made this same journey from Fort Ross. Had her Russian father been sorry to see her go? Had he stayed at the fort, remarried, and had another family? Or perhaps he'd returned to his homeland, or maybe he'd even died. If he still lived at the fort, would he welcome her? Antipina had been her mother's name. Her father was Sergei Ivanov. The priest who'd given her to the Vasquezes left a birth document from Fort Ross with the names of her parents.

Gunther told her he didn't live at the fort, but farmed a nearby homestead. He was friends with William Benitz, another German, who leased the fort. Sutter had bought the fort from the Russians but had lost his claim to it when it was disallowed by the Mexican government. The fort and over seventeen thousand acres around it became the Muniz Rancho and was granted to Manuel Torres. In 1846, Torres leased the fort to Benitz. Gunther helped Benitz run the fort until the two men had gone to the mines together last year. They'd been successful in their diggings and had returned with enough gold for Gunther to buy his own farm. He now traded vegetables and hogs to Benitz for the supplies he needed on his farm.

"It was a good life," Gunther said, but he wasn't a young man any longer and needed a wife to provide sons to work the farm with him. "Daughters would be welcome too," he assured her, especially if they could sing like she did.

"You will also teach our children to read," Gunther insisted, even though Isabella had yet to agree to marry him. "William and Josephine Benitz have hired a tutor for their children. There are books and music at Fort Ross. It's a cultured place. You will like it there."

"But where are the Russians?" Isabella asked when she realized the Germans had taken over Fort Ross.

"They live nearby," Gunther assured her. "If your father is in the vicinity, we will find him."

By late afternoon, they encountered pretty little farms with painted cottages. Chickens scratched in the yards, sheep grazed in the pastures, and hogs lazed in the shade. Dark-haired children ran about with barking dogs. The men they rode with went their own ways, and soon it was just Isabella and Gunther riding together.

Near sunset, they came upon a farm with hogs sleeping all over the place. When they rode up to the barn on their sweat-soaked horses, the hogs arose and began trotting, snorting, and squealing in what sounded like pleasure to Isabella.

"My pigs have missed me," Gunther said with a smile.

Isabella had never seen so many hogs. The smell of them turned her stomach. She would have lost her lunch had she not already thrown it up back at the river. "Please, I must lie down," she told Gunther. She was so tired. She could hardly keep her eyes open and felt so sick.

Gunther helped her from her horse, and she swayed in his arms, nearly fainting. "You are ill." His worried gaze studied her face.

"I am just weary. Please, may we go into the house?"

Gunther tied up the horses and walked Isabella to his cottage across the field from the barn. As he'd promised, it was a pretty cottage surrounded by a garden and flowers growing along the walls. But the smell of hogs drifted on the air and overpowered Isabella's senses. It was the hogs that made her realize she could never marry Gunther and live here.

The house was neat and sparse, a table with two chairs in the kitchen, a parlor that had several sitting chairs, and just beyond that were several rooms. Gunther walked Isabella to a bedroom with a large bed, a washstand, and nothing more. Quietly, Isabella went and laid down on the bed, closing her eyes, hoping to get over the awful smell of pigs and the dizziness that wouldn't leave her.

"I will see to the horses and my hogs and then prepare us a meal." Gunther looked concerned but didn't say any more, just quietly left after closing the bedroom door behind him.

It was dark outside when she awoke. She could no longer smell the hogs. Gunther must have cooked something in the house because she could smell it. Her appetite was finally aroused. Rising from the bed, she felt weak, but no longer dizzy. Using her fingers, she combed her hair as best she could and then braided it in a single plait down her back. She'd sworn never to braid her hair again since Peter wanted it in girlish braids, but she needed to tame her hair to look presentable at Gunther's table.

He was sitting in the parlor, reading a book by the light of an oil lamp, when she came out of the bedroom. Upon seeing her, he broke into a smile. "You are feeling better. The color is back in your cheeks." He quickly left his chair and led her into the kitchen, sitting her down at the table for two.

Gunther lit several candles he'd placed on the table before bringing the meal to her. She thought surely they would eat pork but was surprised to taste venison prepared in a savory stew with carrots and potatoes. He poured hot coffee and proudly presented her with cream and sugar. "I have dairy cows," he boasted. "When you are feeling better, you can milk them with me."

Clearly, he thought this would make her happy. Isabella had never milked a cow in her life and didn't plan to. She didn't tell Gunther that. Instead, she asked, "When can we search for my father? His name is Sergei Ivanov. I do not think he would be much older than you."

The question appeared to surprise him. Maybe he hadn't realized how much older he was than she. He picked up his coffee, blew on it for a moment, took several sips, and then finally met her gaze. "I have been away from my farm for a long time. There is much work I must do. I cannot leave for a while."

"How far is the fort from here?" Isabella smelled her coffee and then regretted it. The scent nauseated her.

"Not far." Gunther watched her. "You do not like the coffee?"

"I grew up drinking cocoa." She pushed the cup away. "May I borrow a horse tomorrow so I can ride to the fort?"

"You should rest tomorrow. And take nourishment. When you're stronger, I will take you to the fort." He stared at her as if he had something more to say, but then focused on his stew and ate as if famished. He finished his plate and waited for her to consume her meal before speaking again.

"I am the oldest of eleven children born in the Grand Duchy of Baden. In the early months of carrying a child, my mother was always sick. I believe you carry a child," he said with a look of sadness.

She set her fork down. It was probably true. "Perhaps the Benitzes would hire me to tutor their children, and I could live at the fort," she said softly. "We could tell the Benitzes I was abandoned by my husband."

"Paul Brondi is not your husband." He set his fork down too, then picked up his coffee.

Outside in the distance, Isabella thought she heard a rooster crow, but rarely did roosters crow in the darkness. Where did the pigs sleep at night? Probably in the same place they slept during the day. In all those holes they'd rooted around the barn. She wanted to argue with Gunther. Tell him she *was* a married woman and that she carried her husband's child, but there was no way it could be Peter's. Perhaps Paul would come find her. Clara knew she'd headed to San Francisco with Gunther. Clara might tell Paul where she'd gone.

"I do not think Paul Brondi will marry you," Gunther said as if reading her mind. "He is a foolish young man. Someone will kill him, and then your child will be fatherless. I will be a good father to your child. I will adopt your son or daughter and make it my own. No one need know we were not married before I brought you here. I told the men we rode with that you were my wife."

Isabella's eyes widened. None of the men had spoken to her on the day-long ride. They'd treated her respectfully and kept their distance. Now it made sense. They'd thought she was Gunther's wife. No wonder they'd treated her respectfully. They believed her married to the big, powerful German. Gunther towered over most men. She felt small in his large bed. The thought of his bed alarmed her. Where would she sleep tonight?

She couldn't sleep with Gunther. She wouldn't. No longer would she surrender herself to a man. She would become a tutor at Fort Ross and raise her child as if she were widowed. Hopefully, she would find her father, and maybe she could live with him.

"My husband abandoned me," she told Gunther, her resolve strengthening. "I am married to Peter Brondi."

Gunther set his coffee cup down. He scooted his chair back and stood up. Quietly, he cleaned off the table and then turned to face her. "I know Peter won you in a card game. Your marriage is not legitimate. You will come to see my offer is good. Your child needs a father. I will be a good father."

Isabella could already see how stubborn he was. Well, she could be stubborn too. "I would like to borrow a horse tomorrow to search for my father."

"When you regain your health, you can search for your father."

"I am not sick. I am fine." She pushed back her chair and stood up.

"You have not eaten in days. You are not well enough to ride to the fort. When I catch up around here, I will take you to the fort myself."

"When will that be?" Isabella pressed.

"When you agree to live here as my wife."

She was shocked. "I thought you were bringing me here to find my father."

"That will come in time."

"Where will I sleep tonight?"

"My house has several bedrooms. You may have your own room until the child comes."

"Was that your bed I slept in this afternoon?"

"Yes," he admitted with that blush back on his cheeks. "I had hoped you weren't expecting. I told myself it was just the sea. And the long horse ride. But I tested you with the coffee. The smell of coffee always made my mother sick when she carried a child."

Isabella hung her head. She didn't want to accept this. Any of it. Not Paul's child. Not Gunther's marriage offer. Not the rest of her life with this stubborn man and his smelly pigs. "I am tired. May I go to bed?" She refused to look at him.

He showed her the way to her room. It was a fine little space with a bed smaller than his bed, but still large in comparison to the bed she'd shared with Paul in Clara's attic. Her traveling trunk had been strapped on one of the horses they'd acquired in Bodega. Now it was here in the room, pushed against a wall. An oil lamp burned on a nightstand beside the bed.

Again, she heard a rooster crow and noticed the window was cracked to let in fresh air. "Why does your rooster crow at night?"

"I don't know. Perhaps the darkness frightens him."

"Are the woods around here dangerous? Do bears and wolves roam here?" She had decided she would steal a horse. Fort Ross was her destination. Not this cottage on a pig farm.

"The bears are fierce and the wolves a problem," Gunther admitted. "We had wolves in Germany. I hunted them as a boy, and I am not afraid of wolves."

"But you fear the bears?" Isabella had grown up with bull and bear fights. She'd even gone on bear hunts with her brother and the vaqueros. The bears in California ran as fast as horses. These huge, fierce grizzlies frightened her. She had hoped they didn't dwell this far north.

"When a bear becomes a problem here, the men gather to hunt it. You do not need to fear bears living here. A bear will go after the pigs long before it comes near the house. The neighbors and I will kill the grizzlies, as we've done before."

Isabella walked to the window and looked out into the darkness. On the breeze blowing though the cracked window, she could smell the pigs. Her stomach turned. She remembered the woods surrounding the farm. How tall the trees were, how dark the forest they rode through to get here. A wave of despondency swept through her. Did she have the courage to ride to Fort Ross alone if she could escape Gunther's watchful eye and steal one of his horses?

Chapter Thirteen

Peter's moccasin boots did not make a sound as he walked the boardwalk. The last time he'd been in San Francisco there had been no wooden sidewalks to escape the mud. Now boardwalks were everywhere, and brick and wooden buildings stood from the top of the steep hills all the way down to the bay. A brisk ocean breeze slapped his face and seagulls squawked overhead. Men filled the streets, along with more women than he'd expected. He saw more bonnets here than he'd seen since leaving St. Louis. Civilization had come to California. Women had arrived. San Francisco was a real city, though rats still scurried across the streets, and sea lions barked in the harbor.

He'd enjoyed his trip down river from Marysville to the delta, and then on to San Francisco. Most of the time he'd spent reading and resting on the boat. He'd been on a few schooners in his lifetime on rivers, but never a sailing ship on the ocean. When he'd booked his passage yesterday, the ship captain said they would make good time to Bodega Bay. There he would secure a horse and continue on to Fort Ross. "It's the best time of the year on the coast," the ship captain had assured him. "You'll have a pleasant journey to the fort."

It took a while to locate the dressmaker's shop he'd heard about last night at the hotel. When he walked through the shop door, a bell jangled, letting the shopkeeper know he was there. He looked around at the dresses of satin and silk lining the walls. No calicos caught his eye, which surprised him. Clearly, this was going to be a costly affair. He just hoped he could find a dress that appealed to him and would fit Belle.

"How can I help you, fine sir?" A small, neatly dressed man came from a back room, walking past a row of rainbow-hued dresses that didn't appeal to Peter.

"I'm looking for a wedding gown." He was never one to mince words. The ship was sailing for Bodega Bay in a few hours. From there, he'd ride a horse to Fort Ross. He'd never been on a ship before and wasn't sure if he'd like it or not. He'd only seen the ocean a couple of times in his life when he rode with Carson down south.

The shopkeeper smiled. "What size is your lucky bride? My wife makes the dresses, but she isn't here today."

Peter glanced around. To his relief, he noticed a creamy gown in the corner on a stand that looked about Belle's size and captured his fancy. Yards of silk the color of a newborn lamb circled the gown on the floor. "I'll take that one."

"That is pure silk and very expensive." The dressmaker's gaze raked over Peter's buckskins.

"I said I'll take it." Peter pulled a pouch of gold from his pocket.

"The goldfields must have done you good. Where are your diggings?" The shopkeeper went over and removed the creamy gown from the wooden rack.

"I supply the miners with meat. They are a hungry bunch with gold to spare," Peter said without a smile.

"You don't look like a farmer. You must be a hunter." Neatly folding up the dress, the shopkeeper walked back to Peter. "You want to feel this silk? It's the finest in San Francisco; I can assure you of that, sir."

"I no longer hunt for a living. I deal in sheep." Peter ran his fingers over the silken bodice. It reminded him of Belle's silky hair and skin. The dress pleased him very much.

"Sheep?"

"They make for slow going over the Sierras."

"You brought sheep over those mountains?"

"A few," Peter said, finally smiling a bit.

"Did you pass Truckee Lake, where the Donner Party wintered a few years ago?"

Everyone knew about the Donner Party in California. An early blizzard had doomed the Donners four years earlier. Nearly half the train had perished in the snowbound mountains. The doomed train was all people talked about in California. Newspapers carried outlandish stories of families eating their loved ones, and the overland trail nearly came to a standstill because of it. Until the discovery of gold changed all that. The trail through the Sierras now boomed with wagons. He was surprised the shopkeeper remembered the Donners with the gold rush on everyone's mind.

But Peter found the deep alpine lake at the bottom of the pass hauntingly beautiful. "I've camped beside the lake," Peter admitted. "It's a pretty place." He wasn't about to tell the shopkeeper that the summer after the Mexican War, riding east with Kearny's army, they'd stopped to inspect the lake cabins surrounded by wildflowers, green grass, butterflies—and bones. Mutilated human skeletons lay in and around the cabins. Kearny had ordered a pit dug in one of the cabins, and they'd gathered all the bones and dumped them into the grave, then burned the cabins, the smoke swirling up over the mountains. It was a solemn affair that haunted Peter still. Sometimes he dreamed about the lake with all those bones scattered around the cabins.

"I've heard wolves and ghosts live at the lake now." The dressmaker walked to the counter and began wrapping up the dress.

"They named Marysville after Mary Murphy. A survivor of the Donner party. Maybe you should send her a dress up there in Marysville."

"I don't know the Murphys, but I've met the Reeds. The entire Reed family survived the ordeal. James found gold, and I've clothed his womenfolk right finely. The Reed family is doing well now. God bless them."

"That's mighty nice for the Reeds. Measure out my gold; I've got a ship to catch."

"Where are you headed? You don't look like an Easterner."

"I'm sailing north."

"To Oregon?"

"You ask a lot of questions. I'm gonna need some women's undergarments too. The finest you have in about that size." Peter pointed to the dress package and pinned the man with his gaze. He knew his stare could be icy when a man displeased him. He wanted to put some fear into this talkative little man. He was tired of yarning on.

"Just trying to be friendly." The shopkeeper hurried to get the undergarments, wrapped them, and then measured his gold on a scale behind the counter. When he returned the pouch to Peter, it was a whole lot lighter.

"I appreciate your hospitality." Peter pocketed what remained of his gold. He had plenty more where that came from.

As the captain had promised, the sea didn't give them any trouble that afternoon as they sailed through the Golden Gate. Peter liked the spray of the waves as he stood on the bow of the ship, following the coastline with his sharp gaze. He was thankful the Lord had given him good eyes. Spotting game had never been a problem. The captain mentioned an early autumn storm had passed the week prior. Had Belle sailed in bad weather? Had the German comforted her? Had they shared the same cabin?

He quickly pushed the thoughts from his mind. He hadn't allowed himself to contemplate Belle's relationship with Paul for very long, and he wasn't about to ruminate on her time with the German. She'd ended up with other men because he'd left her. What had he expected to happen to her, living in a brothel?

When darkness overtook the ship, he dined with the captain and several other passengers—all men. The passengers enjoyed wine with their dinner and brandy and cigars with the captain before he returned to his post. The captain didn't drink the brandy, only smoked a bit and then excused himself to return to duty. Peter denied himself wine at dinner and brandy afterward, and took his cigar to the top deck, where he stood alone under a blanket of bright stars.

The battle not to imbibe at dinner had left him trembling with a prayer on his lips. After that unseen force had knocked the whiskey from his hand at Clara's Place, he feared God and prayed to keep his wits about him. Nothing good came from drinking. He wanted to be done with that. The taste of smoke had never appealed to him, and he tossed the cigar overboard when he walked to the rail.

The ship rose and fell on the waves. He licked the salt from his lips as the sea misted his face. Thoughts of the years he'd wasted nettled him. What had he accomplished aside from seeing California become a part of the union?

It's all chasing the wind, Jedediah had said.

Now he was chasing Belle and wondered if that was any better. He really didn't know Belle at all. She'd gotten in his blood, and he didn't know what to make of it. Why was she constantly on his mind? He told himself he was a fool, but that didn't help. He'd spent a small fortune on the silk wedding gown and didn't know if she'd even agree to wear it. Perhaps she'd wear it for Paul. Or the German.

His heart recoiled at the thought of Belle making a life with another man. But maybe a future at Fort Ross with the German would be best for her. Clara said the German was a farmer, well-off from his jaunts to the goldfields. Belle deserved whatever happiness she could find. Being among her own kind at Fort Ross would spare her from the hardships of a half-breed life. Most white men had an aversion to half-breeds, often treating them poorly. Paul had accused Peter and Jedediah of thinking less of him because of his Indian blood, and maybe somewhere deep in Peter's heart it was true. He remembered the day long ago he'd told his father, "I don't like that dirty little Indian boy. You love him more than me."

"That dirty little Indian boy is your brother. I am Paul's father. He's no dirtier than you, and his blood runs red just like yours. Let me prove it to you." Jedediah had fetched Paul from inside the cabin. He'd carried the boy over to where ten-year-old Peter was chopping wood with a vengeance because he didn't want Paul or his Indian mother sharing their cabin. He didn't like living with Indians.

Jedediah took out his knife and cut Paul's finger. The little boy didn't even flinch. His eyes were on Jedediah, and he remained absolutely quiet in Jedediah's arms. Then Jedediah grabbed Peter's hand, knocking the hatchet from it, and sliced his finger open too. He pressed Paul's bleeding finger to Peter's bleeding finger. "There. It's done. Now you're blood brothers. I love you both for the sons you are to me." Then Jedediah carried Paul back to his mother and left Peter to finish chopping the wood alone that cold winter day.

Paul's mother disappeared the following week, and Peter never forgot the lesson Jedediah had taught him. He had a scar on his finger to remind him and had developed compassion for Paul after his mother abandoned him. He took Paul to his own bed that night when Paul wouldn't stop crying about his mother. Peter had let Paul hog his covers and curl against him when it was cold for several years. Had Paul been old enough to remember that day Jedediah made them blood brothers? Neither of them had ever mentioned it to each other, and why he recalled it so clearly now, he didn't know.

Paul had faced torment, not sure of who his father really was. Peter believed this more than anything had sent Paul down a bad road. Jedediah had said Maggie's love had saved Paul. That her father, the minister, had led Paul to the Lord before he married them. "Your brother turned his back on the

Lord because Maggie died. He was a changed man until trag-edy on the trail took his dreams."

"Do you think this makes me forgive him?" Peter had lashed out at Jedediah. "I don't forgive Paul. And I'm not sure I can forgive you either."

But Peter had forgiven his father. How could he hold what happened with Maggie over Jedediah's dying head?

He was no longer drinking and had nothing to dull his thoughts, and his emotions seemed clearer and sharper than ever. He wasn't minding the sheep or Jedediah, or scouting for Fremont, Carson, or Kearny, or fighting a war. Neither was he on guard against Indians tonight. This journey on the sea left him at loose ends, feeling unmoored, something he wasn't used to feeling at all.

What was Belle doing tonight? Was she at the fort with some kin she'd found? Had she met her real father? Could the Russian still be alive? He'd heard most of the Russians were gone from Fort Ross, but not all of them. Some had kept home-steads around the fort.

If he brought Belle home, he knew it would boost his father's spirits and perhaps restore a measure of health to him. The birth of a grandchild would certainly shore up Jedediah's flagging constitution.

He imagined Belle pregnant with his son or daughter. He didn't much care if it was a boy or girl. A smile hit him in the darkness. *Lord, if you give me young'uns, I'll change my ways. I'll become a new man. I promise I will,* he proclaimed. *I'll even forgive my brother and make amends with Paul.*

After making that promise to God, Peter felt like he should do something to seal this covenant. He got down on his knees on the deck and folded his hands. Turning his face to the stars, a feeling of utter unworthiness came over him. He hung his head in shame. Why he suddenly felt like such a wretch, he didn't know. It was like he was in the hands of God and suddenly saw what God saw. In an instant, his whole life flashed before him. All the men he'd killed. All the women he'd soiled. The fight with Paul that had broken Jedediah's heart. He saw all this in the blink of an eye and began to weep.

"Are you sick, sir?" The captain's hand landed on his shoulder.

Peter had never been so embarrassed in his life. "I don't know what's come over me," he mumbled, struggling to his feet.

"It's a strange night," said the captain. "I've never seen the sea so calm. The stars so close. It's almost as if a man can reach out and take one in his hand."

"I know the Maker of the stars," Peter said in wonder and shame. The knowledge of God flooded him.

He's guiding us tonight," the captain agreed, looking out over the dark sea, then turning his eyes to the sparkling heavens.

Peter had never known anything so surely in his life: God was present on the sea with them tonight.

Chapter Fourteen

Isabella awoke to the crowing of a rooster. It wasn't even dawn yet. Gunther's rooster crowed at all hours, day or night. Isabella was used to roosters welcoming the morning. Sometimes they bid the evening adieu. But they didn't crow in the darkness like this wanton rooster. She'd always liked chickens, but she hated this rooster. Just like she despised the squealing hogs and their stench that made her sick. She couldn't imagine living here. It was worse than Clara's Place. And she carried Paul's child; she was certain of that now. All she wanted was to sleep. She was so tired, and when she was awake she felt ill. Gunther mostly left her alone, spending his days tending to his farm.

During the day, she didn't see him. They'd fallen into the habit of supper together and then her reading to him before retiring to their own rooms. They rarely spoke. Now that Gunther knew she was pregnant, he no longer looked at her with adoring eyes. He was sullen, as if she'd done him wrong. She was determined to take a horse and ride to Fort Ross just as soon as the opportunity presented itself. Most of her belongings she'd have to leave behind in her traveling trunk, which didn't matter. She owned very little. The only thing she really valued was Maria's rosary. That she kept hidden in her skirt pocket.

She'd taken to praying each day. The more she prayed, the more she believed Dios heard her pleas for deliverance. Gunther wasn't abusive, but something cold and dark lived in his house. Each night, she had nightmares. Sometimes she awoke with a shadow beside her bed. The first time it happened, she thought Gunther had come into her room, but the unearthly cold wrapping around her and the terror she felt made her realize the shadow wasn't a human being. The devil prowled in this place. Even the farm animals sensed an evil presence, the chickens too nervous to lay many eggs, the hogs deranged. When she'd visited the horses in the barn, she found them skittish, their eyes rolling around in fear. Every night wolves howled in the nearby woods.

Please send someone to save me, Lord, she whispered, looking out the window. Autumn was upon them. The weather was changing. Some days brought cold gray fog that crept across the land like a living thing. By afternoon, the sun would appear, but the fog usually returned by nightfall. Gunther wouldn't tell her how far he lived from the fort. It could be two miles or twenty—she had no idea. Farms were nearby. She knew that. Perhaps if she could make it to one of the other farms, someone would help her get to the fort. Thoughts of her Russian father were never far from her mind. Now that she'd come this far, she longed to find him.

As the morning wore on, the fog receded from the fields around the cottage, but stood like a gray wall at the edge of the woods. She could see the barn, the hogs lumbering about, some out in the meadows rooting up the grass. A rider came out of the midst and rode towards the house. Isabella sucked in her breath. She hadn't seen another living soul besides Gunther since the men had ridden away before they'd reached the farm a few weeks ago.

Quickly, she changed out of her nightgown and into the only woolen dress she owned. The day was chilly—she could see that from the frost on the window. She threw her shawl over her head and shoulders and practically ran outside to see the lone rider.

Gunther had stopped him in the meadow, and now the visitor was riding away. Gunther was headed back to the barn. Crestfallen, Isabella stepped out into the yard. The rider disappeared into the fog.

Please, oh please, Lord, get me out of here. Perhaps she could follow the rider's tracks through the forest. Surely, he was headed to the fort or some other civilized place. If she hurried, she might catch him. Would he possibly help her escape?

Gunther had disappeared inside the barn. With a prayer on her lips, she made a dash across the meadow. She ran as fast as she could, pleading with Dios to let her reach the rider.

When she hit the fog bank and then the woods where the rider disappeared, she kept on running. Tears streaked her face, but she didn't care. She'd broken free and wasn't about to turn around.

The woods proved dark and misty. A raven squawked and burst from the trees in the wake of her flight. She felt weak from lack of exercise and little food. Keeping nourishment down was a challenge these days. Slowing her pace, she stepped over logs and foliage, looking for horse tracks. She couldn't see more than a few feet in front of her in these misty woods. If she encountered wolves or a bear, she had no idea what she would do. Perhaps she would die in the jaws of a wild animal.

Something alerted her to the fact that she wasn't alone. A slight noise. A sense of someone there. The hair rose on the back of her neck. She swung around to see who was behind her. Strong arms captured her. A hand covered her mouth. It frightened Isabella so badly she couldn't even scream.

Peter couldn't believe he held Belle in his arms. After speaking with the German in the meadow, he'd ridden back into the woods, contemplating his next move. He didn't believe the German when he said he'd never heard of a blue-eyed Creole named Belle. Peter had trusted his instincts all his life. He knew the German lied to him. In the woods, he hadn't gone far. He'd already been to Fort Ross and many of the surrounding farms. Nobody had seen Belle. He'd seen some women at the fort who resembled Belle with black hair and blue eyes. There were also half-breed men with Belle's coloring. A friendly German family lived at the fort and had politely answered all of his questions. Belle had never arrived at the fort.

He picked her up in his arms and carried her over to a log, where he sat down with her in his lap. The shawl fell from her head. Her dark, silky hair tumbled down. Her face was drawn and pale, but remained as beautiful as he remembered. He didn't speak. He just held her, his throat tight with emotion, thanking God he'd found her.

He heard the German coming through the woods before he saw him. He covered Belle's mouth again with his hand to keep her quiet. By the time the man stepped through the trees,

Peter's pistol was leveled on his forehead. He cradled Belle with one arm and welcomed the German by cocking his hammer back.

"You have found my wife." The man approached cautiously now.

Peter wanted to shoot him. Had they already married on their journey here? Well, he'd married Belle first. "Belle's my wife," he said evenly.

The German smiled slightly. "Everyone in Marysville knows your wedding was not legitimate. You abandoned her in a brothel. I have given her a respectable life."

"Well, I'm back. And Belle's mine. Go on home and gather her things. She's leaving with me."

Belle stirred in his arms. He removed his hand from her mouth, hoping she wouldn't resist him before he scared the German away. He wasn't leaving here without her.

"Let her decide between you and me. Bring her back to the house. We will discuss this while she warms herself by the fire. She hasn't been well."

Peter could see that, and it worried him, but he didn't trust the German. The man had already lied to him. He was powerfully built. A rifle hung from his shoulder, but that didn't mean he knew how to shoot fast and clean. The man didn't scare him. Belle moved in his arms. He could feel her gaze on him but didn't look down at her in his lap. He wasn't about to take his eyes off the German. Or lower his gun. "You return to the house. We'll be along in a while."

"Peter?" Belle's voice was soft. Scared. "Am I dreaming?"

"You're not dreaming. I'm here," he whispered, not wanting to share their conversation with the German.

"There's no reason to point your gun at me." The German inched forward.

"If you take another step, you'll see the splendor of God. I've got no use for you. And neither does Belle."

She anchored her hand on his buckskin shirt. He could smell her fear. She didn't trust the German either.

The German stopped walking. "Belle, come with me," he commanded.

Belle shook her head. She didn't let go of Peter's leather shirt.

The German turned and headed back through the trees. His boots crushed the autumn leaves. When a man walked that way in the woods, Peter pegged him for a fool. He would not return to the German's cottage with Belle. He would retrieve her necessities later, after he found a safe place for her at the fort.

"Where's your painted horse? Was that you riding in the meadow?"

Peter motioned through the trees. "The gelding I rode is over there. I left Mel in Marysville. I followed you by schooner and then by ship. I borrowed the black horse in Bodega. I'll return him when we head home."

Belles eyes sparkled with hopeful tears. At least he took her tears as hopeful because they came with a trembling smile.

"Do you want to go home with me?" He liked having her in his lap. She still clung to his shirt. It made him want to protect her all the more.

"I want to go with you, but I haven't searched for my father yet. Gunther wouldn't take me to the fort."

"I'll take you there." He pulled her shawl up around her shoulders and tucked it against the chill. This mist steeped into one's bones. Some places were like this. The spirit cold and unwelcoming. He wanted to get Belle out of here.

"I prayed Dios would send someone to save me," she admitted, "and you came."

"I prayed to find you." He touched his fingers to her cheek. "The fort's not far. Let's get you there." Gently, he set her off his lap. His ears were tuned to the forest. The German had stomped off, but he could always sneak back to give them trouble. And this was a wild land with Indians and fierce animals. He'd rented a room at the fort last night. His chamber had been cold, but the straw bed was wide and welcoming. Right across the courtyard stood a pretty redwood church. He smiled as he thought of the plans he had for Belle and that church.

Chapter Fifteen

It took less than half an hour on horseback to reach Fort Ross. They'd passed two large wooden windmills as they arrived at the fort—the first windmills Isabella had ever seen. They had ridden out of the cold fog as they left the forest near Gunther's land. Around Fort Ross, the day sparkled with bright sunshine. It wasn't warm, but neither was it cold. A soft breeze blew in from the ocean. The fort was built on a jut of land surrounded by deep ravines and the sea, which made it easy to defend. Isabella couldn't believe she was glimpsing the place of her birth with Peter whispering in her ear, "Welcome to the prettiest fort I ever saw. It sure produced the prettiest girl."

A blush seared her cheeks

"Have you seen many forts?" she managed. How could she tell Peter she was probably pregnant? He seemed so happy to have found her. There was still a chance Paul's seed hadn't stuck. Perhaps the stress of living with Gunther had made her ill and kept her monthly flow from arriving.

"I've seen plenty of forts, but none like this one. California is a paradise. The land so fertile you could plant a rock and grow a carrot."

Isabella sensed Peter's happiness but couldn't escape her worries. They rode in silence for a spell. Peter eventually began to hum in her ear, a tune she didn't recognize, but his light-heartedness lifted her spirits.

At the fort, he stunned her by introducing her as his wife to Mr. Benitz and his wife, who held a chubby baby. Mrs. Benitz was a pleasant woman, and Mr. Benitz was polite and welcoming. These Germans were very different than Gunther. The Benitzes invited them to join them for supper. Peter then walked Isabella across the fort's great yard to a housing complex constructed as part of the fort's great wall. He handed her a large package and a smaller one, asking her to wear the clothing in the wrappers after the bath he'd have delivered for her. Leading her up some stairs to a second-story room, Peter left her in a bedroom, where she found his belongings. The bed was made, but she somehow knew he'd already slept there. Her stomach swirled, and she felt light-headed. Sitting down on the bed, she covered her mouth, willing the familiar sickness away.

There was a knock at the door. When she opened it, a Creole man carried in a wooden washtub and then departed. Several Creole women with blue eyes and black hair like hers carried buckets of heated water into the room. When the women saw Isabella, they broke into smiles. They spoke in excited Russian. When Isabella didn't understand, they switched to broken English. At what age had she left the fort? Who were her parents? How long had she been gone from here?

"Antipina was my mother. She died giving birth to me. I left here as a babe."

When she said her mother's name, one of the women nearly dropped her water bucket and then hurried over and hugged her with tears filling her eyes. "Antipina was my sister!" the woman cried. "A padre took you away after she died because it was feared you had the sickness that killed her and you would infect others. The padre said your fate was in God's hands. He was not afraid of the sickness like everyone else. He insisted on carrying you and your wet nurse away."

Isabella couldn't believe she was staring at her aunt. "I didn't know my mother had been sick. I thought she merely died giving birth to me."

"Antipina was very ill when she bore you. She prayed you would live. It's a miracle you did."

Isabella tried to process that she was not the cause of her mother's death, as she'd always believed. She'd thought her mother wouldn't have died had she not been born. She'd carried this burden all her life. A celebration ensued as the women rejoiced over her.

"Is my father here? Sergei Ivanov? I came to find him," she said anxiously.

The women ceased their celebration. By the looks on their faces, Isabella knew her father was gone.

"After your mother died, your father returned to Russia, but then he came back. He was young and strong and handsome when he left, but he was ill when he returned. He is buried beside your mother, just beyond the gorge." The women filled the tub in silence now, allowing Isabella time to grieve for her father. They quietly left one by one, carrying their empty buckets, her aunt the last to depart, promising to come back in a short while.

Isabella washed her hair and body and then soaked until the water cooled. She'd always thought her father didn't want her. And after all these years, finding out her father was buried alongside her mother saddened but satisfied her. She would ask Peter to take her to their graves.

Nothing was unfolding the way she'd dreamed. There would be no reunion with her Russian father, but falling into Peter's arms in the forest was like a dream. She feared she might never get her belongings back from Gunther, but at least she was free. Her rosary was in her skirt pocket. And she'd worn her warm shawl. She'd also had on her best pair of boots. She really didn't care much about the rest of her clothing at Gunther's house. The few dresses she owned had been supplied by Clara. They weren't appropriate for a respectable life anyway. Her aunt had quietly slipped back in and carried away the woolen dress she'd had on for washing.

Drying off, she wrapped the towel around herself and shivered in the room. The fort was constructed of red-hued wood with thick walls and beams and planked floors that held in the heat or cold, depending on the weather. Glass windows allowed in plenty of sunshine from inside the walls of the fort. She tore open the smaller package from Peter, finding the most exquisite undergarments she'd ever seen. Slipping into them, she sighed with pleasure. Never in her life had she worn such unmentionables. The larger package she opened next. She knew it was a dress. Cream colored silk slid out of the wrapping paper. She ran her hands over the fabric in wonder. This dress was made for a princess. The undergarments fit her well; she hoped the gown did too. She wrapped her damp hair in the towel and did her best to dress herself.

Growing up, Indian maids had always helped her dress and braid her hair. Now Isabella did these things for herself. Her life had drastically changed after the American takeover, especially once they'd reached the goldfields. Her life had become a trial each day—until the night Peter won her in the card game.

Her face filled with heat remembering that night with him in the oak grove. The wonder of their union. And then her heart ached all over again. He'd chosen Clara and abandoned her. Did Peter know she'd become Paul's woman? He certainly wouldn't call her his wife if he knew she'd lain with his brother. Despair threatened to steal the relief she'd felt when he arrived. They had hardly spoken at all.

The reality of her situation flooded her. She struggled into the silk dress, trying to gain some warmth. The towel fell from her hair. Her wet locks tumbled down her back and dampened the silk. The gown's skirt went on and on. She became tangled in the yards of fabric. She plopped down on the edge of the bed and sat there as tears threatened to overwhelm her.

Her aunt slipped back into the room without knocking. The woman wasn't very clean, her clothes those of a servant, but she was still beautiful, with midnight-black hair, smooth olive skin, and slanted blue eyes full of kindness. Her features looked more European than Indian. "I've come to help you," her aunt said.

Had her mother looked this way? It dawned on Isabella that finding her mother's sister was a gift. "Did my mother resemble you?"

Her aunt smiled. "Yes, your mother looked like me. I was older, but she was more beautiful. I am Tatiana."

Isabella smiled through her tears. "I was told my father truly loved my mother."

Tatiana came to the bed and pulled a comb from the folds of her skirt. She began to untangle Isabella's long hair. "Everybody loved your mother. She was very special."

"Were my parents really married?" Isabella hesitated to ask such a question, but she wanted to know everything she could about her mother and father.

Tatiana combed her hair without answering.

"So they weren't married," Isabella ventured. The realization grieved her.

"Our father would not allow them to marry. He said Antipina was too young. But really, your father was too much of a rogue." Tatiana laughed softly. "Our parents were very pious. They'd become part of the faithful, and your father was a wild fur trader from the motherland."

"So my mother defied them to be with my father?"

"For a time. But then she returned home carrying you in her belly."

Isabella closed her eyes as her aunt combed her hair. Nothing was turning out the way she'd wanted. "Did my father return with her?"

"No. But later he came. He was very sorry. He loved her."

"Did he know about me?"

Again, Tatiana took some time to answer. She began to pin up Isabella's hair. "He knew the padre took you away."

"Was he sad?"

"We were all sad. Your mother wasn't the only one who died from the sickness. Many died. There was great sorrow at the fort and in the surrounding area when the sailors brought the sickness here. After infecting the fort, the sickness swept through the Indian villages. My mother was not Creole. She was Pomo Indian. Almost all of her Pomo family died."

"Did your parents die?"

"Yes. Only my brother, Vasilli, and I survived the great sickness." Tatiana finished styling Isabella's damp hair. "Your dress is . . ." Her aunt struggled to find the English word. "Magnificent."

Isabella could tell she no longer wanted to speak of the sickness that took her family. "I have never worn anything like it."

Tatiana smiled. "He is waiting for you under the tree out there." She pointed to the window.

Isabella stood up and peered out. Peter sat under an apple tree in the courtyard, reading a book. She hadn't realized he could read. He was no longer wearing his buckskins. Dressed like a gentleman, his short beard was gone, his hair cut short. She hardly recognized him. She returned to the bed and sat down. Peter's appearance reminded her of when he'd come to Clara's and she almost didn't recognize him. That night he'd walked past her on the stairs up to Clara's room, tenderly touching her head like he regretted what he was doing, but he'd done it anyway. So many emotions stirred in her now.

Her parents were never married, her father was dead, and she didn't understand Peter at all. Why come for her now? Why the silken dress and undergarments? They felt luxurious against her skin and were beyond beautiful, but they weren't practical at all. This wasn't a city where people dressed in fine apparel. Even the Benitzes did not dress extravagantly. Why was Peter in gentlemen's clothing out there under the apple tree?

"He won me in a card game," she told Tatiana.

Her aunt quietly picked up Isabella's boots. "Do you have any other shoes?"

Isabella locked gazes with her aunt. "I have nothing else."

"You have an inner beauty that equals your outer beauty. You're like Antipina all over again. Her spirit was so sweet. This man has claimed you. He is strong and rich and handsome. Is he good to you?"

Isabella could see her own face in the lines of her aunt's pretty face. She felt Tatiana's affection. In a way, she was home, but was there any future for her here at the fort with what remained of her family?

"I don't know," Isabella finally answered. "Peter Brondi is a complicated man. I am afraid he will leave me again."

There it was, the truth of the matter. Everybody left her. She recalled the day she'd learned she was adopted. Her sister, Maria, had informed her she was a half-breed. Isabella had never heard the term before. It sounded ugly on Maria's lips. Isabella had gone to her mother, Josefa, who doted on her. "Mama, am I adopted?"

Josefa had smiled her tender smile. "You were chosen by Dios to be our daughter. There is no shame in that. We are all adopted by Dios to become like Jesuchristo, *es el hijo de Dios.*"

Isabella had hoped Maria was just jealous that she had a mother while Maria did not. Maria's mother had died. Josefa had raised them both. "Your mother died too!" Maria had screamed at her one day. This had shocked Isabella. It never occurred to her until that moment that Josefa wasn't really her mother. Or Don Pedro her father. Isabella's skin was darker than theirs, but that wasn't out of the ordinary in Californio families. Her brother, Roman, was dark-skinned. Until he undressed. His skin was fair under his clothing. Isabella's skin was fair too where it never saw the sun, but not like Josefa's and Maria's fair skin. And her eyes were like none of theirs. Nobody had almond-shaped blue eyes in the Vasquez family. They all had green or brown eyes.

Now she stared into almond-shaped blue eyes so much like her own. "I do not think he will leave again," said Tatiana. "The dress you are wearing is a wedding gown."

Why would Peter bring a wedding gown? Dizziness hit her. She rested her head in her hands. Tatiana touched her shoulder. "Do you carry his child?" Her aunt sat down beside her on the bed, wrapping Isabella in her arms. "My only daughter died in the sickness that took your mother. I have sons, but they are grown and gone. I am a widow and will never marry again. I loved my husband, but he died too. Do not give up on love, dear one. Love is life. And life is love."

Isabella gave in to the tears. She didn't want to believe it, but she knew it was true. Love was life. And life was love. But Peter didn't love her. And he would never love her once he knew the truth. "I carry his brother's child," she whispered to her aunt.

Chapter Sixteen

Peter watched Belle walk out of the building. The sinking sun shimmered on her silken dress, creating a warm white light that dazzled him. A Creole servant was at her side. The woman looked like an older version of Belle. Peter stood up from under the apple tree and walked to her side. The servant smiled and walked away. Belle held the long folds of her gown over one arm to keep it from sweeping the ground. Her boots peeked out from under her skirt. Peter's chest tightened. This was the wife God had given him, and he planned to rectify right now his failure in the beginning to make good on their marriage.

"Are you ready for my surprise?" A smile slipped onto his face.

"Must we go somewhere for this surprise? I do not think I can sit a horse in this dress." Her words were soft and tentative.

"We won't go far." He offered his arm to her.

She took his elbow, and he led her to the chapel with its little bell tower and Greek Orthodox cross. He stopped in front of the door, released her arm, and turned to face her.

"Are you willing to speak a vow with me before God?" He took her hands and realized they trembled. For a moment, he thought she might turn him down. She didn't smile. She looked so beautiful his heart ached. He knew he'd wounded her deeply the night he'd spent with Clara. She'd all but begged him to keep her as his wife, and he'd rejected her. He deeply regretted that. Would she reject him now? "Do you want to stand before God with me in marriage?"

She nodded, and tears coursed down her face.

He reached out and wiped the tears from her cheeks. "Why are you crying?"

She hung her head and wouldn't look at him. Her words were so soft he hardly heard her. "I've lain with your brother."

"And I've lain with Clara," he confessed.

She looked up. "Do you love Clara? Are you doing this because you feel sorry for me?"

He wiped more tears from her face. "I am sorry I took you to Clara's. I knew deep down you'd never known a man until me, but I didn't want to believe it. I was a fool. I didn't want a wife I'd won in a card game." He stopped talking. This was hurting him—it must be hurting her.

He took a deep breath and tried again. "I'm sorry. I should have kept you as my bride even if our vows weren't spoken before God. I never should have taken you back to Marysville. An honorable man would not have done that, but I am not an honorable man. And neither is my brother. Do you love him?"

Waiting for her to answer left him holding his breath.

Her gaze roved over his face, her eyes wide and wounded. "I don't love Paul, but what if I carry a child?"

His heart stopped. He removed his hands from her cheeks. "Are you with child?"

She nodded, and more tears ran down her face.

He wanted to comfort her but was losing his own composure. His throat had grown so tight he didn't trust himself to speak. He'd never been comfortable with women. Especially respectable women. But Belle was different. She was everything he wanted in a wife, aside from the Indian blood that ran through her veins. But he'd made his peace with that. She wasn't his enemy. And she wasn't like Paul's mother or Paul. But what if she carried Paul's child?

The thought left him cold.

He reminded himself he'd had her first. There was a chance she carried his child. He considered asking her straight out whose child she harbored. He didn't believe she would lie. But instead, he asked himself: Would it change his decision now to take vows with her? His willingness to make her his wife in every way? To build a life with her from here on forward?

Even if she carried Paul's seed, he couldn't leave her at the fort, where the German would certainly find her. Or another man would swoop in and make her his own. The truth was, when she stepped out into that sunshine wearing that wedding dress the color of a newborn lamb, he knew she was born to be his wife. God had ordained it. A white light had shone on her for a moment that dazzled his eyes, and he took that as a sign from God.

"If you carry a child, then we will be a family."

She wiped her tears and attempted a smile.

Please bless us, Lord, he prayed as he led her into the chapel.

It was a small church with a domed ceiling. Other areas of the fort were busy with activity, but the chapel stood empty. He'd asked Benitz if he could use the church to celebrate his vows with Belle. He hadn't shared how they'd married, other than saying a church wasn't available then and he wanted to speak a vow with his wife before God in a church.

Benitz had smiled and said, "Of course you and your wife are welcome to use the chapel. And we'd love to host you for supper tonight."

Peter didn't want to join the Benitzes for supper. He longed to be alone with Belle. But he didn't know how to turn the man down. Now with the way things were going, perhaps the Benitzes would ease the tension between them. He tried not to think about a babe as he led Belle to the altar. The chapel was bare, but light streamed in the window, and peace permeated the place. Certainty grew in him. Speaking this vow was the right thing to do. Belle dropped her skirt, and it swirled onto the floor in a hiss of silk that sounded like the release of a long-held breath.

Peter released his own breath. He wished a real minister was here. He had no idea how to seal a vow before God with her.

She stared expectantly at him. With her hair pinned back, at least she looked old enough to be his wife. What if, like Maggie, she died giving birth? He closed his eyes, willing his thoughts into order. He'd learned long ago that worrying about the future only marred the present.

"We don't have to do this," she said, mistaking his hesitation.

He opened his eyes. Her gaze was intent on him.

Take care of my lamb.

He recognized that voice. It didn't come from his own thoughts. It sounded just like Jedediah when he read the Bible as they sat beside the fire on cold winter nights.

He realized the words of the Bible had stuck. They'd burrowed deep into his heart like an Indian arrow and killed the man he'd once been. He didn't want to chase the wind any longer. He wanted to make a life with Belle.

"Will you promise to be my wife, forsaking all others and clinging only onto me?" he asked.

"I will," she whispered. Her eyes became more trusting.

"Will you obey me? Will you go where I go and stay where I stay?"

A tear ran down her cheek. "I will." She looked determined now.

"Will you raise our children in the fear of the Lord?" *Where had that come from?* He didn't know the fear of the Lord, but a heavenly presence filled the room. He was being led by the Good Shepherd as he spoke and suddenly realized she wasn't the only lamb in the room. He was a lamb too, and it humbled him. He hung his head. *Forgive me for sinning against Belle. Against You. Forgive me for hating my brother.*

A tear fell from his eye and hit the floor. He couldn't believe he was confessing his hatred for Paul. The realization came to him that he'd always resented Paul. Even before the mess with Maggie. Since the day Paul had arrived with his mother, the Indian woman claiming Paul was Jedediah's son, he'd harbored malice toward Paul. He'd tried to bury it as best he could. When they were young, Paul followed him around like his shadow. He'd soon found it impossible not to like the little Indian boy. It wasn't long before he'd found himself his brother's keeper. Jedediah had given him the chore of looking after Paul day and night. Paul adored him, and he eventually got past being angry over Paul joining the family in New Mexico. Or at least he thought he had.

Why did this deeply buried emotion come up now? He suddenly knew why, like lightning hit his mind, illuminating it. God was putting his holy finger on his greatest sin. How he felt about Paul and all Indians. The sin had shaped Peter into the man he'd become. Each time he killed an Indian, it was like killing Paul. Consciously, he hadn't known this until this very moment. He realized he needed to ask God for forgiveness.

Forgive me for hating Indians, he prayed with another tear traveling down his cheek.

A terrible memory flashed through his mind. A clearing with a cabin. He was riding over to play with his cousin Will. The clearing so quiet. As if all of nature held its breath when he arrived. Even the birds stopped singing. Bodies were scattered all over the place. Uncle Bill was in the pasture, stripped of his clothing. Aunt Emmie Lou lay face down near the cabin, holding a lifeless, wide-eyed baby girl that had been scalped as well. Nine children slaughtered like calves in the field. His best friend, Will, his cousin, among them.

Peter was crying now. He closed his eyes, fighting the memory. Fighting this reckoning with God. "I don't want this . . ." he murmured. "I put this from my mind long ago."

Belle took his hand. He'd almost forgotten she was there. He wrestled, doing his best to control this thing coming over him.

He couldn't control it.

Only God could control it.

He gave himself over to the Good Lord and the pain. In the instant of his surrender, peace like sweet, clean water washed over him. He cried for a moment, his eyes on the floor. Sunlight from above sparkled across the planks.

"I'm sorry for what I did with Paul. I didn't think you were coming back for me." Belle sounded broken. She was crying too.

When he looked up, her eyes were bright with tears.

"I'm sorry for the man I've been. I feared and hated Indians all my life because of what I've seen them do. I treated you poorly on account of your Indian blood. I'd never have treated a white woman the way I treated you. I'm sorry."

She was the first woman to see him shed a tear. It unleashed something in Peter he'd never felt before. Raw vulnerability. Never in his life had he been afraid of dying. But he was afraid of living honest and open this way before God and Belle.

"Dios will help us," she said hopefully.

"Yes, God will help us," he agreed.

A smile curved her lips even as she cried.

It was God who gave him the resolve to stand before Belle with tears on his face. His old self never would have stood for that. Never would he have let her or anyone else see that kind of softness in him. His heart swelled with gratitude. He knew something profound had just happened between God and them.

"Belle do you take Peter Brondi to be your lawfully wedded husband in the eyes of the Almighty?" He was speaking, but it didn't sound like his own voice. It was the voice of a man humbled before God.

Her smile sweetened. "I am Isabella Ivanov." After wiping the tears from her own face, she reached out and wiped the tears from his.

"Will you love me, Isabella Ivanov?"

"I will." Her eyes shone with happiness.

"May I kiss you?"

Her silken dress sighed as she slid up against him. His mouth covered hers, and he kissed her deeply, melding his body to hers. He felt her surrender and her knees give way. Scooping her up, he stared at her face. Long black lashes fanned her pale cheeks. He realized she wasn't well. He carried her from the church and out into the waning afternoon sunlight. Evening was approaching. The fresh air revived her.

"Please take me to the cemetery," she said.

Her request shocked him. He wanted to take her back to his room and tuck her into bed. Her ill health frightened him. "I believe you should rest."

"I'm not ill. I'm expecting," she admitted. "This comes over me from time to time."

Carefully, he set her feet on the ground. People were going about their evening chores in the courtyard. The mercantile across the yard was closing. A man walked out of the shop and mounted his mule, leading a pack mule as he rode off with his supplies toward the gate that would close at dusk.

Peter had forgotten they weren't alone. The world had stopped spinning while they were inside the church; now it turned once more.

"We can walk to the cemetery. It's not far," she told him.

Peter stared at her hopeful face. She was his bride. He didn't want to disappoint her. Bending down, he gathered her long skirt into his hands. "I'll carry this for you. We'll walk slow."

Her smile returned. "You make a fine lady's maid, Peter Brondi."

Her teasing surprised him. His mood lightened. "You make a fine wife, Mrs. Brondi." He led her by her silken skirt across the grounds. People stared at them in their fine clothes, but Peter didn't care. Isabella didn't seem to care either.

The sky was turning rosy when they reached the ridge outside the fort where the cemetery crowned a hilltop. They had to get around a deep gorge, but the day was fine, the landscape almost like a park around the fort. Peter's hands were full of silk and his heart full of wonder. He had a bride. Her name was Isabella, not Belle. She'd wiped his tears and hadn't seen him as less of a man because he cried. She'd cried with him and vowed to love him.

Could she really love him?

Could he love her until the day he died? They hardly knew each other. He'd won her in a card game. She was with child. Perhaps Paul's child.

Perfect love casts out fear.

Peter had heard Jedediah reading that from the Bible. The Gospel of John proclaiming that God's perfect love cast out fear. The peace he'd made with God spread through him.

He looked out over the graves. How would they find her parents' resting place? She seemed to be thinking the same thing. Confusion was on her face. Releasing her skirts, he stepped out to search for stones with inscriptions, but found none. He looked out at the ocean in the distance and saw the sun wouldn't last much longer. Pink streaked the sky. The wind was turning cold. Isabella was a vision with the breeze in her skirts, standing on the hillside watching him walk back to her. He marveled they were really married. He'd made up his mind and didn't care if Old Will wasn't a real preacher. They'd sealed their vows before God in the chapel, and that was all they needed. "I don't know how to tell who's buried under those crosses out there," he admitted.

"It's no matter. I have said my good-byes to my mother and father."

"Are you ready to return to the fort?"

"Must we dine with the Benitzes tonight?"

"I think we should."

"I'm a Creole, like their servants."

Peter gathered up her silken skirt. "You're my wife, and they've asked us to dine with them."

"Perhaps my aunt serves their family."

"Perhaps she does." Peter began walking, leading Isabella by the skirt, wanting to get her back inside the walls of the fort. In his good clothes with only his knife tucked into his boot, he chastised himself for not having his gun. It wasn't like him to let his guard down this way. The whole afternoon had turned him into a man he didn't know.

"Do you care that I'm a Creole?"

Peter stopped. He knew this was important to her. "Your Indian blood doesn't matter to me anymore. The Lord has made us one flesh. You are blood of my blood and bone of my bone now."

"Others may not see it that way. What if the Benitzes see you as a squaw man?"

Peter hated that term. Kit Carson had two Indian wives before marrying his Spanish wife. Folks still called Carson a squaw man. Men who took Indian wives out West were looked down on in polite society. To his relief, society wasn't so polite in California.

"I've never cared what others thought of me." Peter urged her to walk by tugging on her skirt. "I don't believe the Benitzes would have invited us to supper if they felt that way."

"I don't want to be a problem for you."

"Oh, you'll be a problem for me." Peter let her see his smile. "Every man will want my beautiful wife."

Chapter Seventeen

Isabella held the Benitzes' baby, wondering what her own baby would look like. This baby's eyes were round and bright blue. The baby stared at her, so she smiled for him. The child grinned back, and Isabella was charmed. She tried to ignore the sickness coming on. She usually experienced this after eating supper. This happened to her almost every evening. Why did women call it morning sickness when it plagued her most in the evening?

"He likes you," said Mrs. Benitz.

Peter and Mr. Benitz were conversing at the table. A quiet and unobtrusive Indian woman cleared the dishes. Isabella and Mrs. Benitz had ventured to the parlor, where another child, a toddler, played with wooden blocks. The Indian servant watching over the child was silent too. Isabella had grown up with these kind of Indian servants and never thought a thing about it until moving to the goldfields. It had been a shock when men called her an Indian. Isabella had never thought of herself as an Indian until then.

Mrs. Benitz must have sensed her unease as she watched the Indian maid care for the child. The woman reached out and put a hand gently on her arm. "So you were born here at Fort Ross?"

Mrs. Benitz was kind and gracious, but Isabella felt out of place in her home. "Yes, my mother died of the sickness during my birth."

"Probably the pox or measles. Those plagues took so many lives. The Indians dwindled down to hardly any around the fort. My husband and I weren't here then, but the fields suffered with all the workers gone. After the epidemics, Mr. Sutter came and purchased the fort from the Russians. Most folks were happy to leave after Mr. Sutter carried everything away."

Isabella bounced the baby in her arms. Holding him made her think less of how ill she felt. She hoped the sickness would pass. "The fort seems very productive now."

"My husband works hard. And he has good partners. We are slowly replacing the cattle and sheep and coaxing the Indians that survived the epidemics to return. We pay them well so they'll come."

"You pay the Indians?" Isabella's family had always paid the Indians for shearing the sheep and helping herd the cattle and such. Most Indians came and went in freedom at Rancho de los Robles, but she knew other rancheros saw the Indians as their slaves and treated them poorly. The Americans were especially harsh to the Indians. Whole tribes were being wiped out by the settlers and miners.

"We treat the local tribes well, and they are happy to work for us."

The baby was starting to fuss, so Isabella handed him back to Mrs. Benitz. "In the goldfields, they called me an Indian. I am only a quarter Indian, but they saw me as an Indian."

"Gold has uncivilized men. I am glad we don't live near those awful goldfields. Here the Creole people are treated well. Some even own their own farms and businesses. Perhaps you and your husband could settle here."

"I'm sorry, I am feeling ill. I must retire for the evening." Isabella put her hand over her mouth, grabbed up her shawl, and hurried from the parlor. She barely made it out the front door and around the side of the house before she lost her supper. Her stomach heaved until she could hardly stand it. She remained there behind the bushes until her stomach settled.

The night was clear and cold. The wind had stilled. Stars shimmered overhead. A shiver ran through her as she gathered herself and walked back around the house, holding her long skirt over her arm. Fortunately, she hadn't spoiled her dress in the process of losing her meal. There had been no time to change for supper, not that she had anything else to wear until her aunt brought her woolen dress back. She rounded the corner and nearly ran into Peter.

"Are you all right?" His voice was more raspy than usual. His hawkish gaze missed nothing. She had worried him.

"I'm sorry. I'm better now, but can we return to your room so I can lie down?" Being alone with him filled her with angst, but she was so tired. If only she could undo those weeks at Clara's with Paul. Had she known Peter would come back for her, she never would have allowed Paul into her room.

"I told the Benitzes I needed to get you to bed. They aren't expecting us back." Peter wrapped his arm around her waist. "How long have you been like this?"

His question was pointed. Isabella knew it. Was he hoping she carried his child? "Long enough," was all she said.

He didn't press further. They walked back to his room in silence. Oil lamps were burning to guide them to their quarters. Could she allow him to believe there was a chance the child was his? She didn't have the heart to tell him the truth. Exhaustion hit in earnest, and all she wanted to do was close her eyes and escape into sleep. Entering the room, she realized she didn't even have a nightgown to wear. There was only one bed in the quarters. Of course, it was expected she would sleep with her husband.

"I'll let you settle in." He turned and left the room so suddenly Isabella was shocked.

He was gone before she gathered her wits about her. Looking around the room, she saw her woolen gown hanging in a corner. Bless her aunt for being so thoughtful. Perhaps she could sleep in it. Or she could crawl into bed in her unmentionables. Under the covers, Peter wouldn't see her. She wrestled out of her wedding gown, fearing she'd never escape the dress on her own. When she finally loosened enough buttons down the back to wiggle free, she laid the gown over a chair. A few minutes later, she was in bed under the covers, breathlessly waiting for Peter to return.

She waited. And waited.

Where was Peter?

Her eyes grew heavy. The bed was comfortable and warm. She couldn't fight off sleep any longer.

• • •

Peter returned to the room after a long walk around the fort. His emotions were in turmoil. When she didn't deny the child she carried could be his, he was filled with hope. As he walked, he prayed, *Please, Lord, let this babe be mine.* He knew it was his fault she'd fallen in with Paul. Just like his brother stealing Maggie. Paul's child had killed Maggie. Could it happen again with Belle?

He shook his head. *Isabella.* He hadn't even known her real name until a few hours ago. What else didn't he know about her? Her beauty tempted him, but that wasn't going to make for a marriage. And she sure was quiet. It didn't help that he didn't talk much either. Together they'd said only a few words to each other all day. It did move his heart that she'd taken to the Benitzes' baby. He'd never seen her smile the way she smiled for the child, and he'd kept sneaking glances at her holding the infant.

"You sure are taken with your young wife," Benitz had finally said, and a warm flush had filled Peter's face. Benitz had laughed. "The Fort Ross Creoles are a fine race. No shame in a man wanting his bride."

He did want her. Badly. But she was sound asleep when he came back to the room. She was also with child, though she didn't look it one bit. He didn't know what to do about that. The thought of climbing into bed with her suddenly unnerved him.

The desire for whiskey came over him without warning, the pull so strong he could hardly withstand it. The Benitzes had offered him wine at dinner, but he'd politely refused, content to sip his strong black coffee. Now he desperately wanted a drink. He'd seen no saloon at the fort. No place to acquire a drink at the moment.

Lord, help me. The devil is at the door. Please send him away.

He walked over without making a sound and stared down at his sleeping wife. She'd left the oil lamp burning, and her hair was black as midnight spilling over the pillow. Slowly, carefully, he lifted the covers to see the rest of her. Her wedding dress was draped over the chair. The woolen dress she'd worn in the forest hung on a hook on the wall. Just as he'd thought, she was wearing her unmentionables. The sight of her took his breath away. He eased the covers back over her without waking her up. Lord help him, he wanted her.

Give her time.

Had he heard that right? Was that his thought, or had it come from above?

He went to the window and stared out into the night. His thirst for whiskey was easing. He wiped his brow. The desire for Isabella took longer to overcome. How could he sleep with her and not touch her? Before going to sleep every single night, he remembered her sweet surrender to him in the oak grove. He was haunted by thoughts of what she'd done with Paul. A part of him wanted to wipe every trace of his brother off of her. He wanted to reclaim her now and show her he was more of a man than his brother could ever be.

The devil is at the door. Resist him.

The whisper shocked him. There at the window, a battle ensued. He wanted to go to the bed right now and prove Isabella was his. After tonight, Paul would be a distant memory for both of them. Clara too. Nobody would be between them any longer. Becoming one would drive out all the rest.

Wait.

Take her now.

He liked the second voice better. He had every right to have his way with her, even though she was sick. Even though she was exhausted. Even though she carried a babe.

He rested his forehead against the cold glass of the windowpane and closed his eyes. He needed to put her well-being before his own. How long he rested there, he didn't know, but the desire to have her finally faded.

Once he had control, he sat on the edge of the bed to remove his boots. He laid his knife aside and removed his vest and shirt. Stripped down to his britches, he decided that was far enough. Without looking at her, he slipped under the covers and tried his best to go to sleep on his side of the bed. Her scent came to him, and he rolled onto his stomach, burying his face in the pillow, trying not to smell her. She smelled so good.

Her warmth radiated to him. Time passed. He rolled back over and realized he'd left the oil lamp burning. Crawling out of bed, he blew out the lamp and padded back to lie down. This time he settled in closer to her. That wasn't a good idea, and his body awakened. He squeezed his eyes shut and gritted out a prayer. *If you don't stop me, nothing will.*

It hit him that God might find his situation humorous. Was the good Lord laughing at him?

Are you laughing at me?

So you're not laughing, but you're smiling.

Great. I'm glad you think this is funny.

Go to sleep, Peter.

He knew it was the Lord, even though it came to him as his own thought.

Is this how it is? We can talk like men together.

My sheep hear my voice.

Sheep did know their master's voice. Jedediah's herd loved him. Some of the sheep had even taken to Peter. At first, having sheep follow him around, wanting to be near him drove him crazy on the drive to California. But after two thousand miles with those particular animals, he knew every one individually. Some sheep became attached to him. "Those are your sheep," Jedediah had said.

"I don't want sheep of my own," Peter had returned.

"Well, that's too bad. Those sheep have chosen you as their shepherd. Now don't disappoint them."

Are you going to disappoint me, Lord?

No more thoughts came to him. At least the need for whiskey had flown and his desire to have Isabella eased. His eyes adjusted to the darkness and the faint moonlight spilling through the window. He rolled over to look at her. There wasn't enough light to see her features, but he could make out her silhouette. "I promise to do my best by you. I'll put your needs first, I swear I will," he whispered.

Chapter Eighteen

A man's moans awoke Isabella. It took a moment to remember Peter had rescued her from Gunther. She was no longer in the German's cottage. This room was chilly, but not the kind of cold she'd experienced at Gunther's place. She was under the covers. The bed was filled with Peter's warm presence. Was that him making the tortured sounds? He thrashed about, having a nightmare. Should she wake him?

Suddenly, he yelled, "I won't kill her!"

It startled her. "Peter, wake up," she cried.

He reached out and grabbed hold of her. "I'm not going to kill a squaw!"

Fear choked her. His hands felt like iron, but she raised her voice to match his. "I'm Isabella!"

He let her go. "Isabella?" he sounded confused. She couldn't make out the expression on his face in the darkness.

"Isabella, your wife."

He rolled onto his back, breathing hard, his distress tangible.

Tentatively, she reached out and touched him. Her hand landed in the center of his chest, where his heart beat madly. He wasn't wearing a shirt. His body was damp with sweat and rock-hard with muscle and bone. She jerked her hand away.

"It's best you don't touch me," he rasped.

"Do you have these terrible dreams often?"

"Only sometimes now."

"In the past, you had them more?"

"Most nights," he admitted.

"What are your dreams about?"

He didn't speak for a moment. When he finally did, his voice carried shame. "Killing Indians."

Isabella went cold. Of course he'd killed Indians. He'd ridden with Kit Carson. "Have you killed white men too?"

"Some."

"How many men have you killed?"

"I don't know for certain." His breathing was evening out.

"Would you have killed Gunther if he hadn't allowed you to take me?"

"I suppose I would have."

His answer gave her a comfort she didn't expect. He'd drawn his gun on Mick too, his own friend. There was no doubt Peter would kill for her. She felt safe with him from other men, but was she safe from him? She could see how dangerous he was. She hardly knew her husband at all. When he hadn't drank wine at dinner, she'd been relieved. Paul's drinking frightened her. She didn't want to live with another drunken man.

Peter rasped in the darkness, "Can you stomach a husband who's killed his share of men?"

"Can you stomach a squaw for a wife?"

He rolled onto his side, propping himself on an elbow to stare at her in the darkness. She still couldn't make out his face, but she knew he studied her. "I told you your Indian blood doesn't matter anymore." His voice was soft.

"It matters to me." Her heart beat thickly. She'd finally said it. She hated being Indian. Since the American takeover, men looked down on her for that. She wasn't respected like her sister, Maria. Men thought they could freely have her because she was a half-breed.

"Well, you best get used to it. Hating Indians is a sin. I know that now."

His confession surprised her. "I guess it is."

"We need to tell the Good Lord we're sorry." His voice was so humble.

"I'm sorry," she whispered, hot tears spilling down her cheeks.

"I'm sorry too." He reached out and touched her face. Her tears washed over his hand. "Why are you crying?"

"I wish I was Spanish, like my sister."

"Don't wish for that. You are the way God made you. There's no shame in his image. He did a right fine job creating you." He gently wiped the tears from her cheek.

"Why do you dream about killing Indians?"

"I guess because they killed first."

"When you came to California?"

"When I was a boy in Missouri. They killed my Cousin Will's whole family. I found Will scalped in the field. He was my best friend. Just eight years old, like me. They even scalped his baby sister in her mother's arms."

"That's dreadful."

"I shouldn't hate all Indians because of Will, but I have. Those were bad Indians. There's good Indians too."

"Mrs. Benitz said the tribes around Fort Ross are good. Have you killed any Indians in California?"

"I have, and I'm sorry for it. The men I rode with said the only good Indian was a dead Indian. We did our part to make them good Indians."

Isabella shivered. "Did you kill women and children?"

"Would it make you leave this bed?"

"Maybe."

"It would make me leave this bed. I'd never be able to sleep if I'd done that. I don't kill women and children."

That gave her relief.

"Did Mick kill women and children when you rode together?"

"Mick takes pleasure in killing. Has he bothered you?" She could hear the alarm in his voice, though he spoke evenly.

"Mick came to Clara's."

"Did he hurt you?"

"I became Paul's woman to keep him at bay." It was a relief to get that out. She didn't tell Peter Mick had bloodied her lip. She was afraid he might find Mick and fight him.

Peter's fingers stroked her damp cheek. "I'm real sorry I left you at Clara's."

She closed her eyes, trying not to cry again.

He leaned in close, and his lips found hers. It was a kiss of apology, not of passion. "Let's try to get some sleep," he said after his soft, tender kiss. He rolled again onto his back. For a long time, she knew he wasn't asleep. She longed to comfort him but didn't have the courage to get any closer. She felt like she knew something important now. Indians had killed his family. That explained a lot. It took quite a while to fall back asleep.

When she awoke, Peter was gone. Sunlight spilled into the room. His things were missing. It was like he'd never been there at all. Even her wedding gown was absent. Panic set in. He'd left her again. Tears rushed to her eyes. Would she forever be longing for a husband who didn't want her?

She quickly rose from the bed and donned her woolen dress. The cold made her shiver. Wrapping her shawl around her shoulders, she walked over to the window. The courtyard was busy with activity, the fort humming about its normal business. She didn't see Peter anywhere. Trying not to cry, she turned and found a washbowl on the little table in the corner. She went to it and bathed her face. Peter must have left it for her this morning because the water was still lukewarm. After washing her face, she stared at herself in the mirror on the wall. Combing her hair away from her face with her fingers, she secured it simply with the hairpins her aunt had given her.

Where she would go or what she would do now, she didn't know. Maybe her aunt would take her in. Perhaps she could find a new life here at the fort. At least Peter hadn't bedded her before leaving, like the last time. She didn't think she could handle that again. Why was her heart so torn apart over him? She knew Paul better than she knew Peter. She even carried Paul's child, but it was Peter she longed to make a life with. She didn't care that he'd killed men. His nightmares didn't bother her. She had nightmares too. What bothered her was that she'd fallen in love with him from the moment she first saw him, and he didn't love her back.

She reached into her skirt pocket and was relieved the rosary was still there. She gripped it in her hand. *Please, Lord, don't let him leave.* She knew what had wounded him. Indians. She understood his complicated feelings and realized his feelings for her were complicated too. Had he loved someone before her? Not Clara, but a respectable girl? A white woman? The thought made her ache.

Walking to the door, she reached for the nob just as the door pushed open. Peter stood there. "You're awake." The possibility of a smile played on his lips.

"I thought you left." Her stomach churned, but she did her best to ignore the familiar sickness. Butterflies also swirled inside her. Around Peter, she always felt this nervous excitement.

"We're all packed. Your horse is saddled and ready to go. Do you think you can ride today?"

Relief rolled through her. "You're taking me with you?"

"Of course. You're my wife." He really was smiling now.

"May I say good-bye to my aunt?"

"She is supposed to meet us at the horses."

He guided her by the elbow out the door and down the stairs. Walking into the morning sunshine, Isabella spotted her aunt. Standing beside her was a young girl. As they approached, the girl slid behind Tatiana. Isabella smiled, hoping to ease the girl's fears and happy to greet her aunt, though they were about to say good-bye.

"I have wrestled with this all night." Tatiana pushed the girl forward. "I can't let you leave without seeing your sister."

Isabella was taken aback.

Peter let go of her arm and stepped between them. "How do you know the girl is her sister?" He tried to get a good look at the child, but the girl buried her face against Tatiana's back.

Isabella reached out and captured Peter's hand, pulling him away, hoping to coax the child out from behind her aunt. "Please let me see her."

"Before your father died, he named her Antipina after your mother. She is known as Pina. Her mother is gone. Her death was very bad. Pina hasn't spoken since."

"How long has it been since she spoke?" Peter asked.

"Six years." Tatiana wiped her eyes. Was she crying?

"What happened to her mother?" Peter squeezed Isabella's hand. She wasn't sure if he meant to comfort her or keep her quiet.

"A man killed her."

Isabella put her hand over her mouth.

"Did the girl see it happen?" Peter's voice was gentle.

"Yes." Tatiana looked around nervously, as if someone might be coming. She pulled the girl out from behind her and made the child face them. She was pretty. Dark and petite with sky-blue eyes that dominated her delicate face. In the girl, Isabella saw herself. She didn't doubt the child was her sister.

"Oh, Peter, look at her."

"How old is she?" Peter asked.

"Eleven. She is small for her age."

"Was she injured when she lost her mother? Is she dumb now?"

"No, she's very smart." Tatiana stroked the girl's head. She wore a shawl over her short black hair. She appeared scared to death.

"Who cares for her?" Isabella's heart was bursting. She had a sister of her blood. Love flowed through her.

Tatiana pushed the girl into Isabella's arms. "He does." She pointed to the man striding toward them. Judging by his clothes, he was American or European. "I must go. They will be missing me in the kitchen. If you want to save her life, take her with you." Tatiana hugged Isabella, crushing the child between them, then she hurried away before the man reached them.

The man said something harsh as her aunt hurried past him. Isabella couldn't make out his words.

"Let me handle this. Hold on to the girl if you can." Peter gripped the handle of the pistol tucked into his belt.

"I won't let her go." Isabella locked her arms around the trembling child.

"You there, what are you doing with that girl?"

Peter stepped in front of Isabella and Pina. "She is our relation," he said evenly. "We are taking her with us."

"You'll regret it. That girl is cursed."

Isabella sensed Pina's terror of the man, and her heart bled for her. The child was filthy and dressed in rags. She could feel the girl's ribs under her clothes.

"God will set her free from any curse." The authority in Peter's voice surprised Isabella.

"Well, she ain't free," said the man, huffing as he approached. "You'll have to pay me if you take her."

"That's far enough." Peter pulled his pistol from his belt, but didn't take aim at the man.

The man froze when he saw Peter's gun. "You wouldn't shoot me on account of a dirty little half-breed, would you?"

Peter stiffened. He raised the gun, leveling it on the man's forehead. "I don't see her that way. She needs a bath. That's easy to remedy. What can't be remedied is your cruelty."

"Look, mister, I never met you in my life. I'm not cruel. I've taken care of her since her ma died. You're a fool to take her on. I've had all kinds of problems with her. She's a little witch. I only keep her because nobody else will; they're scared of her."

"That's enough!" Isabella surprised herself with her outburst. "She's my sister. We are taking her."

Peter looked at Isabella. He didn't say anything. She wasn't about to back down and put her hands on her hips, her gaze locked with his. He turned back to the man, keeping his gun pointed at him. "Is the girl your woman?"

Isabella cried, "No, she's too young!"

The man smiled. "That's the only thing she's good for. You already got yourself a woman. You need to leave the girl here." The man spoke to Peter, ignoring Isabella's outrage.

"I should shoot you," Peter said. "I'd feed you to the German's pigs if I could. It's a bit of a ride through the woods to his place. I was just there this morning gathering some things, but I'd gladly strap you to a mule and take you back there myself if I didn't think it would upset my wife."

"You know Gunther?" the man asked. "He likes the girl too."

"You're a sick—" Peter caught himself before cursing. "Turn around and head back to where you came from before I change my mind and shoot you clean through."

A small crowd had gathered. Tatiana was there, along with a handful of other Creoles wearing servants' clothes. A dozen men stood there as well. Isabella didn't know where they'd all come from. She looked around for the Benitzes, but she didn't see them among the curious faces. Pina had her head buried against Isabella's stomach. She wouldn't look at anyone. Isabella kept her arms tightly around her.

"Put her on that sorrel horse with you and start riding out of here," Peter told Isabella. He didn't holster his gun, even though the man was walking away from them, toward the crowd of onlookers.

People murmured amongst themselves. Isabella caught her aunt's gaze, and they exchanged trembling smiles. There were so many things she wanted to ask her aunt regarding her sister, but Isabella knew they needed to leave while Peter had the upper hand. One man he could handle, but what if the other men came against him?

Chapter Nineteen

Peter turned around in the saddle to see how Isabella and her sister were doing. The girl did resemble his wife, but she was darker—or just covered in dirt, he couldn't tell. An hour or so into the ride, they stopped at a rancho, where he borrowed a horse for Pina. The owner wouldn't take payment for the animal.

"Just let the horse go when you reach Bodega, and it will return to me," said the aging Californio.

Peter had learned this was how it was at the ranchos along the coast. Nobody was more hospitable than the Californios. Their horses were trained to follow the trail back to their own pastures when released. A number of times they had to stop so Isabella could be sick. She would race into the trees, and the girl would race after her. He worried about the girl. She had the look of a wild animal about her. She'd obviously been abused. He couldn't get near her without her eyes rolling in fear. This wasn't the way he'd planned to spend his honeymoon—with a mute girl and a pregnant wife.

The day wore on. A dark despair settled over him. His thoughts spun with guilt and shame and confusion. Isabella continued to be sick. After one of their stops, a squawking raven followed Isabella and Pina out of the woods. The big black bird's presence seemed to please the girl. When the bird wouldn't fly away, the girl broke into a smile. The look on her face chilled Peter. And he'd never seen a raven behave that way before.

A half hour later, when he couldn't take any more of the squawking bird swooping around, he pulled out his gun to shoot it. The girl went wild, jerking her horse into a rearing spin that made Isabella scream. "Put your gun away!" Isabella cried. "Can't you see you've upset Pina?"

"Something's wrong with her," said Peter.

"She's been through evil with that awful man," Isabella replied.

"I think evil's gotten into her." Peter watched the girl spin her horse in circles until the animal nearly fell down. The girl didn't seem dizzy at all. The raven continued to fly in circles above her. He'd never seen anything like it.

"That's a terrible thing to say." Isabella kept her voice low so the girl didn't hear her. "She's my sister."

Peter was at a loss as to how to handle Isabella and the girl, so he kicked his horse into a trot away from them. It didn't take the girls long to catch up since he led a pack mule and they were good riders. Thankfully, the raven disappeared. With the sun descending, they finally crossed a long stretch of sand dunes to reach the bay. An ocean breeze blew. The waning day turned cold. The settlement beside the bay wasn't much more than a cluster of farms, some warehouses down by the water, and a handful of ships anchored in the harbor. He hoped *The Frolic* was there. The clipper ship was due to arrive in Bodega, and he planned to be on her tomorrow headed back to San Francisco.

Picking out a grove of nearby pines, he told Isabella they'd camp there for the night. "You can't find a room for us in the settlement?" she questioned. "Pina is shivering."

"The warehouse has rooms, but men sleep there. It's better to keep her away from others. I'll make a fire as soon as I see to the horses."

That satisfied Isabella. She rode close to Pina and told the girl they would warm themselves by the fire shortly.

Peter led them to the pines. Before he could help Isabella down, she was sliding off her mount to hurry over to Pina. The girl jumped down from her sweat-soaked horse and ran off into the trees. Isabella ran after her.

He shook his head. Walking over to Pina's mount, he removed its bridle and tied it to the saddle. With its head free, the mustang spun around and trotted back the way they'd come. When he'd first arrived in California, this had amazed him. That the horses returned home on their own, even twenty or thirty or forty miles. He was used to it now but felt bad for this little mustang. Pina had ridden the horse hard for no good reason. Whenever he and Isabella had stopped to rest their mounts, Pina had run hers across meadows and back again. The animal only got to rest when Isabella ran into the trees to be sick and Pina leaped off the horse and ran after her.

The girl had a demon. He knew it. Indians either revered or greatly feared those like Pina. He didn't fear the girl, but he did worry about the pull she would have on his wife. And he longed to be alone with Isabella, the way they'd been on that first night in the oak grove outside Marysville. Would the girl live with them from now on? Would she always be wild like this, with that unsettling look of something supernatural in her eyes?

Jedediah would know what to do. He'd seen his father stand up to a spirit before that had taken hold of a man. They'd been driving the sheep, and the men had gotten into whiskey. Before he and Jedediah realized it, the men were drunk. They camped for the night, and one of the men went crazy, trying to throw himself into the fire. Peter captured the man and tossed him away from the flames. The man jumped up with a wild look in his eyes, and Jedediah put down the Bible he'd been reading, stepped forward, and commanded, "I see you, demon! In the name of Jesus, come out of that man!"

To Peter's utter astonishment, the man fell to the ground as if dead. Everyone around the fire froze. The man lay on the ground for several moments and then began moaning. Peter went to him and could see he was returning to his senses. He helped the man up and offered him a drink of water. The man thanked him and sat down on a log, looking stunned.

All of them were stunned.

Jedediah returned to his Bible reading. The rest of them, except for those on watch, retired to their bedrolls. It was a long night for Peter. He'd never seen anything like that in his life. Had he ever gotten so drunk that a demon took over? There were nights on whiskey he couldn't remember. When he'd blacked out and awoken somewhere completely new, usually in a brothel with a girl in his bed. He couldn't remember what he'd done with them, but they didn't seem to mind. Once he'd awoken from a stupor and Mick told him he'd nearly beat a man to death. Mick thought it funny. Peter had a black eye and bloody knuckles. The other man barely survived. "Why did I fight him?" Peter asked.

"Cause he gave you the stink eye," Mick said with a toothy grin.

"I almost killed a man because he looked at me funny?"

"Well, he was ugly too," said Mick. "If you hadn't done it, I'd have done it. He needed a good lickin' to rearrange his face."

That fight he didn't remember bothered Peter for a long time. When he woke up with girls, they were always smiling, so he didn't worry much about that. But he'd heard that fight had left the man blind. That must have delighted the devil.

He unsaddled the horses and mule and staked them out to graze. Tomorrow he'd return the horse he'd borrowed along with the mule and horse he'd acquired at the fort to the Bodega stables before they boarded the ship. The horses had gone back and forth between the Bodega colony and Fort Ross numerous times, Benitz had assured him.

By the time Isabella returned leading her sister by the hand, he had a fire crackling. "Did she run a long way?" Peter asked, noticing the girl held something behind her back.

"She caught a rabbit and killed it," Isabella said. "Do you think she's all right?"

The girl was staring holes through him with her bright blue eyes. He certainly didn't think she was all right. He toyed with the idea of doing what Jedediah had done and commanding the demon to come out of her. The look on his wife's face stopped him. "Let's try to get her to eat and bed down," he said. What he really hoped was that Isabella would eat and sleep if the girl did. Isabella looked exhausted.

She let go of the girl's hand, and Pina slowly approached, pointing at the knife strapped to his belt. He didn't want to give it to her. He pointed to the rabbit and motioned with his hand for her to give it to him.

She shook her head and pointed again to his knife.

He figured it would be easy to wrestle the knife away from her if he had to, so he pulled it from his belt and handed it to her. She took the knife and her rabbit and walked off into the trees.

Isabella was about to follow her.

"Let her go. Let's see what she does," he said.

"Do you think she's hungry?"

I think she's crazy. But he didn't say that. "Maybe so." He uncorked a bota and handed it to Isabella. "Drink some water."

Isabella sat down on a nearby log and sipped the water. She watched the trees, anxiously waiting for her sister to return. It didn't take long. Soon the girl was back with a perfectly skinned rabbit and a spit she'd made from several skinny tree branches. She returned his knife and began to cook her rabbit after preparing her spit.

Peter raised his eyebrows at Isabella, and she gave him a weary smile. The smell of roasting rabbit made his mouth water.

When the girl had the rabbit cooked, she ripped off both legs. She handed one to Isabella and kept one for herself. The rest of the rabbit she gave to Peter.

"Thank you, Pina." Isabella reached out to stroke the girl's short black hair. The girl's filthy shawl was wrapped around her puny shoulders.

The girl smiled for Isabella. Peter decided maybe she wasn't as bad off as he'd first thought. After he ate some of the delicious rabbit, he decided she might be handy to have around.

He saved the rest of the rabbit for Isabella. When he walked over and handed it to her, she gave it to Pina. The girl shook her head and pointed to Isabella's stomach. Perhaps the girl understood she was pregnant. It was almost as if she was saying the baby needed to eat. Either that or she thought Isabella was still hungry. Sitting on the log together, the sisters shared the carcass. He left them alone and went to gather firewood. Then he took care of the horses and mule. Leading the animals back to camp, he tied them to the trees for the night, securing the mule close by to alert them to danger. Mules made the best watch dogs.

By the time he stoked the fire, Isabella was asleep in her bedroll, and Pina was watching him like a hawk.

"I know what you're thinking," he quietly told her. He pointed to Isabella. "There's my woman. I'll never touch you."

Pina gave him a nod, letting him know she understood, then she rolled her back to him.

A sudden rage tore through him that a man would misuse a child this way. He had the urge to ride back to Fort Ross and shoot that man dead.

Paula Scott

Chapter Twenty

The ship crashed down on a wave. Isabella covered her mouth, willing herself not to be sick. The cabin door flew open. Pina rushed in, something wrapped in her shawl. "What do you have there?" She approached her sister slowly. Pina needed time to adjust to people.

Pina shook her head and held her bundle tighter.

"We will eat with the captain shortly. You do not need to find your own food on the ship." The rabbit episode had disturbed Isabella. Pina was good at catching and cooking her own food, but there was a wildness about the girl that didn't seem human. As Isabella walked toward her, Pina retreated to the farthest corner of the cabin. Her eyes shone with something that made Isabella shiver.

"Let me see what you have," Isabella said with gentle firmness.

Her sister refused to offer up her bundle.

"You must give it to me." Isabella felt dizzy and sick to her stomach, but she wasn't going to let Pina steal things on the ship.

Pina crouched down around the lump in her shawl. Isabella knelt beside her. "We are here to take care of you." She reached out and pulled on the shawl. Pina pulled back. The shawl came undone. A headless chicken flopped at Isabella's feet. Isabella screamed.

Pina grabbed the chicken and rushed from the cabin.

Isabella jumped up, chasing after her.

Racing across the deck, Pina sprang up into the rigging, holding the chicken under one arm. When she started climbing, she dropped the chicken. It bounced off Isabella's shoulder and tumbled into the ocean. Pina climbed so fast Isabella couldn't catch her.

Sailors stood there slack-jawed, staring at Pina in the rigging.

Pina went straight to the top, where sails billowed like clouds. Isabella was horrified. What if her sister followed the chicken into the waves? "Peter!" she screamed. "Help us! Somebody please help us!"

Strong arms wrapped around Isabella, pulling her down off the rigging. "I have to get my sister!" she cried.

"I'll get her." Peter set Isabella's feet firmly on the deck. Isabella burst into tears. "She killed that poor little red hen."

"She thinks she needs to feed herself. And feed you." Peter captured Isabella's shoulders. "Calm down. Being upset isn't good for you. The ship has lots of chickens. I'll speak to the captain. I'm sure he will understand."

"You don't understand!" Isabella cried. "That hen looks like Señora Poppycock."

"Who's Señora Poppycock?"

"My chicken. Somebody killed her when I was Pina's age."

Peter raised his eyebrows. He didn't say anything, just studied her in concern.

Isabella realized she sounded crazy. "She was such a good chicken."

"I'm sorry," Peter said. She could see he was at a loss for further words.

"Please go get Pina before she falls into the sea."

"Whatever happens, do not climb into the rigging. It's too dangerous."

Isabella pointed at Pina high above them. "My sister is in danger." Her voice trembled.

"I won't let her fall." Peter sprang up into the rigging and began to climb.

The ship rolled with the waves. Isabella found a barrel to hold on to that was tied down. Sailors returned to their chores, but all eyes remained on Peter crawling up the rigging. The captain appeared on deck. He barked an order to the sailors to yank in the sails.

That was a relief. At least a flapping sail wouldn't knock Pina and Peter into the ocean. As the sails quickly came down, the ship slowed on the sea. It was easier to hear Peter calling to Pina without the billowing sails overhead. He was trying to coax her to return to the deck. She looked like a bird up there with her dark dress fluttering in the wind. When Peter had nearly reached her, it appeared Pina might jump into the sea. She let go with one hand and hung from the rigging. Isabella could hardly breathe. Fear choked her. She wanted to scream at her sister to hold on.

Peter reached out and captured Pina's leg. He crawled higher and pinned her to the rigging.

"Get up there and help him!" the captain ordered two young sailors standing near Isabella.

The men jumped onto the ropes and quickly crawled up to Peter and Pina. Peter held Pina in his arms.

The sailors helped him bring her down to the deck. Isabella didn't breathe easy until Peter carried her sister over to her.

"Pina?" Isabella touched the girl's cheek. She appeared to have fainted.

Her sister's eyes popped open. She looked confused.

Peter set her down, and Isabella wrapped her arms around her. The captain came over, his concerned gaze on Pina. "Is she a child of the forest?" he asked.

Isabella found that fitting. Her sister probably could survive the wilds alone. "She was orphaned as a babe. And given to a terrible man. She thinks she has to hunt for her food."

"How odd," said the captain. "Perhaps God can tame her."

"That is our hope," said Peter.

A handful of male passengers stood on the deck amongst the sailors staring at them. Pina had created quite a spectacle. She stood there stiff and silent in Isabella's arms. At least she was docile now. "I'm taking her back to our cabin. Do you mind if we take our supper in our room tonight?"

"I'll have the cook prepare your plates," said the captain.

"Thank you," said Peter. "I'll come down to get them."

"I'd like it very much if you dined with me tonight," the captain said to Peter. "I want to hear about the gold up there near Marysville. Is it really just lying in the streams for a man to scoop into his pan, like they say?"

"Not anymore," said Peter. "It's hard work to get the gold now. Men are breaking their backs for a day's worth of dust in the goldfields."

"I can hardly keep a crew," said the captain. "The siren's song of gold is stronger than the calling of the sea."

"You're better off making an honest living at sea," said Peter. "Many of the men spend their gold on drink and gambling in the gold camps. It's a reckless life that leads to ruin for many a man."

The captain lowered his voice, looking apologetically at Isabella before returning his attention to Peter. "Are there women in the gold camps?" He was young for an officer at sea and clearly interested in the fairer sex. "I've told my sailors San Francisco has the women in California. Running off to the goldfields will only make them lonely."

"Respectable women are hard to come by up in the camps." Peter turned to Isabella. "Go take your sister back to the cabin. I'll be along shortly."

Isabella was happy to escape the men on deck. It felt as if every eye was upon them. She led Pina to their cabin without meeting any of the men's curious gazes. Thankfully, by tomorrow they should reach San Francisco. Isabella couldn't wait to get off the ship. She tried not to think about the chicken Pina had killed. The girl didn't seem to know any better. She was just trying to survive.

Isabella felt like she was just trying to survive too. The babe she carried was making her so sick, and her sister was wearing her out. Any moment she feared Peter would leave them. Then what would she and Pina do? She had no money left. No means to support herself and Pina and the babe when it came. When they reached San Francisco, she would return to Maria's house on the hill above Portsmouth Square. The Oriental house-keeper had said Maria and Dominic were due to return from Boston before winter set in, but that could be weeks from now. She sighed after closing the cabin door behind her sister. When she released Pina, the girl went over and sat in the corner where she'd crouched earlier with the dead chicken. Her sister pulled her knees up to her chest, hugging herself and rocking. Isabella felt sorry for her.

"I'm not mad at you," she told Pina.

Pina didn't look up. She just kept rocking.

Isabella settled down beside her. She put her hand under Pina's small, pointed chin and raised her face to look at her. Her sister's eyes were shinier than she'd ever seen and glistening with tears. The girl's eyes were so blue and wounded Isabella drew in her breath. "I'm not mad about the chicken," she tried again.

Pina nodded, and Isabella knew she understood. "We will feed you from now on. You no longer have to kill your own food. Peter will take care of us. And if he doesn't, I will take care of us."

Her sister's eyes widened with worry.

"You don't want Peter to leave?"

Pina smiled just a little. For the first time, Isabella felt like they were having a real conversation.

"Do you like Peter?"

The smile on Pina's face grew.

"I like him too." Isabella couldn't help but smile. She realized how crushed she would be if Peter abandoned them. "I am praying he doesn't leave." She patted her stomach. "I carry a babe."

Pina nodded, this time without reserve. Her smile widened, and she made a cradle with her arms. Then she stopped and pointed at herself and made a cradle again.

"You want to take care of the baby?" A thrill shot though Isabella.

Pina eagerly nodded.

"I'm so happy you want to help with the baby." Isabella reached out and hugged her. "That will be wonderful."

Pina didn't stiffen as she had the other times Isabella had tried to offer her affection. She leaned into Isabella's embrace. Her sister smelled the way she looked. Filthy.

"I'm going to see if I can find some bathwater for you."

Pina grew wary.

"Don't be afraid. You will like being clean. You will smell nice."

Pina stared at her, and Isabella could almost read her mind. "A little soap is good for a girl. It won't hurt. I promise. When we reach San Francisco, we will buy you a new dress. You will look so pretty."

Her sister needed a haircut too. Someone had carelessly chopped the girl's hair off. At least she didn't have lice like many Indians in California.

The cabin door opened. Peter walked into the room holding two tin plates steaming with vegetables and meat. "How is she doing?" he asked.

"Much better."

"The cook outdid himself. This smells delicious." Peter set the plates on the little table anchored to the floor. The chairs were anchored down too. Everything in the cabin was firmly attached to something.

"I told the captain I would join him for dinner. I thought she would do better without me here."

"She actually likes you." Isabella grinned.

Peter laughed. "I doubt that."

"She told me so."

"She doesn't talk."

"She may not talk, but she communicates just fine."

Peter returned Isabella's smile. "When are we going to communicate just fine? We don't need to talk. There's other ways to express ourselves."

Isabella's cheeks warmed. She couldn't hide her blush. Rising to her feet, she motioned for Pina to get up from the floor. "I'm sure the captain will enjoy your company tonight." She looked at the bed, and her face grew even warmer. How would they all sleep there tonight?

"Don't worry. I'm bedding down in steerage."

So he was good at reading minds too. Pina was already at the table, testing the food.

"Thank you." Isabella covered her mouth. The aroma from the table turned her insides. The ship had risen on a rather large wave and now descended. Isabella's knees wobbled. She wasn't going to be able to control her heaving stomach. Dashing past Peter, she hurried out the door and barely made it to the rail before throwing up.

The spray from the ocean cooled her burning face. She was thankful she'd braided her hair in a single plait down her back. Her braid had fallen forward, but not enough to be soiled by her sickness. She was about to push her long braid over her shoulder when someone did it for her.

She closed her eyes, embarrassed he was there. Peter's warm body was right behind her. One hand held her braid while his other arm wrapped around her waist. "I don't want you to fall overboard," he said near her ear, holding her snugly against him.

Chapter Twenty-One

Peter wanted to hold his wife. Keeping her safe from the raging ocean was as good an excuse as any. He wished she wasn't ill all the time. He worried about her. When she leaned back against him, he savored her resting in his arms. "Are you all right?" he spoke in her ear. Sailors walked the deck. He didn't want to share this conversation with anyone else.

"Yes," she whispered.

The sun cast a rosy glow over the ship. "The heavens declare the glory of God," he said. It was something Jedediah said upon every painted sunrise and sunset. When Peter was younger, it had irritated him. Now he appreciated the sunset and the God who made it so pretty.

She leaned her head back on his shoulder as they watched the heavens turn red together.

"Red sky at night, sailor's delight." He pulled her even closer.

She shivered in his embrace.

"I'll miss you tonight," he admitted.

She put her hands over his on her stomach. He could feel the slight swelling of the growing babe there. Could he accept a child that wasn't his own if it turned out to be Paul's? Maggie had died birthing Paul's child. The magic of the moment disappeared with the sun and the dark thoughts that came over him. As soon as the sun sank into the ocean, the chill of night set in. Isabella turned to face him. "Thank you for saving my sister today."

He tried to smile but couldn't.

Her gaze grew anxious. "I know it's hard having my sister with us. You've been so kind to her. Thank you."

"You don't need to thank me." He stepped away, angry not at her, but at his brother and himself. He'd allowed Paul to swoop in on Isabella like he had with Maggie. Now perhaps she would die bearing his brother's child. The terrible thought came over him so forcefully he shook his head, trying to clear the dark notion from his mind.

"Are you all right?"

"I'm fine." He didn't mean to sound harsh, but it came out that way.

"You felt the babe when you held me. You despise me now. I see it on your face."

"Don't be ridiculous. I'm just tired and I'm hungry. That's all."

"I don't believe you."

"Have you ever believed me? Did you truly believe I wanted to marry you a second time?"

"No," she admitted. "I've been waiting for you to leave again."

"I won't leave."

"Even when the babe comes?"

Now was his chance. *Do you carry my brother's babe?* he longed to ask, but he couldn't. If she confessed it was Paul's, what would he do? Of course she was upset. If he abandoned her, it would be harder now for her to find a husband with a tainted sister and a babe in her belly. Most men would want her because she was young and beautiful, but Pina would frighten almost anyone away with her strange behavior.

Their gazes held for a moment that seemed like forever. "I don't mind a babe," he finally said, though he minded a great deal if it came out looking like his brother. He just couldn't tell her that.

A trembling smile slipped onto her lips. "Pina is excited. She wants to help with the baby."

"I wouldn't trust that girl with a child." He tried to say it gently.

Isabella's devotion to her sister didn't pale. "Pina will be just fine. I think the babe will change her."

"Only God can change her."

"Well then, God will change her. God can change all of us. Perhaps God will make us into a real family."

"With God, all things are possible." Jedediah was fond of saying that too, but when it came out of Peter's mouth, it was not a statement of faith the way his father said it. He doubted the child Isabella carried was his. If it was his babe, she would have assured him of that by now. He realized he was mad at God. And his resentment ran deep. Back to Maggie. Perhaps all the way back to Will and the baby girl scalped in her mother's arms in Missouri.

What kind of God allowed such terrible things to happen to people? Will's momma had always read the Bible to her kids.

Was a prayer on her lips when the Indians killed her? Had she seen the Indians butchering her children before she died? Just thinking about it incensed him.

"Why are you angry?"

"What do you think of a God who allows innocent children to die?" he snapped.

"God crucified his own Son. Why would he spare us?"

"Did you learn that in your Catholic Church?" He'd always thought Catholics didn't know the truth, but she surprised him.

"Where else would I learn it?"

"I don't know. The only thing I know about Catholics is I couldn't purchase land in California five years ago because I didn't belong to the Catholic Church."

"You wanted to purchase land five years ago?"

"I thought about it." The steady sound of the ocean grew louder in his ears as he remembered that hopeful time in his life that had ended so terribly with Maggie's passing and Paul's betrayal.

"Did you hope to homestead?"

"Maybe."

"With a woman you loved?"

Her instincts were too good. It was like she read his mind. He noticed they seemed to do this with each other. He found it unnerving.

He had considered bringing Maggie to California when he saw how lush the land was here. A man could grow about anything in the fertile valleys of the province. The weather was better than New Mexico territory and the Indians not nearly as dangerous. In New Mexico, a man had to deal with Apaches. He hated Apaches, and the Navajos weren't much better.

America had broken treaty after treaty with the Navajos, and they were on the warpath now. The California Indians were peaceful for the most part. Nobody really feared Indians in California.

"I never said I loved a woman," he finally answered her.

"But you did love her." Isabella's eyes shone with unshed tears.

He could see he'd hurt her. "It didn't last."

"Do you still love her?"

After a minute pondering it, he reckoned he did. The ache in his heart grew. "She married someone else."

"Someone you knew?"

"Why are you asking me these questions?"

Her almond-shaped blue eyes glistened. "I want to know."

"She married Paul."

Isabella sucked in her breath. "No," she whispered, shaking her head.

"She did, but she's dead now, so we're done discussing Maggie."

She reached out and touched his arm. "I'm so sorry, Peter."

"About Maggie or about you?"

She jerked her hand away. "I told you I was afraid. Mick came after me," she said defensively.

"Did you have to bed my brother because you feared Mick?"

"I wouldn't be the first woman to let fear rule me."

"And you aren't the first woman Paul's taken advantage of. I guess I'll have to live with that."

"But you don't love me like you loved Maggie."

"I'm not the man I used to be. I don't fall in love anymore."

Isabella's heart was in her eyes. "I've loved you since the moment I saw you ride into Marysville on your painted mare."

The ache in his heart intensified. "I did you wrong in Marysville. That doesn't leave much room for love."

She raised her chin and stepped past him. "I can see you are a stubborn man. I will pray for you."

A strange mix of pain, anger, and hope churned inside of him. "Well, you better fetch your prayer beads. I've heard that's how you Catholics pray."

"I pray however I want to pray." She walked toward her cabin.

"Well, that's where you're wrong, Isabella."

She spun around. "Why am I wrong?"

"Because God is holy. You'd best fear Him and pray on your knees with a humble heart."

"You're the one who needs a humble heart," she shot back.

"I've traveled several hundred miles to find you. I tried to marry you right and proper in a church, even though you carry a child I don't think is mine. That's pretty humbling."

Her haughtiness crumbled. She burst into tears and hurried away.

Once she was gone, he walked the deck, listening to the ocean wash against the ship. He could smell the salt in the air and feel the mist of waves breaking against the bow. It took a while for the stars to appear in the darkening sky. *What am I doing? Why am I even here?* he asked the heavens.

Looking up at all the bright stars, he realized ships sailed by the stars, guided on a path set thousands of years earlier, long before ships came to be. The world was so much bigger than he knew. God so much greater than he could imagine. *I'm not a good man,* he whispered. *Forgive me.*

All he heard in response was the rush of the sea.

Chapter Twenty-Two

San Francisco teemed with immigrants from all over the world. In just a few short years, the city had spread across the sandy hillsides in all directions. Fine brick hotels and respectable restaurants lined the streets now. Isabella held tightly to Pina's hand. They had visited the bathhouse and both wore new dresses Peter had purchased for them. A woman had trimmed Pina's hair. She looked lovely, her blue eyes wide and curious in her little brown face. Her behavior had improved since Peter pulled her out of the rigging. He now trailed after them as they walked up the steep hill to Maria and Dominic's house.

She and Peter hadn't spoken since their confrontation on the ship. It hurt that he still loved Maggie. His relationship with Clara seemed far less threatening now. Clara was a madam. Maggie a respectable girl. What had Maggie looked like? Surely, she was beautiful if Paul had loved her too. No wonder the brothers were at odds. She took a deep breath. Perhaps she and Pina should stay in San Francisco.

Reaching the steps that led up to the front porch of their house, Isabella turned and looked down the hill. Peter walked toward her, the look on his face unreadable. A sea breeze ruffled his wavy brown hair. Since leaving Fort Ross, he'd kept his face clean-shaven, and the dimple in his chin distracted her. He was so handsome in his new buckskins purchased at Fort Ross. His leather shirt was fringed and fit him so finely, displaying his wide shoulders and whipcord waist. Too bad he spent most of his time brooding. She looked past him and out to the rocky island surrounded by the blue waters of the bay. San Francisco was a stunning sight, even with all the mud and teeming humanity. Never in her wildest dreams had she imagined sleepy Yerba Buena could become this cosmopolitan city.

"I know what you're thinking," Peter said when he reached her.

"That isn't possible," she answered him.

"You look at this great city with regret. You don't know where you belong. Should you stay here? If you don't stay, where will you go?"

Her mouth fell open. How could he know?

He smiled—not a happy smile, a sad smile. "You're not the only one who reads faces."

Pina tugged on her hand, pointing to the porch. A young boy stood there. When Isabella saw him, the blond boy bolted into the house. They walked up the porch steps when he returned with his father.

"Isabella!" Dominic cried. "Nicky, go get your mother! Isabella is here!"

The blond boy disappeared once more as Dominic stepped out onto the porch, enveloping Isabella in his arms. He swung her around and then turned his attention to Pina. "Who is this? She looks like you when I first met you."

"My sister, Pina," said Isabella.

"I didn't know you had a sister." Dominic was all smiles.

"I didn't know either." Isabella beamed too.

Dominic offered his hand to Peter. "I'm Dominic, Isabella's brother-in-law."

Peter clasped Dominic's hand, and the two shook heartily. "I'm Isabella's husband, Peter."

Isabella's heart stopped and then beat thickly. So he was willing to acknowledge her as his wife, even after what they'd said to each other on the ship.

Maria raced out the door, nearly knocking Isabella over in her haste to embrace her. "You're home!" Maria cried. "And you look so beautiful! Who is this?" Maria tried get a good look at Pina, who was hiding behind Isabella.

"My father's daughter. We brought her from Fort Ross." Isabella tried to pull Pina out from behind her. The girl clung to Isabella's back and wouldn't let the others see her face. "She doesn't speak." Isabella didn't know how to explain what was wrong with Pina. She wasn't quite sure what plagued her sister.

Nicky had returned to the porch. Isabella couldn't believe how much he had grown and how closely he resembled his father. "Hello, Nicky."

"Hello, Isabella," he answered with a shy smile.

"Come into the house," said Maria. Isabella noticed Maria's thickening middle and realized she was pregnant too. Maria had been pregnant when Isabella left for the goldfields. Had that child lived? She was afraid to ask.

Maria led them to the parlor where an Oriental maid played with a red-haired toddler. "Fang, do you remember my sister, Isabella?"

"Yes, ma'am." Fang smiled, rising to her feet with the red-headed little girl in her arms.

"This is Sally, our daughter." Maria reached out and took the child from Fang.

"Oh my," said Isabella. "She looks just like you, Maria. I knew you'd have a little girl. She is precious."

Maria laughed. "And strong-willed."

"Good thing she has her mother's beauty," said Dominic. "She's going to need a fair face with her fierce temperament."

The little red-haired one drew Pina out from behind Isabella. It was obvious Pina was taken with the child. She watched the little one with longing in her eyes. "May Pina play with her?" Isabella asked.

Maria handed Sally to Pina. A smile spread across Pina's face as she took the tot into her strong, bony arms. Pina grinned at the toddler and the child grinned back.

"I think we have a new nanny," said Dominic.

"Indeed, we do," Maria agreed. "Fang, will you please bring us some refreshments?"

Fang nodded and hurried from the room.

"When did your ship return from Boston?" Isabella asked.

"Just yesterday," said Maria.

"We are home in time for winter." Dominic seemed very happy.

"So you have decided to make San Francisco your home?" Isabella wondered if she and Pina could live here too. She ached for Peter to love her, but she couldn't see that happening, especially once she bore Paul's babe.

"My business is here," said Dominic. "California has become my home."

"What is your livelihood?" asked Peter.

"I'm a ship captain by trade, but shipping suits me. I do not want to raise my children on the high seas. I trade in ships and wares now here in the city."

Maria was staring at Peter's buckskins. She hadn't been on the porch when Peter introduced himself as Isabella's husband. "Dominic, we must pay this man for bringing Isabella home."

Peter's face reddened. "No need for payment. We're married, ma'am."

Maria's mouth fell open.

Dominic laughed. He put his arm around Maria. "We will welcome Isabella and her new husband with a celebration tonight. Where did you marry? Did Don Pedro provide a fiesta for the two of you?"

Isabella didn't know what to say.

Peter took her hand. "We married in the Fort Ross chapel."

"Do you have a wedding gown?" Maria asked in excitement.

Isabella looked at Peter. He'd protected her from embarrassment by proclaiming they'd married at Fort Ross. Now he squeezed her hand. "Isabella's trunk is down at the livery," he said. "Her wedding gown is there."

"I will send someone to fetch it," said Dominic.

"Thank you." Isabella was relieved to conclude how they'd married.

Pina was playing on the floor with Sally. She looked so normal entertaining the child. Sally didn't seem to mind that Pina didn't speak. The two appeared in perfect harmony, sharing toys and smiling at each other.

Maria was all questions. "Are you weary from your journey? Did you come from Fort Ross? Where is Tío Pedro?"

Isabella's throat tightened. How would Maria respond to Don Pedro's death?

"Don Pedro lost his life in Marysville," Peter gently intervened.

"How?" Maria leaned against Dominic.

"He ended his life." Peter pulled Isabella to him and put his arm around her the way Dominic held Maria.

Maria covered her mouth. Her eyes filled with tears.

"When I first met Don Pedro, I was quite impressed with his hacienda and rancho down near Monterey. He threw a fine fiesta for me and my sailors. That's where I met Maria." Dominic smiled, a wistful grin that lit up his face. "Maria danced for me, and I was undone. How did you and Isabella meet?"

Isabella couldn't help it. She began to cry.

Peter pulled her close. "Isabella undid me too." He didn't elaborate.

"Has she sung for you? Isabella has the prettiest voice." Maria was wiping tears from her face.

"I have never heard the Bluebird sing," Peter admitted.

"The Bluebird?" Dominic raised his brows.

Maria looked intrigued too.

A blush seared Isabella's cheeks.

"The miners were quite taken with Isabella's singing in the gold camps. They named her the Bluebird. I hope one day to hear her sing for myself," said Peter.

"You sang for the miners?" Maria stepped out from under Dominic's arm. She linked her arm through Isabella's, pulling her away from Peter's side. "My sister has much to tell me. When we were growing up, we always had a siesta this time of day. Isabella and I will leave you men alone to get to know each other. Dominic, please tell Fang to have the household prepare for tonight's celebration. We will have a fiesta to celebrate my sister's wedding. And please fetch her gown. She will wear it tonight."

"That isn't necessary," Isabella said as Maria led her to the parlor door. She dreaded telling Maria that Don Pedro had gambled her away to Peter. That they'd had a make-believe wedding inside a gambling tent. They weren't even legally married, though their time in the chapel at Fort Ross had been special.

"Of course it's necessary." Maria tugged Isabella along. "We weren't there for your wedding, but we will celebrate tonight."

"Peter and I will get the dress," said Dominic. "And get you all settled in here."

"Thank you." Peter's gaze was on Isabella and Maria. He looked as uncomfortable as Isabella felt. Standing there in his buckskins in this city mansion, Peter was as far away from the mountains as he could get. Isabella felt sorry for him. She could see he longed to be gone from here. Perhaps he'd never been inside a mansion before, and now he'd met her family—at least some of her family.

Isabella had nearly convinced herself she had no real family left except for Pina, but Maria had wiped all that away. Maria and she didn't share blood, but when they were young and made to take a siesta each day, they giggled and told each other stories instead of sleeping. Or they snuck out of the hacienda and splashed in the creek on warm summer days. They'd grown up as the privileged daughters of the *gente de razón* until the Americans overran California. Maybe now that he'd met her family, Peter would finally believe she really had given him her virtue.

Her face grew hot as shame washed over. She reminded herself she'd truly believed they were married. Giving herself to him had been so beautiful, unlike anything she'd experienced before or since. She'd so desperately longed for Peter's love. She'd been so young and foolish. And then there was Paul. She'd tried to forget about what she'd done at Clara's Place. How could she tell Maria she'd lived in a brothel and was now pregnant with Peter's brother's child?

Before Maria led her from the room, she and Peter shared a gaze of regret. They'd both made mistakes. Their eyes locked in remorse. What was he thinking as he stared at her? It unnerved her that he sometimes read her mind. Was he reading now that she regretted giving herself to Paul? Did Peter regret leaving her at Clara's? Did he regret bedding Clara the night after he'd made love to her?

That had broken her heart. It still hurt to think of him with Clara. But Clara didn't carry Peter's babe. How much would it hurt if Peter were having a child with someone else the way she was having Paul's babe?

An ache filled her that she thought would never go away. It was all so awful. Yet Maria had a scar on her face from another man. Every time she saw Maria, the scar stunned her anew. Maria was so beautiful and the scar so ugly. Isabella didn't know the details about that other man, but she knew Dominic had fought a duel with him, and the man was dead. Before they were together, Dominic had married another woman as well. Nicky was that woman's son, yet Nicky called Maria his momma and loved her. Was it possible for her and Peter to ever find the kind of happiness Maria and Dominic had found?

By the look on Peter's face now, she didn't think so.

Chapter Twenty-Three

Peter couldn't believe these were Isabella's relatives. Her sister was a woman of means with a wealthy husband and a mansion on a hill. Where had she come by that terrible scar down her cheek? Even with the scar, she was still a beautiful woman who spoke perfect English with a delightful Spanish accent. He could see she was expecting a child and was well loved by her husband. Never in his wildest dreams had he imagined Isabella's life this way. In the back of his mind, he'd envisioned her born in a tule hut outside of Fort Ross, and perhaps her birth had come about this way, but she didn't grow up in an Indian village. She'd grown up in a grand hacienda, just as she'd told him she had. He'd taken her virginity. Abandoned her in a brothel. He recalled that night at Clara's when she'd begged him in Spanish to be his wife and he'd rejected her. And slept with Clara. He felt like a rogue and just wanted to ride away now. Just keep chasing the wind. Return to whiskey.

And wild living. It would be so much easier than facing this moment.

The last he'd heard, Carson was fighting Indians in New Mexico territory for the United States. He could join Carson and return to scouting and hunting and Indian fighting. He knew how to do all those things. He didn't know how to be a husband to a respectable young woman, which Isabella certainly was.

Dominic wanted to accompany him to the livery, but instead Peter pulled him aside and shared his concerns about Pina with the child. "She's sometimes like a wild animal. It comes upon her unexpectedly. Right now, she is peaceful, but I wouldn't trust her with your children."

Dominic seemed a rock of stability, which probably came from being a sea captain. "Has the girl been abused?" Dominic asked. They spoke in hushed tones as Pina played with the child on the other side of the parlor.

"She has." Peter wanted to share he suspected a demon came upon her from time to time, but broaching the subject just seemed too far-fetched. He would wait and share the notion with Jedediah. His father wouldn't think he was crazy. Jedediah would believe him.

"All right, I will watch the children. Bring your things up here."

"We'll be returning upriver to Marysville by schooner shortly."

"You won't be leaving anytime soon. Maria isn't about to let Isabella go now that she's here. Maria has been so worried about her with Don Pedro. He had a drinking problem. Did you know him?"

Peter looked into Dominic's steady blue eyes. He could lie straight to this man's face and say he'd never met the Californio. That would avert more questions. He'd lied often enough. Another reason to feel the depth of his sins. Since he'd begun to pray, he felt guilty about the kind of life he lived. He decided to tell the truth. "Don Pedro ended his life because I took Isabella from him." He stared into Dominic's eyes, waiting for the condemnation to come.

Dominic put his hand on his shoulder. The two were equally tall and well-built. "Some man needed to take her from him. I'm glad it was you."

The grace Dominic offered surprised him. "I won her with a king of hearts in a card game," he admitted.

Dominic smiled. "By giving you the king of hearts, God was showing you his heart's desire for the two of you."

Grace flooded Peter. Hot moisture filled his eyes. "You're a believer."

Dominic's smile grew. "The Lord is my shepherd. I see he's yours too."

Peter wasn't used to feeling anything but certain in his own strength before other men, but God was doing something inside of him, stripping away his strength, leaving him vulnerable with Dominic. All his life, he'd had to protect himself. Vulnerability was a new emotion. The last time he could recall feeling vulnerable was when he found Will's family slaughtered by the Indians.

"Have you known the Lord for long?" Dominic pressed.

"Not long." Peter ran a hand through his hair. Everything felt in disarray, like the life he knew was falling away, and the life God was inviting him to live didn't fit the man he was. He'd have to change.

Peter wasn't good at changing.

Dominic walked with him down the hall and out onto the porch.

Peter looked back over his shoulder. He could no longer keep an eye on Pina with the little red-haired child. "I don't think you should leave your daughter alone with Isabella's sister. She's not a normal girl."

"I've already prayed for the Lord to watch over my daughter."

Peter realized Dominic had the kind of faith Jedediah had, a simple belief that God was in control of all things and had good in mind for them. "Faith in Christ is new to me," Peter admitted.

"Well, welcome to the family." Dominic patted him on the back.

Peter knew Dominic didn't mean this earthly family, but a heavenly family. A feeling of warmth and peace settled upon him there on the porch.

"Isabella carries a babe." It seemed the right time to say it.

"Congratulations!" Dominic pounded his back again. "My wife is due in a few short months. How wonderful. When will your babe arrive?"

"I don't know." Peter looked Dominic in the eye. In that moment, he knew he could be truthful. "It may be my brother's child she carries, but I'm praying it's mine."

Dominic's eyes widened, but he returned to the rock of stability Peter badly needed. "Maria and I didn't have a smooth courtship. I married another and had Nicky before the Lord saw fit to bring Maria and I together."

Peter was relieved that Dominic didn't seem to be judging him. "It was my fault Isabella spent time with my brother," he confessed. "If I hadn't abandoned her, she never would have been with Paul."

"Does your brother know she carries a child?"

"No." Peter set his jaw. "I hope to never see him again. If I see Paul, I might kill him."

"You'll have to forgive your brother the way the Lord has forgiven you." Dominic's eyes were filled with compassion.

"I don't want to forgive him." Peter leaned against the porch rail. The autumn day was clear and cool with an ocean breeze blowing across the hills. He may as well tell Dominic all of it. "Isabella isn't the first wife my brother took from me. I didn't get the chance to marry Maggie. Paul married her first. Then he killed her with his babe."

He didn't tell Dominic his greatest fear. That Isabella would die having Paul's child. Every time the terrible thought hit him, he prayed the babe was his and that Isabella would live.

"You loved Maggie?" Dominic leaned on the porch rail beside Peter. They felt like lifelong friends, though they'd only known each other less than an hour.

"She was my first love. My only love."

"You don't love Isabella?"

The question struck Peter hard. He looked down the hill at the blue waters of San Francisco Bay. Whitecaps crowned the waves. Just outside the Golden Gate, he knew the sea raged. The captain of *The Frolic* had told him the Golden Gate was one of the most dangerous entries to any bay in the world. How had the Pacific Ocean gotten its name? There was nothing pacific about this sea up here on the northern California coast. And yet San Francisco Bay just might be the finest bay on earth. If a ship could make it through the narrow opening of swirling, deadly currents Fremont had named the Golden Gate, an unapparelled harbor of safety awaited.

He should love Isabella, but did he? Certainly, not the way he had loved Maggie. It came to him that he'd never really had the chance to love Maggie. Yet he and Isabella had become one flesh, body and soul, that night outside of Marysville. And they'd sealed that in the eyes of God in the chapel at Fort Ross. It was so much more than he'd ever had with Maggie. The realization stunned him. Perhaps he did love Isabella. Perhaps he loved her more than he'd ever loved Maggie.

He turned to Dominic. "I do love her," he said in surprise.

Dominic laughed in satisfaction. "I thought so. I first met Isabella when she was just a girl like Pina. She's grown into a beauty."

"Her nature is pleasing too." A smile crept up on him. He loved his wife. That love filled him like sunlight chasing away his dark thoughts.

"Maria will expect us to dance tonight. Do you dance?"

"I've never danced in my life."

"Well, prepare yourself. The Californios dance at the drop of a hat."

"Hide all the hats." Peter wasn't laughing. He meant it.

"Nothing can stop Maria from dancing. Isabella and Maria can dance like you've never seen. These Spanish girls aren't like women from the East. Are you from the East?"

"St. Louis, but I haven't been east of New Mexico territory in some time."

"Do you have anything besides buckskins to wear? I don't want to offend you, but dancing in leather is going to present a challenge."

"Dancing in anything presents a challenge. I'd rather wrestle a grizzly. I'm not dancing."

Dominic laughed, this time with deep, hearty mirth. "You don't know Maria or Isabella. Isabella taught my sailors to dance. I'd never seen anything like it in my life."

"I don't drink anymore," said Peter. "Only whiskey could seduce me into dancing."

"I don't keep whiskey in the house. I'll try to protect you from Maria and Isabella. Maybe you can just waltz a little."

"I've never even seen a waltz."

"What have you seen?" Dominic seemed genuinely interested.

"The wilderness."

"Have you seen the Rockies?"

"I know the Rockies better than most men."

"Are the Indians there as fierce as they say?"

"There are tribes in those mountains that would just as soon kill you than look at you."

"Have you fought Indians?" Dominic hung on his every word.

He'd once felt proud of all the Indians he'd killed. Now all the blood on his hands bothered him a great deal. "Kit Carson was my boss."

"The real Christopher Carson, the Indian fighter?"

"The one and only. He's not as tall as they say."

"How tall is he?"

"He's not tall, but he practically won California by himself."

"So it's true. The man's a legend."

"Indeed, he is. There's no one like Carson. He taught me all I know about the wilderness. I was fifteen when he took me under his wing."

"Where is he now?"

"Back in Taos, I suppose. He has a ranch there, though I heard he's been hired to make peace with the Indians."

"Do you think peace with the Indians is possible?"

"No, but if any man can do it, Carson can."

"Were you here in '46 for the revolt? I heard Carson was part of the Bear Flag revolution."

"The only battle to speak of that Carson and I fought together during the revolution was down at the Battle of San Pasqual. The Californios nearly won that battle with their long lances, but we won the war." Peter still couldn't help the pride that came over him at helping usher California into the Union.

"A Californio on horseback with a lance is a sight to behold. You need to meet Isabella's brother, Roman. He saved my life killing a grizzly with a long lance on horseback."

"I would like to have seen such a feat."

"I can show you my bear rug. It's upstairs in my den. It's nearly ten feet long and just about as wide. I'd be dead if it weren't for Roman."

"Isabella's brother?"

"The finest Californio I ever met. We should ride down to the Santa Cruz Mountains so you can meet him and see Rancho El Rio Lobo. The Vasquez family lost their rancho with the American takeover, but Roman married Rachel, an American with her own vast rancho."

"I thought Isabella was an orphan when I met her in Marysville. She was dressed in rags, and Don Pedro did not treat her like a daughter." He didn't tell Dominic he also thought her a prostitute.

"Drink will do that to a man." Dominic shook his head. "I'm just grateful you're her husband. I know you will take good care of her."

"I don't have a mansion or a grand hacienda." Peter was humbled by how little he had to offer Isabella after seeing the life she could have here in San Francisco. He'd thought himself rich after selling all those sheep. Seven thousand dollars was a fortune to him and Jedediah, but in the presence of real money, it seemed like a paltry amount.

"What kind of life will you give her?" There was no ill intent in Dominic's question. It was the kind of question a brother would ask.

"I have a sheep ranch in the Sierra Nevada foothills." He realized Jedediah had settled that pretty little valley just for him. Built that cabin and barn and kept the herd for his future. All of a sudden, he knew it so surely it about made him weep. He'd never given credit to Jedediah for being a good father. He'd held the years of drinking against him. And the trouble with Paul because Jedediah insisted on raising an outlaw's son as his own. God was humbling him now, that much was certain.

"A ranch in the Sierra Nevada foothills sounds mighty fine. Any grizzlies up there?"

"A few still roam. I'll get a long lance and a fast horse." Peter smiled. "I'm a good shot with a rifle," he assured Dominic. "I've brought down enough bears in my life."

"I suspect you have." Dominic looked him over. "You can borrow some of my britches and boots for the party. We appear about the same size."

"I've got my own britches and I'm not dancing."

Dominic laughed. "Good luck. The Vasquez senóritas will change your mind."

Peter pushed off the railing and stepped down from the porch. He was amazed at how lighthearted he felt. "Thank you," he called to Dominic as he headed down the hill toward the livery stables.

"Don't thank me. Thank the Good Lord. Maybe he will help you dance tonight."

"I'm not dancing." Peter waved.

"Remind the women of that tonight," Dominic called after him.

Chapter Twenty-Four

"I'm pregnant as well," Isabella said.

Maria squealed in delight. "When was your last flow?"

Isabella didn't want to tell her. "I'm not sure. I haven't been regular since the goldfields."

Maria's eyes narrowed. "You did not wait until marriage to make the babe?"

Isabella dropped her gaze in shame. "No," she said softly. She decided right then that she would not confess her sins to Maria. And she could not stay here and give birth to an Indian babe. Between them, her and Paul's child would surely favor their Indian ancestors.

"Izzy, look at me." Maria took her by the shoulders. "This scar," she pointed to her face, "came from a man I lived with outside of wedlock. I chose to be his whore when I could have been Dominic's wife. Lies drove me into the arms of a devil, but Dios rescued me and gave me Dominic, Nicky, Sally, and now another babe. I do not hold it against you that you knew your husband before marriage. Who am I to judge? We are all sinners in need of a savior."

A tear ran down Isabella's cheek. She nearly confessed it was not Peter's child she carried, but looking into Maria's loving eyes, she just couldn't do it. Reaching into her pocket, she pulled out Maria's rosary. "I have been praying." She handed the rosary to Maria.

"You don't need to give it back to me."

"I want to return it. Don Pedro nearly gambled it away. Peter won your rosary in a card game. He gave it back. Now I give it back to you."

Maria took the rosary and pressed it to her heart. "Dios is so merciful to us. We both have such handsome husbands. Tell me about Peter. Is he really a frontiersman? He looks so fierce and wild."

"He rode with Kit Carson."

"No," Maria said vehemently. "Not el Lobo!"

"*Sí,*" said Isabella, slipping back into Spanish. "He's killed Californios and many Indians. He fought against our people in the Mexican War."

"Does he frighten you?"

"Sometimes."

"Has he hurt you?" Maria looked worried now.

Isabella recalled the tenderness Peter had shown her. "No. He has been very gentle."

"He is a man well able to protect you. California has gone crazy. Women are in danger with men from all around the world hungry for women here. If Peter is gentle and protects you, that is good. And he's so roguish in his animal clothes." Maria grinned.

"Those are buckskins." Isabella couldn't help but smile too.

"They are made from animals."

"He has lived in the wilds all his life."

"Is he wild with you?"

"Maria!"

Maria laughed. "You no longer have the sense of humor you once had."

"There was nothing humorous about living in the gold camps. Don Pedro went from bad to worse. It was awful."

Maria's teasing vanished. "I'm sorry. We should never have let you go with him."

Had she never gone to the goldfields, she would not have met Peter. She couldn't imagine life without knowing him, though it had brought her plenty of pain. Like the legendary Kit Carson, Peter was larger than life. After that first night with him, she would have followed him anywhere.

"How did you meet Peter?" Maria had been sitting on the edge of the double bed in the upstairs room she'd given to Isabella. Feeling so tired, as she often did with the babe growing inside her, Isabella lay down on the bed to rest.

"Don Pedro was gambling that night." Isabella hesitated to tell Maria the truth. It was not a pretty love story.

Maria threw herself down beside Isabella. "Tio Pedro did not gamble you away?" She sat back up and slammed her fists on the bed. That was the sister Isabella remembered, always so fiery.

"I was fortunate Peter was the winner. The other man was frightening. He won Don Pedro's gold claim. That's why Don Pedro gambled me away. He was trying to win his gold claim back."

"They could never have done that to a white woman. What terrible men!"

Maria's words struck Isabella with grief. She knew Maria didn't mean to hurt her, but she did. Isabella closed her eyes. All her life, she'd longed to be considered white like Maria. In California, an Indian woman didn't stand a chance. Squaws were treated like horses, bartered back and forth as if they weren't even human, made into slaves or prostitutes by white men. When she was young, she'd convinced herself only a tiny bit of Indian blood flowed in her veins. Living amongst the Californios, she'd never been treated poorly. Adopted children were considered special gifts from God. And many Californios had darker hair and skin. Yet, as she grew older, there was no mistaking the Indian in her. In the goldfields, as much as Don Pedro tried to convince the miners otherwise, she was seen as a half-breed.

"I am sorry. I did not mean to say your husband was a terrible man." Maria looked remorseful when Isabella opened her eyes.

"I wish I was white like you."

"Oh, Isabella, you are beautiful just the way Dios made you. And your husband must be a good man. He married you when he didn't have to. He could have kept you as his concubine, but he didn't. If you were white, perhaps you would have never met Peter because you wouldn't have been in that gambling tent."

It dawned on Isabella that Maria spoke the truth. Respectable white women didn't walk into gambling tents. Every step of her life up until this moment had been ordained by God. Her heritage had been ordained by God. The color of her skin, her eyes, and hair created by God. Who was she to ask the potter why he had made her part Indian?

She began to cry. Maria pulled her into her arms. It was like the night Maria and Dominic had brought the dead baby girl to Rancho de los Robles. Isabella had held Maria that night, absorbing her grief, taking some of the burden of death into her own heart.

Now Maria took Isabella's grief into her own heart. "In heaven, there is no prejudice. The color of your skin won't matter to anyone up there. And it does not matter to Dios. Just think, Isabella, if you lived in an Indian tribe and I was taken captive, you would be respected, and I would be the slave because I am a white woman."

There was nothing that frightened white women more on the frontier than being taken by Indians. Thinking about it this way stopped Isabella's tears. In the goldfields, she had met an African slave named Edmond who had come to California with his owner. Edmond worked for a year to buy his freedom for a thousand dollars. Isabella was so happy to see Edmond go free. Other African slaves were buying their freedom as well with the gold they found in the hills. Yet Indian women could never buy their freedom. But neither could white women rescue themselves from the Indians once they were taken captive. Isabella counted herself lucky Peter considered her his wife. Had she ended up with Mick, she'd probably be dead by now.

"I should not long to be something I'm not," she told Maria. "Now that I am Peter's wife, men will respect me because they respect him."

"I am respected now too because Dominic married me. I do not lower my eyes when I pass those women in their bonnets on the street who still think poorly of me. I spit in their eye."

"You don't, Maria!"

Maria laughed. "I don't. But maybe one of these days I will. Especially Mrs. Green. She has her nose so far in the air she might drown come the rain."

Isabella smiled. "We shouldn't care what those women think of us."

Maria wiped Isabella's wet cheeks, her eyes growing serious. "Do not worry what men think of you. The man you've married wears animal skins. He will kill any man who comes near you. I'm sure he has a very big knife and lots of guns."

"He has several large knives."

"Has he killed any animals with his knives?"

"I don't know, but Pina killed a rabbit with her bare hands. I saw it for myself."

"Are you sure she's your sister?"

"Don't you think she looks like me?"

"When I saw her, it startled me. She looks like you when you were young."

"I do not think my aunt would lie about her being my sister."

"You have an aunt at Fort Ross?"

"My mother's sister, Tatiana. She prepared me for my wedding."

"How wonderful. Why doesn't Pina speak?"

"She lived with a terrible man. We took her away from him. Tatiana said she witnessed her mother's death and hasn't spoken since."

"But she can talk?" Maria pursed her lips. "And she runs down rabbits?"

"I've never seen anything like it. She also killed a chicken on the ship. When I got upset with her, she raced up into the rigging like she wasn't even human. Sometimes I see something in her eyes that frightens me."

Maria got up from the bed. "We shouldn't have left her with Sally."

Isabella sat up too. "I don't think she'll hurt her."

Maria walked to the door. "Try to get some rest. We will celebrate your wedding tonight. I'll go check on Pina and Sally."

"Send Pina up to me. She sleeps with me. I keep an eye on her that way."

"Where does your husband sleep?" Maria's brow furrowed.

"He's used to sleeping on the ground in the woods. I don't think he will mind where he sleeps."

"I'm putting him in here with you. I will take care of Pina. She can sleep with Fang since Fang loves children."

Isabella bit her lip. The thought of sleeping with Peter unnerved her, but she didn't argue with Maria.

"Do you not want to sleep with your handsome husband?" Maria was eyeing her.

"Our marriage is complicated."

"There is nothing complicated about lovemaking."

"You should check on Pina and Sally."

"You should make love to your husband."

Isabella grew exasperated. "Maria!"

"I am only speaking the truth."

"Thank you for taking care of Pina. She is a lot to handle."

Maria smiled. "Get some rest; you are growing a babe." She closed the door as she departed.

"You are growing a babe too," Isabella called at the closed door and then fell back on the bed, worrying about sharing it with Peter.

Chapter Twenty Five

The top floor of the mansion was a ballroom. Peter had never been in a ballroom before. He didn't know rich folks built theirs in the attic. It was a large open room with windows all around and a polished hardwood floor. To a man who crafted wood with his own hands, Peter was more than impressed with the elaborate woodwork adorning the ceiling. Dominic and Maria had brought in musicians. They'd invited all their servants as guests. Peter was surprised by the nationalities represented amongst their household. The Oriental maid, Fang, was holding Pina's hand. Peter noticed a young Oriental man couldn't keep his eyes off Fang. She shyly returned his glances when she thought no one watched them. Their interaction made him smile.

Everyone appeared to be having a joyful time and wore their best clothes. Nobody seemed to be serving. Everyone pitched in to make the party happen. Irish maids and men from Chile. Mexicans, Europeans, and down-on-their-luck

Americans. "Maria finds mouths to feed and brings them all home," Dominic confessed to Peter. "We certainly don't need all these servants, but they seem to need us. Many folks spend all they have getting to California. They arrive in San Francisco expecting to pick gold off the streets. Before they can get to the goldfields, they have to earn some money, and they have to eat. We help them."

Peter couldn't get over this grand affair held in his and Isabella's honor, but the servants seemed to be enjoying themselves the most. "Your servants are fortunate. Do you host parties for others in the city as well?"

"Maria loves parties, but she doesn't like the city's prominent citizens. She didn't come to San Francisco as my wife. When she got here, servants became her friends." Dominic didn't elaborate.

Peter could fill in the blanks. Had a man put that scar on her face? Peter would kill someone for doing that to Isabella. The two sisters were laughing with each other, Maria in a beautiful green gown that couldn't hide her pregnancy, standing beside Isabella in her creamy white wedding gown. Isabella's dark hair was pinned up on the sides and spilled down her back in a long, dark waterfall. She'd never looked more beautiful. To his relief, the dancing hadn't begun yet.

"I would offer you a whiskey for your nerves, but I know you don't drink." Dominic grinned. "The first time I danced with Maria, I was drunk. One thing led to another, and her brother and I got into a fistfight on the dance floor. Maria jumped in and about clawed my eyes out after Roman tried to kill me. I have never gotten drunk with the Californios since. They are a passionate people." Dominic chuckled.

Peter didn't know if he should laugh or not. He couldn't take his eyes off Isabella, so happy with her sister. In this environment, she looked entirely different to him. "How old is Isabella?"

Dominic raised his eyebrows. "I don't rightly know. She looked like Pina when I first met the Vasquezes at their rancho. I'd never seen blue eyes like hers before. Do all the Creoles at Fort Ross have blue eyes?"

"Many do," said Peter. "They're a handsome race."

"Any Russians left at Ross?"

"I didn't see any. Looks like the Germans have taken over the fort."

"So Isabella didn't find her real father?"

"She found him. His grave was beside her mother's." Peter's heart grew heavy. He and Isabella had both lost their mothers in childbirth. He could never forget Isabella walking amongst the crosses in her wedding gown, then standing on the hillside looking out at the ocean with sadness on her face. Life wasn't easy, and often sorrow followed you all your days. He couldn't ever remember a time when he was truly happy. The season with Maggie came close, but that was so brief and ended so badly.

"The Vasquezes were a happy family," Dominic assured him. "The Californios had something special. It's a shame the war destroyed their unique culture."

"War does that," said Peter. War had left him with dreams full of death.

"Are you missing your buckskins tonight?"

"Nah, I like fancy britches. They feel like silk against my skin." It wasn't the truth.

Dominic laughed. "Do my boots fit?"

249

"Your boots aren't soft. I prefer moccasins."

"I've never seen a man waltz in moccasins."

"And you won't see this man waltz in boots."

Dominic slapped him on the back. "We'll see." He walked over to Maria and Isabella, offering his arms to the women. Then he led the ladies back to Peter.

As if on cue, the Mexican musicians began strumming their guitars. Fiddles joined in, but it didn't sound like any fiddling Peter had ever heard before. The servants cleared the dance floor. Dominic bowed to Maria and led her out into the middle of the room. Maria was all smiles for her husband.

When they began to dance, Peter was mesmerized. He'd never seen that kind of dancing in all his life. The only dancing he'd ever witnessed was in brothels and saloons and when the trappers danced with each other after drinking too much. Dominic and Maria moved so gracefully, swirling around the room as if one entity. Isabella stood right beside him, watching as well. "I love seeing them dance together," she said.

"I don't dance," Peter told her.

"I didn't ask you to dance." Isabella didn't look at him.

The urge to take her in his arms suddenly overcame him. Everyone was watching Dominic and Maria. Oil lamps were scattered about the room, but the light was low, and they stood in the shadows. Taking a step toward her, he swooped Isabella into his arms and kissed her with all the passion churning inside of him.

He knew she was shocked but kept kissing her until she kissed him back. He pressed her against his hard frame and kissed her some more. She soon returned his kiss with a passion that astonished and pleased him.

There it was. He hadn't dreamed of that yearning that arose between them. Something soul deep and sizzling with desire. When he finally ended the kiss, he was breathing hard, and so was she. He looked around, realizing the waltz had ended. Dancers flooded the floor as a new tune arose. Dominic and Maria walked toward them.

"I'm sorry," he said, looking into Isabella's shocked eyes.

She put her hand to her lips. His lips were throbbing. He imagined hers must be as well.

"Dance with us," said Maria.

Isabella blinked at him, dropping her hand from her lips to hold his hand as she turned to her sister. "Peter doesn't dance. Let me sing for him instead."

"After a few dances, we will have you sing; the servants are enjoying themselves," said Dominic.

"You have so many servants," said Isabella.

"Many are just passing through," said Maria. "Everyone wants to go to the goldfields. They don't stay here long."

"The goldfields are a hard life." Isabella still held Peter's hand. Hers was so small and soft and warm in the roughness of his palm. Finally, they no longer had Pina between them. She was off with Fang. Since getting off the ship, the girl had seemed at peace. He hoped that wild spirit didn't return to her. It was disturbing to see that in a child, but it strengthened his faith that there was more to this world than a man could see or understand. Jedediah spoke of angels and demons walking the earth. Earthly eyes couldn't see these spiritual beings, but the demons tempted and tried and sometimes took hold of men, and the angels were sent by God to protect people.

"Did you ever look for gold?" Dominic asked, interrupting his thoughts on spirits.

"Nope. That fever hasn't hit me. I hope it never does." Peter was coming to the conclusion that raising sheep just might be the life for him. He had no desire to live in a mansion like this one surrounded by a city. A quiet cabin in the hills was more to his liking.

"I've never wanted to stand in a cold stream searching for gold. I'd rather provide the ships that bring all those fortune hunters and their mining supplies here," said Dominic. "Acquiring the ships is easy; filling the crew is much harder. Everyone thinks they will strike it rich in the goldfields. The truth is most don't, and many a man is ruined chasing after riches."

"Who cares about gold? Gold has nearly ruined California. Let's dance," said Maria.

"My wife speaks her mind." Dominic smiled at Maria and then turned to Peter and Isabella. "If we leave you two alone, I'm afraid you might disappear on us."

Even in the meager light of the oil lamps, Peter could see the blush filling Isabella's cheeks. "We'll stay for the party as long as I don't have to dance."

"You don't have to dance," Isabella quickly assured him.

"I will tell the musicians you are going to sing in a short while." Maria said to Isabella before pulling Dominic toward the dance floor.

Once they were gone, an awkward silence unfolded between Peter and Isabella. She finally ventured, "You are wearing a ship captain's boots."

"That I am." Peter didn't tell her he only wore the boots with the hopes to please her.

"You look like a fine gentleman tonight." She smiled softly at him.

"Do you wish you had married a fine gentleman?" He said it flippantly, but his heart hung on her response.

"I am not a fine lady."

"You underestimate yourself." He squeezed her hand.

Her gaze grew somber. "Would you have married me if you didn't have to?"

He stared into her eyes. It was an honest question. He wanted to give her an honest answer. "I didn't have to marry you. I could have ridden away that night and let Mick have you."

"Mick wouldn't have married me."

Peter felt the tremor in Isabella's hand. "Why didn't you tell me you came from this kind of life?" He waved his other hand out over the ballroom.

"I didn't come from this kind of life. I came from a rancho."

"You came from wealth and privilege."

She smiled, but the smile didn't reach her eyes. "The Vasquezes were deep in debt. My brother had to marry Rachel because of Don Pedro's gambling debts, and still, in the end, everything was taken by the Americans."

"You could have stayed here with your sister. Married a ship captain in tall boots who would build you a mansion in this city."

"I don't want a mansion in the city."

"What do you want?" His throat tightened as he waited. He hadn't shared his dreams with anyone but Maggie, and that had gone so wrong. Jedediah said that with God, all things were possible. Was it possible to build a happy life with Isabella?

"I want a farm with chickens and as many children as God will give us."

"That's not asking much."

"We don't have to have chickens, but I like them."

"I like chickens too. Fresh eggs are my favorite."

"I like milk, so we must have a cow." Isabella was smiling now.

"We'll have two cows and milk them together."

"I don't milk cows."

"Then I'll milk the cows, and you can make the butter." Peter was smiling too.

"I am happy to cook for you and do your washing."

He drew her closer, letting go of her hand to put his arm around her waist. The silk of her dress caressed his fingertips. He slid his hand down her hip and back up to her waist, turning her in his arms to face him. "Will you warm my bed as well?"

She reached up and smoothed the collar down on his fine white blouse. Then ran her hand over his vest. "I like you better in buckskins," she said breathlessly.

"You didn't answer my question." He wrapped his hands around her waist. Slid his fingers up her ribcage and down again in a caress so certain she caught her breath.

He smiled. "I have a farm and a cabin for you."

"You do?"

"I do." His hands slid down to her hips.

"Pina would have to live there too."

"My father lives there already. It's a large cabin. I'll build it even larger for us."

"With enough room for our children?"

His hands returned to her waist. "I would like a dozen children."

"Then I must share your bed."

He pulled her up against his chest, cupped her face in his hands, and kissed her. Heat spread throughout him like a wildfire. She sighed and leaned against him. He ran his warm fingers down her neck and onto her shoulders. His mouth followed the path of his fingers. He kissed back up to her earlobe and whispered, "Go sing for me."

Chapter Twenty-Six

His hands gently pushed her from him. She came to her senses and was relieved to see everyone still dancing, though the music was winding down. Desire coursed through her. The oil lamps flickered. On wobbly legs, she left Peter and found Dominic and Maria. They came off the floor flushed and smiling.

"Are you ready to sing?" Maria asked.

"*Sí.*" She decided she needed to keep her distance from Peter until they both got control of themselves. Something had changed. She could feel it. He was eager to speak of their future. He didn't mention the babe. His touch was full of tender passion, like that first night they were together, but now his eyes were clear and bright and shone with promises.

Was he falling in love with her?

She loved him. She hadn't imagined it. Something powerful knit them together. She just wanted to surrender to that mysterious power and see what happened.

Maria led her over to the musicians. They settled on a Spanish love song.

"But you are singing for Peter. Shouldn't you sing in English?" Maria asked.

Isabella smiled. "Peter understands Spanish just fine." She remembered how shocked she'd been when he spoke Spanish that first time at Clara's. How her heart had stopped and mortification filled her. She couldn't wait to sing in Spanish for him now.

The musicians began to strum their guitars, and Isabella commenced to sing. She closed her eyes and envisioned Peter's face. Remembered his tender touch. Savored the scent of the mountains on him. Her handsome frontiersman on his painted horse.

Spanish love songs were full of yearning, and oh, how she yearned for her husband's love. She regretted letting Paul convince her their marriage wasn't real. She regretted that Clara had come between them and Maggie's ghost lingered still. And what would happen when the babe was born? All the angst, longing, and love Isabella felt fueled her song. She opened her eyes and found Peter's face in the crowd. The look on his countenance matched the trembling of her soul.

Would he want her forever? Or would he leave her like everyone left her?

Tonight, she wouldn't allow herself to dwell on his leaving. She would only think of the kisses they'd shared. Did all women in love feel this way? Overcome with longing? Certainly, the Spanish songwriters had felt this way. She kept her gaze on Peter as she finished the song. He came to her and took her by the hand.

Maria swept over, looking pleased. "Sing some more, Izzy. That was so magnificent—" The look on Peter's face silenced her.

"We have not had a honeymoon yet," he said.

Maria's mouth formed a little O.

Isabella nearly laughed.

Dominic came to her rescue. "Why don't you sing, Maria?" Dominic said as he approached.

"I cannot sing like my sister."

"Then dance for us." Dominic's adoring eyes lingered on Maria.

Maria put her hands on her swelling belly. "Your child is sapping my strength."

"Then let the servants dance. We will retire to our beds." Dominic's eyes twinkled. Like Peter, he wore tall leather boots, a billowing white blouse tucked into his trousers, and a vest. Dressed in similar fashion, the two men could pass for brothers.

"I'm all for retiring for the evening," said Peter. "Thank you for a memorable night. The celebration of our wedding is complete." He spoke to Dominic and Maria, but his eyes were on Isabella.

"We are happy to see Isabella happy." Dominic ushered Maria from the dance floor, following Peter and Isabella to the edge of the room.

But Peter didn't stop walking. He led Isabella right out of the ballroom. They went down one flight of stairs and reached a wing of bedrooms. Guitars and violins came from above, along with the sound of dancing. Isabella didn't mind the noise. She couldn't imagine going to sleep right now. The siesta had helped. She realized the sickness caused by the babe hadn't come over her today. And it was a release not to worry about

Pina. An older maid was seeing to Sally in her nursery, and Pina was safe with Fang. Isabella had enjoyed the fiesta but hadn't missed dancing all that much. She didn't want to put pressure on Peter. She found it somewhat amusing that dancing frightened him when he seemed afraid of nothing else.

He led her to a room that wasn't the one she'd napped in earlier that day. When they walked through the door, she saw her traveling trunk there, along with his saddlebags. The bedroom was decorated nicely, just like every room in the mansion. The bed was large, framed by tall posts draped in fine fabric. A beautiful white nightgown of lace and silk lay on the bed. Isabella suspected Maria had left it there for her. It was something a bride would wear.

"Why don't you settle in, and I'll return in a short while," Peter said when his gaze settled on the sheer white nightgown.

Isabella presented her back to him. All the little buttons down her dress were so hard to loosen on her own. The last time she'd done it by herself, she'd barely escaped the gown. "Please unfasten me?" she asked, her heart pounding.

He leaned in, and his breath warmed her ear and sent shivers racing over her. Slowly, he released each button. His lips traveled down the side of her neck as he unbuttoned her. The dress fell away from her shoulders, and he kissed her naked skin there too. "I have wanted to kiss your bare shoulders since I saw that young miner kissing what is mine," he whispered.

"All the world is a stage, and the men and women merely players," she recited.

"I'm not playing." His voice was raspier than usual. He slipped the dress down her arms and turned her around to face him. She caught the silken gown before it swished to the floor, holding it over the sheer chemise that covered her bosom. She did not want him to see the slight swelling of her abdomen where the babe fluttered.

He reached for the pins in her hair, removing them until her hair tumbled around her in a silken curtain. "I need my hairbrush," he teased.

"I no longer wear my hair in braids because of you." She took the hairpins from him.

"If we have a daughter, she will wear braids." There was a softness in his eyes she'd never seen before. His hands covered hers, holding the dress like a shield against her body. Gently, he pushed the dress down until she let it go. It whooshed to the floor between her slippers and his boots.

Maria had given her the slippers, along with the silk stockings that covered her legs. Silk stockings were a luxury few women could afford in California.

"Do you need help removing your stockings?" he asked, looking down at her legs.

How often it seemed he read her mind. "Certainly not," she assured him, her face burning.

His gaze captured hers once more. He wrapped his arms around her. "How about I untie these?"

The ties of her chemise magically came undone. She reached behind her back to hold her lacy garments together. "I will have no trouble getting into my nightdress now. Perhaps you can return Dominic's boots to him."

Peter knew exactly how to undress a woman. His nimble fingers were like a lady's maid's. He made her so nervous.

A smile grew on his lips. "Would you like to help me remove the boots before I return them?"

Her eyes widened.

"How about you hold my knife while I remove my boots?" He pulled one of his big bowie knives from his boot, handing it to her.

If she took the knife, she would lose hold of her undergarments. "You wore your knife to the fiesta?"

"I wear my knife everywhere." He tossed the knife onto one of his saddlebags.

"Are your guns in your bags?"

"Do you mind? I keep my guns with me too." He picked up a strand of her hair and twirled it around his fingers.

"I doubt you need your guns here."

"You'd be amazed where a man needs his guns." The corner of his mouth lifted in a half smile.

She'd seen that half smile before, under the stars in the oak grove. Her stomach fluttered, and she began to shake in her slippers.

He reached behind her, covering her trembling hands with his own. She stood in his embrace, looking up at him.

"Are you afraid of me?"

"I'm afraid of how I feel when I'm with you," she admitted.

"Don't be afraid." He leaned down and kissed her lips quite softly. She was expecting the passionate kiss of the ballroom, but he pulled back. "If you trust me, let go of your undergarments."

She held tighter for a moment. His hands no longer covered hers. As soon as she closed her eyes and let go of her chemise, he clasped her undergarments and held them together. Then he kissed her passionately, pressing the length of her body to his. He kissed her so thoroughly she no longer cared what happened to her clothes.

Finally, he let her go. "Put on your pretty nightdress. I'll return shortly." He strode to the door without looking back, leaving her standing there with all her clothes on the floor.

Chapter Twenty-Seven

Paul swirled the water in the pan, hoping for the shine of gold. His back ached from digging holes in the banks, and his feet were numb from standing in the cold mountain stream. Mick was a stone's throw away, swishing his own pan. This was called prospecting, testing the dirt to see if it would pay. They'd become partners in the old Californio's claim. With Belle gone, they had nothing to fight over. Mick promised to share his earnings fifty-fifty if Paul helped him dig out the gold. One man couldn't do it alone.

They'd dug hundreds of holes up and down the banks and washed the dirt and clay if they found a hole that would pay. Mining was a lot harder than gambling, and far less enjoyable, but Paul and Mick had gained a bad reputation in the local towns and weren't welcome at the tables anymore. They had to do something to earn a living in California.

They shared a small cabin with windows, a fireplace, and an oven, but winter was almost upon them. Soon snow would cover the diggings until spring. The Sierras were named for their snow-covered peaks. When snow began falling, you wanted to be out of these mountains in a hurry. Miners froze to death here.

Paul found himself thinking about Belle, wondering what had happened to her. Clara said she'd run off with a German to Fort Ross. That didn't surprise him. She'd wanted to find her Russian father. He regretted he hadn't been the man to take her to Ross. He understood the need to look into the eyes of your blood father if he was still alive. He had no idea where his real father was, maybe New Mexico Territory, maybe Texas, maybe dead. Clara said he needed to go and make peace with Jedediah before Jedediah was dead.

Thinking about the man who raised him made that old ache rise up. For years, he'd done his best to think of Jedediah as his real father, but his mother's treachery lingered. The first he'd heard Jedediah was his father was when his mother fled an outlaw she'd said was his father and returned to Jedediah for a spell. His mother hadn't stayed long, and he'd found himself abandoned by her at Jedediah's pueblo in Taos. His mother couldn't stay put with one man, and most men weren't like Jedediah. He should consider himself lucky Jedediah had kept him.

A shiny bit of golden metal, no bigger than an ant, glimmered in the bottom of his pan. Paul stopped swirling and plucked it out. He put the bit in his leather pouch and tucked the damp pouch back into his pocket. They were working a little ravine that sloped down into the stream. There wasn't much clay here, which discouraged him. Usually, clay paid the best, but he'd found enough dust and nuggets to return to the hole this dirt came from and dig in earnest with pick and shovel.

Mick joined him, and they cradled the dirt together. It took two men to work a cradle. One to rock it while the other man shoveled dirt and water into the wooden box. It was the only reason Mick was willing to share his claim.

There was no trust between him and Mick. They watched each other like hawks. At the end of the day—or in the middle of the day if they hit pay dirt and filled up their pouches early— they met inside the cabin at the table and traded pouches. Then they emptied each other's pouches onto a plate and divided the gold evenly.

Once a week, on the Sabbath, Paul rode off to the place where he hid his gold. Lower in the hills below the snowline near the river. Mick mocked him for this, but Paul didn't care. He hoped one day to collect his gold from his hiding spot, a natural cave where he'd dug a hole, and just keep riding into the sunset. Perhaps head down south or back to New Mexico territory. He stomached Mick for one reason only. Gold.

The Sabbath was his favorite day. He could escape Mick. For some reason, Mick feared God enough not to rock a cradle or pick up a shovel or pan on the Sabbath. Instead, he drank his fill of whiskey in the nearest tent saloon. Then Mick paid for a woman's company if he found a willing dove and rode back to the cabin before nightfall.

Paul spent the day traveling to his cave and then looping back through Nevada City for some whiskey, returning to their claim before the wolves began howling in the hills. He hated wolves. He wasn't a hunter like Peter or Mick. When he saw a wolf, he never tried to shoot it. With his luck, he'd just wound the animal, and then it would attack him. Mick did all their hunting, and Paul did the cooking at the cabin. He could manage a rifle just fine, but he didn't like killing things. Unlike Peter, he'd never killed a man. He always said he was a lover, not a fighter. He remembered telling Maggie this, and she had laughed at him until he married her and showed her just how good a lover he could be. Maggie was still a terrible ache in his life. Perhaps because when he'd gained Maggie, he'd lost Peter, and then he lost Maggie and Jedediah too. Everyone he loved was gone from his life. He sorely missed Belle as well. He'd fancied himself falling in love with her when he'd had to leave Marysville in a hurry.

He pushed the sadness from his mind, but his thoughts lingered on Belle. He wouldn't admit now to loving her. He was afraid if he admitted he loved her, she would die just like Maggie. It was a darkness of thinking he couldn't control. These awful thoughts that came over him plagued him for days. Hard work helped ease his depression.

He shoveled for a while, and Mick rocked the cradle. They found some gold. It made them both happy. Paul was taking his turn at rocking the cradle when two men rode up the ravine on mules. They led two more mules weighted down with mining supplies. "Greasers." Mick spat when he saw them. He stopped shoveling and walked toward the men and mules.

Paul stood up and stretched his back. He felt like an old man with all the aches and pains since he'd taken up mining. One of the men got down from his mule, but Mick refused to shake the man's hand. Paul couldn't hear exactly what they were saying, but he could see Mick was now arguing with him.

The man on the mule drew a pistol. Paul didn't waste any time getting to the cabin for a rifle. When he returned, Mick was walking backward with his hands in the air. The mounted man still held his pistol leveled on Mick. The other man was climbing back onto his mule.

"We'll return tomorrow," the man stepping into the saddle said. "This side of the ravine is ours. I got a claim to prove it, so you best be digging on your side of the creek tomorrow."

Mick made his way over to Paul. The two men turned their mules around and headed out of the ravine. Paul was lowering the rifle when Mick jerked it from his hands. A moment later, a rifle blast stunned Paul. Mick shot one of the men in the back. The mules bolted. One man fell from his mule. The other held on and disappeared down the canyon with the runaway mules.

Mick cursed in frustration. "I'd hoped not to have to bury them greasers."

"What'd you do that for?" Paul stared at Mick like he'd lost his mind.

"They ain't taking my claim. No-good greasers. Chileans. Nobody cares about them."

Paul had seen men die before, but never shot in the back. He walked up the bank and down the creek to the man face-down on the ground. He was afraid Mick might shoot him in the back too. He'd learned Mick was like an animal. You didn't want to show any fear around him. Fear brought out the bully in Mick. It was best to be friendly and confident with Mick. Just go on with your business and try not to rile him.

When he reached the man, a bright red stain was spreading on his white poncho. He could see the man was already dead. He looked down the canyon for the other man and mules. They were gone. The ground was all torn up from the stampeding mules carrying a heavy load. This man wasn't the first to be killed over a gold claim. He doubted anyone would be around to investigate. Especially on account of the men being from Chile. If Mick had killed an American, there might have been some vigilante justice, but Chileans were like the Chinese and Indians up here. A dog was treated better than them in the goldfields.

Mick put down the rifle and came to Paul carrying two shovels. "Drag him on down the canyon. We ain't burying that greaser near our cabin."

Paul thought he might throw up. He grabbed the man just above his boots and pulled him as if he was dragging a plow through a field. He kept walking until Mick told him to stop. The day was so clear and blue; Paul couldn't believe it had brought death to their door.

"Let's get him into the woods," Mick said.

Paul dragged the man into the trees and didn't stop until Mick said, "Hold up here."

Mick tossed him a shovel. "I sure hope the ground's softer under these pines. It should be easier digging here in the shade."

He had no desire to speak to Mick. Slamming his shovel into the ground, he dug until sweat beaded on his brow. Birds sang in the pines and an afternoon breeze picked up, rushing through the treetops, creating a pleasant sound. Paul tried not to look at the body. Just an hour ago, that man was alive. Planning on getting rich, perhaps with a legitimate claim in his saddlebags. If the claim hadn't been legitimate, he doubted Mick would have shot that man in the back.

When the hole was deep enough, Mick grabbed the man's legs and dragged him over to the hole. Before dumping him in, he went through the dead man's pockets. Watching Mick steal from the dead sickened Paul even more.

"Well, looky here." Mick held up a flask. He uncorked it and smelled the contents, then took a swig, grinning when he finished drinking. "That's mighty fine whiskey." He corked the flask and tossed it to Paul.

Paul caught it, but the last thing he wanted was to drink from a dead man's flask.

Mick stopped what he was doing and studied Paul. "You got a problem, Paul?"

Paul shook his head.

"Well then, drink up. It's good whiskey."

"I ain't in the mood for whiskey." The Chilean had probably spent months on a ship getting to California. Maybe he'd left behind a wife or sweetheart waiting for his return. The dead man didn't look very old. Paul doubted he had offspring, but someone would grieve this man; at least he hoped a grieving would happen.

Would anybody grieve if one of these days Mick shot him in the back? Or some irate gamblers caught up with him and strung him from a tree like they'd threatened to do in Marysville?

Paul had never contemplated his own death. Why he did so now confounded and unnerved him. A raven squawked in the trees, and he jumped.

Mick laughed. "He's coming to get the spirit." Mick rolled the body into the grave.

"Who's coming to get the spirit?" Paul looked around. The raven squawked above them again.

"Old Lucifer." Mick stood up and gazed into the shadowy woods with a smile on his face. "He's here. Feel that frost on the back of your neck? That's the devil breathing on us. He's coming for souls today."

Paul looked around. All he saw were woods for miles. He did feel that unearthly cold Mick spoke of now that he'd stopped digging. The sweat running down his back chilled him.

"You're shaking like a little girl." Mick laughed. "I never saw Peter shake in my life. We buried our share of bodies together. I don't believe you're really a Brondi. You ain't like Peter at all."

The words pierced Paul. It was true. He wasn't a Brondi. And he wasn't like Peter. Not only did he not have Peter's courage, he didn't have Peter's bent to do the right thing when it needed to be done. "I don't believe my brother buried bodies with you. Peter doesn't kill for no good reason."

"We buried plenty of men with Fremont and Carson, and we buried all them bones up at the lake. Folks cannibalized each other in the snow. Boiled themselves some brains and sat down and made a banquet of their dead, the Donner Party did."

Paul threw down his shovel and walked away. The raven squawked even louder. Mick's mocking laughter trailed him through the trees. It reminded him of the devil's laughter. He picked up his pace, wanting to get out of these dark woods in the worst way. He was making good time back to the cabin when he met up with the wolf.

The big gray beast had his nose to the ground, trotting along, following the scent left by dragging the man's body. The animal looked up about the time Paul spotted it. They both froze. The wolf's lips curled back. Paul didn't even have his knife on him. He glanced around for a weapon but didn't even spot a rock to pick up. The wolf growled. Slowly, he walked backward, keeping his face to the wolf. The beast crept forward, its yellow eyes gleaming.

Paul continued to walk backward the same way he'd come. He wasn't about to turn his back on a wolf. Mick had a knife. And the rifle. He needed to get back to Mick.

"God, help me," he prayed out loud. The forest was so quiet. Even the birds had stopped singing, and the breeze in the treetops had stilled with the wolf there. When Paul stopped, the wolf stopped and hunkered down low like it was about to spring upon him.

The wolf didn't move until Paul moved. He walked backward again, careful where he placed his boots. He didn't want to stumble, fearing if he did the wolf would pounce upon him and rip out his throat.

"Jedediah says you're the God who made the heavens and earth. Who am I that you would be mindful of me?" The words of his boyhood gave Paul courage. He spoke them aloud. "That you would shield me all day long, Lord."

The wolf stopped snarling. Occasionally, it would stop and sniff the ground, probably smelling the blood that had dripped from the dead man. Once or twice the wolf licked the dirt. But it kept following him.

"Your blood covers me, Lord. I'm putting my trust in you. I'm sorry I'm a sinner. Forgive me, Lord. Save me, Lord." How long he walked backward praying, Paul didn't know. He heard Mick cock the rifle before the shot rang out. The wolf yelped in surprise and sprang into the air. Then it was gone in the timber.

"I just winged him. Couldn't get a good shot with you in the way." Mick gathered up the shovels he'd dropped to shoot the wolf. He handed the shovels to Paul and tossed the rifle over his shoulder.

"I was hoping you'd get here before the wolf got me."

"It ain't like a lone wolf to attack a man," said Mick. "Unless it's gone mad. Something was wrong with that beast."

Paul felt like the day had gone mad. Mick wasn't the least bothered he'd just killed a man in cold blood. In the distance, thunder rolled. Looking up through the thicket of pines, Paul saw blue sky, but the breeze was rising once more and had a different feel to it now. A winter feel.

"Storm's coming." Mick quickened his step. "Let's finish cradling that pay dirt before the rain hits."

Autumn thunderstorms were like this in the mountains. Swift to come. Swift to go. Snow hadn't fallen yet, but maybe this storm would bring it to the mountains. Paul kept an eye out for wolves. Mick was right; lone wolves usually didn't bother men. The pack was probably nearby. He whispered a prayer of thanks that he hadn't died today. He wasn't ready to meet the Lord, and he sure as the storm was coming didn't want to meet the devil. Of that he was certain.

Part Three

"And in that day, I will answer, declares the Lord,
I will answer the heavens, and they shall answer the earth.
And I will sow her for myself in the land.
And I will have mercy on No Mercy,
And I will say to Not My People, 'You are my people';
And he shall say, 'You are my God.'"

Hosea 2:21–23.

Chapter Twenty-Eight

Peter spotted the sheep before they reached the cabin. The herd grazed on a ridge as storm clouds gathered overhead. Isabella rode beside him on a horse he'd purchased for her in Marysville. Pina rode behind Isabella, holding the collie pup between them. The pup had kept Pina occupied on the trail. He'd also purchased another mule. Isabella's traveling trunk was strapped to its back. Mel had been so happy to see him and had moved out confidently for home, following the Yuba River into the hills.

They'd camped last night about halfway home. Peter didn't want to push the girls too hard, especially with Isabella expecting the child. Since they'd left San Francisco, they'd had no time alone together. Pina was always between them. Keeping her calm on the schooner crossing the bay, and up into the delta, then the Sacramento River had been difficult. The girl suffered screaming nightmares. Isabella suffered nightmares too.

For some reason, his nightmares had abated. Perhaps when he'd made his peace with God, the Lord had granted a healing of his memories. No longer did he relive war and death when he slept; he'd turned that guilt over to his Maker. For the most part, he felt at peace with his past and hopeful about his future. To his surprise, his animosity toward Indians was gone. And love for his wife was steadily growing. In San Francisco, they'd lived as husband and wife for several weeks in the mansion, sharing lovemaking at night and enjoying the days with Dominic, Maria, and their delightful children.

While Pina played with the little ones, he and Isabella had taken long walks around the city and down to the wharf, where Isabella loved watching the sea lions frolic in the bay. They'd visited a seamstress to clothe Isabella and Pina in dresses practical for farm life. Both girls now wore calico and bonnets, with sturdy shawls wrapped around their shoulders. He could not offer them a life in a mansion like Dominic did for his family, but Isabella didn't seem to mind. She was happy to follow him home to Jedediah and the sheep.

Thunder rolled, interrupting Peter's thoughts. Thankfully, they would reach the cabin before the storm unleashed. Not much snow fell in these foothills. It was California's mountains that were blanketed in snow, but once winter set in, the grass up here didn't grow until spring. Thank the Lord for early springs in California. By February, the sheep would fatten with lambs in their bellies, and by March and April lambing season would begin. This would also be about the time Isabella would give birth. He'd begun fervently praying the child would be his.

On the ridge, Jedediah waved the dogs out to round up the sheep. His father hadn't spotted them yet. How would his father feel about the girls moving in? Certainly, he would rejoice that a grandchild was on the way. He hoped Jedediah could get rid of the demon plaguing Pina. It wasn't there all the time, but came and went like spirits were prone to do, especially at night. On the schooner, Pina had become wild again. He and Isabella had held on to her to stop her from jumping overboard. He'd prayed for the spirit to leave her, and it finally did somewhere in the delta. After that, she'd mostly slept as they sailed up the river.

In Marysville, after retrieving Mel and the pup from Lickedy, he'd handed the fur ball over to Pina to keep her busy on the trail. The pup had grown in Lickedy's care and was twice as big as when Peter left him there. Still, he wasn't much to speak of and easily fit in Pina's bony arms.

When Jedediah finally saw them, his father waved in welcome.

Peter waved back.

"Is that your father?" Isabella asked.

"Yes. Looks like his bachelor ways have gotten the better of him." Peter was concerned about Jedediah's dishevelment. His hair and beard had grown long and scraggily; his clothes, even from a distance, appeared in need of a good washing. He leaned on a staff, as if tired, and let the dogs do the work.

"Does he live up here alone?" Isabella's eyes widened.

"He has the sheep and dogs." Peter could see the little golden collie pup frolicking around his father's feet. "And look, there's your mule." Peter pointed to Old Amigo following the sheep.

"He looks very old." Isabella leaned forward in the saddle, studying his father as they rode toward him.

"The mule or my father?"

"Your father."

"It isn't age; he's sick. I'm hoping you and Pina will give him a reason to live."

Pina leaned around Isabella to get a look at Jedediah and the sheep. She held tightly to the pup and appeared frightened. He didn't like the wildness rising in her eyes, but at least they were nearly home. Surely, Jedediah would know what to do to help the girl.

When they reached Jedediah, he was smiling. "Welcome home," he said to them all.

Peter stepped off of Mel and embraced Jedediah. When he pulled away, he saw Jedediah's eyes shone with tears.

"You found your wife." Jedediah's sparkling eyes were on Isabella. Pina hid behind her in the saddle. "Does she come with kin?"

Pride rose up in Peter as he presented Isabella to his father. She would make a fine wife, of that he was certain. "She comes with a sister. That is Pina hiding behind her."

"Well, let's get everyone home before it rains. Winter is coming. I can feel it in my bones." Jedediah turned and whistled for the dogs to drive the sheep in earnest.

Isabella's horse shied when the sheep began to run, but Isabella handled her mount like a vaquero. Pina clung to her and the pup, and they all three stayed in the saddle.

"You got a girl who knows horses." Jedediah grinned as he watched Isabella rein in her skittish mount.

"She was raised by the Californios. She rides better than I do." Peter's smile matched Jedediah's as he climbed back up onto Mel. He led the girls to the cabin and had them go inside as he untied Isabella's trunk from the mule and carried it into the house. Then he took the horses and the mule to the barn. He unsaddled the animals and fed them and then helped Jedediah settle in the sheep and the old mule. The two mules brayed at each other.

Rain fell as he and Jedediah walked back to the cabin together with their collie pups trailing after them. The pups tumbled over each other in playful abandon around their feet. Peter was filled with a sense of well-being. Bringing home a wife felt right. Thunder cracked in the distance, and the wind picked up. He smiled at the coming storm clouds.

"My bones tell me it's going to be a wet winter," said Jedediah.

"I'll split some logs for the fire." Peter put his hand on his father's shoulder. "It's good to be home, Pa."

Pina took an instant disliking to Jedediah. She stayed as far away from him as she could. Peter was grateful Jedediah had insisted they build a loft in the cabin. Pina went right up the ladder and wouldn't come down. He and Isabella arranged a bed up there for her and hoped for the best. She ate her dinner up there and refused to join them that evening around the fire.

The following morning when Peter rose at dawn, his father looked like a new man. Jedediah had shaved and trimmed his hair. "Sorry I slept in," said Peter. "I'll go feed the animals."

"I already fed them," said Jedediah. He looked healthier than he had in years. Maybe it was the happiness on his face that made him look stronger.

The rain had passed, but looking out the window, Peter could see winter was upon them. The sky was gray with storm clouds. Inside the cabin, it was warm and cozy. Jedediah had stoked the fire, and the collie pups slept near the hearth. He looked up the ladder that led to the loft but didn't see Pina or hear a sound up there. He was grateful she hadn't had one of her screaming fits during the night.

"I've been praying for the girl," Jedediah said, looking up at the loft too.

"Something comes over her," Peter admitted. "She's had a hard life, but it's more than that. I believe she has an unclean spirit that comes upon her."

Jedediah poured Peter a cup of coffee, and they sat down at the table. His father didn't say anything.

"What are you going to do about the spirit?" Peter pressed. He'd always liked Jedediah's coffee. He sipped it gratefully, trying not to burn his tongue.

Jedediah pinned him with his hawkish gaze as he sipped his own coffee. "What are *you* going to do about it?"

"I pray for her. I've made my peace with God. But I don't know what to do about Pina."

Jedediah smiled. "Made your peace with the Lord, huh?"

"I have." Peter smiled. "I guess I'll keep praying for the Good Lord to heal Pina."

"Fasting helps." Jedediah's smile disappeared. His eyes were serious. And shining with knowledge Peter didn't have.

"I don't want you fasting. I'll fast," said Peter. His father was skinny enough. He didn't need to go without eating.

"Part of receiving is believing. Do you believe the Lord wants the girl well?"

"I don't rightly know. I wish the Lord would see fit to make you well."

"I'm doing just fine," said Jedediah. "I plan on living to see my grandchildren."

Peter smiled. "Isabella's with child."

Delight came over Jedediah's face. "That's mighty fine news."

"I knew you'd be happy."

"When do you expect the babe?"

Peter tried not to think about Paul. "In the springtime, I suppose." He prayed again the babe would come out with a Brondi cleft in its chin. It was good to see the cleft in his father's chin again after all these years of both of them keeping beards.

"We got a lot of pregnant ewes. I sure hope another mule will help keep the wolves and coyotes away."

"How's the old mule doing with the sheep?" Peter stood up and walked to the hearth. He retrieved the coffeepot, returned to the table, and refilled both of their cups.

"He's happy with the herd," said Jedediah. "But pretty old and slow, like me."

"The young mule should help." Peter returned the coffeepot to the fire and joined Jedediah once more. "I'm going to add on to the cabin come spring. I'm hoping the Lord sees fit to fill it with children."

"A cabin full of young'uns sounds mighty fine."

"I'm sorry for all the time I wasted chasing the wind. I'm not proud of my past."

"The Lord will repay you for the years the locusts have eaten. He's repaid me plenty for the folly of my youth."

"You're a good father." Peter blinked hard. He needed to say it, though baring his soul to Jedediah left him feeling raw and uncomfortable.

"You're a fine son." Jedediah reached out and covered Peter's hand with his own.

Peter closed his burning eyes, savoring the moment of reconciliation with his father.

"Thank you, Lord," Jedediah whispered, patting Peter's hand.

"I best get the sheep out to graze before the next storm comes." Peter rose up from the table. He blinked hard to clear his eyes.

Jedediah stood too. "I'm praying Paul comes home," he admitted.

Peter nodded but didn't say anything. Paul coming home was something he wasn't ready for. Might never be ready for. What would happen if Paul came home and wanted Isabella back?

Chapter Twenty-Nine

Isabella tried to coax Pina down from the loft. It had been a week, and still she wouldn't remain in the same room with Jedediah. For some reason, she was terrified of him.

The first morning, she'd scampered down the ladder and raced out of the cabin. An hour later, Isabella had found her cowering in the barn. She had both collie pups with her, which made Isabella feel better. When Jedediah came to the barn, Pina returned to the cabin. When he was in the cabin, she retreated to the barn.

At night, she hid in the loft. Sometimes Isabella awoke to her screams. Peter was always out of bed first and beat Isabella to the loft ladder. Isabella would climb the ladder to the sound of Peter praying over Pina. Her sister rocked back and forth, awake and silent on her bed. Thankfully, Pina had come to trust Peter and wanted him there. Isabella was growing to trust Peter too.

He wasn't the same man who'd won her in that card game. His anger had vanished, and he smiled often. He made tender love to her at night and cared for her, Pina, his father, and the sheep during the day. His quiet strength was a balm to Isabella's fears.

Jedediah milked the cow and did all the cooking. He taught Isabella how to make butter and cheese. He also taught lessons from the Bible. Pina avoided Jedediah's Bible reading like the sound of his voice alone might kill her. Sometimes Jedediah would read the Bible out loud at night by the fire. Pina would bang on the wall in the loft to drown out his words of scripture.

"Why aren't you eating?" Isabella asked Peter that night at supper. She'd noticed he skipped meals and it bothered her.

"I'm fasting for Pina," he said, and Jedediah nodded his approval.

"I think she's in the barn." Isabella had gained a hearty appetite now that she was past the morning sickness. Her waist was thickening. She could no longer hide her pregnancy. Because Peter was at peace about it, she felt at peace too. But there was no peace for Pina. Her sister was worsening.

Jedediah pushed his plate away and stood up. "It's time," he said.

Isabella had no idea what Peter's father was talking about.

Peter and Jedediah locked gazes, and Peter rose from the table too. "I'll fetch our Bibles." Peter went to get the books.

Isabella was even more confused. "What are you going to do?"

"I think you should stay here," Jedediah told Isabella. "Pray for your sister. It's time the Lord sets her free."

Peter returned with Jedediah's Bible and his own. The two men walked to the door. Peter had been reading his own Bible daily, usually at night before he went to sleep. He spent most days out in the hills with the sheep unless a storm was brewing.

"Where are you going?" Fear rose in Isabella.

"To help Pina," said Peter.

"I'm going too." She hurried over to where her shawl hung on a peg on the wall.

"No," said Peter. "It's better you stay here. We will bring Pina back when it's over."

"I want to go with you." Isabella wrapped her shawl around her shoulders.

Peter looked to Jedediah. "Should she come?"

Jedediah turned to Isabella. "The devil frightens folks. You might want to stay here."

"My sister is not the devil." Isabella was growing terrified. Talk of the devil had always scared her to death.

"Pina is not the devil," Jedediah agreed. "But a demon has a hold on her. It's time for Pina's deliverance."

"We need a priest." Isabella felt the terror clawing at her throat. "We must find a priest for this."

"The Holy Spirit is all we need," said Jedediah. His calmness soothed Isabella some.

Peter stepped over and put his hand on her cheek. "Stay here and pray," he said before kissing Isabella's other cheek. He put his arm around her and led her over to a chair by the fire. Urging her to sit down, he placed his Bible in her lap. "Read Psalm 23." He helped her open the Bible to the psalm he wanted her to read and pointed to the text. "Read this until we come back."

Jedediah headed out the door.

"I'm frightened." Isabella's eyes filled with tears.

"That's what the devil wants." Peter put his hand on top of her head. "Please, Lord, keep the devil away from my wife. Let her know you are with us."

"I don't like this. We shouldn't speak of the devil." Tears filled Isabella's eyes.

"God doesn't want us to fear the devil. He only wants us to fear Him. The devil can do nothing God does not allow."

"Why has God allowed my sister to be tormented by an evil spirit?"

"I don't know, but I believe God wants Pina healed."

Isabella looked down at Psalm 23 on the page. *The* LORD IS MY SHEPHERD; I SHALL NOT WANT. She looked back up at Peter. "I want my sister to be free of evil."

He smiled. "God wants that too. Let me go help Jedediah. Pray for the best."

Once he was gone, Isabella read from the Bible. *"He maketh me to lie down in green pastures; he leadeth me beside the still waters. He restoreth my soul; he leadeth me in the paths of righteousness for his name's sake. Yea, though I walk through the valley of the shadow of death, I will fear no evil; for thou art with me; thy rod and thy staff they comfort me."*

She stopped reading and stared into the fire. She did feel comforted. Reading the scriptures out loud helped calm her fear.

"Thou preparest a table before me in the presence of mine enemies; thou anointest my head with oil; my cup runneth over. Surely goodness and mercy shall follow me all the days of my life and I will dwell in the house of the LORD FOREVER." Would goodness and mercy follow her all the days of her life? *Please, Lord, let it be so.*

Hours later, Peter returned carrying Pina in his arms. Her sister looked sleepy. Jedediah followed them into the cabin, carrying his Bible. He looked tired too. Jedediah proclaimed that Pina was healed, and then he went to bed.

Isabella and Peter helped put Pina to bed and then sought their own bed. Peter was even quieter than usual. After blowing out the oil lamp, she knew he lay there awake.

"Is everything all right?" she finally asked in the darkness.

"It's fine."

"You don't sound fine."

"I don't want to talk about it."

"Did you see the devil?" Isabella whispered. She hated even mentioning the devil.

"No, but I saw a soul delivered."

"Did it scare you?"

"It put the fear of God in me."

"Wasn't the fear of God already in you?"

"I've never seen anything like that in my life. My father has a mighty faith. The devil didn't like it. I saw what the devil can do."

"I don't want to talk about the devil. I just want my sister healed."

"She's healed." Peter sounded so certain.

"Did she speak?"

"No, but she's free from the demon."

"Is she still terrified of Jedediah?"

"No, that was the demon who feared Jedediah. The demon's gone now."

"Will it come back?" Isabella couldn't help but shiver.

"I hope not."

"What will we do if it does?" Isabella snuggled close to Peter.

"We will fear God and pray for His protection." He put his arm around her and held her close.

His warm strength felt so good. She nestled against his chest. Nights with Peter had become her favorite. She loved the smell of him, the strength of him, his tender touch. For someone so big and strong, Peter could be so gentle. Rain pattered the tin roof. "Is another storm upon us?"

"It felt like rain was coming. And maybe snow too."

"I hope Pina will stay in the cabin instead of running to the barn all the time."

"If she goes to the barn, it will be on her own accord now. Her will is her own."

Isabella listened to the rain strengthening on the tin roof. "You really believe all of this is true? That angels and demons walk this earth with us?"

"I know it's true. Jesus is real. The devil is real. I saw it with my own eyes tonight."

"You sound scared." Isabella stroked his warm, hard chest. She could feel Peter's heart thumping there.

"I am scared." He sounded so humble. "Please, Isabella. Let's try to sleep."

Her eyes finally grew heavy. She stroked Peter's chest for a while, and his heart settled down under her hand, but she knew Peter was still awake well into the night.

Chapter Thirty

It pleased Peter when Pina became Jedediah's little shadow. She even minded the sheep with his father on sunny winter days when Jedediah felt strong enough to walk out with the herd. The collie pups were always with Pina and Jedediah. They were no longer fur balls but had finally grown legs and long noses. Jedediah was showing Pina how to teach the collies to gather up the sheep. He also taught her and Isabella Bible lessons at the kitchen table at night. They passed their first Christmas celebrating the Lord's birth with a turkey dinner. Pina had hunted with him that frosty morning, and he couldn't get over how she could call turkeys, clucking just like a hen, which brought in the toms. He'd shot a big tom, and Pina had run over and carried it back to him so proudly. He'd marveled at her strength. The turkey was nearly as big as Pina. She'd been grinning from ear to ear, but still wasn't speaking. She did make noises now. Shushing the collies when they yapped. Whistling at the

Mexican sheep dogs, just like Jedediah. And laughing. It was so good to hear Pina laugh. She did so often.

"She's smart as an old coyote," Jedediah said. "Pina may not speak, but she knows everything."

"Do you think she remembers that night in the barn?"

"In the Lord's mercy, I believe Jesus has kept her from remembering her deliverance."

"I wish I didn't remember." Peter didn't want to recall how Pina had crouched on all fours, gnashing her teeth and scurrying around the barn in the most unnatural way as Jedediah commanded the demon to leave her. The deliverance had left him awake the rest of that night, praying for the Lord to forgive his sins and protect them all from the devil. The spiritual realm was more real than he'd ever imagined, and it put the fear of God and the devil in him.

"I'm going to teach Pina to be a shepherdess like Rachel," Jedediah was saying. That night in the barn didn't seem to bother him at all.

"Who's Rachel?" They were walking amongst the herd, checking the ewes for signs of early labor. It was still too soon for lambs. Peter hoped the days would warm with spring before the lambs hit the ground.

"Jacob's wife. I thought you were reading the Bible now?"

"I am."

"Abraham's grandson, Jacob, married Rachel. She herded her father's sheep." Jedediah continued on about the people of the Bible. Peter knew it was going to be a long conversation, but he didn't mind his father's rambling about the Bible anymore. He was happy Jedediah was still with them and felt strong enough to follow the sheep across the hills.

Oaks and pines dotted the land. Some hills were steep, others gently rolling with new green grass. Streams watered the meadows. Peter loved California. It was a Garden of Eden. He carried his rifle over his shoulder. One of their old Mexican sheepdogs had been wounded by a bear that came too close to the sheep last week. Pina and Isabella had managed to nurse the dog back to health, but it still wasn't strong enough to leave the barn. The collie pups were learning how to mind the sheep but offered little protection. The other old Mexican sheepdog did his best to guard the flock by himself. Fortunately, the two mules did a pretty fair job of keeping predators away.

Isabella and Pina were heating water in the yard to wash clothes when he'd left the cabin. Out of the blue, he felt the need to pray for them. The need grew stronger and wouldn't leave him. "I think we should drive the sheep home," he told Jedediah.

"You worried about that bear coming back?" Jedediah asked.

"No, but I got a feeling I don't like."

"What kind of feeling?"

"I'm not sure," said Peter. "I want to go check on Isabella and Pina."

"Head on back and I'll get the goats to lead the sheep home," said Jedediah.

Two goats with bell collars always led the sheep. Anywhere the goats went, the sheep followed, trailed along by the two mules. Peter knew all Jedediah had to do was convince the goats to go home and the sheep would trot after them with no trouble.

He began striding back to the cabin.

• • •

Isabella and Pina were hanging clothes on the line when Mick rode up. Clearly, he was surprised to see her. "Where's Jedediah?" he asked, his gaze roving over her and Pina.

"Jedediah's asleep in the cabin. He's been sick," she told Mick. "I don't want to wake him. He needs his rest." She lied because she was terrified.

Mick smiled. It wasn't a pleasant smile. "I'm sure Jedediah won't mind if I feed and water my horse." Mick's saddle creaked as he stretched out his legs. "It's been a long ride. Jedediah is like a father to me. He'll be happy to see me."

"You're welcome to look after yourself at the barn." Isabella's heart pounded. She didn't know what to do.

Mick looked her over again, his gaze lingering on her protruding stomach. His smile vanished. When he headed to the barn, she and Pina ran into the cabin. Isabella grabbed Jedediah's rifle down off the hooks, and Pina pulled out a knife that she kept hidden under her skirts. By the time Mick returned, the girls were ready for him.

Mick acted friendly upon entering the cabin. He said he was only here to check on Jedediah's welfare. Isabella tried to stop him, but he searched both bedrooms and found them empty. When she told Mick to leave, his friendliness vanished.

He jerked the rifle from her hands. "I've got a scar on my head because of you." He yanked off Isabella's bonnet and loosened her hair.

"I'm with child," she backed away from him. "Peter will be back any minute. He won't want you here."

Mick smelled like a wild animal. He stepped over and yanked Iabella against his big, hard body. Wrapping his hands in her hair, he held her still, his mouth lowering to hers.

Isabella didn't see Pina coming at them, but Mick did. Instead of kissing her, he swung around and captured Pina's wrist as she tried to stab him in the back. He called Pina an awful name, taking the knife from her.

"Don't hurt her," Isabella pleaded.

Mick pushed Isabella away and grabbed Pina. He sat down in Jedediah's chair and threw Pina facedown across his lap. After tucking the knife into his boot, he yanked Pina's skirts over her head and spanked her with his bare hand. Pina never made a sound.

Isabella grabbed Mick's arm, trying to stop him, but Mick shook her off without any trouble. He was so much stronger than her. "I'll punish the girl worse if you don't let me finish here."

It dawned on Isabella to pray. She dropped to her knees and folded her hands, praying earnestly for Jesus to help them right there at Mick's feet.

Mick stopped the beating. "You're tough as nails," he told Pina when he yanked down her skirts and set her back on her feet. Pina remained silent before him without a tear in her eye. Pina turned and ran out of the cabin when he released her. "Indians ain't really human," Mick said. "You can't hurt Indians much."

Isabella ached for her sister. She hoped Pina would run to Peter and Jedediah. "You hurt her. You're a terrible man."

"That half-breed tried to kill me. I should have cut her throat. Were you praying for me, Belle?"

"God will punish you."

"I ain't afraid of God." Mick grabbed Isabella's hair and pulled her to her feet. "Is that girl your sister? She's got eyes just like you. Never seen blue eyes on an Indian before."

"She's from Fort Ross."

He lifted her hair and ran his mouth over her neck. "I ain't eaten all day. I'm mighty hungry."

Isabella shivered in repulsion. "Let me go, and I'll fix you something to eat."

"It's a shame you're expecting. I don't like my women already bred."

Isabella pulled away from him. To her surprise, Mick let her go.

"I want bacon and potatoes and carrots, if you got 'em." Mick straightened his gun belt.

She moved quickly to tempt him with food, all the while praying Pina would bring Peter back.

He stoked up the fire. "It's cold in these hills. I've been wintering down in the valley. When did you move up here with Brondi?"

Should she answer him? Mick was so unpredictable. Maybe she should keep him talking. "We've been here a while. You're gonna need to fetch the bacon, potatoes, and carrots down in the cellar for me." She pulled out a pan to cook in.

Mick finished stirring up the fire and then did her bidding. She thought about bolting for the door but didn't want to make Mick mad again and knew she couldn't outrun him while pregnant. He soon came back carrying a piece of pork, several potatoes and carrots, along with the knife he'd taken from Pina.

"That's Jedediah's knife." Isabella took the food he handed to her.

Mick smiled. "Well, you make sure and return it to Jedediah for me." Mick offered her the knife, his eyes raking her face, a half smile that looked more like a sneer on his lips. "You sure are a pretty thing."

She put down the vegetables and accepted the knife. If only she had Pina's courage to bury the blade in Mick's back. Instead, she picked up a potato and began peeling it.

Mick reached out and ran his fingers through her hair. "I usually don't like Indians, but I like you, half-breed."

Isabella continued to peel the potato without meeting his gaze. She prayed he would leave her alone.

"You know how many Indians I've killed?" She could feel Mick's hot breath on her. "Only about a dozen more than Peter. He won't kill squaws. And I never thought he'd marry one. Of course, you ain't full squaw. What are you?"

Isabella put down the potato she'd skinned and picked up the other one. *Please, God, save me.* Her hands shook so badly she could hardly peel the potatoes. "My father was Russian. My mother was half-Russian, half-Indian."

"Give me that knife. You're going to cut yourself." Mick took the knife from her and finished the potato. "You must have gotten those blue eyes from the Russians. I killed a Russian once. He died with courage. Your little sister has that Russian courage. I didn't beat her much because I didn't want to scare that out of her. I like courage in a woman."

Isabella didn't respond to his taunting.

"Paul and I are partners now in my gold claim. Do you miss Paul?"

"I'm married to Peter." She tried to move away from him.

He dropped the potato and yanked her back against his side. "I was there. That ain't marriage. Peter won you with my card. You ain't a wife. You're a Brondi whore."

Anger came over Isabella. "Get out of my way and let me cook."

He took her by the shoulders, trying to kiss her again, but she turned away from him. His lips landed on her ear, making a smacking sound. She grabbed the knife.

He took the weapon from her and began to calmly slice the bacon off the hunk of pork. "I sure do like you. Mixing Russians and Indians makes for a pretty half-breed squaw."

Isabella stepped away, trembling all over, praying more fervently. *Oh, Peter, please come! Please, Dios, let Peter come to me.*

Chapter Thirty-One

The day was cold, but Peter warmed quickly running for the cabin. By the time he reached the homestead, it was late afternoon. He burst through the door with his loaded rifle in hand.

"Hello, Peter, you look ready for a gunfight."

He didn't have to see Mick to know he was there. He recognized his voice. The cabin smelled like fried bacon. Mick warmed himself beside the fire. Isabella was clearing the table. Her hair was flowing down her back, like she wore it for bed. When she turned around, her eyes were bright with fear. Pina was nowhere in sight.

"If you hurt her, I'll kill you." His gaze returned to Mick.

"He didn't touch me," Isabella said too quickly.

"Where's Pina?"

"The girl tried to stab me. I put her over my knee and gave her a good whuppin'. She ran off."

Peter leveled his rifle at Mick.

Mick held up his hands. "You wouldn't shoot an unarmed man. That's not like you, Pete."

"You're armed." Peter slowly stepped into the cabin, keeping the rifle aimed at Mick. He walked to Isabella. "Are you sure he didn't hurt you?" He kept his eyes on Mick.

"I'm fine," Isabella whispered. He could hear tears in her voice.

"Get up," Peter told Mick.

Mick smiled. "It's a cold day. She made me a warm supper. I didn't hurt her."

"It will be a cold day in hell when my wife serves you again. Get up." Peter waved the barrel of the rifle at Mick.

"We used to be friends." Mick slowly rose to his feet. "You're making me sad, Pete."

"My wife doesn't like you." Isabella stepped behind him, pressing her body against his back. He could feel her trembling.

"You figure out whose babe she'll bear?" Mick's sneering smile returned.

"Mine." He pressed back against her, hoping to comfort her, his eyes never leaving Mick.

"You sure about that?" Slowly, Mick walked to the door with his hands raised in surrender.

"I'm sure." Peter nudged Isabella further back in case Mick drew on him.

Mick laughed. "I'll have to tell Paul I found Belle. Maybe he can come and see the babe for himself."

"The babe will look like me."

"You always were full of confidence." Mick made it to the door.

"Don't come back."

"Where's your old man? I thought this was Jedediah's cabin."

"He'll be here shortly."

"Well, I'm glad your Pa's still alive. Paul will be happy to hear it."

"Where is Paul?"

Mick laughed. "I thought you hated your brother."

Peter gritted his teeth. He didn't trust Mick to stay away from the cabin. Now he'd worry about Isabella and Pina when they were there alone. "I don't hate Paul. What are you doing in these parts?"

"My claim ain't far from here. About half a day's ride up the hill. I was hoping to spend the night with Jedediah tonight."

"You can reach Nevada City before dark if you ride hard. Where's your horse?"

"In the barn with Mel. I've been waiting for you. I see I waited in vain for your hospitality."

"Nevada City will be a whole lot more hospitable than here. I'd get to riding if I were you."

Isabella ran outside, calling Pina's name. Peter accompanied Mick to the barn to make sure he rode away, then he returned and helped her search for Pina. They couldn't find her anywhere. They heard the bells on the goats before they saw Jedediah and the sheep coming down the hill. For a sick old man, he was moving fast. Pina was helping him along.

"There she is!" Isabella cried.

"She must have followed the sheep's trail to find us. I returned a faster way and missed her on the trail," said Peter.

"How did you know to come home?"

"I had a feeling you were in danger." He slung his rifle over his shoulder and put his arms around her.

"I prayed you would come."

"Are you sure Mick didn't hurt you?"

"I'm fine."

Peter put his hand on her stomach. "Is the babe fine?"

Isabella pressed her cheek against his chest, holding on to him. "The babe's just fine."

Afternoon was turning to evening, the sun sinking onto the hills, casting a rosy glow over the cabin and barn. They'd had some snow days earlier, but it was gone now. Spring wasn't far off. Peter reached down and tipped Isabella's chin up. He looked into her eyes. "I'm sorry I ever rode with Mick. I was a fool. I'm sorry he was my friend."

"Let's forget about the past. Neither of us are who we used to be. We'll start over."

"I can't imagine life without you." Peter leaned down and kissed her.

The sound of the bells grew louder. Peter pulled away. "Go in and warm yourself by the fire. I'll check on Pina."

It wasn't long before Pina joined Isabella in the cabin. Isabella hugged her and asked if she was all right.

Pina smiled and nodded.

"Does your backside hurt?"

Her sister shrugged. She didn't seem injured. She patted Isabella's stomach as if her main concern was the babe.

Isabella smiled. "The babe is kicking. Can you feel it?" She placed Pina's hand where the baby moved.

A look of wonder came over Pina's face. She leaned in and pressed her cheek to Isabella's stomach. The babe rolled. Pina smiled with happiness. Isabella laughed. She was so relieved Pina wasn't hurt.

"Let's prepare supper," she said, feeling lighthearted. God had heard her prayers and had protected them from Mick.

Chapter Thirty-Two

Spring was upon them, along with lambing season. Peter spent long days with the herd. Sometimes Jedediah accompanied him to the pasture. Other days Pina helped with the ewes. Peter didn't want Isabella left alone at the cabin. Her time of delivering the babe was nearly upon them. Each day, he prayed the babe's birth would go smoothly. And that the child would be his. He wouldn't allow himself to ponder the babe being Paul's.

They'd settled into family life far better than he'd hoped. As soon as lambing season ended, he planned on expanding the cabin. Jedediah seemed a little stronger than he'd been a year earlier. He hoped his father would remain with them to enjoy his grandchildren. Jedediah was busying himself these days proudly building a cradle. For a long spell, Jedediah hadn't mentioned Paul. Peter was grateful for the reprieve. He didn't want to go find Paul. He just wanted to build a life here with Isabella. Raise their children. Savor the peace God had given them in this little valley.

Fortunately, with all the new spring grass, they didn't have to go far to graze the sheep. He was nearby in case Isabella needed him. On the days Pina was with him in the pasture, he sent her to the cabin often to check on Isabella.

Pina still didn't talk, but she had a way of communicating with her hands and eyes that they all understood. Her hearing was incredibly sharp. She sensed danger sooner than most people. When it came to the sheep giving birth, Pina instinctively seemed to know when a ewe needed help delivering. Peter was teaching her how to reach up into a laboring ewe that was in trouble and turn a lamb into the proper position. Pina's small hands were perfect for this job, and she was getting good at feeling the difference between forelegs and hind legs and how to guide a lamb into the right position inside its mother so it could be easily delivered. A number of wobbly white lambs were already on the ground, frolicking around their mothers amongst the green grass and wildflowers covering the hills.

The new lambs delighted Peter. Somewhere over the months of his return here, he'd embraced being a shepherd. He'd come to love the sheep and the little family God had given him in Isabella, Pina, and his father. A sense of well-being like he'd never known had settled upon him, and he counted each day as a blessing. He looked across the field and thanked God for this life.

He'd had his eye on a young ewe for a while now, and he spotted her on the ground. She'd been down for over an hour, laboring to bring forth her lamb. He decided it was time to assist her. Striding to the creek, he washed his hands, then returned to the ewe on the ground. She roused when he approached, raising her head off the grass to look at him. He could see in her eyes she was relieved he was coming to help her.

"Easy, girl," he said in a gentle voice. "Let's get this lamb turned for you." He knelt down and reached up into the sheep. The ewe's body contracted, and he waited for the contraction to pass. His hand touched a tail. Not good. He did his best to turn the lamb, but it wasn't cooperating. The hind legs felt large, and foreboding washed over him. He pinched the lamb's leg but got no movement from the lamb. It was dead or dying. The ewe watched him with surrendered eyes. He didn't like this about sheep. They gave up far too easily.

"Come on, girl. Don't give up." She closed her eyes and refused to push during another contraction. She couldn't be that weak. Just this morning she'd looked strong and healthy in the barn.

He tried once more to turn the lamb. There was no extra room in her womb. The lamb was lifeless and refused to roll. It was a big lamb.

Pina appeared at his side. She tapped his shoulder. He removed his hand from the ewe and moved over to let Pina kneel down to put her hand inside the ewe. The ewe's breathing had grown shallow. Peter went to the ewe's head and spoke to her.

"Don't give up." He rubbed his hand over the her head. She didn't open her eyes. Peter watched her stomach contract, but the ewe didn't labor. His eyes met Pina's, and she shook her head sadly.

"The lamb's too big for this young ewe," he told Pina. During the next contraction, he tried to press on the ewe's stomach, sweeping the pressure toward Pina's hand inside the ewe.

It did no good.

But Pina refused to give up.

Peter pulled some twine from his pocket. He should have done this sooner, but he had hoped to save the lamb. Now they'd probably lose the ewe as well. He returned to his place beside Pina and handed her the twine. "Can you tie it to a hind leg? We'll have to pull the lamb out of her."

Pina did as he told her, and soon he was pulling the twine as Pina did her best to get both hind legs into the birth canal. By the time they got the dead lamb delivered, the ewe was gone as well.

Tears filled Pina's eyes.

The only other time he'd seen her cry was after her deliverance in the barn.

"You did real good. This happens sometimes with a ewe's first lamb. We did what we could for her."

Should he have helped the ewe sooner? Doubts filled his mind, but he didn't voice them to Pina. He didn't want to upset her further.

He looked around the pasture and saw another ewe down and in labor. "Go check on her."

Pina leapt to her feet and ran to the other sheep. *Please, Lord, let that one be born. Grant us a live lamb today.*

He took hold of the dead ewe's hind legs and dragged her down the hill and as far away from the herd as he dared, leaving Pina with another laboring ewe. Either the coyotes or wolves would find the ewe's body, and she'd be gone by sunrise.

A sickness settled in his stomach. He hated losing a fine, young ewe. It was like losing a part of his future.

You will lose Isabella too.

The awful thought came out of nowhere and sounded like a dark voice he didn't want to hear. He shoved the thought away and swiftly returned up and over the hill and across the pasture to where Pina was caressing a newborn lamb. This lamb was large, but it was moving. The ewe was rising to her feet.

Pina looked determined to see this lamb live.

"Another big lamb," Peter said, shaking his head. "We may have to part with one of the rams." He suspected it was their largest ram that had sired these big lambs. Normally, that wasn't a problem, but they had a new batch of ewes birthing for the first time. Young ewes and large lambs were not a good mix.

He heard Jeremiah's whistle and turned to look down the hill toward the cabin. Jeremiah was headed their way in a hurry. A wave of dread washed over Peter.

Pina jumped to her feet.

The ewe had begun cleaning the lamb.

After one last look at the lamb, Pina ran toward Jedediah. She didn't stop when she reached him, but raced on toward the cabin.

Peter was running too before he even knew he was running. Fear washed over him in waves. He knew Isabella was in trouble. He could feel it in his bones.

When he reached Jedediah, his father said, "She's been laboring since this morning. She swore Pina and me to silence. She didn't want to worry you. But her water's broke now, and she's having trouble. She's asking for you."

Peter let out a curse. "You should have told me. See to the sheep," he commanded his father. He turned and ran.

When he reached the cabin, he plowed through the front door. Silence filled his ears. In a few long strides he was in their bedroom. Pina was bathing Isabella's forehead with a damp rag. A grimace was on her face.

Pina moved out of his way to let him lean over Isabella. "Why didn't you tell me?"

She smiled. "I didn't want to worry you. The sheep are lambing. You need to be with the ewes."

"I need to be with you." He pressed his lips fiercely to her forehead.

A contraction hit, and Isabella's whole body lifted off the bed in agony, but she didn't make a sound.

Gently he took her by the shoulders and eased her back against the mattress. "Don't fight the contractions. Breathe. If you feel like you need to push, hold your breath and push hard."

She closed her eyes and let out a low moan.

Pina moaned too.

He looked at Pina. "Go heat some water." The girl's blue eyes were wide with fear.

He was fighting terror himself. He put his hand on Isabella's belly. It felt like a rock, tight with a contraction that didn't seem to end.

Finally, her body eased. "How long have you been having contractions?" He picked up the rag Pina had dropped back into a water bucket. The water was cool in the pail. He squeezed out the excess water and ran the rag across Isabella's forehead.

"Since yesterday. But not like this."

"Yesterday?" He was stunned.

"It wasn't difficult . . . until this morning."

He couldn't believe she could hide this from him during the night. He knew she hadn't slept well, rising often from their bed, but she'd been doing that for weeks. Over and again he'd asked her if she was all right. She'd assured him she was fine last night.

Several hours later, he was doing the same thing, washing her face with the rag. Isabella was pushing, but it didn't seem to be bringing the babe down into the birth canal. He'd begun to pray. Mostly pleading with God to release the babe from her body. The last thing he wanted was to reach up inside her to see what position the babe was in. He could see how weary Isabella was. Her moans had intensified. Pina's eyes were on him. "Go wash your hands and boil more water," he told her.

When she returned, he said, "Isabella, Pina is going to check the babe's position. We need to know if the head is down." He tried to remain calm. Inside, he was a mess. He'd shoved his hands deep into his pockets. They'd begun to shake badly. He kept thinking about the ewe they'd lost this morning. He feared Isabella would die too.

Pina's eyes were wide with worry, but she looked determined. Peter stayed up at Isabella's head, staring into her eyes, trying to comfort her.

"Don't be . . . afraid," Isabella whispered to him when her contraction passed.

He wanted to deny that he was afraid, but his throat closed tight. He couldn't speak. He removed a hand from his pocket and reached for her hand. They clasped hands, threading their fingers together, both their hands trembling. Tears filled his eyes. "I love you," he whispered.

A smile lit her face. When the next contraction hit, she bore down hard. Those whispered words had renewed her strength. She pushed with all her might.

He looked down at Pina and could see she wanted to speak. Her lips moved but no sound came from her mouth. She'd climbed up onto the bed with Isabella to do what she needed to do. "Say it," he urged.

Paula Scott

Her face convulsed. Pina moaned instead.

Isabella moaned in agony too.

"Fo . . ." Pina managed.

"One or two?"

"T-t-t-t . . ." Tears streaked Pina's cheeks.

"You must grab both feet and gently pull during her next contraction."

Pina did as she was told.

"Stop pulling when the contraction ends." Peter's heart was bursting from his chest. He was desperately praying. Terrified of losing Isabella.

Pina nodded, biting her lip in concentration.

Isabella bore down several more times. Each time, Pina tugged on the babe. Peter began to pray out loud, pleading for the babe to come forth. Speaking life over the child. And life over Isabella. "In the name of Jesus, I proclaim this child will live. And my wife will live," he commanded. Something rushed through his spirit. A will greater than his own. A life force he could feel flooding his body and the room. "Jesus!" he proclaimed with overwhelming hope.

"Je . . . s . . ." Pina parroted, tugging the babe from Isabella's body.

Isabella's moan turned into a scream.

Pina screamed too. The babe landed in her lap. She picked it up and swept its mouth with her finger. Peter had seen her do this with a newborn lamb that wasn't breathing. Like the lambs born earlier in the day, the babe was large. When it finally began to cry in Pina's hands, Peter cried out, "Thank you, Jesus!"

"Jesus!" Jedediah hollered from the doorway. He raised his hands in the air. "Praise you, Lord!"

312

"Our Father in heaven," Isabella said.

"Hallowed be thy name," Peter joined her in prayer.

Pina tied off the cord and cut it with a knife. Then she held up the crying boy so Isabella could see the child.

"Our Father has given us a son," Isabella said, smiling and weeping and looking at Peter.

"A fine son," Peter agreed, tears coursing down his face.

Everyone cried, even Jedediah.

Pina began to wipe the babe clean. Peter marveled that she knew what to do. Perhaps she'd helped women at the fort. She swaddled the babe and handed it to him, then helped Isabella finish the birth process.

Peter looked at the babe in his arms and noticed the cleft in his son's chin. The Brondi cleft. Just like Jedediah. Just like him. He cried harder, overjoyed that the Lord had given him a son afterall.

Chapter Thirty-Three

Isabella stared at the babe Peter placed in her arms. Gratitude filled her that the babe was alive. And she was alive. Though he had dark hair, the babe didn't look like Paul, but she knew it was his. Peter was all smiles, his face wet with tears. He cupped her cheek so tenderly. "I love you, Isabella. You have given me a fine son. What should we name him?"

Jedediah finally came into the room as Pina was cleaning up. "I think you should name my grandson after his father," Jedediah said proudly. He came over and stared down at the babe. "Look at that. The Brondi cleft. And those are Brondi eyebrows for certain." Jedediah chuckled with happiness. "He looks like a little hawk."

A wave of guilt washed over Isabella. She didn't have to tell them the truth. The babe was a Brondi. Wasn't that enough?

Her gaze locked with Peter's.

"Should we name him after his father?" Peter's smile widened.

She could see he believed with all this heart the child was his. She closed her eyes, agony filling her. How could she not tell Peter the truth?

"Isabella?" Peter's voice rasped. "Are you all right? Pina, is Isabella all right? Something's wrong."

Isabella could hear the angst in Peter's voice. She opened her eyes and looked around the room. Her sister had saved the babe's life and probably her life as well. "Pina," she called.

Pina came to her side. Her sister's eyes were wide and blue and full of love. "You can speak. Tell them I'm fine."

Pina shook her head. She didn't want to speak. She looked a little worried.

Isabella smiled. "You don't have to speak. Thank you for saving the babe."

Pina burst into a smile. She nodded happily and returned to her cleaning.

Isabella turned to Peter, standing on the other side of the bed. His gaze was locked on her. Jedediah stood by his side. She looked down at the babe and could see the resemblance clearly. The child was certainly a Brondi. He was perfectly formed. And fair of skin. He'd stopped crying and stared at her with dark blue eyes. A wave of love washed over her. How could a moment so beautiful be so awful?

"Do you want me to name the babe?" Jedediah teased. His concerned eyes went back and forth between Peter and Isabella.

Isabella took a deep breath. Tears filled her eyes anew. Her heart broke. *I know you are here. Help us, Father . . .* She fixed her gaze on Peter. "He is Paul's son," she finally said.

Peter's face crumpled, and he closed his eyes.

Jedediah put his hand on Peter's shoulder. "Paul's son?" Jedediah studied the babe.

Peter opened his eyes. What Isabella saw on his face frightened her. "Name him Paul," Peter said as he shook off his father's hand.

"You know what this means," Jedediah's voice trembled, "Paul's a Brondi."

Peter spun around and headed for the door.

Pina stopped cleaning the room and stared after him, her eyes wide with alarm.

"Please don't leave," Isabella cried. Her voice startled the babe, and he began to wail.

Jedediah reached down and took the boy into his arms. He tucked the babe close to his chest, bowed his head, and his shoulder's shook with sobs.

"I'm happy for you, Jedediah," Peter called from the door. "I truly am. You have a son. But I don't."

"Peter, please don't go!" Isabella struggled to rise from the bed. Fear and heartbreak filled her.

Pina rushed over and pushed her back against the pillows. "N-no," Pina struggled to speak.

Peter was gone. The babe wailed in Jedediah's arms.

Isabella closed her eyes, her heart shattering in a million pieces. She'd nearly convinced herself Peter would accept the babe no matter what. The past months with Peter had been so breathtaking. So filled with love. She thought he loved her enough to never leave. She was wrong.

Jedediah gained control of his emotions and handed her the baby. "I'll talk to Peter. He'll come to see God works everything for the good of those who love Him."

Tears coursed down Isabella's cheeks. She wanted to believe that. Could God really work this for good?

As soon as Jedediah left, Pina checked Isabella for bleeding. She looked satisfied as she tucked fresh bedding beneath Isabella and covered her with an extra blanket.

To calm the babe, Isabella tried to feed him. He finally settled down at her breast and fell asleep. She couldn't stop crying. She'd gained a son but lost her husband.

Pina wouldn't leave and kept checking to make sure Isabella didn't lose too much blood.

Isabella had no idea what time it was. She could see out the window that darkness had descended. Sometime during her labor someone had lit an oil lamp in her room. It burned steadily, like a promise from God that light would return. Eventually exhausted by not only her labor but her broken heart, she quietly cried herself to sleep.

When she awoke, Pina was curled in a blanket at the foot of the bed. Her sister was asleep. The babe slept in Isabella's arms. The oil lamp still burned. To her relief, she heard the murmur of Peter's and Jedediah's voices in the other room. She knew a fire crackled in the hearth because the cabin felt warm. She tried to make out what the men were saying but couldn't decipher their words. She must have dozed off again. When she awoke, the babe was stirring in her arms. This time he nourished himself at her breast and then went back to sleep. She no longer heard the men's voices. Pina still slept on at her feet.

She wished she had Maria's rosary to hang on to as she recited the memorized prayers of her childhood. After saying the prayers for a spell, holding her son, she settled into silence. Jedediah had been teaching her and Pina that they could pray just by sharing their hopes and fears with their heavenly Father in their own words. When she was desperate, Isabella had always done this, but most of the time, when she wasn't desperate, she prayed her memorized prayers.

Tonight, she was desperate for Dios to hear her. *Please don't let Peter leave. Please help him accept the babe. Please don't let him stop loving me.* Her throat closed tight, and she stopped praying. It hurt too much to pray. She lay there a while, just staring at the oil lamp. It never wavered in its steady light. A warmth began to spread from the light. It came to her, bringing a warmth and peace she'd never known. The light became brighter. And brighter.

I will love you. I will never leave you. I accept the babe.

Could that really be Dios whispering to her? The oil lamp brightened until a swirling white light filled the room. The light was so beautiful. So warm and peaceful, but Isabella didn't feel worthy enough to look at the light. Every bad thing she'd ever done came back to her in an instant. She looked down at Pina, but her sister slept on. The babe slept too. She was the only one awake with the warm white light engulfing her.

Ask for forgiveness.

The thought was so gentle.

Forgive me, Father.

You are forgiven.

In that instant, Isabella knew with every fiber of her being she had a heavenly Father. She felt His love envelope her. The swirling white light surrounded the bed. She realized she didn't need anyone else to love her. God loved her. She knew her heavenly Father loved her because Jesus loved her. Jesus died for her. She began to weep in gratitude. She closed her eyes and suddenly felt sleepy.

When she awoke again, the light was gone. The oil lamp burned, putting off it's normal golden light. Had she dreamed the swirling white light? The warm, peaceful encounter with her heavenly Father? If she had, the peace it brought hadn't left her. She still felt sure of her heavenly Father's love. It erased every need she had for an earthly father's love. God's love was enough. Somehow the Holy Spirit had been in her room whether she dreamed it or not. If Peter didn't return, she would be all right. She would miss him, but she would make it. She would raise her son, and hopefully Jedediah would teach him to be a man like Peter.

She realized she no longer hurt over Peter leaving her that first time. Over his indiscretions with Clara. Or his youthful love for Maggie. All of it had just faded away in the presence of the dazzling white light. She also realized she was no longer angry at herself for bearing Paul's son. For giving herself to Paul as a way to survive at Clara's. Jesus had died for all her sins and mistakes. She was forgiven so she could forgive herself.

Chapter Thirty-Four

After spending several hours with Jedediah, Peter slept in the barn. Perhaps it was his way of punishing himself by spending a cold, miserable night with the animals. If it weren't for the two collies curled up on each side of him in the straw, his night would have been a whole lot colder. He knew he should return to Isabella and beg her forgiveness, but he just couldn't bring himself to do it. He'd been so certain God had answered his prayers, convinced when he saw the Brondi cleft in the babe's chin that the big, fine boy was his. After talking with Jedediah, he realized he'd been so convinced because he'd convinced himself long ago that Paul wasn't really his brother. That was the root of his sin. He hated his brother.

At dawn, he walked out of the barn and stared at the sunrise. He knew what he had to do. Red sky at morning, sailors take warning. The sky was filled with red clouds lined with golden splendor. It was a spectacular sunrise that gave him pause. He should pray, but he didn't. Jedediah had prayed enough for both of them last night. Peter was happy for his father. After all these years of loving Paul regardless of his parentage, regardless of Paul's rebellion and rejection of Jedediah's love, Jedediah could now go to his grave knowing Paul was truly his son.

But that wasn't enough. Paul needed to know Jedediah was his father. The last thing he wanted was for Jedediah to die without reconciling with Paul. And he was jealous of his father's love for Paul. Had always been jealous of that love. Peter had wept last night admitting that to Jedediah, "For a long time, I thought you loved that dirty little Indian boy more than me."

His father had smiled. "I thought I taught you not to call your brother a dirty little Indian boy."

"Well, he's no longer a dirty little Indian boy. He's the father of Isabella's son. What do I do with that?"

"You forgive your brother."

"I don't know if I can," Peter had admitted. A part of him wanted to forgive Paul. The other part of him was filled with hate and envy and heartache. Paul had the most beautiful baby boy he'd ever seen. The boy was a Brondi through and through. Would he have to give up Isabella now? Did she and the babe belong to Paul?

Maybe Paul deserved the cabin he'd helped Jedediah build. Maybe Paul was supposed to be the shepherd. Perhaps Paul was to build a life with Isabella, and maybe Peter's fate was a lifetime of chasing the wind.

The thought arrowed through his heart, ripping it apart. He didn't have the courage to face Isabella to say good-bye. He'd gone from a man who'd once feared nothing to a man who feared everything. That was the beauty of having nothing. There was no fear of losing it. Now that he had it all, he was losing it all, and he ached so badly he found it hard to keep breathing.

He was saddling Mel when Jedediah walked into the barn.

"You need to go see your wife," Jedediah said. "That was a hard birth. She needs your love to strengthen her."

"I don't have any love to give her." Peter felt empty and broken.

"You're looking at yourself and all you see is loss. You need to look at the Good Lord and see your gain."

"The Lord didn't give me a son. He gave Paul a son. I've gained nothing."

"You've gained a brother."

Peter led Mel from the barn.

Jedediah followed him. "You need to let go of your pride and go love your wife. And then go love your brother."

"I don't know if I can do that."

"Why do you envy Paul? You always have." Jedediah trailed after Peter, but he didn't want to listen. He just wanted to leave.

Outside the barn, he rounded on his father. "You were a mean drunk when I was a boy. I remember you beating me. Reeking of whiskey and beating me until I couldn't see straight. That's what I remember about you. When Paul came along, you threw out that bottle and became a good pa. It was all about taking care of that little Indian boy. What about me?"

"Everything I have is yours. It's always been yours, Peter." Jedediah tried to put his hand on Peter's shoulder.

Peter shrugged him off. "Paul's going to end up with everything. I hope that makes you happy, Jedediah." He looped the reins over the saddlehorn and swung up on Mel.

"Paul only ends up with it all if you leave and let him have it."

"How can I stay?" Peter looked over at the cabin. "Everything I love is in that cabin. And it's not mine anymore."

"That's the lesson God has for you," said Jedediah.

Peter's brow furrowed. "What lesson?"

"You think on it a while." Jedediah handed him a small sack he'd been holding. "I figure you're hungry. Brought you some food for the ride."

Peter took the sack and tied it to his saddle. Yesterday was a blur. He couldn't remember the last time he'd eaten. "Thank you. Good luck with the sheep."

"I don't believe in luck." Jedediah's gaze pierced him.

Peter nodded a farewell to his father. He turned Mel around and urged her into a gallop. He no longer believed in luck either. He knew God controlled everything and had given Isabella and the babe to Paul. He'd been hoping and praying for a life with her and the babe when God was orchestrating something else. Something mighty fine for Paul.

What was the lesson Jedediah spoke of?

The old envy rose up in him stronger than ever. Paul always was the lucky one. Now that he knew the truth, he realized it was never about luck. Just like Jedediah, God favored Paul. And that just wasn't fair. Paul hadn't done a thing to earn God's love.

What had he done to earn God's love?

Could God's love even be earned?

He rode for hours, higher into the hills, pondering God's love. Oak trees gave way to ponderosa pines. The air grew colder. He came to the realization that there was no earning God's love. He couldn't make sense of God's love. God's love was something far beyond him.

• • •

Mick shoveled dirt and water into the box, splashing grit into Paul's eyes as he rocked the cradle. "You think it's yours or Peter's bastard?" Since Mick had seen Isabella with Peter at Jedediah's cabin, he'd been needling Paul about her.

"I think we should dig a new hole." Paul wasn't about to discuss Isabella and Peter with Mick.

"This dirt's still paying." Mick slopped more water onto the dirt, splashing Paul's face. "I never thought I'd see the day when your brother took up with a squaw." Mick laughed.

"I say we find a new hole. This one's played out." Paul didn't want to think about Belle and Peter. It was too painful. When Mick told him they were living at Jedediah's cabin together and that Belle expecting a child, he was shocked. He'd spent the winter trying not to waste his gold. Most of it he kept buried in the cave along the river. He'd even taken a job in a mercantile in Sacramento City, working for an old shopkeeper who needed help stocking shelves and lifting heavy supplies. At least it granted him a free place to sleep until the snow melted in the goldfields and he could meet up with Mick again. He didn't make much at the mercantile, but he didn't spend much either, except on whiskey and sometimes a dove on his days off when he visited the saloons along the waterfront. He missed Belle and had thought about returning to Marysville, hoping to find she'd returned there. But he knew he'd done Peter wrong. Why couldn't he stay away from Peter's women?

By March, in the wake of heavy rains, the Sacramento waterfront flooded, along with the mercantile. Paul made it to Sutter's Fort, purchased a horse, and headed up to Marysville just to see if Belle might be there. The growth of the city astonished him. In less than a year, ten times the number of dwellings had sprung up. Most of the tents were gone, replaced by brick and wooden buildings. Horse-drawn carriages cruised the streets, and the bonnets had arrived on the wooden sidewalks. Seeing women in bonnets reminded him of Maggie.

He stopped at Clara's in search of Belle. Clara was all smiles. That was the thing about Clara, she never held a grudge. She was happy to serve him her finest whiskey and provide a dove for the evening. Clara had a new singer, but she wasn't near as pretty or talented as Belle. The men didn't seem to mind. Gents packed the place, cheered on the singer, and the mood was lively. Clara said Belle had never returned. "Good riddance," said Clara. "That Creole was more trouble than she was worth."

Disappointed Belle was gone, the next day he gathered supplies and purchased a pack horse to return to the diggings. He figured he'd run into snow but could ride out the rest of the winter in Nevada City, where he and Mick had agreed to meet on the first Sabbath in April.

May was upon them now. They'd had a pretty good run the previous summer. Paul finally had a big wooden box of gold buried in his cave, but the ground was finally playing out. Mick wasn't ready to give up on the old Californio's claim yet. "Look at the clay we've found today," Mick said.

"We ran into clay yesterday, and it didn't pay." Paul stopped rocking the cradle and rose up off his knees, stretching his aching back and legs.

Mick leaned on his shovel for a rest. "I had a woman read my palm in San Francisco. She predicted I'd come into real riches this year."

Paul walked up out of the shady creek bed and sat on a bank in the bright sunshine, listening to the creek sing on by. Once upon a time, he'd loved singing creeks. Now all he saw was work when he looked at a pretty creek. Gold digging was backbreaking labor. He was tired of it. "God don't like palm reading," he told Mick.

Mick left his shovel standing up in the mud beside the cradle. "Do you think I care what God likes? God never helped me. My pappy was a preacher. I couldn't wait to get out of St. Louie and away from him." Mick sat down beside Paul on the bank.

"How do you know God hasn't helped you?" More of late, Paul had been thinking about God. He recalled his brief days with Maggie. Her faith had been so inspiring. He'd even tried to embrace religion for himself. Putting his trust in Jesus until Maggie and his son died on the trail. Standing at her grave, he'd turned his back on God.

"My pappy always said God helps the helpless. I ain't helpless." Mick pulled out his silver flask. He'd been drinking out of it since he'd taken it off the Chilean he'd murdered in the fall.

"Well, we've about dug up this whole creek bed. I think we've found all the gold there is to find here."

"We'll find more," said Mick. "I know it. The palm reader told me so." He guzzled from his flask.

Paul caught a glimpse of a rider coming up the ravine. The man didn't look like an Indian, but he rode a fine Indian pony. He was dressed in buckskins, and his brown hair flashed golden under the glare of the sun. The way he sat in his saddle, Paul knew he was a man of importance. A strange feeling of foreboding hit Paul.

"Well, I'll be . . ." Mick lowered his flask and let out a curse. "Your brother's come to see us."

Paul jumped to his feet, and so did Mick.

Peter crossed the creek and rode right up to them. "Howdy, boys."

Mick put his hand to his gun. "Don't howdy me. The last time I seen you, you weren't hospitable."

"Well, I'm hospitable today." Peter nodded to Paul. "It's good to see you, Paul."

Paul realized his hands were shaking. He shoved them in his pockets. "Hello, Peter."

Peter smiled, but Paul wasn't sure if it was a real smile. "I came to get you. It's time you made amends with Jedediah."

"Just like that?" Paul tried to sound like he didn't care, but the thought of seeing Jedediah again and being forgiven by his father and Peter filled him with hope. He couldn't wait to be done with Mick and on to something else. Perhaps on to forgiveness with the only men who'd ever meant anything to him, Jedediah and Peter.

Chapter Thirty-Five

The babe didn't have a name. Isabella just couldn't bear to name him without Peter. The infant ate and slept most of the time. She did the same. Pina took good care of them both. Jedediah grazed the sheep close to the cabin. Spring rains interspersed with sunny days kept the grass growing fast and tall. The meadow was lush for the ewes and their lambs. With Pina always after him to eat, Jedediah had gained weight too. He seemed healthier than when they'd arrived in autumn.

Pina was now speaking a little. Only a word or two here and there, but each time she heard her sister's sweet voice, Isabella thanked God for Pina's healing. Since the night of the babe's birth, when she'd seen the swirling white light, Isabella felt close to God. She prayed night and day, asking for his hand on everyone she loved, especially Peter.

Walking over to the bedroom window with the babe upon her shoulder, she could see sunset approaching. Still sore from the birth, she moved slowly across the room. The sky glowed with waning light. She heard the collies barking. What had upset them? They never barked at the sheep, just nipped silently at the sheep's hind legs to move them to the barn or out into the fields.

Across the pasture, two riders approached. Excitement filled her when she recognized Peter's painted horse. She didn't know the other man wearing a hat pulled low on his head, but Peter on Mel she couldn't mistake. She whispered a prayer that God would restore them. More than anything she wanted to return to the way they'd been before the babe arrived. Living as husband and wife in a state of bliss. Walking gingerly to the living room, she sat down in the rocking chair beside the fire. Peter had crafted this rocker with his own two hands. Pina kept the cabin warm feeding the fire. The babe dozed in her arms. Why had Peter brought a stranger to the cabin?

She didn't wonder for long. The cabin door opened, and Jedediah walked in, followed by Peter and the other man. Her heart stopped when he removed his hat. Paul. He'd lost weight and looked thin and unkept, but there was no mistaking him. Her gaze flew to Peter. His eyes were unreadable. He didn't smile.

"Good to see you, Belle," Paul said quietly. He wasn't his charming self. He didn't smile either.

Her heart thudded, but she managed to return Paul's welcome. Pina came from the kitchen, her blue eyes wide with wariness on Paul.

Jedediah came to Isabella. "May I hold my grandson?"

Isabella handed him the babe with trembling hands.

Jedediah walked over to Peter and Paul. They stood side by side, their faces somber.

Jedediah showed them the child. "He's a fine young'un. God's gift to this family. We are a family. We're all Brondis here."

Isabella's heart pounded harder. She couldn't take her eyes off of Peter. He wouldn't look at her. Neither would Paul. They both stared at the babe.

"This child needs a father." Jedediah tucked the babe against his chest.

"The babe's a Brondi," said Paul. "No doubt about that. Look at the cleft in his chin." Isabella could hear the sorrow in his voice.

"You sure about that, Paul?" Jedediah showed him the babe once more.

Paul leaned over the child. "No mistaking it." He stepped back and put his hand on Peter's shoulder. "Congratulations, you got a fine son. He looks just like Jedediah." Paul gritted out a laugh.

Isabella could see Paul was hurting. Why hadn't they told him the babe was his?

Peter stepped away from Paul. He looked at Isabella and then back at his father. "You going to tell Paul, or do I have to do it?"

"Tell me what?" Paul glanced between Jedediah and Peter.

"He's your son." Peter was hurting too. The brothers both looked broken. Isabella ached for all of them.

Paul turned to her.

A tear ran down Isabella's face.

"Is it true?" he asked. His voice trembled.

She nodded, causing more tears to streak her cheeks.

Paul turned back to the babe. "May I hold him?" He held out his arms.

Jedediah placed the babe in Paul's grasp. The child awoke and began to whimper. Paul looked into the child's blue eyes beneath those hawkish Brondi brows. The babe had black hair like him, but his cleft was as deep as Jedediah's.

"He looks like you." Paul looked up at Jedediah and then studied the babe more intently.

"Welcome home, son," Jedediah said.

Paul seemed to be in shock. He tucked the child to his chest. His shoulders began to shake. Soon he was weeping over the child.

Peter left the cabin.

Isabella rose up to go after him.

Pina caught her at the door. Shaking her head.

"Please let me go," Isabella cried. "I have to see Peter."

Pina stepped aside but followed Isabella out into the sunset. Red spilled across the sky. Geese migrated overhead. Isabella barely noticed the birds or the beautiful sunset.

Peter strode to the barn. He didn't turn around when she called his name.

Pina ran after Peter and grabbed the fringe of his buckskin jacket, yanking hard.

He turned around. "Leave me alone, Pina."

"No!" Her rebuke came out clear and firm and shocking.

The sound of her voice froze Peter.

Isabella ignored the pain in her body to reach them. She'd hurt so badly since bearing the babe, but her heart was hurting more.

Pina released Peter's jacket and stepped out of Isabella's way.

"Please, you promised not to leave me ever again," said Isabella.

"Paul deserves a father. The babe deserves a father. What do you want me to do?" Peter rasped. His eyes mirrored her pain.

"I want you to stay." She reached out and grabbed his buckskin jacket with both hands, pressing her body against his. "You are my husband. You promised never to leave me again." Tears clogged her throat. She couldn't bear the thought of losing him.

He wrapped his arms around her, burying his face against her hair. She realized Peter was crying.

"God will help us," she said on a sob of her own. "I know our heavenly Father will help us."

Peter's shoulders shook. They wept in each other's arms. After a few minutes, Peter scooped her up and carried her back inside the cabin. Pina was waiting to open the door for them. He strode past Jedediah and Paul, still holding the babe, and took Isabella to their bedroom. Pina followed them and opened that door too. Then she closed the bedroom door behind them.

It was just Peter and Isabella. He gently set her feet on the floor. His cheeks were wet with tears. "I want to do right by you and the babe. Tell me what to do." His eyes raked her face.

"You're my husband. Don't ever leave me." She wrapped her arms around his neck and pulled his head down so she could kiss him. She tasted the salt of their mingling tears. Peter returned her passionate kiss. He pressed his hands to her cheeks, pulling away so he could look into her eyes.

"Paul will want his son."

An ache grew in Isabella's chest. "I know."

"I don't know how this is going to work."

"The Lord knows."

Peter finally smiled. "When did you get so certain about the Lord?"

"I saw the light."

He laughed.

When she didn't laugh, his smile slowly disappeared.

"I met the Lord. Maybe I dreamed it, but I saw the light. I know it's all going to work out just fine."

"I'm glad you know that." Peter turned from her and walked over to the window. "Where's Paul going?"

Isabella joined him at the window in time to see Paul headed for the barn.

"I've got to go talk to my brother."

"Yes, go," Isabella urged.

The babe began to wail in the living room. Isabella swung around. Peter followed her out of the bedroom. She took the babe from Jedediah as Peter headed for the door.

"I think you should let Paul go," Jedediah said to Peter. "He'll be back when he's ready."

Peter took one look at his father and walked out the door.

Chapter Thirty-Six

Paul had cried on his father's shoulder like a little boy. The relief he felt knowing Jedediah was truly his father knew no bounds. He had a father and he had a son, and he thanked the Good Lord for both. He'd asked Jedediah's forgiveness for all the wasted years between them.

Jedediah just kept saying, "Welcome home, son."

Welcome home.

He wasn't sure how that would all play out, but he knew he had a home now even if he couldn't live there. One look at Belle's face and he saw she loved Peter. Everyone called her Isabella. All this time and he hadn't even known her real name. That filled him with shame. She'd borne him a fine son that looked like Jedediah. For that, he would be forever grateful, but Belle belonged to Peter, had always belonged to Peter.

Paul didn't allow Peter to persuade him from saddling his horse. "I made my peace with Jedediah," he said in the barn when Peter found him. "It's best for you and Belle that I go."

"You haven't made your peace with me." Peter sounded determined.

Paul tightened the cinch on his saddle and then turned to face his brother. "Do you want to make peace?"

Peter came at him, and Paul braced himself for a fistfight. He didn't want to fight, but he wasn't gonna let Peter kill him. He raised his fists, but Peter plowed right past his defenses and hugged him tight. "I have a brother."

Paul could hear the joy and tears in Peter's voice.

Paul began to laugh. Then he cried. Then he laughed some more as Peter squeezed the breath out of him.

The two stood there a good long time just holding each other. Neither spoke. There was nothing to say. Paul finally pulled away. "I best get going. I don't like riding in the dark. You know I'm afraid of wolves."

Peter nodded, wiping his face. Paul had never seen Peter cry, even over Maggie.

Paul could tell his big brother had changed. There was love in Peter's eyes. Seeing that love about undid him. He led his horse from the barn. Peter followed him. "You tell Belle I said good-bye. You got a fine family. Take care of my boy. He don't need to know you ain't his pa. Knowing he's a Brondi is good enough."

"When he's older, I'll tell him you're his pa," Peter said.

Paul mounted his horse. "I thank you for that." Paul could barely talk. His throat burned with tears, and his chest ached. He had a father. A brother. And a son. It was the happiest day of his life.

Peter nodded, and Paul nodded in return. There was no better man than Peter to raise his son. He knew with all his heart that leaving was the right thing to do. He pressed his boots to the sides of his horse and sent the gelding on his way.

When he looked back, Peter waved to him. Paul waved in return and then urged his horse into a gallop. He'd said good-bye to Jedediah already, promising to return the following spring for a visit.

"I may not be here," Jedediah had said. "You better make your peace with God if you want to guarantee seeing me again."

Paul had forced a laugh. "You better be here next spring. My boy needs a grandpa."

Jedediah had said he'd talk it over with the Good Lord.

"Put in a special word for me with the Lord," Paul had said before he left.

He rode hard until he reached Nevada City. The moon was full, and he had no problem getting there. He spent the night at Bicknell's Block. The new brick hotel wasn't cheap, but the gold he spent didn't matter. There was plenty stored up at his cave, and he'd be there tomorrow to collect it. Where he'd go after that, he didn't know. To his surprise, he slept hard and awoke the next morning in a hurry to move on.

A sunny afternoon was upon him when he reached his cave. As he crossed the wide, shallow creek, he couldn't believe fate would have it that Mick was there waiting at his cave. Mick's horse was tied to a tree. Mick was just sitting there on the bank like he was enjoying the sunshine.

"You came just in time. Now we can divide up the gold and go our separate ways."

"What gold?" said Paul. If Mick knew where his gold was, he wouldn't be sitting here waiting. Mick would be long gone already—with his gold. Paul reached down and cocked his pistol.

Mick laughed. "I followed you the last time, but you didn't know it. You been taking more than your share. Let's even up the gold, and I'll be on my way."

Paul cautiously got down from his horse.

Mick stood up, his hand on his own gun. "Take your hand off your pistol, Paul. You're no match for my draw, and I don't want to kill you."

"Until you find my gold," said Paul. "Then you'll kill me."

"No, I ain't gonna kill you. I just want to even up and be on my way."

"We did that already at the cabin. We've been even since last year. I took my fair share; that was all I took."

"I don't see it that way," said Mick. "I brought my gold. You go dig your gold out of that cave, and we'll trade what we have."

Anger boiled over in Paul. "I ain't trading with you. I spent all winter working in Sacramento City for some old man who treated me like his dog. You went to San Francisco and lived high on the hog. That's why I got more gold than you."

Mick put his hands on both his guns.

Paul only had one gun. He knew he didn't stand a chance against Mick. His mind whirled with what to do. He took his hand off his pistol.

"That's the Paul I know. Let's just be friendly, and we'll get along fine." Mick eased his hands off his guns.

Paul turned around and headed toward the cave. Mick followed. When Paul reached the entrance to the cave, he grabbed hold of his pistol and spun around. With the hammer still cocked, the gun fired before Paul could pull it clear of his holster. The bullet tore through his thigh and blew out the other side. Paul buckled to the ground.

Mick let out a string of curses.

Paul rolled in agony at the entrance of the cave.

"Why did you do that?" Mick growled. "Instead of killing me, you about killed yourself."

It took several minutes for Paul's mind to clear enough to understand what Mick was saying. "Show me where you buried the gold. I'll dig it up quick, and we'll get you to a doctor."

"I don't believe you." Paul's leg was on fire. He'd never felt such pain in his life.

"You don't have much time. Show me where it's buried." Mick reached down and pulled Paul to his feet.

Paul groaned and allowed Mick to drag him into the cave. His only chance was relying on Mick. He figured Mick might kill him once he showed him where his gold was, but if he refused to show the gold, he was certain Mick would let him bleed to death. "Tie my leg off, then I'll show you where it's buried."

Mick took off Paul's belt. He grabbed Paul's gun and fired at the cave wall till it was empty. He tucked it into his own gun belt, then he used Paul's belt to tourniquet his leg above where the bullet had entered his thigh.

Paul cried out in pain.

"I still don't believe you're a Brondi," said Mick.

"Well . . . believe it," Paul gritted out. "I'm a Brondi."

Mick looked at him. "Something change your mind?"

"I got me a . . . son," Paul growled.

"Well, congratulations." Mick pulled Paul back onto his feet. "Where's the gold?"

Paul pointed to the base of the boulder. Each time he'd come here, he'd dug all around the cave, disturbing all the dirt so a man couldn't tell he'd dug under the boulder. He'd packed down all the dirt so a man couldn't see the difference.

Mick eased him to the ground and walked out of the cave. He returned with a shovel and quickly set to digging. It wasn't long before he'd unearthed Paul's box.

"Let's get going," said Paul. He could feel the blood still trickling out of the wounds on his leg, but it no longer spurted freely, so that was good. Nevada City wasn't that far away. "I saw a doc's office at Bicknell Block. Take me there."

"We're going to Marysville." Mick walked past Paul, carrying the shovel and box of gold.

"I won't make it all the way to Marysville." A sense of doom came over Paul.

"Yes, you will. Peter made it a lot farther when he was shot, and he was worse off than you. You'll make it."

"Take me to Nevada City, or I ain't sharing my gold."

Mick's laughter filled the cave. He just kept on walking.

Paul tried to stand up but fell back to the ground. If Mick took the horses, he was done for. He struggled to his feet, yelling for Mick as he hopped out of the cave on his good leg. He about lost his britches without his belt.

Mick was strapping the box of gold to his horse. He finished what he was doing before he turned around. "You're enough to please the devil." He grinned at Paul.

Paul grabbed his pants, yanking them up as he fell to the ground. He cursed Mick from there.

"You better start talking sweet if you want to ride to Marysville with me."

"I ain't riding to . . . Marysville." Paul gritted out. "It's too far. That will kill me."

"I seen lesser men than a Brondi go farther with a gunshot worse than yours," said Mick.

"Split the gold here. Give me my gun . . . and my horse."

"We go together or you don't go," said Mick.

"I ain't going to Marysville." Paul tried to get up.

Mick untied Paul's horse.

Paul thought he was going to abandon him, but Mick led the gelding over. "You don't get the gold or your gun until we get to Marysville." Mick hefted Paul up onto the saddle.

Paul cried out in pain, grabbing the saddlehorn and holding on with all the strength he had left in him.

Mick put the reins in his hand. "You can follow me to Marysville or head for Nevada City on your own. If it wasn't for Jedediah, I'd kill you for trying to kill me."

"I wasn't trying to kill you. Just stop you from taking my gold. Why Jedediah?"

"I hated my own pa. Jedediah always treated me like a son. So I'm paying Jedediah back by giving him back his son. You said you're really a Brondi, so I'm letting you live."

"Give me half the gold." Paul wrapped his hands around the reins.

Mick walked to his horse and pulled a substantial pouch from his saddlebags. He returned to Paul, tucking the heavy pouch in Paul's saddlebags. "You come and get the rest of your share when you heal up."

"Where you gonna be?"

"I'm making my way to San Francisco. Met me a woman there this past winter that turned my head. Gonna buy her a dancing dress." Mick slapped Paul's gelding on the hind end.

When the horse bolted, Paul nearly lost his seat in the saddle. By the time he gained control, his mount had plowed back across the creek and was following the trail to Nevada City.

Paul grew dizzy and weak from blood loss very quickly. A thirst for water overwhelmed his pain. He stopped his horse and tightened the belt on his leg. After drinkling from his bota, he urged the gelding on. Somewhere on the ride, he began to earnestly pray. As it grew darker, he realized he'd never make Nevada City tonight, but maybe he could make it to Peter and Jedediah's. The cabin was closer than the city. Jedediah was good as any doctor, and he knew the bullet was already out of his leg. All he needed was to stop the bleeding and time to heal.

He clung to the horse and did his best to find his way back to the cabin in the dead of night. Fortunately, there was a lot of moon left. He could see his way pretty good. The hours blurred together. Sometimes he knew he was riding, and other times he blacked out. He drank all his water way too soon. Thirst began to drive him half-mad.

Please, Lord, spare me. It became his endless prayer. *Let me see my son again. Let me see my father. Let me see my brother. Please, Lord, let me live. Please spare me.*

When he hit the ground, it jarred Paul awake. His horse trotted off. He was alone in a dark meadow. He lay there for a while, staring up at the stars. *I'm sorry for all I've done. Let me live and I'll give you my life. I'll change my ways. I promise I will, Lord.*

The stars seemed brighter than ever as Paul lay on his back staring up at them. The night was clear and cold, but not cold enough to freeze him. Thank the Lord for springtime.

For a while, he slept in the soft, sweet-smelling grass of the meadow. He dreamed of his son, with the fine Brondi cleft in his chin. Then he dreamed of his other dark-haired boy that he'd buried along with Maggie on the way to California. Had that baby boy been born with the Brondi cleft, it would have saved Paul from wasting the last five years. He would have known he was Jedediah's son and not ridden away thinking that outlaw was his father. There still would have been the bitterness between him and Peter over Maggie, but Paul knew God would have healed that sooner or later.

He awoke knowing God was real. God was good. And God was there with him in the meadow. He didn't know how he knew, but he knew.

"I want to see my father and brother one more time," he said out loud, feeling more peaceful than he'd ever felt in his life. The morning sun was rising, the meadow filling with golden light. Paul heard bells.

He rose up on his elbow and saw a herd of sheep coming down the hill. They followed two goats that had bells around their necks. He lay back down and passed out again. He awoke to a barking dog and realized he was surrounded by grazing sheep. Another dog appeared beside him and joined in the barking.

Jedediah's collies.

He tried to sit up, but he was too weak. *Thank you, Lord, I made it home.*

Paul drifted off to sleep and awoke in Jedediah's arms.

"I'm here, son. I've got you." Jedediah cradled Paul against his chest. He was clasped in Jedediah's arms but couldn't see his father's face. "I need to get you up on this old mule," his father said. Jedediah's voice comforted him.

"Thank you, Pa." Paul hoped he spoke loud enough for Jedediah to hear him call him "Pa."

Jedediah was lifting him up, but suddenly he stopped, gasping for breath. Jedediah fell back against the mule. Paul fell too. The mule brayed and stepped away from them.

He could hear Jedediah gasping for breath.

"Pa? Are you all right?"

"Just . . . give . . . me a moment." Jedediah struggled to speak. "I got a . . . mighty sharp . . pain."

Paul struggled to stay conscious. Jedediah's arms relaxed around him. "Jesus!" he called. Suddenly, he knew the Lord was there. He saw Jedediah standing with Jesus. Jedediah was smiling. The meadow filled with warm white light. He heard bells in the distance. His pain was gone. Immeasurable joy filled him.

Chapter Thirty-Seven

Peter spent the morning working on the cabin. The babe would need his own room when he grew older. He prayed the Lord would see fit to give them more children. And now that Pina was becoming a normal girl, perhaps she'd want her own chambers downstairs. He was grateful Jedediah was strong enough to take the sheep out to pasture today so he could start building onto the cabin. He'd always had a knack for carpentry and enjoyed the process of working with wood. He realized how happy he felt and thanked God for his many blessings.

His father was happy too. Jedediah had found new strength to shepherd the herd farther afield. He figured Paul would return eventually. He was just grateful his brother was allowing him to be the babe's father and Isabella's husband. They hadn't named the babe yet. Isabella said she wanted him to name the child, and he was leaning toward calling the boy Jed, after Jedediah. That's who the babe really looked like, though his black hair took after Isabella's and Paul's Indian hair.

Holding Isabella in his arms last night, together in their bed while the babe slept in his cradle, was all Peter needed in the world. Just knowing Paul hadn't come between them was enough. And making peace with his brother had healed something in Peter he hadn't thought could ever be healed.

The spring morning was full of birdsong, just like Peter's heart. As the day wore on, a surprisingly warm wind began to blow. Peter warmed up quickly as he split some logs. The warm wind felt so good he removed his buckskin shirt.

Isabella came out onto the porch, holding the babe. When she saw him bare-chested, she stopped and stared at him.

"Am I indecent?" he asked with a grin. The sun felt so good after the cold days of winter. He just wanted to soak it in for a while and let that warm breeze caress his skin.

"You're a beautiful creature," Isabella said as she came to him, giving him a smile. "I thought that the first time I saw you, riding into Marysville."

"I didn't ride into Marysville without my shirt on." He put the hatchet down and reached for the babe.

She handed him the boy, and he pressed the swaddled infant to his chest and leaned back against the log that was propped up on two sawhorses he'd built for his carpentry. "It's a mighty fine day."

"You're a mighty fine man." She made herself comfortable beside him on the log. "Did you decide on a name yet?"

Peter sighed in pleasure. "I think Jed would fit the boy well."

"I like Jed." Isabella smiled.

He leaned over and kissed her lightly on the lips.

She leaned in, and he kissed her some more, not so lightly. Passion flamed inside of Peter. He couldn't wait until she healed up from the birth. He missed becoming one flesh with her. It wasn't just physical satisfaction he gained from his wife. A deep spiritual and emotional connection came from joining his body with hers. Perhaps this was the mystery of a man leaving his father and mother and joining himself to a wife, though he hadn't left Jedediah.

He chuckled at the thought. He'd never dreamed he'd settle down with Jedediah and a wife and a little Indian sister that hunted better than he did. If Carson and Fremont could see him now, being fed by Pina when he was once the best hunter in the camp, they would laugh at him. He left most of the hunting to Pina now. He'd taught her how to use his rifle, but she preferred capturing rabbits, quail, and other birds her way. Just yesterday she'd brought in a big tom. Rocks were Pina's weapon of choice, and she could call turkeys right up to her in the bushes where she waited with her pile of stones. Maybe Pina would never be a normal girl. He laughed. He didn't mind. He'd never have to hunt again.

"What's so funny?" Isabella's eyes were soft and full of love. The babe slept peacefully on his shoulder. The warm wind caressed his face.

"My family."

"Why is your family funny?"

"I never thought I'd live with Jedediah, letting him tell me what to do. And I don't hunt anymore. Your sister's a better hunter than I am."

"That's not true. You bring in the venison."

"Not very often. I'm kind of getting used to rabbit."

Isabella wrinkled her nose. "Do you think Pina will ever marry?"

"If she grows up to look like you, and hunts better than me, what man wouldn't marry her?"

Isabella laughed.

"I want to have your child," she said, no longer laughing.

He touched her cheek. "I pray you bear me a passel of young'uns, so I best get back to work." Looking beyond Isabella, Peter noticed a black gelding grazing down near the creek. The animal still had a saddle on. His instincts kicked in. Something was wrong. He handed the babe back to Isabella. "Take the baby into the house. Bolt the door behind you. Don't open it till I return."

"What's wrong?" Isabella's eyes filled with fear. She cradled the sleeping babe.

"I don't know. I think that's Paul's gelding." Peter threw on his shirt and grabbed his rifle from the ground.

"Please be careful."

"I will. Go into the house," Peter said calmly. "Make sure Pina's there too." He didn't want to frighten her more than he already had.

He stood guard until Isabella was inside the cabin, then he slowly walked out to capture the gelding. When he got close enough, he could see one side of the horse and saddle were smeared with blood. His heart constricted. He hoped Paul was all right.

He looked all around but didn't see or sense any danger. The gelding seemed happy to be caught. The horse was dragging his reins, and one leather strap was broken. Peter quickly took Paul's gelding to the barn. He removed the bridle and saddle and turned the horse out in a corral. Then he saddled Mel.

He followed the gelding's trail to the sheep meadow. When he arrived, the collies began to bark. The mules acted disturbed, and the sheep mostly milled instead of grazed. He cocked his rifle in his lap. The day was so fair, the meadow so pretty, it didn't seem possible danger was here. But he remembered riding up on Will's family in their meadow, and his heart began to thud in his chest. He began to pray.

The sheep had formed a circle in the meadow. The collies stopped barking and kept the sheep clustered together. The mules stood guard, and the Mexican sheepdogs were on high alert, standing a ways off with their hair raised on their backs in warning. He guided Mel slowly through the sheep until he saw the two bodies. Right off, he recognized Jedediah. It took a minute to realize the other man lying there was Paul.

Taking up his rifle, he sprang down from Mel, scattering the sheep. The collies went to work, rounding the sheep back up. "Easy, girls," he spoke to the ewes. He'd seen dead men before. He knew Jedediah and Paul were gone. "God help me," he breathed, falling to his knees beside his father and brother.

Out of nowhere, that warm wind he'd enjoyed so much at the cabin hit him. It hadn't been blowing in the meadow when he arrived, but he felt it now. On his face. Rustling through his hair. Hitting his mouth. He opened his lips and felt the Spirit of God rush through him. The Lord's peace had arrived on the wind. Jedediah still had his arms around Paul. Blood soaked Paul's leg and hands and arms. He reached out and loosened the belt on Paul's thigh. Upon examining Paul's empty holster, Peter realized the bullet had torn through the holster and entered Paul's leg. Peter had seen this before. Men drew too quickly and shot themselves instead of shooting their enemy.

"Paul . . ." He took a deep breath. Again, he could swear that warm wind was the breath of God on his face.

Paul had accidently shot himself, but what had killed Jedediah?

He studied his father there on the grass but saw nothing out of the ordinary. Jedediah's eyes were closed, and a peaceful look was on his face. Paul's face was peaceful too. The two looked like they were sleeping in the meadow. The sheep bleated, but he hardly noticed.

He needed to get his father and brother home.

They are home.

The whisper came on the wind and comforted him. He recognized it wasn't from his own thought. It was the voice of the Good Shepherd. He felt like a sheep.

Rising to his feet, he looked around. Mel waited close by, like she always did for him. He never had to tie her up. She wouldn't leave him. He went to Mel and untied a rope from his saddle, and then he found the old mule with blood on its side. Jedediah must have tried to put Paul on the mule. He took another deep breath. Swallowing down more unexplainable peace.

Fixing a halter out of the rope, he put it on the old mule and led the animal over to Mel. He tied the mule to her and retrieved Paul's body. Paul was no longer was bleeding. He'd bled out there in the meadow.

He carried Paul in his arms, remembering how he'd carried the dirty little Indian boy—his brother. "You turned into a fine man," he told Paul. "You got Brondi bones. You're big and strong now." A tear ran down Peter's face. "I've decided to name your son, Paul Jedediah Brondi. What do you think about that? I think it's a fine name."

Gentle as he could be, he draped Paul over the mule. The old mule didn't move. He went to Mel, got another rope, and tied Paul onto the animal. Then he did the same with Jedediah, tying his father to the young mule. The young mule looked scared. He hoped the mule wouldn't get to bucking with Jedediah. He mounted Mel and whistled for the collies. "Move out!" he called. All four dogs went to work. The collies herding the goats and sheep, the Mexican sheepdogs bringing up the rear, allowing no straggling lambs to fall behind. The young mule stayed right on the old mule's tail. It was a slow train, Peter keeping a pace that wouldn't exhaust the young lambs. All the ewes had given birth by now. The herd had nearly doubled itself this year.

All the way home, the warm wind blew. Peter no longer chased the wind. He realized the wind was chasing him. *"Surely goodness and mercy shall follow me all the days of my life. And I will dwell in the house of the Lord forever,"* Peter whispered Psalm 23 as he brought his father and brother home.

That night, he dreamed of Paul and Jedediah in the meadow. He rode up on Mel just as he had that day, but instead of finding their bodies amongst the sheep, the sheep weren't in the meadow. Paul and Jedediah stood there alone waiting for him. They looked to be the same age. Jedediah young, strong, and handsome. Paul healed and all spruced up. Golden light flooded the meadow and haloed his father and brother. That warm wind was blowing. The sky somehow glittered like dust dancing in sunlight. The closer he got to Paul and Jedediah, the more the golden light turned white. Glittering dust swirled all around. But it wasn't dust. Peter knew that. This was a clean place. A fresh place. A new place. This meadow was heaven.

He pulled on the reins, and immediately Mel was no longer beneath him. Just thinking about getting off her had made Mel disappear. Slowly, he walked to his father and brother. Welcoming smiles were on their faces. Suddenly, he noticed butterflies. Dragonflies. Birds of every color. A flock of snow geese soared right above his head. It was as if the whole meadow had come alive in an instant.

Joy filled him, and he laughed. Beyond Paul and Jedediah, an elk herd walked out of the glittering mist. Deer sprang through the meadow grasses. It was almost as if they flew past him, leaping in the air. Every animal he'd ever hunted suddenly appeared. Bears. Wolves. Mountain lions. Nothing frightened Peter. The animals were all in perfect harmony.

He heard bells and then singing. A heavenly choir. The voices of angels. Yet when Jedediah spoke, Peter heard his father as if his father's voice was the only sound in the meadow. "Don't you worry about Paul and me. We'll be waiting for you over yonder." Jedediah pointed toward a river of crystal-clear water. The River of Life. Trees heavy with fruit lined the river. As soon as Jedediah pointed to the river, he and Paul stood there on the other side.

Peter walked toward the sparkling river, wanting to get to Jedediah and Paul, but before he made it there, a sky-high gate of gold appeared. Then he woke up.

Peter heard the babe nursing beside him in the bed.

"Are you all right?" Isabella's sweet voice came to him. Her hand reached out to touch him.

His shoulders shook with a sob of joy and sorrow.

"I'm sorry. I know how much you loved them."

He could hear tears in Isabella's voice.

"Don't cry. The Good Lord just let me see Jedediah and Paul. They're in heaven. It's a beautiful place."

"But you're crying." Isabella stroked his shoulder.

"Oh, Isabella, it's true. Heaven is our home. I can't wait to get there."

"You promised not to leave me again." Her hand gripped his shoulder.

"I did promise you, and I won't leave until the Good Lord takes me from this earth."

"I hope he takes me first. I don't ever want to live without you." Isabella's voice was thick with love. The babe continued to nurse, undisturbed by their talking.

"I think we should call the boy Paul. If he was a Jed, he'd be interrupting us by now. When Paul was a little boy, he interrupted no one. Paul was the quietest boy I ever saw. Paul Jedediah, it's a fitting name for the boy."

Isabella was silent, her hand resting on his shoulder.

"I don't mind anymore that Paul fathered the babe. I'm glad he did. It's like a piece of my brother is still here, and my father died happy knowing Paul was truly his son."

Isabella stroked his shoulder. "You wouldn't have ever known Paul was your brother without the babe. I think God did that. He took our sin and gave us glory."

Peter smiled in the darkness. "He took a gambling tent and gave us a wedding." He reached out and found the child's soft head. The babe had fallen asleep between them. "I never figured God could do it, but He gave both Paul and me a son." Peter moved his hand from the babe to Isabella's face. It was wet with tears. "We are never alone. The Good Shepherd doesn't leave His sheep. Ever."

"Will the life of a shepherd please you?"

"A life with you pleases me." He ran his thumb across her open lips.

She picked up the babe and moved the child to her other side so there was nothing between them.

Peter pulled Isabella into his arms. "I love you," he said against her silken hair.

"I loved you first," she whispered.

"I never deserved it." He pressed his lips to hers. Peter wouldn't take more than a kiss tonight. They would grieve. They would heal. And then they would love.

THE END

A Note From Paula

Thank you so much for reading *Chasing the Wind*. Seeing this novel in print is a dream twenty-five years in the making. I was in my early twenties, living in Germany, when I first envisioned my California Rising series. There was no Internet back then, and my parents sent me California history books through the mail. When we moved back to the states, I gave birth to our second daughter and would bundle up my two little girls and head to the Marysville Library. The library's California room was an oasis of history. I spent hours there poring over the journals of original California settlers and wrote my first draft of *Until the Day Breaks*. A quarter of a century later, *Chasing the Wind* completes my California Rising series. My Grandma Helen would be proud of me. She loved *Until the Day Breaks*, which I read to her since she was losing her eyesight back then. Grandma Helen always wanted me to become a famous author. I can still hear her voice, "You can do it, honey. Do it for your grandma."

I wish my Grandma Helen was alive so I could put *Chasing the Wind* in her hands and tell her the story, but I'm thrilled to give it to Grandma Helen's sister, my Aunt Gracie, for her ninety-ninth birthday. Aunt Gracie reads my books and has encouraged me to keep writing. I also want to honor my mom,

Carolyn, and her twin sister, my Aunt Marolyn. These amazing ladies taught me to love reading. I would never have become an author if I wasn't a reader first. Thank you, Mom and Aunt Marolyn, for turning off the TV and telling me to read.

To share the California history I love, I needed to create a character who lived it. Isabella is a sheltered girl, so I couldn't impart much history through her. But my hero, Peter Brondi, has all the freedom in the world to experience California's turbulent times. While researching history, I found the frontiersman Kit Carson the ideal historical figure for the conquest of California. So I modeled Peter Brondi after Carson. When I first began researching for *Chasing the Wind,* I deemed Carson a heartless killer. He was known as the greatest Indian fighter of all time. Responsible for the deaths of thousands of Indians, Carson helped slaughter the peaceful California Indians along the Sacramento River during the Bear Flag Revolt. He killed Californios and Mexicans alike. Carson had so much blood on his hands. But the more I read about Carson, the more I developed compassion for this man determined to protect his family and see his nation win the West.

The Californios called Carson *el Lobo,* the Wolf. They feared Carson more than any other man. A quiet, soft-spoken Missourian of smallish stature and sharp blue eyes, Carson never learned to read. This embarrassed him. He wanted California for the Union and was a hero of the Mexican War. Above all, Carson was a patriot. He loved his nation.

I have no idea if he loved the Lord, but Carson did value religion. In his early thirties, he left the Presbyterian Church to join the Catholic Church in order to marry fourteen-year-old Josefa Jaramillo, the daughter of a wealthy and prominent Mexican couple in Taos, New Mexico. This may sound strange to us today, but grown men married girls in those days due to the fact that men established themselves before starting their families and girls were considered adults at an early age. Women regularly died in childbirth. Most folks did not live to be old. It was a different time with different social norms. I was very aware of this while crafting my story. I wanted to stay true to history while not offending the sensibilities of modern-day readers. Isabella, my heroine, is a teenager in my story, but I never reveal her age. Peter is in his late twenties, about Carson's age when he married his first wife, an Arapaho Indian girl named Singing Grass. It was rumored Carson gained his first whiff of fame in the gun battle he fought with another mountain man to win the beautiful Singing Grass's hand.

I envisioned Peter and Isabella's love story out of the ashes of Carson's youthful love for Singing Grass, who died soon after giving him two daughters; only one girl lived. Carson's second wife, a Cheyenne woman, divorced him within a year the Indian way, by setting his belongings and his young daughter outside of her tent. No children came from that brief union. Carson then took his little daughter back to Missouri and left her with his family. His greatest desire for his daughter was schooling. He wanted more than anything for his daughter to learn to read. For the next eight years, Carson split his time between St. Louis with his daughter and his trapping duties in Taos, New Mexico. During this time, he married the captivating Josefa and had eight more children with her through the years. When Josefa died at forty years of age, after complications from having their final child, Carson was devastated. A month later, in his fifty-eighth year, he followed his beloved Josefa to the grave.

My California Rising stories are romances, but the actual lives of the California settlers were far from romantic. Unlike the Californios, who enjoyed a relatively rich, easy lifestyle by appropriating the already established mission lands and resources before the American takeover, the American settlers faced many hardships homesteading in the Golden State. Guns and grit tamed the territory, and death was always at the door. Many settlers brought their own livestock to California. In 1852, an American frontiersman named Dick Wootton, known as Uncle Dick, rounded up nine thousand sheep in New Mexico and drove them from Taos to California to sell to the miners. It was a successful endeavor, and Kit Carson did the same in 1853.

In my story, I have Peter and Jedediah drive their sheep in 1850 across the desert and over the mountains. The loss of the two Mexican sheepdogs to a rabid wolf happened during Uncle Dick's drive.

Marysville was a brand-new city in 1850, mostly tents along the river, but I depict Clara's Place there already. The brothel/saloon I envisioned as Clara's was actually constructed in 1851 beside the Yuba River in Marysville. That building, The Silver Dollar Saloon, still stands in Marysville today and it's fun to have lunch there at the corner of D and 1st Streets next door to the Bok Kai Temple. The Silver Dollar Saloon is one of the oldest historical landmarks in Marysville, and until 1972, the former owners ran a brothel on its second floor.

Fort Ross is now a historical park about an hour's drive from Bodega Bay, which is several hours north of San Francisco. I love visiting the park and walking through the fort, which has been preserved so well. I stood in the middle of the little chapel originally built in the 1820s at Fort Ross and said a prayer that I could write this story well. The wooden chapel has a small belfry and was the first Russian Orthodox structure in North America outside of Alaska. In 1836, Father Ioann Veniaminov came to the settlement and conducted sacraments of marriage, baptisms, and other religious services. Father Veniaminov later became Bishop of Alaska, then Senior Bishop of the Russian Empire.

Unlike the Spanish, the Russian priests in North America baptized only the Indians who demonstrated a knowledge and sincere acceptance of Christian belief. I envisioned Isabella's Pomo Indian grandparents and her young Creole mother as having sincere Christian beliefs, but I didn't get into that history of Indians being converted to Orthodox Christians much in the story. The people of mixed Indian and Russian heritage at Fort Ross were known as Creoles. Like the Creoles of the south, some had mostly European blood and others were mostly Indian. Just a little bit of Indian made you a Creole, but around Fort Ross, Creoles owned land and were respected by the white population for having largely accepted the Orthodox faith and culture. The blue-eyed, black-haired Creoles of Fort Ross were known for their beauty and intelligence—and weak constitutions. Many Fort Ross Creoles died young, probably due to tuberculous, though at the time they didn't know why the Creoles weren't as hardy as the full-blooded Russians or Indians.

It was wonderful to stand in the Fort Ross chapel and imagine Peter and Isabella committing themselves to God and each other there. My husband and I held hands and prayed in the chapel in 2017. This chapel was destroyed in the 1906 earthquake. Between 1916 and 1918, it was rebuilt. On October

5, 1970, the chapel was destroyed again in an accidental fire. Following Russian Orthodox tradition, some lumber from the burned building was used to reconstruct the chapel in 1973. The chapel bell melted in the fire and was recast in Belgium using metal from the original Russian bell. On the bell is a small inscription in Church Slavonic which reads, "Heavenly King, receive all who glorify Him."

I pray somehow, in some way, this story will glorify Him. I really wanted to convey the Father's love for us. We are all sinners in need of a savior. I do my best to depict sinners the way they truly are, human and sinful. And I pray that I depict God the way he really is, holy, compassionate, merciful, and ready to love us when we turn to Him. The week before finishing this novel, I was struggling with the ending of the story. I knew Paul and Jedediah were going to die, I just didn't know how they would die. In church on Sunday morning, I prayed, "Please Lord, give me the ending of *Chasing the Wind*."

After church, we headed to my parents' ranch. I'd printed out another hundred pages of my manuscript to edit while we were there. I try not to work on Sundays, but my husband and our sons were going to watch football. Sitting down to edit my book on a cold winter day wouldn't bother anyone, I supposed. For some reason, two of our boys decided to go hunting at the ranch. They took their grandpa's pistol and off they went. I saw our sons walking down in the pasture and said a quick prayer that God would keep them safe. My dad has never let the boys take his pistol out before. But at fifteen, our son John is very responsible. He carried the gun, so I took a deep breath, sat down, and began editing beside the fire. An hour later, John came howling into the house. "I shot myself! I shot my foot!"

I dropped my book and ran to him. His foot was covered in blood. Spurting blood, really. I screamed for a towel. My mom, Oma, threw me several towels and my husband, Scott, appeared at my side. I was trying to get John to sit down on the kitchen floor. Blood was smeared across the tile. Wrapping a towel around John's foot, I realized it immediately filled with blood. I grabbed another towel and wrapped it tight too. "Someone get me duct tape," I yelled. This is so not me. I usually am worthless at the sight of blood. I'm not a nurse, that's for sure. "Let me see the wound," said Oma, the nurse in the house.

I kept pressure on the wound. "We need to get John to a doctor." The towels were warm and squishy with blood. I held John's foot in both hands, pressing hard to stop the bleeding.

"We're going to the hospital," Scott said. He scooped John up into his arms, and I trailed along holding tight to John's foot. Our seventh grader, Joey, met us at the door with duct tape. He looked scared to death. "Are you okay?" I asked because he'd been with John.

Joey nodded, his face white, his freckles standing out like spattered mud on fresh snow. "John's gonna be fine," I told Joey as I grabbed the duct tape from him. Joey just stood there in shock, staring at me. Scott laid John on the front seat of the truck. I began securing the bloody towels around John's foot with duct tape. Scott jumped behind the wheel and backed out of the driveway. By now John was saying, "My finger slipped on the hammer when I was unloading it. I'm sorry. So sorry. So so sorry," he said over and over again. He was holding on to his cross necklace and praying. I wrapped the duct tape tight around the towels and held his leg in the air, putting pressure on the wound. It was a long drive to the hospital.

That Sunday night staring at the ceiling, I just wanted to stop. Write no more books. Have no more weird accidents when I'm trying to meet a deadline. Just stop. "God, help us," I prayed. "Thank you that our sons are alive. That hunting accident could have been so much worse." The miracle was the bullet went right between John's bones and exited the bottom of his foot without causing any real damage. Thankfully, the bullet was only a .22 caliber. The doctor said the duct tape to stop the bleeding was a brilliant idea and that John was lucky. All the nurses told us our son was lucky. "You got Glock foot," said the male nurse who washed John's wound and dressed it. "A lot of rookies shoot their foot with their Glocks." This was news to me. I didn't realize shooting yourself in the foot was so common. So I googled it. In WWI and WWII, soldiers would shoot themselves in the foot on purpose so they could go home and not die in battle. In the Old West, shooting yourself in the foot or the leg while drawing your gun was a common accident.

Of course, you all know now that Paul accidently shoots himself while drawing his gun, leading to his death in the story. The beautiful meadow where I envisioned Paul and Jedediah dying is a real place up near present-day Nevada City, which boomed into a town during the Gold Rush. The first "easterners" built a cabin along Deer Creek in Nevada City and staked a claim in 1849, just a year after the discovery of gold at Sutter's Mill. Nevada City was originally called Deer Creek Diggins, but the fast-growing town soon became known as Caldwell's Upper Store, after the man who opened the town's first general store. By 1850, people decided the town needed an official name. Nevada was chosen—Nevada is Spanish for "snow-covered"—because it had been a particularly snowy winter that year.

I love Nevada City. The National Exchange Hotel (also known as the National Hotel) in Nevada City opened in August 1856 under the name of Bicknell Block. The town's first hotel, saloon, stagecoach stop, and mail center were all known as Bicknell's Block. In my story, I have Bicknell Block there in 1851, but it was five years later when it really opened. In 1977, the hotel was placed on the National Register of Historic Places and is considered the oldest continuously operated hotel west of the Rockies. I sure would like to know if the original Bicknell of Bicknell's Block was related to my husband, Scott Bicknell. History is so fascinating! Thanks for taking this journey with me.

Love,
Paula

Made in the USA
San Bernardino, CA
08 May 2018